At last! Finally, we get to read th__ _
Fairfax and Mr. Frank Churchill! __ _b,
welcomed, believable story that reveals ___ and
their opinions of everyone in Highbury. She has clearly explained
the complicated background of their falling in love and secret
engagement. The book is full of laughter, love, annoyance, and
desperation; all the emotions of young love impatient to marry. I
loved *My Dearest Miss Fairfax*!

-Arlene S. Bice, author; editor of *Jane Austen, an anthology of thoughts & opinions*

Austen portrays Jane Fairfax as a worthy and slightly dull
supporting character in a novel studded with leading actors.
Jeanette Watts repositions her as the passionate and independent-
minded heroine of her own story. Funny, wise, insightful – and
remarkably gripping, given that we all know how things will turn
out in the end – this is a gem of a book that will send readers back
to Emma with quite a new perspective.

-Joceline Bury, *Jane Austen's Regency World*

This tender, lightly-handled but moving story reveals Jane's
perspective, on her romance with the exasperating Frank Churchill,
but also her feelings towards Emma herself, which are not always
positive! Other delights include her perspective on her dear but
infuriating aunt Miss Bates, and on Mrs Elton. Always true to Jane
Austen, but revealing the inner world of Miss Fairfax, this is not to
be missed. Brava, Ms Watts!

–Harri Whilding, author of *Out There In the World* and *Every Wand'ring Barque*

Also by Jeanette Watts

Wealth and Privilege

Brains and Beauty

Jane Austen Lied to Me

A Woman's Persuasion

My Dearest Miss Fairfax

Jeanette Watts

To Astrid, who probably doesn't even remember the conversation that inspired the insight that allowed me to understand Jane Fairfax enough to write this book.

Part One

CHAPTER ONE

Jane Fairfax wished she could truly be a good person. Barring that, she settled for keeping quiet when she had nothing good to say. Which could be frequent.

She did wonder, frequently, whether this was really a wise strategy on her part. It never seemed to fail; if there was going to be a party of any size greater than three, the person most likely to chatter away at her with an insipid monologue was sure to seek her out and make her an auditory captive.

At the wedding breakfast of her dear friend Miss Campbell to Mr Dixon, her captor seemed to be a relative of Mrs Campbell's. Jane was not quite sure if it was Mrs Campbell's cousin, or a brother, but it was some male relative of indeterminate age and relation to the bride. He was clearly a fussy man, childless and wifeless, who no doubt was going to remain so all his days. Jane had the vague impression he had been married once. Perhaps his wife had been the love of his life, and he could not bear the idea of marrying again. Or perhaps he was never able to find another woman willing to put up with his nonsense.

"So, indeed, I said, why not simply repaint the whole thing?" her companion was saying. She assumed she was overdue for some sort of verbal reaction. "Indeed," she repeated.

While her companion happily enjoyed the sound of his own voice, she allowed her eyes to drift around the party. The Campbells, who had raised her as if she were their own, were blessed with a happy wealth of well-informed, judicious, warm-hearted family and friends, which created the largest wedding breakfast Jane had ever heard of. Aunts, uncles, cousins, nieces, nephews, neighbors and friends were all collected in small groups. In the bits of conversation she was able to hear, she discerned words such as

"Beethoven," "Shelley," and "Leipzig."

She sighed to herself. While others were talking about music, literature, and politics, of course she ended up listening to a one-way conversation about the intricacies of putting up a fence.

Knowing that the bride's father, Colonel Campbell, did not necessarily approve of the practice of "enclosure," enriching the privileged few at the expense of large numbers of small farmers, she was extremely grateful when the newly-made Mrs Dixon came to her rescue. "My dear Uncle Roberts, I am sorry to impose upon you, but I desperately need to steal sweet Jane away. I have been embraced so many times, my hair is a disgrace, and she is the only one with fingers clever enough to put it back to rights."

"Well, of course, my dear, of course!" the now-named Uncle Roberts gallantly dismissed the two young women. "We cannot have the bride disheveled on her wedding day!"

Sophia Dixon took Jane by the arm with one last sweet smile, and drew her away. "You looked like your ears could use a respite," she murmured when they were a safe distance away.

Jane's heart was bursting with love for her foster sister. "Thank you. He's a gentleman of the old school, to be sure. I certainly could not get up and walk away. But he never seems to pause to take a breath of air. He must be a very accomplished singer."

Sophia giggled a little, and gave Jane's arm an affectionate squeeze as they retired to their room, where Jane could re-pin Sophia's drooping curls. "You are the most tactful person the world has ever known."

"That's only because I am the meanest, most uncharitable person the world has ever known," Jane answered. She paused in the process of reattaching the orange blossoms to Sophia's light brown hair, and gave her a mournful look. "How on earth am I going to get by without you? You are the only person in the world who can watch me listening to a conversation without saying a word myself, and know exactly what I am thinking."

Sophia twisted in her chair, and wrapped her arms around Jane's slim waist. "That's because no one in the world knows you as well as I do," she said. Jane laid her cheek on the top of Sophia's head, and for a moment the two girls remained there, without a dry eye between them. "Are you sure you cannot come with me to Ireland? I am sure Mr Dixon would not object. Or, at least, if a bride cannot overcome her husband's objections when they are newly married, it speaks ill of her ability to have any influence over him later in life."

Jane had seen all the sketches Mr Dixon had shown them of his home in Ireland, and she desperately wanted to go. "You are a dear, sweet, generous friend," she answered. "But I would be imposing too much. I was supposed to have left your family to start supporting myself when I turned eighteen. I am twenty one now. As wholeheartedly as I love you, and your parents, it is time I proved to be a credit to all of you by using the education your parents gave me."

"It does not seem right," Sophia's voice was muffled, because she had buried her face in Jane's dress. "You are prettier than I am, and smarter, and you sing and play better than I do, and when you apply your needle to a project, it comes out looking as you intended it to. I am the plain one, and the dull one. It does not seem right that I am the one with a rich, clever husband today."

"That's the world we live in," Jane shrugged pragmatically. "Your father had the means to provide for you, but not for us both. If my father had lived, things would be different. As it is, I can only be grateful. Just imagine if your father had not found me, and raised me because of his love for my father. I would not be fit to be a governess and to make my own way in the world. I would have grown up in poverty with my aunt and grandmother in Highbury, in terribly reduced circumstances."

"I am glad your father nursed my father through the camp fever." Sophia looked up at her, smiling through the tears in her eyes. "I suppose if your father had lived, we would still have been great friends, and we would have been each other's bridesmaids, and settle on estates a mile apart, and our children would have grown up together."

"I am sure you are right," Jane agreed. "Well, now I have made a mess of it," she said when they finished their mutual exchange of affection and Sophia's arms released her waist. "I have mussed your hair all over again."

CHAPTER TWO

One could search the world over, and never find more excellent people than Colonel and Mrs Campbell.

The Colonel had served under Prince Frederick, Duke of York and Albany in Britain's coalition with Russia, Prussia, Spain, Holland, and Austria. Jane's father, Lieutenant Fairfax, had been serving under Colonel Campbell in Flanders when the Colonel fell dreadfully sick with camp fever. Lieutenant Fairfax nursed him through the illness, only to die in action a few months later at Hondschoote.

The Colonel was not the sort of man to forget an officer under his command who had saved his life. His lieutenant and nurse had been married only a couple of years, with an infant daughter almost the exact same age as the Colonel's own child.

When William Pitt the Younger sued for peace with France and the Colonel was finally able to return home to his own wife and daughter, he sought out the child of the man who had saved his life.

He found that child, Jane, now completely orphaned. Her mother had died not long after her father, and Jane was living in a small village called Highbury with her grandmother and a maiden aunt.

The child was pretty, well mannered, and intelligent. She was doted on by her relatives, but he could see they were not financially well-positioned to raise a child. He needed to do something to help her: he owed it to Lieutenant Fairfax. After returning home to London and talking it over with his wife, Colonel Campbell returned to Highbury with an invitation for Jane to visit for a fortnight.

His daughter Sophia took an immediate liking to Jane. After the first visit, the child was constantly begging for Jane's return. For the next three years, short visits turned into long visits, which turned into longer visits. By the time the girls were eight years old, the two were inseparable. The Campbells decided to ask Mrs and Miss Bates if they could have the responsibility of completing Jane's upbringing.

The change from Highbury to London could not have been more drastic. In Highbury, dinnertime conversations were dominated by Aunt Bates's cheerful discussion of the comings and goings of the neighbors. At the Campbell dinner table, there were discussions of poetry by Coleridge, or Wordsworth, or Scott. Colonel Campbell read from the newspaper, and they discussed the change from Prime Minister Addington to Prime Minister Pitt. The Colonel explained to the two girls the difference between Whigs and Tories. Jane was quite certain her aunt, and even her grandmother, had no idea the two parties of Parliament even existed, much less what they stood for.

Mrs Campbell had her share in the education of both girls as well. She taught them everything a woman should know that involved needles: knitting needles, embroidery needles, sewing needles. She taught them how to curl the papers for delicate and fanciful paper filigree, how to turn all sorts of finished fancywork into decorations for fire screens, or slippers, or clocks, or any number of other household items.

There were other parts to education that were more serious. Sophia would need to understand how to manage a large number of people, since it was hoped she would make a good match when she came of age. Then she would have a household to manage. Jane would more likely be the one educating the daughters of rich men, and it might fall to her to educate those daughters on how to make a budget for all the foodstuffs, linens, clothing, and servants' wages that were part of household business.

When it came to dancing, and music, and French and Italian, Colonel and Mrs Campbell hired the best tutors that could be found in London. While the younger generations seemed less concerned with the importance of a graceful curtsey and proper way to give or receive an object, Colonel Campbell was a military man. These matters of deportment were still important. Everyone could still tell simply by the way a person walked into a room whether that person was educated or not. And he made sure no one would ever doubt that Sophia and Jane were both educated young ladies.

While both girls bloomed as their natural graces were honed to perfection, Jane surpassed Sophia at the keyboard. Sophia was at best an indifferent student of music. But Jane captivated anyone within earshot when she sat down at a pianoforte.

Jane loved music. No problem in the world was so large that it could not be fixed by placing her fingers upon the ivory keys. There were Scotch and Irish airs to soothe the nerves, and concertos to help one think, and dance tunes to delight family and friends. Mozart was good for days when she was feeling unhappy, and Beethoven's newest music was sure to make a good day even better. Sophia's favorite music was a book of Russian folk songs arranged for four hands, and they would play together. Jane tried to coax her into more challenging music, but with only mediocre success.

Their piano teacher, Mr Muzio Clementi, dreamed of sending Jane to the continent to perform professionally. "If Babette Ployer can conquer the crowned heads of Europe, so can Jane Fairfax," he insisted.

Colonel Campbell flatly refused to entertain such an idea. "There is nowhere in Europe that is safe from Napoleon's greedy eyes. Our Jane would no sooner arrive in Vienna, and his armies would be arriving a week later."

Mr Clementi made one last effort. "Then let me take her to France. She can make her fame in Napoleon's wake."

This was so out of the question, Colonel Campbell nearly went looking for a different music teacher.

With each passing year, when Jane would dutifully pay her visits to her aunt and grandmother, she felt her good fortune more and more thoroughly. It was not merely the matter of her relatives' lack of material things. People in Highbury spent their time thinking about themselves, not larger subjects. They gossiped about each other, instead of discussing literature, or music, or philosophy, or the events of the world.

There was one young lady who always made Jane intensely grateful to the Campbells. Her name was Emma Woodhouse. She was the daughter of one of the richest men in the county, almost exactly the same age as herself, and her every utterance contrasted starkly with Sophia's sweet determination to keep up with Jane's mind.

When Jane had a thought that Sophia was not following, she would frown, and make Jane explain herself. Mrs Campbell once told her in confidence, "You are a clever girl, Jane. Perhaps too clever. The world does not care for smart women. But when you use your intelligence to help explain things to people who don't understand as quickly as you do, I believe you will be loved and respected. People will appreciate you sharing your gifts with others."

But when Jane was forced into the company of Miss Woodhouse, which was frequent, because they were as close in age as she was to Sophia, she quickly learned that discussion of any interesting topic was out of the question. Jane did not think Miss Woodhouse was stupid, necessarily, but ignorant and lazy. There seemed to be no topic of interest to Jane that Miss Woodhouse seemed to have the least bit of real knowledge about.

While Jane deplored Miss Woodhouse's lack of substantial education, she did admit there were good points to her character. She was generally well-mannered, generous, and took the privileges that came with her family's wealth very much for granted. Because of her position in society, almost no one offered her any challenge to attempt to use her brain.

There was one gentleman in Highbury, a neighbor of the Woodhouses, who seemed to try. But he did not have much success. Jane could not be sure if it was due to Miss Woodhouse being incapable of or disinterested in improvement, or if it was because Mr Knightley's rather gruff, tactless manner was unlikely to inspire improvement in a young lady who had no real incentive to do so.

Every year, every visit to her relatives brought home the realization that, had Jane been raised there, she would have grown up to be a very, very different person.

CHAPTER THREE

Jane enjoyed weddings as much as anybody, but it never failed: whenever there was a wedding, within a week, she was sick with a cold.

It did not seem to matter what time of year it was, or whether she had been out in the rain recently, or whether she had eaten any of the wedding cake, or whether she had taken sugar with her tea. Everyone had a pet theory as to why she would catch cold, but the one constant was, she always caught it.

Mr and Mrs Dixon planned to spend a fortnight at the Campbell household after the wedding before leaving for Mr Dixon's home in Ireland, but when Jane took ill, it was suggested that the Dixons, the Campbells, and Jane should all go down to Weymouth instead of remaining in London.

Jane protested that no one should change their plans on her account, but she was overruled by the other four, and soon they had arrangements for comfortable quarters at Weymouth.

"A course of heated sea water baths, and some good sea air, and you shall be right as rain in no time," Mr Dixon assured her. "Mrs Dixon would never countenance my taking her away when her bosom friend is ill."

The wedding plans and upcoming trip to the coast stalled her efforts to find a position for herself with a respectable family. Every time she sat down to start writing the letters, something came up, and they did not get finished. They were still sitting in her correspondence box, a few lines away from embarking upon her new life. When she pulled them out one evening to review and finish them, it was Mrs Campbell who stopped her.

"If you leave immediately after we lose dear Sophia to her new home, the house is going to be much too empty," she implored her. "Why don't you stay with us just a little longer? Losing you both at once would be too awful to bear."

"At the very least," the Colonel added his plea to his wife's, "I would like to have you create a supply of slippers and smoking caps for me before you go. With all due respect to my excellent wife and daughter, yours always fit better."

"That is, after you finish the mitts you are currently knitting for your grandmother," Mrs Campbell smiled.

"You see, my dear? We simply cannot do without you yet," the Colonel insisted.

Jane's heart swelled with love for the endless kindness of her benefactors. "It would be heartless of me not to leave you well equipped."

Weymouth might only be a small seaside town, but it was the watering place favored by the king until his delicate health overpowered him and he was forced to allow his son to rule as regent while he remained shut up in Windsor. The little coastal town bustled with activity, with people, and with shops.

While Weymouth was not London, Jane and Mrs Dixon and Mrs Campbell enjoyed detouring from their strolls on the Esplanade into the shops. They walked back and forth several times from Miss Anthony's millinery shop on Conygar Street and Miss Hyde's on St Mary Street before they decided the Misses White made bonnets that surpassed either of the other two shops.

The day after their arrival, while Mr Dixon set off with his easel and sketching materials for an afternoon by the shore, Colonel Campbell had business matters of his own. Mrs Campbell was having tea with an old schoolfellow, leaving the two girls to amuse themselves among the shops. Sophia was on a buying spree, while Jane tried to keep her from overspending her new allowance from her husband.

"I am trying not to buy everything in sight. I don't know what will be available in Ireland," Sophia had a pair of gloves in each hand. "Do I really need both of these? I know I will not be able to buy French silks the way I can here, but how difficult will it be to get anything else I need?"

"You are going to Ireland, not to Arabia," Jane pointed out in amusement. "They also wear gloves in Ireland."

"Still, you never know." Sophia's eyes got wider. "Mr Dixon tells me I have a music room waiting for me with a harp, and a pianoforte, and even a guitar! We should go over to the music store. Since I was not blessed with your musical talents, I need to start collecting music that is within my ability to play."

"You sell yourself short. You are nowhere near as terrible as you always say you are," Jane protested, as they set aside the gloves and left the shop.

"Well, it is hard for me to believe I possess any of my own talents with a musical genius in the house with me."

"There is one good thing to come out of our impending separation. Your musical talents will immediately improve with my absence," Jane offered loyally.

"I already dislike performing, and once I get to Ireland, I won't have you to shield me from the obligation to play in front of people." Sophia shook her head. "Without you around to make me practice all the time, my music is going to suffer dreadfully. You know I don't like the sound of my own playing, since I never sound like you."

"There won't be anyone there to compare you to me. So you need not, either. And I don't believe you will neglect your music so much. If that were true, we would not be on our way to the music store because you want to buy more music," Jane laughed at her. "But I will write you absolutely every day to implore you to practice, if that will help."

"You know it will," Sophia laughed with her. It was the first time they were able to talk about the near future without tears.

The music shop was impossibly cluttered, but Jane and Sophia were able to find a selection of ballads, dance music, and sonatas that pleased them. There was only a handful of other people in the shop, but the proprietor fussed about as if there were scores of people lined up to make purchases. He hovered over a hapless shop clerk who was trying to wrap a parcel and make change and answer another patron's question all at the same time.

"The Italian arias are by the window – over to the right," the clerk answered the patron's question, apparently incorrectly.

"No, no, the French music is beside the window," he contradicted his clerk. "The Italian is farther to the left. Watch how you tie that bundle, that knot is going to come undone. How many pence did you give back?" There was a peculiar thwacking sound, when he smacked the clerk on the back of his head. "That should have been a farthing, you dolt. That package looks terrible. Start over and wrap it up again."

"The package is quite fine, I assure you." The customer at the counter was a tall man, with a profile that struck Jane as rather perfect. "There is no need to berate your poor clerk on my behalf. See? I am able to pick up the bundle by the strings without any problems. Your clerk did a perfectly fine job." He seemed to have the air of a Greek statue about him. Or maybe Michelangelo. He had an air of harmony and good humor about him, which was odd, when he was in the process of confronting a shopkeeper about his lack of manners. "There is certainly no call for striking him." The speaker looked around, and his eyes rested on Jane's. "Especially not in the presence of ladies."

"Well, as stupid as this fellow is, your knot will break before you are halfway home with your parcel, and then you will be back here, demanding your money back when the music ends up in the mud," the shopkeeper growled.

"I am sure I am capable of delivering music to my aunt without mishap," the gentleman answered with the same combination of assurance and amiability. "I promise you, should there be any accidents, I shall take responsibility for my own clumsiness, and I will happily pay for fresh music. Now, I must implore you to leave off this abuse of your poor clerk, who seems to be doing his job perfectly well." Once again, his eyes met Jane's. "These ladies are being kept waiting, and I am sure they would prefer to spend their time giving you their money, instead of watching you perform any display of violence."

"Indeed," Sophia was beside Jane, and staunchly assisted the gallant stranger. "I have quite worn out my friend's feet with shopping all day, we should like to be on our way, if your clerk will be so good as to wrap these up."

"Well, I definitely don't want you having anything happen to your package, I will have to wrap it up myself so that this idiot does not make a mess of it." The proprietor pushed the clerk out of the way, and handled the exchange himself.

The handsome stranger exchanged looks with the girls. There seemed to be nothing more any of them could do to prevent the abuse of the hapless clerk. The stranger bowed to them and left.

CHAPTER FOUR

Jane and Sophia broke into uncomfortable giggles the moment they were out of the music shop and back on the street.

"Oh, my goodness, what a horrible, horrible man!" Sophia exclaimed. "Imagine, treating his clerk like that!"

"I did not know what to do," Jane admitted. "I cannot believe he did not mend his ways when the gentleman asked him to refrain. I kept trying to think of what I could do to help the man, but if the gentleman was unable to curb such behavior, what could I possibly do?"

"We should have just turned around and left the shop," Sophia said.

That stopped both of their giggles. They stared at each other guiltily.

"That is what we should have done," Jane agreed.

Sophia looked down at the brown paper parcel of music she was carrying in her arms. "I should not have bought any of this. I should have put it down on the counter, and walked away." She looked back at the shop. "Do I take it back?"

Jane groaned. "I suppose we should," she agreed. "But I don't want to face that awful man again. And what if he takes it out on his clerk again? He might be the sort that will blame everyone else for his poor behavior."

Sophia hugged the bundle to herself and frowned. "Would you mind if we head back? I have a headache, now. Why don't we return to the inn and order some tea."

Jane nodded in agreement. "I am a bit tired. I would like to lie down."

The wind sprang up as they walked. A gust took everyone strolling on the Esplanade by surprise, blowing curls, ribbons, skirts, and one unsecured bonnet hither and thither. A second gust also brought with it a few pages of music.

The girls hastened to stop the flying sheets, then looked around uncertainly for their owner. When their gallant gentleman from the music shop nearly ran them over, darting out from East Street, capturing two more escaped pages, they could not help but laugh.

"Oh, dear," Jane said, as they handed over the music they had captured. "I guess maybe the proprietor was correct in his estimation of your parcel, even if he is incorrect in his manners."

The stranger smiled as he accepted the pages. "I suppose I really should go back to the shop and apologize. But truth be told, I am reluctant to set foot in there again."

His eyes were brown, and filled with warmth. The polish with which he collected the music from her showed that he had studied with a dancing master every bit as much as she and Sophia had. Not that there was any question he was a gentleman.

"We were just discussing the same sentiment!" Sophia admitted.

"I hope that unpleasant man has not completely spoiled your day," he said. "If you find you are in need of something to sweeten the afternoon and put all thoughts of that awfulness in the past, I highly recommend a stop at Mr Lovelace's pastry shop. Princess Amelia and Princess Charlotte have declared his confections the best in the entire kingdom."

"Thank you for the recommendation, we were just going back to our inn to order some tea," Jane replied.

"A cup of tea is a capital idea. And, if you will excuse me, my aunt is no doubt waiting for her tea until I return with her music." He touched his hat and bowed, then disappeared up the street whence he had dashed.

Jane and Sophia both stared after him for a moment. "What a perfect gentleman!" Sophia exclaimed as they resumed their journey down the Esplanade. "I don't suppose we will ever have the good fortune to be properly introduced."

CHAPTER FIVE

A cup of tea, some quiet time lying down, and Sophia's headache was sufficiently alleviated to contemplate the rigors of dressing for the ball being given at the Assembly Rooms that evening.

Mrs Campbell had learned from her schoolmate that Princess Charlotte was in residence at Royal Lodge, and she had stated her intention to come to the ball.

"Why on earth do you suppose she is here? I thought she referred to Weymouth as 'this odious place?' " Sophia asked while Jane was curling her hair with the curling tongs. "If she wanted a bit of sea air, why not go to Brighton with the Prince Regent?"

"Your father read all about this last summer in the papers," Jane reminded her. "After she reversed her decision to marry William, Prince of Orange, her father refused to allow her to come to Brighton with him, and sent her here instead."

"Is that when her father had put her under house arrest, and she ran out into the street, and a stranger put her in a hackney cab and sent her to her mother's residence?" Sophia recalled. "It all sounds like the sort of thing one would read in a novel, not the newspapers. My goodness, that took a lot of courage. I cannot imagine fighting with my father the way she has defied hers."

"It is hard to imagine two men more opposite than your father and the Prince Regent." Jane possessed her share of the popular disapprobation for the King's eldest son. "No doubt the princess owes a great deal of her popularity to that escapade. I certainly admire her! She has pluck, and fortitude, and she knows what she wants. She is willing to 'stick to her guns – hold to her convictions and rights.' Samuel Johnson would approve. I concur, she seems like a heroine in a novel, not a flesh and blood woman of eighteen."

"It requires fortitude to be a member of the royal family – and heir to the throne," Sophia commented. "Can you imagine, everything she does, everything she says, is watched, commented upon, either approved or disapproved, repeated, and examined."

"It must be taxing to have one's every syllable marked upon and repeated." Jane finished with Sophia's curls, and examined the collection of feathers available to finish off her creation. "Not only when at home, but everywhere you go. I know I get very quiet when I visit Highbury, and I spend hours listening to silly gossip by very silly people. If I were Princess Charlotte, I think I would be afraid to ever utter a word. Even in private, there is some servant listening and repeating every mean thing that's ever said."

"Speaking of taxing," Sophia looked up at Jane with concern. "The reason we are here is to take the sea air for your health. Are you certain you are well enough to be going to the ball? I don't wish to be selfish. I want you there with me, but if you would rather stay home and rest, don't feel like you have to come."

Jane smiled fondly down at her friend and shook her head. "Once I am a governess, I will not be able to attend balls. Especially not balls with our future monarch! Until I am so sick I cannot raise my head off my pillow, I am not going to miss one single moment of society!"

She was sorry she said it when Sophia's eyes became glossy with tears. "No, no, this is no time for tears," she hastily continued. "We have known since we were eight years old that you would grow up to marry a gentleman, and I would grow up to teach a gentleman's children. This is no time to feel sorry for ourselves. We are going to enjoy every moment while we are here, and we can do our crying while you are on your way to Ireland and I am applying for positions in respectable households."

Sophia took the handkerchief Jane offered her, dabbed her eyes, and smiled. "You are right. If you can be brave, I can be brave. Just like Princess Charlotte is brave. We all do our duty."

The assembly rooms were crowded and warm. Everyone wanted a chance to be presented to the princess. The men were hoping perhaps they would be asked to dance with her. The women merely wanted the chance to see her gown, and maybe to exchange a word with her that they could take home and repeat to their friends.

The Colonel and Mrs Campbell seemed singularly delighted with the crush of people; they had no idea so many of their acquaintance were currently in Weymouth. Despite it being November, any number of friends were there for the warm sea baths and the healthful nature of the sea breezes.

"Every sailor knows that there is nothing better for one's health than the salty air!" Colonel Campbell's friend, Colonel Walton, told them after they had exchanged astonished greetings.

"What a shame we served in the army, not the navy, then!" Colonel Campbell replied. "Perhaps we would know a larger number of healthy people!"

"Well, if we were among the healthy people, we would not be here having this delightful reunion!" Colonel Walton laughed. "Look, Major Elsey and his daughters are here!"

Among the military men there was a vast network of acquaintances. Jane, Sophia, and Mrs Campbell were introduced to friends, and neighbors, and cousins, and friends of friends. The network of personal relationships also extended over a vast geographical territory, ranging from Cornwall, to Dover, to Yorkshire. The laughing collection of former comrades-in-arms grew, as voices were recognized and more greetings were exchanged, and introductions were made so that wives and children were included in the melee.

"Campbell! How are you?" an extremely dignified-looking tall gentleman approached to clap Colonel Campbell on the shoulder.

"Churchill! You old dog! What are you doing all the way down here? I thought you said you never had any reason to leave 'God's Own Country' once you went home!" Colonel Campbell grinned affectionately at the taller man.

"Well, the coast of Yorkshire is not much known for its sea bathing, I will admit, so I am accompanying my brother's family all the way down here on behalf of his wife." He turned to include the three people standing behind him. "You remember my brother and his wife, don't you? And their nephew Frank Weston? I mean,

Frank Churchill. When he came of age, he elected to take the Churchill name. Which is excellent, since I am well beyond marrying years, and Mrs Churchill is in too ill health to be bearing any more children. So we are grateful to have this excellent fellow carrying on the family name."

Jane and Sophia uttered simultaneous gasps of recognition. The young gentleman standing among the Churchill family was the very gentleman from their encounters in the music shop and on the Esplanade!

The young Mr Churchill made his own indications of astonishment, and then all three of them burst into laughter.

"Well, it is about time we had a proper introduction," Mr Churchill said, with a very proper bow. "We have had a very busy day together."

"I trust you were able to deliver the music to your aunt without any further mishap?" Jane inquired after they had finished making their curtsey.

"Indeed, thank you. This is the excellent lady in question." He turned courteously to a squat woman with a stern face, wearing a very large turban that made her round face seem rounder, and a dress of an unfortunate shade of pink with ruffles that made her ample bosom seem even more ample. "Aunt Churchill, this is…" he stopped with a laugh, then turned to Colonel Campbell. "My apologies, Colonel, can I trouble you to make the introductions? I myself have not been properly introduced yet."

The Colonel was only too pleased to oblige. "Colonel Churchill, Mr Churchill, Mrs Churchill, Mr Frank Churchill, this is my wife, Mrs Campbell, our daughter Mrs Dixon, her husband Mr Dixon, and my daughter's particular friend, Miss Fairfax."

"How do you do!" Mr Frank Churchill laughed as they all rose from their proper honors. "I am so glad we can now be formally acquainted. I had recounted the afternoon's adventures to my aunt, and she asked to know more about the two ladies who were so good as to help rescue her music."

"Thank you, indeed," Mrs Churchill spoke to Sophia and Jane. Jane had the immediate impression that Mrs Churchill was one of those people cursed with a face that seems to be frowning even when its owner is in a perfectly good mood. Her face was frowning, but her voice was friendly. "Without your help, my nephew believes parts of Weber's Piano Sonata No 1 in C Major would have been lost to the sea."

"That would have been a catastrophe," Jane agreed. "I am so glad we were able to help a fellow musician. I hope someday soon we might hear you play!"

"I never play in public," Mrs Churchill demurred. "The music soothes my nerves, but I almost never go out in the evening. It taxes my strength too much. I made an exception tonight for Her Royal Highness. If she can tax her strength to come among her people, I can tax my strength in order to see her. But no doubt I will suffer tomorrow."

"I hope not!" Sophia exclaimed earnestly.

Any further pleasantries were halted by the announcement that Princess Charlotte had arrived, and the group turned obediently to face the passage that had been cleared for the princess down the center of the hall.

Princess Charlotte had brown hair and blue eyes, and her mouth, cheeks, and chin loudly declared her the granddaughter of the King. She colored a little at the cheers that went up as she entered the hall; then, in another gesture that made people think of her excellent grandfather, she took great care to greet the people lined up to pay their respects to her. A word here, a question there, a protest to elderly women and men to rise from their bows and curtseys and save their knees and backs.

It was, Jane was sure, impossible to be in the same room with her and not love her.

For the millionth time in her life, Jane silently thanked the Campbells for their rigorous education. A curtsey seemed like such a simple concept; bend your knees, and straighten them again. The dancing master had made her and Sophia do it over and over again, for year after year, until nothing was so easy and graceful as the sinking and rising, like a boat on the ocean in some light, rolling waves. As she watched the line of people when the princess approached them, she could see the differences in education. So many people from so many walks of life and parts of England were assembled here at the watering-hole. Money did not automatically mean distinction. Neither did birth, rank, nor the county one resided in. Only education gave a person the means to walk into the room, or give appropriate honors to one's betters, and wordlessly indicate to the world that one has breeding and manners.

Princess Charlotte stopped when she reached Sophia, who had managed to get in the front row, and smiled at her. "Your hair is the most charming thing I have ever seen, Miss…?" she looked inquiringly at her attendant.

There was a somewhat amusing chain of whispers, then her attendant made the introduction. "Mrs Dixon, Your Highness."

"Well, Mrs Dixon, you have the most clever maid."

"She is – not my maid. My particular friend does my hair. Might I please be allowed to present Miss Fairfax?" Sophia answered.

"Why, of course." When Princess Charlotte smiled, she looked like her grandfather all the more.

Jane found herself pulled forward by Sophia and pushed from behind by Mrs Campbell all at the same time. Princess Charlotte indicated that she might rise from her curtsey, and then looked her in the face. The two of them were almost exactly the same height.

"You are as pretty as you are clever, Miss Fairfax. I assume you also arranged your own hair as well as Mrs Dixon's?"

"Yes, Your Royal Highness." It was impossible not to return the warm smile with one of her own.

"They are both a work of art," the princess declared, and then she moved along and the interview was over. Pushed close together by the admiring crowds, no one noticed the two friends gleefully clutching hands, in a silent promise to squeal together in excitement like two little girls when they had a private moment to themselves later.

When the princess passed into the assembly room itself, people began moving and talking among themselves again. Mr Frank Churchill was the first to congratulate the friends on their attention.

"Well, after that gracious notice, the two of you are going to be the belles of the ball," he predicted amiably. "I had better take advantage of my proximity while I have any sort of advantage. Might I engage Miss Fairfax for the first two dances, and Mrs Dixon for the following two dances?"

"I should be delighted, thank you," Jane answered. She took the arm he offered to escort her into the ballroom, while her head buzzed with excitement and confusion. She would not honestly be able to say which was more thrilling, her compliment from the princess, or the way Mr Churchill looked at her when he asked her to dance.

CHAPTER SIX

There is nothing so delicious as the preparations for bed after coming home from a ball, when two girls giggle with delight over their conquests, and revisit every compliment said by every gentleman.

As Jane entered the inn, she realized that such days had ended for her, forever, when Miss Campbell became Mrs Dixon. As she climbed the stairs behind the Dixons, she steeled herself for the moment she would have to say the awful words, 'good night.' She was determined to be cheerful and nonchalant.

The three of them were surprised by a summons from Mrs Campbell, sitting by the fire in the front parlor. "After you dispose of your wraps and overshoes, why don't you come back in here? The lady of the house is bringing us a jug of negus, so that we might sit a while and let the events of the evening sink in. I declare I am not the least bit tired, and I have not had nearly as exciting an evening as the rest of you."

Mr Dixon had been called upon to dance with the princess, as had Mr Frank Churchill. The friends had their compliments from the princess to review with satisfaction, and all of them had plenty to say about the dances chosen, the quality of the musicians, the acoustic qualities of the room, and the abilities of the dancers.

"It is so interesting dancing in a spa town with people from all over the country!" Sophia was a more avid dancer than Jane. "I swear, we completely collapsed with laughter during the cotillion. Everyone in our set was from a different county, and had a different idea of what the changes were. My partner and I assumed we were doing a ladies' chain, but the couple across from us thought it was a right and left, and our side couples were turning their partners. It was a mess!"

"You can see why cotillions are going out of fashion," Jane pointed out. "Quadrilles and country dances are less likely to create so much confusion."

"Which is a terrible shame, I was always partial to French cotillions," Colonel Campbell chimed in. "Although Mrs Campbell is no doubt more sorry to see the minuet leaving the ballrooms. She was particularly admired for her minuet. Gentlemen of the highest ranks would ask her to dance with them. If they danced with her, everyone would watch her, and the gentleman's lack of grace would pass unnoticed."

"Well, perhaps so," Mrs Campbell said. "But no one wants to spend hours at a ball just watching others. People want to be dancing."

"You were admired for your minuet?" Sophia asked her mother. "You never told us that."

"Well, I was a popular partner." Mrs Campbell was actually blushing a little.

"You never danced any later than the third couple," her husband pointed out. "I was never able to dance with you, myself. After all, I could hardly confront dukes and earls and my commanding officers and insist that I dance with my wife."

"At least when we learned how to waltz, I always waltzed with you," she smiled at him.

"It is an indecent dance, but at least being married, we made it a little more respectable," he smiled back at her. Then he looked around the room. "Why is everyone else smiling at us like that?"

"It is fun, hearing about your romantic past," Mr Dixon looked up from his sketchpad. "If you would both do me the favor of waltzing for us, I will start a fresh sketch."

There was space in front of the pianoforte in the corner. Jane elected to get up and play a waltz, and the Campbells waltzed for them. They continued the conversation as they danced.

"Perhaps I could have married higher above my station in life, but I have been very happy to be married to a man who suits my temperament," Mrs Campbell said. "I know there are those ambitious persons who think otherwise, but there is more to matrimony than money. I might have had finer clothes and carriages if I had married someone else, but I would not have been happier. To the contrary, years with an unsuitable partner would have accumulated into misery by now."

"Well, my captain was not your only conquest," the Colonel pointed out.

"Speaking of conquests," Mrs Campbell suddenly changed the topic, "Jane certainly had her share of them tonight!"

"A few dances is not a conquest," Jane protested. She kept her eyes on the keyboard, but she could feel her cheeks getting warm. She smiled self-consciously, and tried not to think of one particular gentleman holding out his hand to collect her for his dances.

"We may not have to worry about finding you a position as a governess, if any of these fine swains tonight is content with an accomplished, beautiful wife," the Colonel speculated.

"Your face is your fortune," Mrs Campbell agreed. "Perhaps it will be enough to gain a fortune."

"It won't be. Gentlemen require a woman of means," Jane shook her head. "They may dance with me and give pretty compliments, but the dance invitations and compliments will cease once they learn I am a penniless creature. They certainly won't be offering me proposals of marriage."

The Colonel's face clouded. "I am sorry I was not able to do better by you, my girl."

Jane looked at him with love, and her fingers faltered on the keys. "You have done very well indeed by me!" she declared firmly. "I would be an ignorant girl in Highbury with a head full of nonsense and no firm guidance, without your influence. Now I am equipped to live in the world and handle whatever it may send me. I will never be anything but grateful for all you've done for me. I promise I will make you proud."

The eyes of the entire Campbell family were misting over. "You do make us proud," Sophia was the one to speak at this emotional juncture. "And, mark my words, a few years from now, you will be Mrs Calvin Hitchcock, or Mrs James Grismer, or Mrs Frank Churchill, and we will be sitting on the lawn watching our babies play together."

CHAPTER SEVEN

Jane dutifully rose early every morning to accompany the Colonel to the spa for the hot saltwater baths that were meant to cure his hearing loss and her cold. She feared that the treatments were much more effective for her cold than they were for his hearing.

"I am certain the ringing is much less severe," he assured her when she asked, but when she watched him throughout the day, she was sure there was no change in the number of times he needed to ask people to repeat themselves, or the number of times he gave the noncommittal answers that convinced her he had not heard the question.

Nonetheless, it was hard not to enjoy the many delights of the town. The proprietress told them about all the best places to shop for smuggled French silks, and Sophia was well equipped with enough fabric for a couple of years' worth of new gowns, plus some fine fabrics for her husband's waistcoats.

There were walks along the Esplanade, walks in the sand next to the water where the sea bathing machines would put in during the summer months. The party went wherever there were items of interest that Mr Dixon wanted to sketch, so they roamed the ruins of Sandsfoot Castle, admired the new statue of His Majesty King George, shopped along St Thomas and St Mary Streets for presents for Jane's aunt and grandmother as well as for Mr Dixon's parents and various other family members. But they never went back to the music shop.

As busy as the days were, the nights were even more so. There were dinners, concerts, whist parties, and any number of evening visits to be attended. Music was a frequent part of these entertainments, and Jane was often called upon either to perform at the pianoforte to amuse a room full of guests, or to play a handful of simple tunes so that the assembled company could dance. Dance music was less challenging, so a larger handful of young ladies would take turns at the pianoforte, giving everyone a chance to line up with a favorite partner. But Jane was always called upon to play and sing.

As she had predicted, the young gentlemen discovered that her face did not have any other fortune attached to it, and swiftly fell away to court more monetarily gifted faces. There was, however, one notable exception.

Mr Frank Churchill did not seem to care that she would bring nothing but her own self to the marriage contract. As other gentlemen vanished like mist in the sunlight, he took advantage of the greater opportunities to be at her side. He sang duets with her at evening entertainments, turned the pages for her while she played for the dancers, and danced with her when other ladies were providing the music. He happened upon her and Sophia while they were shopping and carried her parcels, and fetched umbrellas for them when it was raining.

Jane enjoyed his attentions very thoroughly. He was more than merely ever-present; he was always ready with good conversation, a clever wit, a well-bred opinion. They could discuss Lord Byron's poetry, or the success of British forces in burning Washington but the failure of the navy at Baltimore in the war in the Americas, or speculate on the proceedings at the Congress of Vienna. After all, even in Weymouth Colonel Campbell received the daily papers, and read them aloud every evening for discussion over the dinner table. Other households said grace at dinner; Colonel Campbell introduced a topic for discussion.

Using the excuse that both Jane and he were born in the same small village of Highbury, Mr Churchill became an almost daily apparition in their lives. On the days he did not show himself, he offered an excuse for his absences.

"We are here for my Aunt Churchill's poor health," he told her as they were seated beside each other at a dinner being thrown by Colonel Walton. "I know there are those who say the majority of her illness is confined to the insides of her head, but they are unjust. I will confide to you honestly that yes, in her past I have seen her fancied ill with no real causes for complaint. But this is different. I am truly worried about her."

"I assume she is taking the hot saltwater baths? Do you think she is deriving any benefit from them?"

"Even with the most solicitous of care, she has her good days and her bad days. I swear, there are days her poor nerves cannot take any more. I will sit and read to her, and some days that is about the only thing that will soothe her."

Jane was impressed by his patience and compassion. "You are a dutiful nephew."

"I will not deny it, she is a difficult woman," he admitted. "But she has always been exceedingly good to me. I know my duty. And I embrace it."

Jane smiled. "I am glad you have each other. Everyone needs kind and understanding people in their lives."

"Kindness and understanding are vastly underrated by a great majority of people," he agreed. "So many people enter the married state thinking only of money and status, and very little about compatibility and understanding. Society treats marriage like a business venture, which is almost vulgar."

Jane was pleased to hear him echoing Mrs Campbell's sentiments. "It is rather vulgar, when you present the matter like that," Jane agreed with him.

"But you do see what I am saying, don't you? There is money, a contract, and, not to be too crude but –" he dropped his voice to a low murmur. "A buyer and a seller."

Jane's eyes got large. She answered him in an equally low voice. "Do you realize what you are comparing marriage to?"

His eyes were looking intently into hers. It was a little hard to focus on his words. His face was too beautiful to be quite real. "Am I wrong? Sometimes it seems to me even worse than that. It is not that uncommon for the bride to be not only chattel, but unwilling chattel."

Jane stared back at him. "I feel fortunate that I have never witnessed that sort of a marriage. Not that I have witnessed so many weddings," she admitted.

"Come, now," Colonel Walton's wife noticed their heads together. "Whispering at the table is a poor show of manners. What are you two conspiring about?"

"You have caught us out, Mrs Walton," Mr Churchill lied smoothly. "Miss Fairfax and I have been discussing which duets we might sing this evening. She has been suggesting several Italian pieces, but I am begging her to at least start with 'Robin Adair.' It is one of my favorite songs. She is protesting that we sang it just the other night, and that people might get tired of hearing it. I put it to all the company at the table: are you tired of hearing us performing Irish ballads, and what is your opinion of that one, in particular?"

The table was unanimous in declaring that the two of them gave such a delightful rendition of 'Robin Adair,' they must indeed sing it again.

"But we should not get ahead of ourselves," Mr Churchill took a sip of his wine. "We have hardly begun to savor this dinner, this is no time to be talking about what happens after dessert. Please forgive my disgraceful manners, Mrs Walton. Your dinner is exquisite."

"You are forgiven, dear boy, if you tell me what you think of the pressed duck."

That night, Jane and Mr Churchill sang several Irish and Scottish songs together, to great approbation. Jane did not mean to show off so much, but when Mrs Walton invited Sophia to take a turn at the pianoforte, her husband came to her rescue.

"Oh, would Miss Fairfax play just one more?" Mr Dixon would implore her. "There was this lovely Italian air I overheard her practicing yesterday morning, it really was entrancing."

Knowing Sophia's distaste for performing before an audience, Jane plunged into 'just one more' several times over. "It is no punishment to play such a wonderful pianoforte," she confessed afterwards to Mr Churchill. "The softness of the upper notes is everything I could ever ask for."

"I am reasonably certain the quality of the instrument is nearly irrelevant, when it is your fingers upon the keys," he answered. "I do believe you bring out the best of everything you play."

"You are too generous, Mr Churchill, but I do try."

"I am not speaking to be generous, I am merely stating a fact," Mr Churchill answered loyally. "But I do hope there are many wonderful instruments in your future."

CHAPTER EIGHT

Jane was playing the pianoforte in the front parlor and Sophia was sewing on buttons when Mr Dixon came hurrying home late one morning. "I don't suppose both you ladies can be interrupted for an afternoon's excursion?"

"What sort of excursion?" Sophia asked.

"I am told that the best way to see the likeness of the King at Osmington is from the water, so I have engaged for us all to take a little boat trip to go see it!" Mr Dixon told them enthusiastically. "Are your parents about somewhere, my dear? Do you suppose they would like to come with us?"

"They are gone to the apothecary at the moment," Sophia told him.

"Can you both be ready to depart within an hour?"

"Yes!" both girls answered at the same time.

"Well, then, you make ready, and I will run down to the apothecary's to ask if they would be interested in going," Mr Dixon was already dashing out the door before Jane stood up from her stool at the pianoforte and Sophia had put down her sewing.

When they returned to the parlor with wraps and bonnets and sensible shoes, Mr Churchill was standing with Mr Dixon, who exclaimed, "Look what I found at the apothecary's! I have convinced him to join our little expedition, as well as your parents."

"How very delightful!" Sophia exclaimed. Jane was glad that Sophia was able to express pleasure for the both of them; her tongue was tied into a knot. All she could manage was a smile.

"Such fortuitous timing," Mr Churchill returned their smiles. "I was ordering some powders for my aunt when I saw the Colonel and Mrs Campbell coming in. And then Mr Dixon ran in to ask if they would like to make the boat trip out to see the White Horse, and, well, here we all are!"

"We shall be a very merry party, with Mr Churchill to join us!" Mrs Campbell also returned to the parlor. "I have exchanged my bonnet for something less likely to be blown away by a sea breeze while we are miles from the shore. Besides, the feathers would not survive such a journey."

"Lead the way!" Colonel Campbell directed Mr Dixon, and they marched cheerfully out into the street and down to the docks.

It was sunny and breezy as they walked to the pier. The skipper of the yacht Mr Dixon had hired greeted them cheerfully. "You could not have picked a more perfect day for an outing. The breeze has been a bit gusty, but that simply means it will be a nice, quick ride. We should be able to sail farther along the coast than I can usually take passengers for an hour."

The skiff was large enough to accommodate eight people, so their party had plenty of room when they climbed down into the boat. It was so arranged that Jane sat at the back on one side, preceded by Mr Dixon and Sophia. Mr Churchill was across from her on the other side, with Mrs and Colonel Campbell.

The skipper instructed Mrs Campbell and Mr Dixon on their jobs. "You are part of the crew for this trip," he told them. "That sail up front, that's the jib. When we come about, that means you unwrap that line right in front of you. And you, when we are turned around, you will pull in your rope, and wind it on the cleat, in a figure eight, just like the missus has hers done up right now, you see that? The lot of you, even the ones not in charge of the jib, when we come about, you need to duck. You see how low the boom sits? It will easily hit you in the head when it swings past. It moves very quickly. Now, everybody ready?" He released his lines, two boys on the dock unwrapped two other ropes, and they were away.

Jane had never been on a sailing boat before. It was exhilarating. They were gliding along the water, moving with the wind. The air smelled of water, and salt, and fish, and sunshine, just like it did when walking on the beach, but yet at the same time it was different. It was – cleaner. More intense. Jane felt cleansed and purified as the wind and salt water spray blew against her face.

They were moving so fast! She was sure she had never been moving so quickly in her life. She and Sophia had lessons in how to ride, but she was convinced no galloping horse ever moved this quickly. All three women shrieked with glee when a gust of wind caught the sails, and the small boat shot forward with an extra burst of speed.

"Do you like mathematics, Mr Churchill?" Jane asked as she watched the curve of the taut sail, and noticed the calm skill with which their skipper managed the extra power being transferred from sail, to boom, to rigging, to the line in his hand, and then relaxed again when the gust had passed.

"I like it all right, I guess. I think I do better with words than with numbers. Why do you ask?" Mr Churchill answered with a quizzical look.

"Tonight at dinner I shall ask Colonel Campbell to explain the mathematics of how sails work," Jane told him, looking back up at the sail. "What happens to the wind when it reaches the sail, how the sail captures the wind to propel us forward. He always knows. It is the sort of thing he did in the army. He is exceedingly good at it."

"Well, I suspect I would make a terrible army officer, in that case," Mr Churchill laughed. "But it would indeed be interesting to hear the explanation."

She took a deep breath, and tried to sound natural. "I will try to arrange an invitation for you to come to dinner, then, if you think your aunt and uncle can spare you." There, she did it! She invited him to dinner. Then she gasped and laughed with the rest of the group as a large wave lifted the boat, and it rocked sideways. It was exciting and a little alarming, but Jane trusted in the expertise of the owner of the boat. They were clearly in no danger.

The White Horse truly was best seen from the water. The silhouette of King George III on horseback was carved into the chalk of the hills rising behind the town and farm fields.

"They say His Majesty objected to the fact this shows him riding away from the town, not toward it, and that is why he hasn't been back," the skipper told them, bringing the boat around and dropping the sails, so that they could float on the waves and admire the view.

"Well, that cannot be," the Colonel objected. "They did not even start carving this until a few years after His Majesty's last visit to Weymouth."

The merry group grew quiet. The king's health and mental well-being had suffered so much that three years ago, his son and heir was appointed prince regent. The king was still the king, but he was unable to truly rule his kingdom.

Mr Churchill cleared his throat, then began singing "God Save the King." Jane quickly joined in, followed by the Dixons and the Campbells. Even the skipper joined in.

When the last note faded away over the waves, the sober silence that followed was broken by a whistle from the skipper. "I have sung that song more than a few times in my life, but that was the first time I sang it with a bunch of real musicians! Was that a four part harmony we were singing?"

Everyone laughed, and the somber mood was lifted. "Yes," Jane assured him. "That was four part harmony."

"Well, three and a half parts," Mr Dixon amended. "I was only pretending to sing. Colonel Campbell was the one truly carrying the baritone part."

"Well, then, shall we continue up the coast a little ways?" The skipper reached up and began raising the sail again. "As I said, swift sailing today, so I can go a little farther up the coast before we have to turn back."

As the boom was rising into place, however, another strong gust burst upon them. The rope was ripped out of the skipper's hands, and the boom swung wildly from one side of the boat to the other. Jane had been looking at the King's silhouette riding the white horse on the hill, and not at the business of sailing.

It all happened in a flash. Before she could turn her head at Mr Churchill's shout of warning, she was hit on the back of the head. Next thing she saw, her face was only inches above the water, she was drenched by a large wave, and she inadvertently took in a large gulp of salt water.

Then she was back on the boat, sprawled awkwardly with her head on Mr Churchill's knee, the small of her back against the legs of the skipper, and Mr Dixon was hovering above her, his hand still clutching onto her pelisse.

Through the water in her ears, she could hear everyone

shouting. The back of her head was throbbing. The sky overhead was very blue, and the sun was in her eyes. "I do believe I am still alive," she reassured everyone. "I think I am going to need some help getting out of this undignified position."

Hands lifted her, and she was back on her seat next to Mr Dixon. Everyone was staring at her in concern. "I am a little the worse for wear, but that would seem to be all."

The skipper shook his head. "You took quite a crack to the skull, there, miss. If it is all the same to everyone, I am going to cut our excursion short and return to port. This young lady needs some dry clothes and a hot toddy. We don't have a physician in town, but we have several very good surgeons. I recommend Mr Small. He's on St Thomas Street."

Jane coughed, and nodded. The large gulp of salty water was not making her feel very well. Now that she was wet, the breeze was also making her cold.

The others were all talking at once. Jane pieced together what happened from what fragments she could string together. "Thank goodness you had such quick reflexes, Mr Dixon!" "If you had not caught her by her habit, she would have fallen straight into the ocean!" "It all happened so fast, I had not even realized Jane was in danger until it was over!" "It was all instinct, really. The boom came at us, Miss Fairfax was next to me one moment but not the next. I reached out and grabbed whatever was in my hand. I am glad it was her, not just a handful of sail or rigging or something."

Mr Churchill was unbuttoning his coat. "You are shivering. Take off your wet coat, put mine on."

Her fingers felt slow and stupid, but her pelisse only had three buttons, and she was soon able to get them undone. She was trying to shrug herself out of the wet garment, but the wet fabric of her coat clung to the wet fabric of her dress. She was glad when both Mr Dixon and Mr Churchill came to her aid.

"That was the biggest fright I have ever had in my life!" Mr Churchill told her as he helped her get her arms into the sleeves of his coat. "Is there anything else I can do for you until we get back to dry land?"

She was clenching her teeth together. Afraid to say anything for fear of them chattering, she shook her head, and tried to smile at him.

The rest of the trip back was a blur. She was cold, there was wind, there were voices. When her wet dress started to soak through Mr Churchill's dry coat, it became less and less of a barrier against the breezes. She was glad they were still brisk, however. She knew the stronger the wind, the sooner she would be back on dry land and able to get into dry clothes.

The moment the skipper navigated his craft back to the dock, she was hurried out of the boat and up the street. She was dimly aware of Mr Churchill taking his leave of her, of their arrival back at the inn, of more voices, of the taste of brandy. She was ushered into a hot bath, but there was a cold compress on the back of her head.

Eventually, Sophia and Mrs Campbell helped her into her nightdress, into her room, and into her bed.

CHAPTER NINE

Mr Churchill called on Jane the next day as she held court in the parlor. The maids already had his coat cleaned, and returned it to him freshly pressed, but while he was appreciative when they delivered it, all his concern was for Jane.

"It looks as good as new! I would happily have sacrificed it, if need be, to ensure that Miss Fairfax survived her ordeal unscathed." He sat on the chair next to the sofa where Jane was reclining, her pillow consisting of a mustard plaster that was meant to reduce the swollen lump on the back of her head.

No amount of pain was sufficient to stop the tingling thrill that went down her spine at the sight of him. "Thank you for your contribution to my survival," she held out a hand to him. "My apologies for not getting up."

He took her hand and bowed over it. "The whole point of calling upon you, dear lady, is to see how you are recovering, not to inconvenience you and increase your discomfort. How is your recovery proceeding?"

"My head is aching, and the lump on the back of my head is throbbing, but the surgeon said some time, and some rest, and I will be better," Jane told him. "I have spent the majority of the morning reassuring the Campbells, and the Dixons, and the proprietress of the inn, and the maids, that I am convinced I am going to survive yesterday's ordeal. So, now I will reassure you, too."

"But is it safe to assume that you are expected to keep quiet for the next several days?" he inquired with a smile that made Jane suspect he had some plot up his sleeve.

"She is to stay as still as possible, until the swelling goes down," Sophia confirmed.

"I feel so terrible," her husband added from behind his ever-present sketchpad. "We proposed coming to Weymouth to improve Jane's health, and instead, I have contributed to making it worse," he concluded ruefully.

"It was an accident," Jane reminded him. "Until the breeze decided to turn against me, I could swear that sailing made me feel as if I had never been ill a day in my life."

Mr Churchill was smiling even more broadly now. "Well, as everyone is determined to keep Miss Fairfax as quiet as possible, and entertained in her seclusion..." he produced a small volume from his coat pocket. "Did I hear tell that no one here has read Lord Byron's 'Lara' yet? My aunt gave me leave to bring it to read to you, Miss Fairfax, if you were of a mind to be entertained. She enjoyed it immensely when I read it to her last week. Would you be interested in having me read to you, to take your mind off your headache?"

The offer was received with enthusiasm and gratitude by everyone in the parlor, and Mr Churchill obliged them with a spirited oration. Jane's stomach fluttered the entire time, and she could feel her cheeks growing warm every time he looked up and smiled at her.

After Mr Churchill's visit, the entire family was smiling at Jane speculatively. "Has that young man spoken to you, yet?" Mrs Campbell asked.

"You mean...?" Jane realized exactly what she meant. "Oh, no. Mr Churchill has been a most kind and attentive friend, but I believe his duty to his aunt prevents him from making any designs for himself. And surely my lack of fortune would be a strong objection to Mr and Mrs Churchill."

"My dear," Captain Campbell laughed, "Mrs Churchill should have no means to object. Her father was a gentleman, to be sure, but her own claims to family and blood are about equal to your own. No doubt she was a very spirited adventuress in her youth, to claim the affections of Mr Churchill. And, speaking of the excellent gentleman, since he married a woman with no fortune, how could he object to his heir, who recently went to the trouble of honoring him by taking his name, behaving in the same manner as himself?"

"His aunt's ill health may make her very reluctant to part with her favorite nephew," Sophia pointed out. "That was a very excellent reading he gave us. He is clearly very practiced, and I am sure he gets his practice keeping his aunt amused."

"He told me the other day that his aunt refused to allow him to go abroad, in order to finish his education," Mr Dixon volunteered. "I will add to my wife's concerns on that score. If she won't let him travel abroad because she cannot do without him even briefly, she may not support the idea of parting with him longer than that."

"Well, surely Enscombe can absorb a daughter as well as a son?" Colonel Campbell objected. "Marriage usually means the wife moves in with her husband. Mrs Churchill would be gaining a nurse, not losing one."

Jane's head was starting to throb again. "Can we please find a different topic for speculation?" she asked. "Why do you suppose Lord Byron would not admit to the publication of 'Lara' for almost a year?"

She was interested in Lord Byron's motivations, but she was even more interested in halting everyone's speculations about Mr Churchill's intentions. Her own speculations were already more than her heart could bear. They were certainly enough to prevent her from sleeping a wink all that night.

Mr Churchill's relationship to his aunt and uncle, especially his aunt, became much clearer over the course of the next week.

While the entire family watched with interest for his next call, one was not forthcoming for an entire week. After several days had elapsed, a note arrived from him instead, addressed to Colonel Campbell, inquiring after the entire family's health, and Jane's continued improvement in particular. He wished that he were in a position to invite them all to come pay a call upon his aunt and uncle, when Jane felt ready for visiting.

Alas, my aunt's health has not been as much improved by the sea air as we hoped. I have suggested that your cheerful company would do wonders for her spirits, but she has declined that suggestion. She has been keeping me much occupied with escorting her to the spa for her treatments, fetching powders from the apothecary, reading to her, writing letters for her, and posting said letters for her. I am sorry to have missed your excellent company these past several days. I have been anxious to know how Miss Fairfax's head is improving. Abandoning my acquaintance at this juncture seems unpardonable; I wanted to let you know I mean no disrespect. I know you understand that my duty to my aunt and uncle supersedes any personal wishes of my own.

This is surely a temporary situation, and I shall see you and your excellent family again soon!

"Well, there you go, Jane!" Sophia exclaimed when her father had finished reading Mr Churchill's letter. "Mr Churchill is as much in love with you as ever, and worries every moment you are out of his sight."

"Surely you exaggerate," Jane protested with a blush.

"I doubt it," Colonel Campbell grinned at her, and then turned his smile on his wife. "I did not have a moment's peace after I met Mrs Campbell. She was the most beautiful creature I had ever laid eyes on, and there were so many other swains buzzing around her. I truly did have to worry every moment she was out of my sight. Who knew what other suitor was trying to press his advantage while I was not there to demonstrate that I was a much better candidate for her affections?"

"I did not have that many other suitors," Mrs Campbell protested, laughing.

"Oh, no?" Colonel Campbell raised both eyebrows. "There was Lieutenant Pickering, and Alexander, and Stockton, and Patterson, and Powers. Most of my regiment was in love with you."

Mrs Campbell opened her mouth to protest, considered the list of names the Colonel had just rattled off, and then paused. "Well," she amended whatever she had been about to say, "none of that lot were real contenders. You clearly outshone them all."

"You see what I mean?" the Colonel turned to the rest of his family. "A suitor has to press his advantage. Alexander was smarter and better-looking than all the rest of us, and Patterson was richer, and Powers was a much better dancer. I had to be more persistent, to charm the most beautiful girl I had ever seen into thinking I was worth having."

Mr Dixon looked fondly at his wife. "Well, I am glad your daughter accepted me, even without your advice."

Sophia smiled back at him. "Well, unlike my mother, I am not the most beautiful girl in the world, but you were willing to take me, as I am."

Mr Dixon laughed. "No man on earth with any sense is going to tell his wife she is not the most beautiful girl in the world! But, regardless of your lack of vanity, you will be one of the most frequently-drawn women in the world." He turned his sketchpad around. He was drawing her in profile where she was sitting in front of the window, with the morning light streaming in, touching her hair and her cheek.

"How beautiful!" Sophia exclaimed.

Watching the Campbells and the Dixons, Jane did hope that there was something to their speculations about Mr Churchill. She wanted to look at a man the way Mrs Campbell and Mrs Dixon watched their husbands, and it must be nice to be looked at the way Colonel Campbell and Mr Dixon regarded their wives. More specifically, she would love to be able to share with Mr Churchill the sort of warmth and sense of belonging that the loved ones in her life enjoyed.

CHAPTER TEN

When Jane was feeling well enough to attend a whist party, she was thrilled to discover that the Churchills were also in attendance.

"I am most gratified to see you back out in society," Frank Churchill echoed her sentiments. "I trust this means your poor head has recovered from your misadventures?"

"I am tolerably well," Jane answered. "Still a little delicate, perhaps. I might not have engaged in something so rigorous as dancing. But cards are a quiet activity, and not too taxing. I assume that is how your aunt is able to manage to be here as well?"

"My aunt's poor health has prevented her from going out most evenings, but she will make every attempt to be sociable if there is a card game involved," Mr Churchill agreed.

"How fortunate for us that she is an avid card player!" Sophia returned from depositing her wraps. "We have missed seeing you, Mr Churchill."

"I do apologize for absenting myself," he said with a bow. "It was certainly not my inclination to neglect your family. But, as the poor nephew and only heir of a well-situated relative, well, my time is not really my own."

"It is a very delicate situation," Jane agreed. "I understand that very well."

"I am sure you do," he smiled his appreciation. "Our situations are not terribly dissimilar. The needs of others take so much precedence over our own. It can be very awkward and distressing from time to time." He took the seat beside her, and leaned forward earnestly. "Since you are from Highbury, Miss Fairfax, are you acquainted with Mr Weston?"

"Why, yes," Jane answered. "He seems a very kind man."

"He is my father. Since I was very small, I have only seen him when he comes to visit while my aunt and uncle are in London. He has recently remarried. My mother passed away when I was very young, and it is my duty as his son to pay a visit to my new mother. But my aunt has not seen fit to spare me for the journey to Highbury."

"That is the problem of being useful," Sophia commented. "The family cannot bear to part with you. It was meant that Miss Fairfax should have left us years ago to take up life as a governess, but somehow we still have not been willing to let her start looking for a suitable position."

"But at least the Campbells have never prevented me from paying my duty to my grandmother and aunt," Jane added, slipping her arm around Sophia's waist for a sisterly squeeze. "I have not been there for a couple of years, but I almost always visit once or twice a year. My absence these last two years was due to selfishness on my part, not a lack of generosity on the part of the Campbells."

"She says that," Sophia countered, "But surely we could have been more generous, or more insistent, or something."

"I don't see how," Jane responded. "Your parents have always been completely generous with everything within their means."

"Generosity of one sort can unintentionally lead to a lack of generosity of a different sort," Mr Churchill observed. "My aunt and uncle have been very generous in naming me their heir. But I confess it does make me feel beholden. I am sure my aunt does not mean to keep me from my duty to my father. But how do I pay my respects to Mrs Weston as a new bride, without my aunt and uncle's approval? I resort to letters, which I hope will be my proxy in giving my respects."

"My Aunt Bates wrote extensively about your father's marriage. He married Miss Taylor, the governess of Miss Woodhouse? Perfectly respectable. She must be a lady of forbearance and understanding, having lived with the Woodhouses for many years! Surely she will show you the same sympathy and patience that I believe she shows them. You must have explained your situation well enough to earn her forgiveness for the slight."

"I like to believe so," he answered. "I hope so. I would not wish to give offense."

The announcement came for them all to take their tables, cutting off any further discussion of Highbury and their similar circumstances.

CHAPTER ELEVEN

It was a gray, breezy day, but Sophia was determined to get in one more shopping trip before the Dixons departed for Ireland. Her parents looked skeptically at the skies, and declined to join her, and Mr Dixon was busy making their travel arrangements. So it fell to Jane to accompany her to the silk merchants, the milliners, and any shop on St Thomas and St Mary Streets to which they had not paid at least a cursory visit.

"Do you think I should get a couple more pairs of gloves, after all? You know how quickly I ruin my gloves," Sophia asked anxiously as they perused the selections of pre-made items in a surprising number of shades.

"You do have the most remarkable ability to acquire stains that defy the most tenacious laundress," Jane giggled. "I still want to know how it is that you could spill one cup of punch that splashed both our dresses and gloves, and mine came clean, but yours were ruined."

"It is my one true talent," Sophia answered. "I keep warning Mr Dixon that I am going to be a most trying and expensive wife, but he will not believe me."

"Nor should he," Jane replied staunchly. "You are a most sweet and amiable wife, and he adores you. How could he not? You are quite perfect for each other."

"Speaking of Mr Dixon, I promised to replenish his art supplies!" Sophia exclaimed. "I nearly forgot!"

"Well, then, buy four more pairs of gloves, and then we can go take care of that errand, before we get distracted by any more purchases," Jane suggested.

The gloves were purchased, along with a large selection of colored silks for embroidery and several handkerchiefs, and then the friends turned their steps back up the street.

The art supplies purchased and sent to their lodgings, they stood looking up the street, undecided upon their next direction.

"Hello, there! Fancy finding the two of you still shopping!" Mr Dixon came around the corner and laughed in delight to find them.

"We just ordered all your art supplies," Sophia told him. "I got crayons as well as watercolors. And a dozen new sketchbooks."

"Excellent, my darling. I have been going through more sketchbooks lately, and being married to you, I can foresee that I shall continue to require more sketchbooks than I used to."

"Sooner or later you will tire of me as a subject."

"I doubt it. Or, if that happens eventually, it will only be because someday our children will no doubt absorb a great deal of my attention as new subjects."

Jane smiled at their flirtation, and wondered if she should wander over to look in the shop windows and let them be alone together. As she scanned the street looking for a window that could occupy her, her eyes fell on a most welcome sight walking up the street towards them. "Mr Churchill!"

"Hello, Churchill!" Mr Dixon greeted him as Mr Churchill approached their party.

"Dixon. Ladies." Mr Churchill looked very glad to see them. "What brings you out on this increasingly blustery day?"

"Some last shopping before we set sail for Ireland. You are just in time. I was about to ask my wife and Miss Fairfax if they would join me in the examination of a lovely inlaid table I am thinking about getting for the front hall. It is a bit of a walk; all the way to Chesterfield Place. But I did not want to buy it without my wife's opinion. Would you like to join us?"

Jane's head had been less and less pleased with her morning's exertions, and the extension of their shopping trip daunted her. Now that Sophia was no longer alone, she was not needed to escort her. "Would you mind terribly taking the detour to drop me off back at the inn? My head is not entirely happy with me, if you might excuse me from rendering an opinion?"

"Of course!" Mr Dixon's forehead furrowed with a concerned

frown. "Or, better still, since it is not on the way, Churchill, would you mind seeing Miss Fairfax home? I would be remiss to force Miss Fairfax beyond her endurance."

"I am completely at Miss Fairfax's disposal," Mr Churchill answered gallantly.

"Thank you," Jane answered gratefully. "If it is not too much trouble."

"Not in the least!" Mr Churchill answered. "I have finished with my aunt's errands. A longer walk before I return will do me good."

"Thank you, Churchill! You are a good sort." With a nod to him and Jane, Mr Dixon took his wife's arm, and they turned in one direction, while Mr Churchill and Jane turned in the other.

Mr Churchill offered her his arm. "Shall we?"

The Esplanade was almost completely deserted. The skies were distinctly grayer, and the breeze, which had been brisk that morning, was blowing with greater determination than before.

Without a word, simply understanding each other and enjoying the chance to walk together, they walked down the steps to the beach, and strolled down the sand where the bathing machines were parked in a row, waiting for better weather.

"When do you leave?" Mr Churchill asked her, his steps getting even slower than the slow pace necessitated by the sand.

"The Campbells and I are staying two more days, after the Dixons leave for Ireland. Then I return to London with the Campbells."

Their steps slowed to a halt between two of the bathing machines. "I will not be far behind you. My aunt and uncle are thinking of leaving within the fortnight. My aunt has not entirely made up her mind yet on a particular date. But the servants have been folding our clothing to make it ready to put in the trunks. At least the both of us will be here for the ball tomorrow night. I am glad I shall have the opportunity to dance with you again before we part ways."

Mr Churchill caught the end of one of the long ribbons from her bonnet, which were flying madly in the strong breeze. He toyed with it for a long while, then looked up into her eyes. "Do you believe in love at first sight?" he asked.

"No, I don't suppose I do," Jane answered. Her heart started beating harder. That was a lie. Maybe her breath was catching in her throat because she was lying: she fell in love with him the moment she saw him, rescuing the poor store clerk. Or maybe it was because he was standing so close to her, just on the other end of her bonnet ribbon. She felt her cheeks growing warm, and tried to talk herself out of blushing. He was not standing any closer to her than when they danced together, or sat on the same bench at the pianoforte. Why should it fluster her that he was wrapping the end of her bonnet ribbon around his fingers like that?

"Neither did I." He tied a knot into the very end of the ribbon, then caught the other flying ribbon, and did the same to its end. "I thought love requires mutual respect and understanding, and complementary temperaments that can only be discovered with a judicious application of time and conversation."

Jane hid her trembling hands inside her muff. She wished there was a way to hide the fact that she was trembling all over. "I understood you from the first moment I saw you," she admitted, her voice little more than a whisper.

Mr Churchill looked up from her ribbons, and she was bowled over by his beautiful, soul-piercing, intelligent eyes. "And I knew from the moment you looked at me, that you understood me like no one has ever understood me before." Now he had both her bonnet ribbons in his hands, and he gently tugged on them. She was not even sure which one of the two of them took a step forward, but the distance between them was shorter. She thought he was going to kiss her. If he did not, she was going to have to be the one to kiss him. The thought made her blush harder.

But he did not kiss her. His eyes stared intently into hers. His eyes were dark brown, but being so close, she could see that there were actually several different shades of brown. The outside edge was darker than the middle, and there were flecks in his eyes that seemed almost black. "Please tell me you understand me, now," he whispered.

"I think I do," she answered as softly as he asked.

"So, as soon as I can get permission, you'll marry me?"

"What?" Jane asked, stupidly.

"I told you how it is with my aunt and uncle. I am not a free agent. Will you wait for me, will you agree to a secret engagement, and as soon as I can get permission, we can make our engagement known?"

Jane's head was spinning. She was shaking, she was hot and cold at the same time, she was frightened, she was elated. *He wanted to marry her!*

"Yes," she answered. "Yes, I will."

There was no telling who kissed whom. They met in the middle.

CHAPTER TWELVE

Jane had never spent so long at her dressing table as she did before the ball at the assembly rooms, the night before her departure. *She was engaged. Mr Frank Churchill had asked her to marry him, and she was engaged!*

As she pulled out all the hairpins and started over with some fine braids to loop around the knot at the back of her head, she pondered the wisdom of confiding in Sophia. She would want to know. She was sure Sophia would be glad for her. She was a pragmatic soul, and would surely advise her that a secret engagement to a man as destined to be as wealthy as Mr Frank Churchill made for a much better future than that of a governess. She would be a wealthy man's wife, not a highly educated hermit with only small children for company.

But, she debated with herself, if she told Sophia, Sophia would tell her husband. Between the two of them, one of them would talk the other into telling the Colonel and Mrs Campbell. Could four people keep the secret from spreading any further?

The Dixons would be in Ireland. If they told anyone in Ireland, it could hardly matter. But the Campbells were going home to London. Could Mrs Campbell resist the urge to confide in her bosom friend, Mrs Baldwin? Could the Colonel keep the same secret from his best friend, Colonel Bishop?

She despised the idea of keeping such an important secret from the people she loved best in all the world. But, because they loved her, they would be excited for her and might share with others in their excitement. Or, worse, what if they disapproved? She did not imagine that they would. But was she absolutely, completely sure of that?

There was a knock on the door, then Sophia came in. "Jane? Do you need help with your dress? Father has sent for the carriage."

Jane pushed the last pin into her hair. Yes, that would do. "Your timing is perfect, thank you! My hair would simply not behave tonight."

Sophia smiled at her fondly. "You look ravishing. You always do. I am not sure I have ever seen you look so lovely."

"It is our last ball in Weymouth! I am determined to have a wonderful time," Jane answered, wishing she could say more. For now, she would not.

Frank Churchill was waiting for her when she arrived. He had now been a convenient sixth with their party on multiple occasions, escorting Jane following the Campbells and Dixons, and it seemed so natural as he greeted them and slipped into place as they entered the hall. "Have a care, you are sparkling tonight," he murmured under his breath. "Almost as if you had recently become engaged to the love of your life."

Jane did not dare look at him as she smiled. If she did, the entire world would know their secret.

Perhaps they were still too obvious. Mrs Campbell and Mrs Dixon were smiling speculatively at Jane as they laid their wraps aside and took a last look at their hair in the glass. "Mr Churchill seems very taken with you," Mrs Campbell observed. "Perhaps with a little encouragement from you, your future might be very different than we had imagined."

Jane internally squirmed. What was she supposed to tell them? Her mouth moved a moment before any actual sounds emerged.

"Is he in a position to be making any offers?" she asked. "If he only recently took his uncle's name and became his heir, what sort of stipulations might there be towards any marriage prospects?"

"Mrs Churchill can hardly be in a position to object, she herself came from a family of no consequence," Mrs Campbell reminded her. Jane wondered where Colonel and Mrs Campbell had received their information. This was the second time they brought up Mrs Churchill's past. They had clearly been making inquiries.

"The way Mr Churchill looks at you, he is surely of a mind to propose to you, if he can," Sophia observed.

"What is in his mind, and what he is able to say and do, may be very different things," Jane pointed out. "His aunt requires a lot of his attention. We also have his uncle's wishes to consider."

"It is a shame they are not here tonight," Sophia shook her head. "If you were able to charm them as much as you have already charmed Mr Frank Churchill, surely all three would be delighted to welcome you to their family."

"I would not object," Jane admitted as they moved back into the hall to collect their escorts. The words took on special meaning as her eyes met Mr Churchill's, waiting with Colonel Campbell and Mr Dixon for their reappearance.

They walked into the hall just as the call was made to start a new dance; with a slight bit of hurry the six of them were able to claim the top of the set. Mrs Campbell was called upon to name the dance, but as she did so, her shoelace broke. There was a bustle of confusion, mother and daughter hurried away to fix the problem, their husbands left with them, and Mr Frank Churchill and Jane ended up at the top. It fell upon to Jane to call the dance; she picked The Duke of Kent's Waltz.

The music started, they honored each other and set off. They made a right hand star with their neighbors, a left hand star, they took hands down the center, cast around their neighbors, then met in the middle and stepped forward and back. "Clever girl," he whispered in her ear as they changed places, "you named the dance," they passed again, "which allows for the greatest amount of contact," he finished when their hands met for the final turn. Jane smiled her answer over her shoulder as they started over with a new couple.

The refreshment room was fairly empty when Mr Churchill escorted her in, after they had danced with each other, the Campbells, the Dixons, and other partners of their acquaintance. Jane wished they could open a window, but she knew how everyone would object to her catching cold. She plied her fan and thanked him when he brought her a glass of punch. He sat beside her, sipping his own glass, surveying the room to calculate how much they might be overheard by other attendees. "I have an idea."

Jane kept her eyes on the rim of her punch glass. "Yes?"

"We both have a connection to the village of Highbury. My father has recently been married, and I am overdue to pay a visit to make the acquaintance of my new mother. Your grandmother and aunt reside in Highbury?"

"Indeed, they do," Jane answered.

"I approached the idea of marriage with my aunt yesterday, after I left you. She was not fond of the idea. I fear this might take all my powers of persuasion, which, as you know, are considerable."

Jane had to laugh at that statement. "Yes, I am very familiar with them."

"I think this is going to take some time. She is a stubborn woman, but once I acquaint her with an idea long enough, I can almost always talk her around until she thinks any idea of mine was hers in the first place."

"What does this have to do with Highbury?" Jane asked.

"Well, we need time for the idea of marriage to germinate inside my aunt's head. While we are waiting for those seeds to sprout, we can spend the time together in Highbury, instead of separated in Yorkshire and London. I already tried out the idea of getting my aunt to London, but it will be easier to convince her to let me go to Highbury to visit my father than it will be to convince my aunt to go to London. She is not fond of the city."

Jane's spirits sank. "Do you think your aunt is really going to object to me so much?"

He took her hand in the process of taking her empty punch glass, and gave it a heartfelt squeeze before letting go. "My dearest darling Miss Fairfax, it has nothing to do with any objection to you. My aunt is a difficult, selfish woman, and I have foolishly spent my life making myself agreeable to her. So now, she has come to rely on my company so completely, she is reluctant to share it with anyone. I could tell her Princess Charlotte has asked me to marry her, and she would object in the most stringent of terms. I will write you to let you know how I am getting on, but do consider the idea of visiting Highbury."

By the time they regained the ballroom, they had memorized each other's post-offices where they might send letters.

Part Two

CHAPTER ONE

My dearest Miss Fairfax,

I wish I had better news to write to you.

I told you before we said farewell that my aunt was unenthusiastic when I approached her with the general idea of my getting married. I am fairly convinced that, in her head, she has been planning for me to remain a bachelor for the rest of her life. When I bring up the subject of marriage, she insists that since she is dying, I should spend my time with her; I can devote myself to other people – including a wife – after she is gone.

Since she has spent the last twelve years of her life on her deathbed, I can only assume she will spend the next twelve years of her life also on her deathbed.

I will own that my aunt is a difficult woman, but I insist that my own stubbornness, and my love for you, is stronger than her ability to be obstinate. Bear with me, my angel of patience. I am sure once I get her used to the idea that she can share me with another human being, without her feeling neglected, I can get the necessary permission to make you the next Mrs Churchill.

I am glad to hear you have been able to procure a visit to Highbury; while I have no excuse to go to London, I have been endeavoring to get to Highbury to call upon my father's bride for some time. Surely my persuasive forces, when I have double the reason to be there, will prevail to

bring me to you sometime very soon.
Every day apart from you is agony, you must believe me
when I say I shall see you soon!

Your devoted slave,
F. C. Weston Churchill

Jane walked to the post-office in Highbury every day. Some days, it was to send or retrieve letters for her grandmother and aunt, Mrs and Miss Bates. Most days, it was to send a letter to Sophia, to Colonel Campbell, or to Mr Churchill.

Arranging to come to Highbury had been easier than she had anticipated; Sophia had been so homesick upon reaching Ireland, she begged her parents to join her at her new home, Baly-craig, only weeks after she had arrived. The invitation had included Jane as well as the Campbells. Even very recently, Jane would have once again postponed her new life as a governess and gone with the Campbells. She would dearly have loved to see Ireland, as well as her bosom friend again. But now she had her own affairs to see to. The excuse of wishing to see her aunt and grandmother was sound, especially after nigh on two years' absence. No one argued with her need to fulfill her family obligations.

Mr Frank Churchill thought that it would take him as much as a month to persuade his aunt to allow them to get married. Just to be safe, Jane asked for a three month visit. She had worried that the request for such a long visit would raise eyebrows; she had forgotten how simple-minded and good-natured her relatives were. She was grateful to be received with nothing but enthusiasm.

Jane could tell on the very afternoon of her arrival that it was, however, going to be the longest three months of her life.

There were those who professed to prefer the country to the city. Jane was not one of them. Or, at least, she did not prefer the country at Highbury. When she was younger, she mostly appreciated that her aunt was talkative but good-natured. But now, as an adult, Aunt Bates's verbosity and generosity of feeling combined into a perpetual assault on Jane's ears.

That evening, Jane watched the clock while her aunt cheerfully pattered away, gossiping about this neighbor, and then that neighbor. She went for a full seventeen minutes before she required any verbal input from anyone else in the room.

While Jane listened to the long monologues about who had written to whom, and the generosity of the neighbors who had given them various foodstuffs, and complimenting Jane's needlework, and penmanship, and fussing over her health, she missed the conversations at the Campbells' dining room table, in their drawing room, or out in public in their company. Jane realized there was far less stimulus in the country; they could not discuss concerts or lectures, when there were no concerts or lectures to attend. There was less access to books, and fewer newspapers. Hence, a letter to one of the neighbors would provide a week's worth of discussion.

Highbury seemed to thrive on gossip. It was not merely her aunt. When Jane's arrival necessitated a parade of callers to welcome her back to Highbury, and then Jane was required to accompany her aunt and grandmother on the return visits, she was subjected to day after day of conversation that was comprised of nothing but gossip, with hardly a breath of substance.

It afforded her some amusement that her aunt could talk so long about a letter, without ever saying a thing about the actual contents. She praised the handwriting. She praised the style. She praised the frequency with which the correspondent wrote. Jane wondered idly what a "bad letter" would be, since her aunt was consistently praising people's correspondence for being "a good letter."

While these endless conversations mostly left Jane mentally numb, her interest was strongly piqued when Mr and Mrs Weston called upon them.

She had remembered Mr Weston as a very kind man. Now she watched him with intense interest, noticing the familial resemblances, a few mannerisms, and a cheerful way of looking at the world. Both father and son had a profound sort of trust in the universe. Somehow or other, things would work out. Jane wished she could have so much faith.

Mrs Weston was every bit as patient and generous as Jane had reported to Mr Churchill. Jane could not help but warm to her immediately upon the renewal of the acquaintance. She wished she could confide to her that someday soon, Jane would be able to call her 'mother.'

At least the inevitable topic of letters came up, and when Jane accompanied the Bateses for their return call upon the Westons, the much-talked of letter was produced, and Jane was able to read it for herself.

It took all her strength not to caress the words upon the page, to put the paper to her lips. His hand had held this piece of paper. He had worried that his letter was an inadequate substitute for the visit he knew was his duty to his father's new wife; she could reassure him from both the words on the page and the loving way the recipient, and his father, and the entire village accepted his apology, that he had nothing about which to worry.

Most well-beloved Mr Churchill,

Your father and Mrs Weston did me the honor of calling upon me to welcome me back to Highbury yesterday, and my Aunt Bates and I returned their visit today.

Please ease any fears on your part that your letter is not sufficient to placate your family; indeed, every single person in Highbury has read your letter, and admired it, and exclaimed over it, and declared you a most excellent young man, and they are most satisfied with your very proper feelings.

Rather than dismissing your need to pay your visit, however, you ought to know that everyone is wild to see you. You are everyone's favorite subject of gossip. The only topic I hear about more in a day is whatever food has arrived for us from one of the neighbors. Mr and Miss Woodhouse, Mrs Cole, and Mr Knightley have all been most charitable to my aunt and grandmother. I have known most of my life that they live on the charity of others, but now, somehow, it bothers me more than it ever did. Perhaps because I am no longer a child, perhaps because I have not witnessed it for longer than a fortnight since I was eight years old.

I hope you are able to make headway with your aunt's permission quickly. I am missing your quick wit and conversation more than I can tell you! I am still subject to frequent headaches, just as the doctor in Weymouth warned me would happen, but I am sure a mere two hours of your company would help them vanish with greater speed.

Your adoring,
J. Fairfax

CHAPTER TWO

On Jane's third day back in Highbury, Miss Emma Woodhouse came to welcome her home.

Aunt Bates received her with the usual profusion of gushing thanks for the latest gifts of food from Hartfield, and how kind and thoughtful Miss Woodhouse was, and how fortunate they were to have such thoughtful neighbors.

Miss Woodhouse's elevated stature as the wealthiest caller ever to climb the stairs to the little apartment quieted Miss Bates's ever-active tongue from time to time. At least long enough for Miss Woodhouse to get in a word, now and then.

"My father would love to be able to welcome Miss Fairfax back to Highbury; since he is so little away from home, can I trouble you, Mrs Bates, and Miss Fairfax to come to Hartfield on Thursday evening?" Miss Woodhouse asked as she settled on the sofa and accepted a cup of tea.

"Oh, yes, that would be so lovely! Mr Woodhouse is so good to think of poor Jane's return to us! My mother was saying to me the other day how much she loves being in your drawing room with a good game of quadrille. Nothing gives us more pleasure. You are so gracious to think of us, inviting us over so often whenever your father is well enough to play cards. I am so grateful. And I know you and Jane would like the chance for a nice long visit. Bless me, I know how attached the two of you are to each other. How could you not be, when you are only three months apart in age, and both of you such beautiful and accomplished young ladies! Since this is our first time laying eyes upon Jane in two years, I know the two of you have so much to talk about! Dear me, what a pleasant evening Thursday evening is going to be for all of us!"

Inevitably, Jane's and Miss Woodhouse's eyes met, and both of them smiled. Jane could only assume that Miss Woodhouse disliked her as much as she disliked Miss Woodhouse. But they did have this in common: the entire village always assumed that the two of them must be special bosom friends because they were the same age. That assumption irked Jane, and it must annoy Miss Woodhouse equally so. Perhaps more so, since Miss Woodhouse was an heiress, and she would be assuming that Jane was on her way to becoming a governess.

"I am pleased you will be able to come," is what Miss Woodhouse said when Aunt Bates stopped for a sip of tea. "Of course, if Miss Fairfax will bring her music, we would all love to hear her play."

Jane was assuming she was expected to say something in acquiescence, but her aunt accepted for her. "Bless me, Jane would love to play. We don't have a pianoforte for her here, you know, which I am sure is such a hardship for her, for she is so very fond of music! She would be at the pianoforte all day long if we had an instrument. But of course that is completely beyond our means. Mother and father had an instrument when my sister and I were children, and you know my sister was very musical. Jane gets her talent from her mother. It is so kind of you to give Jane the opportunity to play. I am sure she misses it dreadfully. And you have such a beautiful instrument, much nicer than the one we did have when I was a girl. It is probably much nicer than the one Jane had available to her at the Campbells. It might be the very nicest instrument she has ever played upon in her life."

Miss Woodhouse took advantage of Miss Bates stopping for air to conclude, "Excellent. I will send James for you."

The remainder of the fifteen-minute visit was spent listening to Aunt Bates's praise of Miss Woodhouse's thoughtfulness, and what a lovely carriage Mr Woodhouse owned, and what a treat it was to ride in it, and how wonderful James was; he always helped Mrs Bates in and out of the carriage, since of course her knees weren't what they used to be.

One of the last of the Highbury residents to call upon Jane came later that same afternoon. Mr Knightley owned Donwell Abbey. He was a neighbor to the Woodhouses at Hartfield, but in a different parish. He was moderately tall, moderately handsome, quiet, and very gruff. Jane supposed him to be well-meaning, and possibly much better-read than most of the residents of Highbury. But his lack of polish meant his manners usually left something to be desired. He seemed to be honest, but lacked the tact to turn his blunt statements into welcome criticisms. It seemed to Jane he was much more comfortable with his tenant farmers than he ever would be in London society.

He happened to pay his call while Miss Bates was not at home. Jane had been writing a letter for her grandmother, whose eyesight was less sharp than in former days, but whose hearing was not quite as deficient as Miss Bates thought.

"I never get a word in anyway; I just stop listening," Mrs Bates confessed to Jane when they had a moment alone.

Pen and ink were laid aside, however, when the maid announced they had another visitor. Jane helped her grandmother stand up as Mr Knightley was ushered into the room.

"Please don't get up on my account, Mrs Bates," Mr Knightley protested when he saw her rising in order to give him a curtsey. "Surely we know each other well enough to forego that formality."

"My knees are not as far gone as my daughter says they are," Jane's grandmother said after executing a fairly acceptable rendition of proper honors.

"I am sure of it, Mrs Bates," Mr Knightley chuckled. "It is kind of you to allow your daughter to think you are completely dependent upon her. You give her a purpose in life."

Even though Jane might be in complete agreement with Mr Knightley's assessment of the familial assumptions, she somehow resented his implicit criticism of her aunt. Several sharp things passed through her mind to say. She settled upon, "Would you care for tea, Mr Knightley? I can ring for Patty."

"Oh, no, please do not trouble yourself on my account," he protested, sitting in the chair she indicated for him. "I happened to have business here in town, so I thought I would come and welcome you back to Highbury, and apologize for not having come sooner. My estate has been occupying my full attention. I kept meaning to make the trip in to see you, and then it was suddenly too late to call."

Jane tried to imagine anyone in London making the excuse that they were too busy and distracted by their own affairs to pay their necessary calls. It made her smile. Which was just as well, she ought to be smiling, anyway. "No matter, you are here now. I trust all is well at Donwell Abbey?"

"It is, indeed. Everyone is prospering. My manager has been pressuring me to enclose my fields, but I have no interest in displacing my tenants in order to increase my own profits."

Jane appreciated his sentiments. "It is honorable of you to be thinking of the greater good, instead of your own personal gain. I do fear for England as a whole. When so many landowners are removing tenants to raise more sheep, where are all those people supposed to go? Instead of a nation filled with respectable farmers, we are going to be a nation of dispossessed poor, desperately looking for a way to survive."

"I agree!" Mr Knightley sat forward in his chair. "When a farmer has no land to farm, what is left for him? How is he expected to feed his family? If we don't put an end to these practices, we are going to see a rise in crime the likes of which this nation has never seen before. What are we supposed to do, ship them all to Botany Bay and Van Dieman's Land?"

"More prison hulks in the Thames?" Jane agreed. "What do we do when there are so many of them it impedes the ability of merchant vessels to get in and out of London?"

"My thinking, exactly!" Mr Knightley exclaimed. "A landowner has an obligation to the people on his land. Violating that responsibility to increase profits is bad policy, and we are going to suffer for it."

Their interesting conversation might have lasted longer, but Miss Bates arrived, and the remainder of Mr Knightley's call was occupied with Miss Bates's profuse thanks for the honor of his visit, and how difficult it was for her mother to go out anymore, on account of her knees. Jane was surprised to be honestly disappointed when Mr Knightley's call came to an end.

CHAPTER THREE

Thursday night, the Woodhouses' carriage arrived, the Bates ladies were handed in, followed by Jane, and they were soon deposited at the Hartfield front door.

Hartfield was a grand manor, the kind of place that required a full complement of farmers to work the adjacent lands, an army to trim the gardens, and a large staff of servants to maintain the house and its occupants. Jane had been in other country estates where the task of upkeep outstripped the means of the owners to ensure good repair, but the Woodhouses were wealthy enough that such concerns were not an issue.

When Jane was being perfectly honest with herself, she was terribly jealous of Miss Woodhouse. She had absolutely everything that money could buy: clothes, carriages, a very beautiful pianoforte, and all the freedom that over-indulgent and affectionate parents could give. Her mother had died only a year or so after Jane's own mother had died (another reason why everyone in Highbury assumed that the two of them must of course be extremely attached to each other), but while Jane was an orphan, Miss Woodhouse still had a father to pet her and spoil her and make much of her somewhat paltry talents.

It took her a lot of effort to smile graciously as Miss Woodhouse welcomed her to her home. She felt more charitable as she helped Miss Woodhouse establish the ladies and Mr Woodhouse in the drawing room.

Mr Woodhouse was, in a way, an amalgam of her grandmother and her aunt. Fussy, sickly, constantly harping on worries with little substance behind them, and trying to cope with the various unpleasant consequences of getting old. He was oddly likeable. When she paid him her respects, he took her hand gently between both of his, expressed his concerns at the rumors of her poor health, and rattled off a litany of cures she ought to try. He was kind-hearted and generous, with little ability to affect any real improvement in his own life, much less others.

"My dear, since you are ill, you must sit beside the fire. But not too close! While it would not do to take a chill, excessive heat is almost as bad! Perhaps worse. Emma, where is the fire screen? We cannot have Miss Fairfax going home more ill than she arrived."

"It is right here, papa!" Emma spoke to him in affectionate, soothing tones. "Of course I will see to Miss Fairfax's comfort."

Miss Woodhouse handled him with so much patience. Jane could see the kindness of the father reflected in the daughter, and it spoke well of the both of them. She resolved to try to be more charitable in her thoughts towards Miss Woodhouse.

"Oh, of course you will, Miss Woodhouse, you always are the soul of thoughtfulness!" her Aunt Bates was gushing. Jane groaned inwardly. Once her aunt started talking, she never stopped. "We are so worried about poor Jane, you know, she has come to us from the Campbells because they are so worried about her health! As if her delicate constitution was not bad enough, that boating incident certainly did her no good. Since she has been with us, bless me, mother and I have been so anxious. You should see how little appetite she has. This morning for breakfast she had nothing but a piece of bread with the smallest bit of butter on it, and then at dinner, you could see through the slice of mutton she ate. Mother and I are so worried for her!"

"I should send over some gruel, Miss Bates," Mr Woodhouse declared. "It is the best thing for one's health. If Miss Fairfax were to confine herself to a basin of gruel for supper, I am quite sure she would be restored to health very quickly!"

"You are so generous, Mr Woodhouse!" her aunt thanked him profusely, while Jane tried to smile. She hated gruel. "Indeed, we have been so worried about poor Jane. When the sea air of Weymouth was not sufficient to restore her health, we wondered what we could possibly have to offer here in Highbury? But of course, simply being away from London must surely be an improvement to one's health and spirits…"

Jane stopped listening while her aunt and Mr Woodhouse diagnosed what was wrong with her, and then, even worse, her aunt started producing the caps and workbags Jane had made them since her arrival in Highbury. She was suddenly desperately homesick for London. The smoky skies and crowded streets would be worth it for the music, the dancing, and most of all, the conversation with people she enjoying conversing with. Almost no one in Colonel Campbell's circle ever talked of one's health. When they did, it was with a jovial dismissal of ills as an inconvenience, the price one paid for having been in the army. And one never brought bits of needlework to show off to the neighbors.

Mr Knightley's arrival contributed something of a relief. Instead of discussing what was wrong with her, there were discussions of why Mr Knightley was only just arriving.

"My deepest apologies, but my manager had some pressing issues for me to resolve. I trust you are enjoying each other's company without me?"

Jane could swear his eyes had lingered upon her as the group exchanged their greetings. Her thoughts retreated back to London as Mr Knightley was required to elaborate upon the farming troubles that had delayed him.

She had to pay attention, again, when music was called for. As the guest, Jane was called on to go first, if she thought her health would stand the rigors of performance. Jane would have to be on her deathbed before she would pass up the chance to play on such a beautiful instrument. As she touched the keys with the first strains of Mozart's Sonata Number 18 in D Major, she acknow-ledged that, even were she dying, she would still be playing. Some things were more important than the inconvenience of one's health.

Musically ignorant as the company might be, the praise and applause and insistence that she play another piece was still pleasant. It was not the same as the appreciation she'd received in Weymouth, from people with much more discerning ears, but it was modestly gratifying.

After she finished, Miss Woodhouse took her place on the piano bench. Jane smiled politely while she played one of Pleyel's German Dances. She had the entire length of the piece to think of something complimentary to say. It made Jane's homesickness for

London all the more acute. There were so many accomplished musicians in London! An evening's soiree with intimate friends was a chance for real musical excellence, a chance to learn from one's peers, a chance to discuss fingering techniques and the excitement over Beethoven's first new sonata in five years.

When the music had finished, Jane and Miss Woodhouse accepted the small glasses of Madeira from Mr Knightley's stock that he was pouring for everyone. Once they made sure their elders were comfortably situated, they settled themselves in a corner.

"Well, what did you truly think of my playing?" Miss Woodhouse asked.

"Pleyel is one of my favorites: it is hard to listen to you without thinking of wildflowers and blue skies," Jane responded. "Have you ever been to his shop in London?"

"No, I have never been to London," Miss Woodhouse responded.

Jane was surprised. "What? Never?"

"I cannot imagine why I should want to go to London, everything I could ever want or need is right here in Highbury," Miss Woodhouse answered. "I certainly don't need to go there to buy music, or to hear someone else play a pianoforte. But enough about music! Do tell me, Miss Fairfax, I am dying to hear more about Miss Campbell's wedding! What can you tell me of Mr Dixon, who has carried off your bosom friend to Ireland? I hear he is a very congenial man! What can you tell me of his character?"

Jane's mind clamped down as hard as her jaw. She hated gossip. She hated small minds that were capable of nothing but gossip. She hated Miss Woodhouse, who clearly possessed such a small mind, she was capable of thinking of little more than gossip. She tried, she really tried, to think better of Miss Woodhouse. But it was impossible. She was unbearably stupid. A different kind of stupid than her Aunt Bates, but every bit as unbearable.

When she thought of Mr Dixon, she could not separate him from his sketchbook, from the look he gave her surrogate sister when he had sketched her with the sunlight streaming through the window onto her profile. "He has an excellent character."

"Did you enjoy his company? Is he good at conversation?" Miss Woodhouse persisted.

"Miss Campbell thought his company and conversation good

enough to consent to become Mrs Dixon," Jane answered, beginning to wonder at Miss Woodhouse's questions.

"So, you think it is a suitable match?" Miss Woodhouse asked next.

Jane wanted to stand up from her seat, face Miss Woodhouse, and shout in her face, "What are you driving at?" She wondered if some day, she would have the power to do what she wanted. Well, that day was not today. "Very suitable," she answered mildly. "He is an excellent and amiable gentleman, and Miss Campbell – now Mrs Dixon – is an excellent and amiable lady. I cannot imagine a more suitable match."

"You were all of you together at Weymouth, after the wedding? I understand that Mr Frank Churchill had been at Weymouth at the same time as you. Are you aware that he is the son of Mr Weston, one of our neighbors here in Highbury?"

"Yes, so I was informed," Jane answered. Her stomach churned a little.

"Did you see much of Mr Churchill while you were in Weymouth?" Miss Woodhouse asked.

"We were a little acquainted," Jane answered.

"So you did meet him?" Miss Woodhouse seemed to have no end to the questions.

"Indeed, I did meet him on multiple occasions at Weymouth," Jane admitted.

"Was he handsome?" Miss Woodhouse asked next.

"He is reckoned to be a very fine young man," Jane answered.

"Is he agreeable?"

"I do believe he was generally thought so."

"Did he appear a sensible young man; a young man of information?"

Jane's mind dissolved into memories. Mr Churchill's face when she met him, horrified over the lack of manners at the music shop. Mr Churchill as they discussed mathematics during the ill-fated boat ride to see the White Horse. Mr Churchill when he visited her after the dreadful accident on the boat. Mr Churchill when he proposed. "At a watering place, or in a common London acquaintance, it is difficult to decide on such points. Manners are all that can be safely judged of, under a much longer knowledge than I have had of Mr Churchill. I do believe everybody found his manners pleasing."

Until they were called upon to give opinions on Mr Woodhouse's new slippers, the conversation between Jane and Miss Woodhouse never improved.

CHAPTER FOUR

The next morning, an entire hind quarter of pork arrived from Hartfield, setting off a flurry that seemed to upset the entire household.

"Bless me, what generous neighbors we have! Such a huge bit of pork, it will feed us all for a week, at least!" Aunt Bates gushed. "There is so much, we shall have to have Mrs Goddard over for dinner. Of course, she prefers boiled pork, and we can salt the leg, but then how should we dress the loin?" She looked at their servant, Patty, who served as cook, maid, laundress, and all-around useful girl. "Take this to the kitchen, Patty, and start salting the leg."

While Patty was scuttling out of the room with her cooking task, Jane's grandmother frowned in concern. "I don't think we have a salting pan large enough."

"Surely we must, Mother," Aunt Bates frowned back at her in equal concern. "Oh, dear, what are we to do if our salting pan is too small? I had best go down and see."

Jane pitied poor Patty. The entire piece of meat would be spoiled by the time her aunt figured out what to do with it. "Shall I go down, instead?"

"You go to the kitchen, I shall go put on my bonnet and spencer. You check on the salting-pan, and I will come speak to Patty and then go to Hartfield to thank Mr Woodhouse."

Such an uproar over a piece of meat! Jane thought to herself as she started for the kitchen. Patty was back in the passage – without the pork – before she had made it down the stairs. "Mrs Cole sent a note for Miss Bates," she told Jane, handing off the note and scurrying back to the kitchen.

Aunt Bates entered the same passage only seconds after Patty had quit it. "Did I hear the bell?"

"You have a note from Mrs Cole," Jane told her, handing over the folded paper.

Aunt Bates broke the seal, opened it and read the note right there. "Mr Elton is getting married!" She exclaimed, grabbing onto Jane's wrist excitedly.

"Who is Mr Elton?" Jane asked, trying to smile and show interest.

"Oh, you remember, the vicar. The one living in our old home. Mother!" Aunt Bates dragged Jane by the wrist back into the parlor. "Mr Elton is to be married!" she shouted.

Jane's grandmother looked up. "Hopefully that is a good thing. The Vicarage is surely suffering without a mistress."

"A Miss Hawkins, from Bath," Aunt Bates read from the letter. "Jane, go and put on your things and come with me to call on the Woodhouses. We have to thank them for the pork, anyway, and they will be eager to know such exciting news!"

"Will you be content to be alone while we go out, Grandmama?" Jane asked, hoping she would prefer Jane to stay home with her and allow Aunt Bates to make their social calls for them.

"Go ahead," her grandmother answered. "I will stay here."

At least Jane had to own that her aunt was a brisk walker when she was on her way to impart gossip. They hurried to Hartfield, her aunt talking the entire way. Jane retreated inside her thoughts, piecing together what she could remember of the history of the Vicarage. There had been an occupant after her grandfather passed away, and before this new vicar. She was trying to remember his name. Carter? Carson? Carlson? It was something like that.

When they reached Hartfield, they were shown directly into the drawing room. Aunt Bates did not even pause in her chatter as she changed from talking to Jane, to talking to the Woodhouses' servant, to entering the room and talking to Mr and Miss Woodhouse.

"Oh! My dear sir, how are you this morning?" she asked as she curtseyed. "My dear Miss Woodhouse – I come quite overpowered. Such a beautiful hind quarter of pork! You are too bountiful! Have you heard the news? Mr Elton is to be married."

The reaction of the rooms' occupants was amusing. Miss Woodhouse started and blushed, making Jane wonder if she had had designs upon the vicar for herself. Mr Knightley looked annoyed. Mr Woodhouse looked as though he would rather talk about the pork than the upcoming wedding.

"There is my news: I thought it would interest you," Mr Knightley covered his irritation with a smile. Clearly he had also paid a call to Hartfield to bring the same gossip.

"But where could you hear it?" Aunt Bates protested. "Where could you possibly hear it, Mr Knightley? For it is not five minutes since I received Mrs Cole's note."

Jane stopped listening, for fear of blushing. It was a trifle mortifying, having her aunt arguing with her betters over who had heard a certain piece of gossip first. But then, Mr Knightley was arguing back with her, saying he was with Mr Cole when he got the news from Mr Elton, himself. So Mr Knightley was no better. She was relieved when her aunt changed the subject back to the pork.

"You really are too bountiful. My mother desires her very best compliments and regards, and a thousand thanks, and says you really quite oppress her."

Well, maybe she was less relieved. While of course her aunt put words in her grandmother's mouth, she wished she could be a little less obsequious. Her grandmother had some dignity about her, which her aunt was entirely lacking.

"We consider our Hartfield pork," Mr Woodhouse replied, "indeed it certainly is, so very superior to all other pork, that Emma and I cannot have a greater pleasure than-"

"Oh! My dear sir, as my mother says, our friends are only too good to us," Aunt Bates interrupted him.

Jane was clenching her teeth. Would Mr Woodhouse tolerate the lack of good manners, if he had not been very close friends with her grandfather?

Mr Knightley seemed to get over his annoyance, and be lording it over both her aunt, for having heard the news before her, and over Miss Woodhouse for some reason. If Jane cared to wonder what was distressing Miss Woodhouse, her best guess was that

Miss Woodhouse had been planning on marrying Mr Elton, and he had slipped out of her grip.

Jane did not know what to say when she was called upon to contribute to a conversation that consisted of gossip about the marriage of people she had never met. "No, I have never seen Mr Elton. Is he," she paused. What was she supposed to say in this insipid conversation? What had Miss Woodhouse asked her about Mr Churchill? "Is he a tall man?"

At least her question released her from having to say anything for a while, as Miss Woodhouse and Aunt Bates talked about Mr Elton, and then just about everyone else. Unfortunately, it did not last very long, before Miss Woodhouse demonstrated better breeding than Aunt Bates, and tried again to engage her in the conversation. "You are silent, Miss Fairfax, but I hope you mean to take an interest in this news. You, who have been hearing and seeing so much of late on these subjects, who must have been so deep in the business on Miss Campbell's account. We shall not excuse your being indifferent about Mr Elton and Miss Hawkins."

What exactly was Jane supposed to say to that? Because her dearest friend just got married, she was supposed to take an interest in the marriage of two strangers? "When I have seen Mr Elton, I dare say I shall be interested. But I believe it requires that with me. And as it is some months since Miss Campbell married, the impression may be a little worn off."

She was glad for her aunt jumping in to continue the gossip. If she had to be present while they were speaking of people she did not know, she would rather not participate. But this time her aunt dragged her back in. "Jane, do you know I always fancy Mr Dixon like Mr John Knightley? I mean in person –tall, with that sort of look – and not very talkative."

Why, Jane wondered, would her aunt assume Mr Dixon was anything like Mr Knightley's younger brother? She thought longingly of her friends. Who cared what they looked like? When out of their hearing, Mr and Mrs Dixon were both discussed as equally plain, Colonel Campbell had weather-beaten skin and a bit of a perpetual squint (though he had kindly eyes). But if she was told to sketch a portrait of what a mother looked like, she would draw Mrs Campbell's smiling face. To Jane, the Dixons and the Campbells were the most beautiful people in the world. Although, she amended loyally, Mr Frank Churchill would look as beautiful to strangers as he did to loved ones. "Quite wrong, my dear aunt; there is no likeness at all," she answered.

"Very odd! But one never does form a just idea of anybody beforehand. One takes up a notion, and runs away with it. Mr Dixon, you say, is not, strictly speaking, handsome."

Jane was now feeling very contrary, and decided to give her listeners the gossip as she heard the gossip from other gossipers. "Handsome! Oh, no. Far from it. Certainly plain. I told you he was plain."

"My dear, you said that Miss Campbell would not allow him to be plain, and that you yourself-"

Jane did not want this conversation going on any longer in this company. "Oh! As for me, my judgment is worth nothing. Where I have a regard, I always think a person well-looking. But I gave what I believed the general opinion, when I called him plain."

It worked. She had confused her aunt into ending the visit. "Well, my dear Jane, I believe we must be running away. The weather does not look well, and Grandmama will be uneasy."

Miss Woodhouse made a gesture as if to invite them to stay longer, and then she would send for the carriage, but thankfully Aunt Bates declined. "You are too obliging, my dear Miss Woodhouse; but we really must take leave. This has been a most agreeable piece of news, indeed. I shall just go round by Mrs Cole's; but I shall not stop three minutes; and Jane, you had better go home directly. I would not have you out in a shower! We think she is better for Highbury already."

While her aunt continued to chatter her goodbyes, Jane gave everyone a silent curtsey. She was surprised when Mr Knightley also rose, made his honors, and joined them at the door. He looked at her as if to say his goodbyes when there was a break in the farewell speech, but then her aunt prevailed upon him to see her home.

Jane could not quite suppress a sigh of relief when they were outside of Hartfield, her aunt had scuttled off to visit Mrs Cole, and suddenly she was alone with Mr Knightley.

"Are you quite well enough to walk?" he asked her solicitously. "Your aunt is clearly terribly worried about your health."

Jane was tired of everyone fussing about her health. So, she had been having frequent headaches ever since the accident on the boat. It was no reason so many conversations had to revolve around what she ate or whether she should curtail her activities more. Taking a walk outside in the fresh air made her feel better than all the fussing about making sure she stayed warm and dry.

"I am tired, Mr Knightley," she admitted in a moment of candor. "But it is a kind of fatigue few people in Highbury would understand. Perhaps you might. I am tired of people fussing over me. I am tired of people talking about my health, instead of more interesting topics. I am tired of being watched all the time."

Mr Knightley's arm shook under her hand, and she realized he was laughing at her. "I am terribly sorry, Miss Fairfax. But I am afraid I must advise you to simply get used to attention. Being the granddaughter of the old vicar, you are automatically a member of this community. Everyone takes an interest, because you are one of us. Because you are one of us, you are going to be watched. Especially since you are by far the most interesting person in Highbury. If I may be so forward as to say it, you are the most beautiful and accomplished woman to grace this village. People may not understand just what it is that makes you so remarkable, but they recognize beauty and achievement."

Jane gave a different kind of sigh. "Very pragmatic advice, Mr Knightley. What I cannot change, I shall simply have to accept with as good a grace as I can muster."

"You would seem to be in command of a great deal of grace, Miss Fairfax. I have every faith in you," Mr Knightley concluded as he left her at her door with a bow.

CHAPTER FIVE

Most well-beloved Mr Churchill,

I am in a perfect state this morning, but there is no one here I can talk to about it. So I am going to be "frank" with you. Highbury is awful!

I love my aunt, truly I do. But oh, the incessant talking! Not that I mind talking. I enjoy a good conversation. But there is no conversation to be had under this roof. A conversation implies back and forth, give and take. My aunt simply chatters away, repeats herself three times, and only has about four subjects of conversation: excessive gratitude for the kindness and generosity of the neighbors, gossiping about the neighbors, Grandmama's hearing, and my poor health.

The rest of the village is not much of an improvement. My aunt is not the only one who adores gossip. Everyone here thrives on it. Who had dinner with whom, and what people look like, and who is interested in marrying whom. When there is music, they talk the next day about how well the performer played and how well she looked doing it. No discussion about the actual music at all. They won't discuss Pleyel, or Haydn, or Handel. They will discuss the hairstyle I was wearing while I was playing!

It is more than just the neighbors. My aunt only

employs Patty, who needs to be cook, maidservant, laundress, and scullery maid all in one. So of course all of it is done poorly. I have hardly eaten since arriving here. Some of it is nerves. I am so unhappy, I simply cannot convince myself to eat anything. It does not help when I sit down, and the food is so terrible. Of course Patty does the best she can, and with such limited resources, what would I expect? I own that my palate has been spoiled by my life with the Campbells. I used to laugh about it when I would come for a fortnight's visit once a year over Christmas, but the idea of three months of this! This is awful.

I am sorry everything I have to say is mean-spirited. I am so homesick. I am so anxious for your arrival. If not for you, I would be in Ireland with Sophia right now, discussing Waverley, and Queen Mab, and The Times. Not that I am reproaching you, my darling. I know what a difficult time you are having, too! But please, please hurry. If ever you wanted to play a heroic knight coming to rescue a damsel in distress, here is your opportunity!

Your own,
J. Fairfax

Jane set down her quill as her aunt called her to dine. "Jane! Are you ill? Bless me, you have not had a thing to eat other than a bit of tea so far. Come, I still have baked apples from Mrs Wallis. So very obliging, Mrs Wallis! I know there are people who think Mrs Wallis rude, but we have never known anything but the greatest attention from her. Mr Knightley was so generous to give us so many apples. Mr Woodhouse believes there is no fruit as wholesome as an apple, and highly recommends a baked apple. Mrs Wallis surely agrees, since she bakes so many for us at a time. Come try a bit of baked apple. You must be hungry by now, and you need strength if your health is ever going to improve."

Jane finished writing her letter as her aunt was talking, then capped her ink with a sigh. She wanted to write to Sophia, too. It could wait. She might as well try eating something. A baked apple from Mrs Wallis might be better than most of the food Patty cooked.

"I am here, Auntie," she said from the doorway. "Let me try Mr Woodhouse's recommendation."

She sat listlessly at the table, while her aunt brought her a dish with two apples. They were not beautiful, but Patty had warmed them for her. She took a bite. They would have been better with a sprinkling of cinnamon and nutmeg on top, but Mrs Wallis was not of the same class as Colonel Campbell. At least she had drizzled a little bit of honey on them, and the added sweetness was pleasant.

"What do you think?" Her aunt was hovering over her anxiously. "Are they baked enough? Mr Woodhouse made us promise to have them baked three times, but Mrs Wallis only baked them twice. She told me twice was quite sufficient, but you know how particular Mr Woodhouse is."

The bell rang, and Jane was saved from a further discussion of baked apple recipes. She took another bite. Is it really a recipe, she wondered, when one is giving directions on how many times a pan of apples is put in to bake? Or does a recipe require more instructions on what ingredients are combined together?

Her aunt reappeared with Mr Knightley behind her. "Look who has come to call, Jane! Mr Knightley!"

Jane made to stand up, but Mr Knightley hastily stopped her. "I did not mean to interrupt your breakfast. I merely wanted to call and see if you are feeling less fatigued today."

"Bless me!" her aunt answered. "I do believe she is more, not less so this morning! She did not have a bite to eat, only the smallest bit of tea! But now, you see, she is finally eating, thanks to your generosity! These are your apples from Donwell. Mrs Wallis baked a pan for us, and you see how Jane likes them! I do not believe she likes anything so well as these baked apples. Thank you so much for your generosity. You are so thoughtful. The sack you sent has lasted this long, you see. There never was such a keeping apple anywhere as from one of your trees."

"I am very gratified that Jane is enjoying them so much," said Mr Knightley. Jane had taken another bite while her aunt was talking, but put her spoon down. It was strange, having him standing there, watching her eat.

"Would you care for one?" she asked, hoping he would say no.

"No thank you, I merely wanted to call and see for myself how you are faring." Mr Knightley shifted his hat to his other hand.

"Since you are enjoying my apples so much, I should send more." He looked at Aunt Bates. "You must be about to the end of your stock? I am sure you must be."

"Oh, no need to trouble yourself about us! We still have ever so many! I believe we have an entire half dozen. They should all be kept for Jane. We still have the entire pan of baked ones, these will still last us a very long time!"

"I will send you another supply. I have a great many more than I can ever use. William Larkins let me keep a larger quantity than usual this year. I will send you some more," Mr Knightley overruled her objections.

Aunt Bates objected again. "I cannot bear that you should be sending us more. You have been so liberal with us already."

"Indeed," Jane agreed. She hated the extent that her aunt and grandmother lived on the charity of the town. Pork from Highbury, apples from Donwell. Her presence under this roof was making matters worse; now the neighborhood was having to feed her, as well as her aunt and grandmother. Well, at least, as her aunt had said, she was not eating much. "My aunt is correct. You have been so very generous already, please do not trouble yourself on our account."

"It is no trouble! I do not eat many apples, I would rather have them enjoyed by you than spoiling in my larder. They will be good for nothing if no one is eating them. I will have William Larkins bring some by." Before Aunt Bates could protest again, he had bowed and left.

Jane picked up her spoon to finish the apple, and put it down again. "Oh, Auntie! Why did you admit to Mr Knightley that the apples were so nearly gone! You should have told him that we still had a great many left."

"My dear, I did say as much as I could. We do have ever so many apples left."

"There was no need to be so specific about having a half dozen left!" Jane wailed. "A half dozen may seem like ever so many to you, but he will calculate that there are three of us, but only one of him, so as a gentleman he should deprive himself in order to please three ladies. Now he is going to insist on following his word."

Jane was correct. That evening, William Larkins delivered a very large basket of apples.

Jane had been writing to Mr Churchill, and had missed the entire event. When Patty served them a bit of boiled pork with a baked apple, the subject of the delivery came up. "We have more apples," Jane's grandmother told her when Patty put their plates down. "Saw him from the window."

"And such a good thing mother saw him!" Aunt Bates exclaimed. "William Larkins had given them to Patty, and would have left again without my thanking him. Fortunately mother pointed him out to me so I ran down to talk to him. William is such an old acquaintance, you know! Sadly, he could not stay long. But it is no matter. I was excessively disappointed, but Patty filled me in on the details. Dear me! Such a large basket of apples! At least a bushel. Patty said that William said that it was all the apples of that sort his master had. Mr Knightley sent us all of them! He did not keep back a single one for himself. Mrs Hodges was quite put out at their being all sent away. She could not bear that her master should not have another apple tart this spring. William told Patty not to say anything about it to us. Mrs Hodges would be cross sometimes. Perhaps it is simply in the nature of cooks to be cross. I was shocked to find Mr Knightley had given us all of them! We must not let Mr Knightley know the extent of his generosity, since we are not supposed to know. Oh, dear, I thought I should keep this knowledge from you, Jane. But, there it is."

Jane put her fork down and fought down tears. More charity. She had been a charity all her life. At least with the Campbells, she had had an illusion of dignity. She never felt pitied. Here in Highbury, she was the sickly, pitiful granddaughter of a pitiful poor widow and niece of a pitiful spinster.

She desperately wished for a pianoforte. At every other moment of distress in her life, as long as she could remember, at least, she had been able to sit down in front of a row of keys, and banish unhappiness with beauty. Now, the poverty of her family deprived her of her most cherished of all comforts. This was the life from which Colonel Campbell had rescued her. She spent the rest of the evening writing a letter to him.

CHAPTER SIX

My dearest Miss Fairfax,

At long last, I have triumphed! Not the ultimate triumph of securing my aunt's permission for me to get married, alas. But at least I convinced her to part with me for a fortnight to come to you in Highbury. Thank goodness for the convenience of you living in the same village as my newly-married father!

I am writing to you from Oxford, and I write my father as well to inform him of my arrival. I am a little anxious to make a good impression upon my new mother. Despite your assurances of her patience and good will, if I fail in pleasing her, it will make it much harder to stay so near to you.

Regardless of my reception by anyone else, my darling, the only one that truly matters is you. In order to preserve the secrecy of our engagement, I will rush to you as quickly as possible without the appearance of any hurry. I hope to be there by dinner time tomorrow, and I will immediately start looking for reasons to call upon your grandmother and aunt – and you, since at least we can admit to a casual association in Weymouth, and therefore it would be my duty to call and renew the acquaintance.

Would that I could travel all night, and you could be gazing upon me, instead of this letter! I am your impatient and devoted lover,

F.C. Weston Churchill

Jane set down the letter with a mixture of elation and despair. Mr Churchill was coming to her! The clock was going to be her enemy for the next several days. He had failed to get his aunt's permission to marry. They were going to have to see each other for a fortnight, pretending to nothing more than a casual acquaintance. How on earth could one sickly old woman cause so much anguish?

Aunt Bates's voice summoned her to come and help her grandmother get dressed, and began a litany of items that could use Jane's clever fingers for repairs. Old women required maintenance, and could be tricky to manage. Mr Churchill's ability to change his aunt's mind could be no greater than her ability to get her own to stop talking continuously.

Once her grandmother was up and dressed, Jane managed to maneuver herself into the window seat with a basket of mending. Of course she needed to be in the window, able to see people coming and going up and down the street; the light was best there. Her aunt fussed and worried that the brighter the light, the worse it might make her headaches. Jane reasoned that, because her eyes were young and strong, she would risk the headache today in order to save her eyesight in the future.

Jane knew it was going to take all of her willpower NOT to sit in the window all day, for the next several days, watching for Mr Churchill. He would come to her as soon as he could. It might be three days. It might be longer. She took her time with her basket of mending, since it was still several hours until dinnertime. He would have to come through Highbury on his way to Randalls, the Weston's home. He did not say how he traveled. On horseback? By post? Did his aunt and uncle keep their own carriage? Jane did not know. It was frustrating, all the things she did not know about the man she was going to marry.

Looking out the window, she stabbed herself in the finger. It couldn't be! Her finger was bleeding, she put it in her mouth to stop the bleeding and prevent it from staining her grandmother's white shift. It was not....it was! Mr Weston and Mr Churchill were striding up the street. Mr Weston pointed Frank in her direction, then he turned to walk the other way while Mr Churchill came striding to them!

She examined her finger. The bleeding seemed to have stopped. She was torn between the urge to watch him approach, hoping he would look up and see her at the window, and the urge to retire to her room and tidy herself up. Should she change her dress? His rapid approach answered the question. He looked up, and saw her.

Their eyes met. They both smiled, aware that they were in public, where anyone could see them on the street and in the window. But the rest of the world did not matter. For that moment, everything else vanished. He was there, she was there, no trouble could touch them.

It might have been a matter of minutes, or only a matter of seconds. He touched his hat to her, and turned to come inside. Jane remembered to breathe, remembered there were sounds in the world, remembered there were other people in the universe. "We are about to have company," she told her aunt and grandmother as casually as she could manage.

"Bless me! We have such wonderful neighbors, who are always so good to pay us such attention," Aunt Bates stood and fussed with her cap and her dress. "Who is coming? We had a visit from Mrs Goddard only yesterday, and we are seeing Mr and Mrs Cole tonight. You don't suppose Mr Elton has returned already, to ready the Vicarage for his new bride?"

Before Jane had a chance to answer the question, the caller was standing in their parlor. "Miss Fairfax! Lovely to see you again. My father informed me you were here in Highbury, visiting your grandmother. Would you do me the honor of presenting me?"

Jane did not know how she was going to manage to maintain this fiction that they were mere acquaintances. "Mr Frank Churchill, may I please present my grandmother, Mrs Bates, and my aunt, Miss Bates. Grandmama, Aunt, this is Mr Frank Churchill. He was in Weymouth with his aunt and uncle while I was there with the Dixons and Campbells."

Aunt Bates dipped in a small curtsey, then came forward to take his hand warmly. "You are Mr Weston's son! My goodness, we have not seen you since you were all of two years old. Is that not right, Mother? Mr Churchill would have been little Frank

Weston back then. When poor Mrs Weston – the first Mrs Weston, that is – your poor mother, Mr Churchill – dear me, it is all so complicated – when Mrs Weston died, and Mr Weston agreed to allow Mrs Weston's brother, Mr Churchill, to take over the raising of young Frank Weston, who could have imagined that not quite twenty years later, here you would be standing, Mr Frank Churchill, now. Bless me, it makes it sound as if you were no longer from Highbury. But, you know, Mr Churchill, we will always consider you part of us."

Waiting for the moment when her aunt needed to pause for a breath and a change of topic, Jane jumped in, "Do have a seat, Mr Churchill, and tell us, how are things at Enscombe? Is your aunt improved for having tried the sea air?"

"Oh! Is your aunt in poor health? What ails her? I trust that the sea air was more successful for your aunt than it was for our poor Jane! The Campbells are such generous people, before the Dixons left for Ireland they took Jane to Weymouth for her health. But, I suppose you would know that, since of course you met Jane there."

Mr Churchill looked at Jane, and smiled, as her aunt continued to ask questions without allowing any opportunity to answer. She smiled back. Her aunt could talk all she liked. It did not matter. He was here, in the same room with her. Life was perfect. She would find a way to see him to the door, to have a moment's privacy with him.

Forty-five minutes later, her plans were dashed by the arrival of Mr Weston, come to collect his son. "I am so sorry to disturb you, Miss Bates, but did my son happen to mention where he meant to go upon quitting you?" he asked, then turned at Mr Churchill's laugh. "Ah, there you are, my dear boy! When you weren't at Randalls I feared perhaps you were lost. I realized perhaps I should not have left you alone, until you have time to become better acquainted with the town."

"Bless me! We did not mean to detain Mr Frank Churchill so long that you needed to come and retrieve him," Aunt Bates exclaimed. "It has been such a delight to become reacquainted with him."

Jane nearly giggled from mortification. Mr Churchill had hardly said a word for the entire forty-five minutes he had been held captive by her aunt's talking. At least the two of them had been able to sit together on the sofa after she'd arranged for Patty to serve tea. It made it harder to look at each other, but they had been able to sit side by side, nearly touching, occasionally brushing fingers when they would both reach for the teapot or a biscuit. Jane was sure his timing was deliberate.

Mr Churchill rose from his seat, and bowed to them. "I do apologize for the alarm, father, I am sure you were expecting me to arrive home before you. I hope I did not overstay my welcome, Miss Fairfax. Mrs Bates. Miss Bates." He retrieved his hat, which had wandered onto the side table at some point during his call, and, with a last look at Jane, departed.

Mr Weston bowed after Mr Churchill had left the room. "I shall have to call upon you another time, to collect your impressions of my son!" he exclaimed with a proud smile.

"You are always welcome, Mr Weston, to be sure!" Aunt Bates called after him as he followed his son. Then she sighed happily. "Such excellent and attentive neighbors we have here in Highbury. I cannot imagine living anywhere else in the world with such excellent people as the ones who live here in Highbury."

"Indeed," Jane answered drily. They were charitable, to be sure, to allow their ears to be assaulted by her aunt on a fairly regular basis. She would give them that.

CHAPTER SEVEN

Good morning, my dearest, darling Miss Fairfax!

The irony of being so close to you, and yet here I am writing you a note instead of speaking into your perfectly formed ear!

I spent a good deal of yesterday in Highbury in the company of my new mother and Miss Woodhouse. I found endless excuses to walk up and down the streets, in hope that you might come around the corner on some small errand. I spent as much time as I could on your particular street, hoping you might appear at the window, but alas, my timing was never so fortunate.

Miss Woodhouse is every bit the hopeless gossip you made her out to be! I thought we might as well use that to our advantage, and I have started an intrigue which should divert suspicion from us for some time, at least.

It all happened by accident. I was downplaying your charms in order to force her into singing your praises; she thinks your complexion is divine, and the character of your face has a peculiar elegance, and as to your musical skill, you play charmingly. I was somewhat incensed at such paltry praise for your musical genius, and was attempting to elicit stronger praise for your skill. But the conversation took a different direction.

Miss Woodhouse is now rather firmly of the belief that there might have been some sort of affection on the part of Mr Dixon towards you. She does not think that you were in the least bit improper; she complains about how very reserved you are. The longer she expounded upon the subject of your reserve, the harder it was for me to restrain myself from exploding with laughter.

I know you will chide me for using her ill, but since my new mother is so strongly connected with Miss Woodhouse, I will be thrown into her company frequently during my visit. I might as well embrace the inevitable, and use the acquaintance to our advantage. I will say that I don't believe Miss Woodhouse is a malicious sort, and will be like to laugh at the joke when we can make our engagement public.

I wanted to confess the scheme to you, my darling. There is little doubt we will be in public together in circumstances where the safest thing I can do to protect our secret is to reinforce this notion of my indifference to you. Please ignore anything hurtful I might say in the process of eliciting compliments for you from the mouths of others. If I am unable to speak them to you myself, I might as well induce your neighbors to be my messengers.

Your devoted slave,
F.C. Weston Churchill

Jane's mouth was unable to decide if it should be smiling or frowning. Unable to do both at the same time, it alternated from one to the other. She did not approve of Mr Churchill using Miss Woodhouse to throw suspicion off of them. It was not a gentlemanly way to treat a lady. But at the same time, she was not fond enough of Miss Woodhouse to care if he put her to some use. Convinced of their mutual dislike of one another, there was some amusement in Mr Churchill forcing Miss Woodhouse into praising her complexion. It was useless for him to try and get her to comment upon musical matters; Miss Woodhouse's musical talents were limited, and she would not be capable of much understanding beyond an awareness that Jane played better than she did.

Mr Churchill was also perfectly right that, being Mrs Weston's son, and Miss Woodhouse being Mrs Weston's former charge, they were going to be thrown together frequently. As he said, might as well embrace the inevitable.

Jane folded his letter, kissed it, and slid it into her bureau with his other letters when she heard the bell ring. She took a quick look in the glass to make sure she was presentable for company, then went into the drawing room.

Mr Knightley was turning down her aunt's offer of tea. "I happened to be in town, and thought I would stop in to inquire after everyone's health." He bowed to Jane as she walked into the room. "I trust you are settled in by now, Miss Fairfax? How are you enjoying Highbury?"

Aunt Bates answered for her. "Our dear Jane is improving, now that she is back among us! Nothing is so good for one's health as the air of home. When she wrote that she was coming, and was ill, I was sure we were going to have to send for Mr Perry. I know the dear man would have seen to her without charging us, and even though he is ever so expensive, we would have found a way to pay the dear man. He is terribly generous, but an apothecary has expenses to meet. But just being here, I swear, Jane's looks have improved immensely. She is still so pale, but then, she has always had such delicate skin."

Mr Knightley was studying Jane's face a little too intently for Jane's comfort. "Indeed, we must all of us in Highbury do what we can for Miss Fairfax's good health. I would say you are looking very well this morning, Miss Fairfax."

Jane opened her mouth to say thank you, but she was too slow in responding. "I was just saying how well she looks!" Aunt Bates commented. "I think her complexion always looks best in the morning. Not that she does not look well in the evenings, but dear Jane is such a morning person! I am a little concerned about Tuesday evening! The Coles have invited us to spend the evening! Such delightful neighbors! It is so good of them to think of us. They are having a dinner party in the new dining room, did you know? We have been invited to spend the evening after dinner. But I am so concerned about walking home with Jane afterwards. Mr Woodhouse puts such a store by not being out in the evening air! It is not such a long walk, and the walk there will surely do Jane good, but I have been wondering if perhaps Jane ought to stay home with mother. I hate to deprive her of such lovely company, and of course she is such a favorite with everybody -"

"Allow me to put your worries at ease, Miss Bates," Mr Knightley interrupted. "I will be at the same party. I have a carriage at my disposal, and I was planning on hiring horses for the evening. Once I have been deposited at the Coles for dinner, I will have the carriage come to collect you and Miss Fairfax. There is no sense in my having horses for the evening and not putting them to use. My carriage can collect you for the evening, and bring you back home at whatever time you should wish to leave."

"Bless me! What kindly, thoughtful neighbors we have! Did you hear that, Mother? Mr Knightley is going to come to our rescue on Tuesday, so that we don't have to worry about poor Jane's health." Aunt Bates could hardly keep her seat for excitement. Jane half expected her to jump up and embrace Mr Knightley.

Mr Knightley seemed to be half expecting the same thing. "Miss Bates, would it be terribly rude of me to change my mind about that tea? Last winter while I was calling upon you, I had a bit of a tickle in my throat, and you had prepared a concoction for me that quite carried away any soreness. I don't suppose I could trouble you for a bit of your magic potion right now? I realize I have been talking all morning, and I fear my throat is beginning to feel it."

"Oh! Oh dear, of course I will see to it myself! I am quite sure Patty has put up the proper herbs by now. You stay where you are, Mr Knightley, I will see to it. It is the least I could do, to repay your generosity." Aunt Bates was still talking to him when she was already out the door.

Mr Knightley looked at Jane in the ringing silence that followed the door closing. "I hope my dodge was not too transparent, Miss Fairfax," he said. Jane still did not quite like the way he was looking at her. He looked – much too interested for comfort. "I truly did call to see how are getting on, and I did want to hear from *you* how you are getting on. Are you feeling better? Are you in need of Mr Perry's services? Pray, be blunt."

"There is no need to call for Mr Perry," Jane assured him. "And truly, there is no need for you to send your carriage for us. I enjoy walking. You yourself must understand that, since you do not keep your own horses and you walk everywhere."

"But I am not a lady," Mr Knightley pointed out. "A lady dressed for an evening's entertainment should not have to worry about arriving with her shoes in a sorry state. There is no telling what the weather might be. There is also the question of the night air on your return journey. Your aunt's concerns do have some merit. I simply insist on putting my carriage at your disposal for the evening. Wearing yourself out, and being sick the following day, would be folly."

"It would seem you give me little choice in the matter, Mr Knightley," Jane responded.

"I do, indeed, Miss Fairfax."

The door opened, and Aunt Bates returned, Patty following with the tea tray. "I have your tea, Mr Knightley, in this pot. I made enough so that poor Jane can join you. She is more prone to headaches than to any complaint of the throat, but there is no harm in seeing if it will help the one, as much as the other. The other pot is for mother and me. And since we are having tea, I thought we might as well bring up the cake."

Jane accepted the cup of tea that was poured for her with the same resignation that she accepted Mr Knightley's offer of the carriage. Her aunt would spend all Mr Knightley's visit focused on her health if she did not. At least instead she continued fawning upon their visitor. "It is so good of you to offer us your carriage for Tuesday evening, Mr Knightley. So generous, indeed. I am so looking forward to the evening. I understand Mrs Cole has invited Miss Woodhouse and Miss Smith. Jane, you have not met Miss Smith yet. Such a very pretty girl. A parlor border of Mrs Goddard's. Miss Woodhouse has taken such a fancy to her."

"Miss Woodhouse could make much better use of her time than spending it on Miss Harriet Smith," Mr Knightley commented darkly.

Miss Bates looked confused. "Oh, Mr Knightley, if there is anyone in all Highbury who is as grateful for Miss Woodhouse's attention as me and Mother, it is Miss Smith."

"Oh, I am sure Miss Smith is grateful for Miss Woodhouse's attentions. But that does not mean those attentions are not misguided in the first place."

"Oh, Mr Knightley, how can you possibly object to something as sweet and lovely as their friendship?" Aunt Bates objected. "It does my heart good to see Miss Woodhouse with a friend her own age. Since my dear Jane hasn't lived in the village since she was small, Miss Woodhouse has spent most of her life without any companion except her dear father, and her dear Miss Taylor, who of course is now Mrs Weston and no longer under her own roof. And neither of them is her own age! Now, at last, she has Miss Smith with whom to share her secrets, and go for walks, and every other thing that is natural for two young people to do together. My Jane has been blessed to be with Miss Campbell all these years, and Miss Woodhouse when she is home for visits. But Miss Woodhouse has had no one. Now, not only has she Miss Smith, but also Mr Churchill! Everyone in the village has noticed how readily the two of them have become fast friends. Why, Mrs Cole says that the two of them were thick as thieves when they came into Ford's so that Mr Churchill could buy gloves. And then they seemed to walk up and down Highbury from one end to the other, over and over, because they could not bear to part company."

Jane had to clench her teeth together to avoid laughing. She was glad Mr Churchill had already sent her the letter with his translation of these actions. They could have been upsetting, if she had not known his true motives. She looked down at her hands in her lap, wishing she had brought out her embroidery before she sat down. Of course, in this awful, gossip-ridden small village, everyone was watching what everyone else did and then ran to the neighbors to make reports. This village needed a bookstore, so that people had something else to talk about.

"Mr Churchill stands to be an even worse friend for Miss Woodhouse than Miss Smith!" Mr Knightley exclaimed. "Did you not hear what he did this morning? At breakfast, he sent for a chaise and dashed off to London – to get his hair cut!"

Even Jane stared at Mr Knightley at that pronouncement. "All the way to London? For a haircut?" Aunt Bates was exclaiming.

"Yes, indeed," Mr Knightley gave a snort of disgust. "First, he slights his father's bride taking so long to come and pay his respects to her, and then as soon as he arrives for a fortnight's visit, he leaves again. To get his hair cut! It is the most extravagant, vain, ridiculous nonsense! Mr Weston is amused, but I assure you,

Mrs Weston feels this insult. Fine sort of man for Miss Woodhouse to be associating with! She has her own streak of vanity, she does not need encouragement from weak-headed individuals to make her more so."

"Dear me!" Jane had never seen Aunt Bates so distressed she was at a loss for words. She could understand why – Mr Knightley had, in short order, expressed his disapproval of this Miss Smith, and then of Mr Frank Churchill, and then of Miss Woodhouse. Aunt Bates was of a disposition to like all people, and these were three people that she would never dream of criticizing.

Jane's hands had balled into fists. Mr Knightley's derision was not to be borne. She could not, however, think of a way to defend Mr Churchill.

"Perhaps you are being a bit unkind, Mr Knightley?" she prodded as gently as she could manage. "Miss Woodhouse is a generous and amiable soul. I do not believe I have ever seen a woman with so much to recommend her, who is so unimpressed by what she sees in the looking-glass." Her mind flew to Mr Churchill's letter. Well, if Emma would defend her in the face of his insults, the least she could do was repay that in the face of Mr Knightley's criticism. It was, after all, the truth.

She decided not to try to defend the other two recipients of his criticism. She did not know Miss Smith, and she did not trust herself to say a word about Mr Churchill.

"Well, perhaps it is more pride than vanity," Mr Knightley acknowledged. "Nonetheless, it should not be encouraged by keeping company with ill-advised friends."

Jane imagined herself pointing out to Mr Knightley that he was probably more guilty of the sin of pride in criticizing Miss Woodhouse's companions than Miss Woodhouse was of being prideful in making friends with people who no doubt had their share of human failings. Fearful of betraying her secret, she mentally apologized to all three people, none of whom deserved Mr Knightley's censure. She merely smiled when Mr Knightley rose to bow, thanked her aunt for the tea, and left.

CHAPTER EIGHT

Jane was returning from Ford's with a new packet of embroidery silk to the surprising sight of a wagon pulled up in front of her grandmother's front door. Curiosity spurred her steps until she could hear the conversation in progress.

"No, no, there must be some mistake," Jane heard her aunt saying. "You must have the wrong place. We have not ordered anything from Broadwoods. I don't know what Broadwoods is."

Jane practically ran to the front door. John Broadwood and Sons made pianofortes. Good ones. "Good morning, may I help you?"

A tall man with a rumpled coat handed her a piece of paper. "I am trying to make a delivery from Broadwood's for a Miss Jane Fairfax?"

Jane's breath caught, and her heart started beating hard enough, she could hear it in her own ears. "I am Miss Fairfax."

"Well, then, we have a pianoforte for you." He gave an impatient look at her aunt. Jane could only imagine the conversation that had taken place before her arrival. "Where do you want it?"

"In the drawing room, please. Just up the stairs. I will run and clear a space for it." She looked at the large crate in the wagon. It looked huge. She hoped it would even fit up the stairs! She gripped her aunt's arm. "Would you please find Patty, and ask her to come and help?" She ran inside, not waiting for an answer.

She ran up the stairs, and looked around the small drawing

room, gasping. How large was a pianoforte? Surely it would fit on the wall across from the window, where the table stood. She scooped up the contents of the table, and hastily removed them onto the sofa. She pulled out a chair, and carried it across the room. They could figure out how to rearrange the furniture later.

Patty scurried in, wide-eyed. "Miss Bates says you are getting a pianoforte?"

"So it would seem." Jane remembered Mr Knightley's complaint that Mr Frank Churchill had gone to London simply to get his hair cut. Apparently he got his hair cut on Great Pulteney Street. How on earth was she going to explain this? "Come, help me move the table."

Once the table and chairs were moved, Jane directed Patty to sweep the floor, while she made sure there was a clear path from the door to the wall. A pianoforte. Mr Churchill had sent her a pianoforte. He was crazy. He was amazing. Was it possible to love someone as much as she loved him?

Grunts coming from the stairwell announced the arrival of the instrument. What was she going to tell people? In this town full of gossips, half the town already knew about this. By dinnertime, every single person in town would be talking about it. This was a terrible idea.

Two men slowly came into the room, the beautiful mahogany cabinet of the instrument between them. "Over there," Jane pointed, then realized they could not see her. "The wall across from the windows."

They gently lowered it down in the middle of the wall. "Will that do, miss?" the tall one asked her.

"Yes, thank you, that's perfect," Jane answered. She had no idea if it was going to be a good idea to have it in the middle of the wall or not.

"Be right back, then," the two men disappeared back down the stairs. Jane looked after them in surprise. What else? She had barely turned around to examine her gift, when they re-materialized with a matching bench, and another large parcel wrapped in brown paper.

"Here's your music, miss." She took the package from him, and watched while the two men set about tuning the instrument.

Aunt Bates came back in the room. "Bless me, what a surprise!

Jane, were you expecting this?"

"No, Auntie, I confess I am completely astonished," Jane admitted.

"I don't believe we have ever owned such a beautiful thing in all my life. Such a cunning instrument! You learned on a grand, I am sure, at your lessons, but it is so nice that there is such a thing as a square pianoforte. A pianoforte like the one Mrs Cole bought would completely fill up our entire drawing room!"

While her aunt continued to talk, Jane put her parcel down on the table and opened it with shaking hands. Mr Churchill knew her tastes and ability, perfectly. There were piano compositions for her from Ludwig van Beethoven, Franz Schubert, John Field, Johann Hummel. Arias in Italian. Several other songs that Jane knew he intended for future duets with her. Their voices had blended so well together in Weymouth. As a metaphor for their future life together, it was a rather nice one.

"There you go, miss, all set. Sign here, please?" Jane was not even sure what she signed. The delivery men left. She stood in front of the instrument.

"Mother has been at her nap for ever so long, I need to wake her. She is going to be so sorry she missed all this excitement," Aunt Bates said. "I should have woken her up, but I was so excited myself, I did not think of it. She is going to be so excited."

Jane stopped listening as her aunt talked all the way to her grandmother's room. It was exquisite. The large square, six-legged pianoforte was much more compact than the full-sized grand at the Campbell's house. But the Campbell's instrument was not inlaid with rosewood. Mr Churchill had been terribly, terribly extravagant! What was he thinking? How was she going to explain this? She started listing the most musically inclined people in Highbury. Who among them would take one look at this, and know instantly just how exceedingly expensive it was?

She took her first real breath since she had come around the corner, down on the street. No one. Mr Churchill was taking a terrible risk, sending her such a gift. At least she did not believe there was anyone in all Highbury who would understand the full extent of his extravagance.

She was going to have to scold him heartily. She heard Aunt Bates and Grandmama coming back, and knew if she was not playing, she would never get to hear its quality for herself. She touched one of the ivory keys. The note rippled through the air like sunshine after a rainstorm.

It was an emblem, a monument of Mr Churchill's love for her. He had chosen the most exquisite pianoforte in the store, to signify that he thought her the most exquisite woman in the world. How was she supposed to scold him for that?

"See, mother?" Aunt Bates and Grandmother came in, as Jane seated herself on the bench. "Is it not the most beautiful thing you've ever seen? It is such a surprise, I declare. Jane is quite at a loss to who could possibly have sent such a gift."

In order to avoid having to make any speculations, Jane began playing.

CHAPTER NINE

Most well-beloved Mr Churchill,

Your pianoforte came yesterday. But then, considering the nature of gossip in this village, I am assuming you already know by now.

It is every bit as handsome as you are.

My aunt has talked herself into believing that the pianoforte is a gift from Colonel Campbell, and I am saying nothing to confirm nor deny her assumption.

I am thrilled, and terrified. Please do not do anything so extravagant again, especially without warning me! At least we should be cautious enough to lay a groundwork first, before any further such displays, so that there is an explanation.

I love you so much, my dear, handsome, impetuous, generous Mr Churchill! I cannot wait until we are able to abandon all secrecy and admit the nature of our relationship. I do not believe the residents of Highbury will be as amused as you think they will be once our secret is out. While it is of little matter to me, your father will always be your father, and I hate the thought of you losing his – and Mrs Weston's – goodwill.

I am counting the hours until I can gaze upon your face at Mrs Cole's party. The pianoforte is an excellent diversion that makes the wait more bearable; I do understand why you sent it. I still urge you not to send any more such gifts that I cannot explain.

Your own devoted
J. Fairfax

Tuesday seemed to drag on endlessly. Even with Mr Churchill's diverting gift in the drawing room, Jane was disheartened to rise from her music to help her grandmother and discover it was only ten o'clock in the morning. She checked over the dress she planned to wear that evening. She repaired the gown her aunt was planning to wear.

There was an early afternoon visit by Mrs Cole, which tried Jane's peace of mind to the utmost. Neither her aunt nor Mrs Cole would leave off the subject of the mysterious arrival of the pianoforte.

"Jane had a letter from Colonel Campbell only last week, and just think, not a single mention of any gifts from beginning to end!" Aunt Bates exclaimed to Mrs Cole as they stood admiring the instrument. Jane was trapped at the tea table, cutting slices of cake, wishing she could be playing the instrument in question and drowning out the conversation. It would have been harder for them to speculate if they were forced to politely listen to her play.

"Is that so, Jane?" Mrs Cole asked as they finished admiring the instrument, and she accepted a slice of cake and sat down. "Not a word to go along with this surprise?"

"I suppose there must be another letter on its way, and the pianoforte arrived before the letter," Jane tried to shrug nonchalantly. "Or else the delay is deliberate, and the Campbells meant to surprise me. I could easily see the Colonel enjoying a little laugh at my expense." She mentally asked the Colonel his forgiveness for such a falsehood. While he was a generous and jovial man, he was not given to practical jokes.

"It is such a handsome gesture! So very, very generous! But then, we have such very generous friends," Aunt Bates launched into her usual enthusiastic discourse on her favorite topic. Her obsequiousness might be less grating in smaller doses – after all, each neighbor did not hear the speech as frequently as Jane did – but it made her cringe.

"Would you care to hear me play, Mrs Cole?" she offered as

soon as she was able to make herself heard.

"Why, of course, my dear!" Mrs Cole exclaimed. It was a relief to put a temporary stop to the gossip, but as Jane launched into Beethoven's Sonata No. 27, she realized that showing off the quality of the instrument might only serve to fuel the gossip even further, instead of dampening the flames. But then, Mrs Cole was not a musician. Hopefully she would give the credit to Jane's playing, and not the exceptional quality of the instrument.

At last, it was dinnertime. Jane was able to take a few hasty bites and then retire to her room to attack her hair with the curling tongs.

Her feelings found expression in her hair. Instead of merely a few ringlets to frame her face, she allowed her fancy to continue into a profusion of curls around her face, her ears, all around to the back of her neck. She even managed a few curls among the loose knot of her hair pinned to the back of her head. Well, and why not? She had the time. Her lowly status as the granddaughter of Mrs Bates did not earn her an invitation to dinner, only to come to visit for the evening, when the other guests left the dinner table for the drawing room. The particular friend of Miss Campbell never had to face this sort of indignity.

For the millionth time since her arrival in Highbury, she mentally thanked Colonel Campbell for his kindness and generosity. Then she mentally apologized to him for the speculations the wagging tongues of Highbury were no doubt heaping upon him even now, assuming he was the sender of Mr Churchill's pianoforte. She determined to treat the gift as a metaphor. The village would not be able to understand the full scope of Colonel Campbell's generosity. But they could understand an expensive present. She did not mind them understanding her wholehearted gratitude. That part was absolutely true.

She had not realized how long she had been sitting at her dressing table, lost in thought. But she was not dressed when Aunt Bates summoned her to say Mr Knightley's carriage was waiting for them. She asked her aunt to do up the ties on the back of her dress, which seemed ample excuse for her not being ready.

The ladies were already in the drawing room when they arrived. Their hostess greeted them graciously. Mrs Weston was there, and Mrs Gilbert, and Miss Woodhouse, who was talking with an exceptionally pretty girl whom Jane did not know. Upon introduction, she was the Miss Smith to whom Mr Knightley took such a strong objection.

If Jane thought she could simply hide behind her Aunt Bates's endless talking, she had grossly miscalculated. All the other women in the room took precedence over Aunt Bates. Her aunt could drown out the other women in chatter individually; but when Mrs Cole, Mrs Gilbert, and Mrs Weston all gathered around to press her for details about the new pianoforte, physically excluding Aunt Bates with the contracted size of a circle which included Jane but excluded Aunt Bates, Jane was trapped.

"Mrs Cole told us all about the surprise that arrived for you yesterday!" Mrs Gilbert started the attack.

Mrs Weston was the only musician in the group. "Broadwood makes such superior instruments! It is a square pianoforte, of course, not a grand. Are you pleased with its tone? You must be used to playing on grands."

Jane did not get to answer before Mrs Cole joined in. "Have you received another letter from the Colonel yet, to tell you about the gift? Have you written him to thank him for it?"

"I started a letter to my excellent friend, Colonel Campbell, but I have not finished it yet," Jane answered. "I will confess, words fail me a little at present."

"My word, I would have no idea what to say if I was the one receiving such a generous gift. Although, I suppose I could say that our new pianoforte is something like a gift. Mr Cole really bought it for our guests to play, since I am not musical. I do hope at least one of our girls proves to have some talent for it. Their governess can play a little, I shall have to encourage her to start sitting them down and teaching them the keys when I am out visiting, and don't have to hear them banging away." Mrs Cole gave a little start. "Why, you are going to be a governess, so you should know. Are they too young to start musical training?"

Jane clenched her teeth together. A governess was possibly the worst kind of servant to be. Other servants were expected to be mostly invisible, but at least they had each other. The governess was expected to be equally invisible, seen only when bringing the children in to see their parents. But she was supposed to be educated, and respectable. Too good to mingle with the servants, too lowly to mingle with the employers. In exile with only the children for company. "Mozart composed his first piece at age five. I believe his father was sitting him at the harpsichord as soon as he was old enough to sit up on his own."

"Dear me, imagine my daughters as gifted as Mozart! But, I assume when you accept a position, you will take your instrument with you? Or will you leave it here with your grandmother? I suppose it depends upon whether you are allowed to play wherever you will be. If you are in a part of the house where you won't disturb anyone, and have the space for an instrument, without having one already made available for you..." Mrs Cole shook her head. "While a generous gift, perhaps it is not such a practical one. What was Colonel Campbell thinking?"

"Surely only to give Miss Fairfax pleasure. She is like a second daughter to him," Mrs Gilbert chimed in.

While Mrs Cole and Mrs Gilbert were more curious about the giver, Mrs Weston, being more musical than the other two, was more curious about the gift. "You still have not reported on the qualities of your instrument," she pointed out. "Are you pleased with the touch? How are the pedals?"

Now that the ladies had had their share of monopolizing Jane, Aunt Bates was finally able to squeeze her way into the circle. "To be sure, Jane has been so pleased! She has spent so much time playing since it arrived! Mother was saying the other day how very wonderful it is to have music in the house."

Mrs Gilbert and Miss Cole moved off to greet the Miss Coxes when they arrived, but Mrs Weston was gently persistent in asking more questions of Jane, despite her aunt's insistence in joining the conversation. "I have not seen many square pianofortes, how do you feel it compares with other instruments you have played?"

As Jane allowed her aunt to continue answering, making it unnecessary for her to have to talk, she realized that Miss Woodhouse was watching her from across the room. A wave of dislike washed over her. While it was difficult to answer the awkward questions being posed by her well-meaning neighbors, at least they made a point of congratulating her on her new instrument. Miss Woodhouse's enmity would not even allow for enough manners to come say the basic pleasantries about it. Well, at least it was one fewer person Jane had to talk to about it, one fewer person she had to lie to.

It was something of a relief when Mrs Weston, discouraged that she could get no answer from Jane because Aunt Bates insisted on answering all her questions, moved away. The door opened, and Mr Frank Churchill hurried into the room. His eyes immediately looked for hers. Jane met his eyes, then hurriedly dropped her gaze before she gave away too much. She would tell any lie, about anything, to anyone. He was worth it.

She saw him consciously slow his steps, so that he could approach more casually. But he came straight for her. "Miss Bates, Miss Fairfax. I trust you are having a good evening?" When Jane flashed him a quick warning look, she saw understanding in his eyes, and he swiftly moved past them and kept walking. He made a point of finding a seat near Miss Woodhouse. Considering what a horrid gossip she was, Jane was glad of it. She had the feeling Miss Woodhouse had been watching and listening to every word that had been said, and having Mr Churchill charm and misdirect her was a good idea.

Since he could not talk to her, Mr Churchill settled for talking to Miss Woodhouse loudly enough so that Jane could hear him. He talked about Enscombe, and society in Yorkshire, and how isolated he was, since his aunt's health and personality made her disinclined to be social. He had already told her some of his circumstances, but while talking loudly to Miss Woodhouse in veiled terms, he was able to tell Jane more about her future life in Yorkshire, and promised that as soon as he could, he would persuade his aunt to allow their marriage.

Jane listened to his performance, tried not to smile when he teased her with veiled references which she understood and Miss Woodhouse did not, and studiously kept her eyes focused on the rest of the room. The other gentlemen arrived, and the drawing room filled with conversations. Mr Cole interrupted Mr Churchill's conversation with Miss Woodhouse.

Mr Weston and Mr Gilbert entered, still debating some topic of parish business, until Mrs Weston drew Mr Weston aside for some more private words. The Miss Coxes were talking to Miss Woodhouse's pretty friend. Mr Knightley seemed to be continuing a debate with Mr Cox from dinner, but Jane was uncomfortably aware that his eyes seemed to wander back to her very frequently. She smiled at him, since after all he was so kind as to send his carriage for her and her aunt. She got the distinct impression that if it had been just her aunt, he would not have been so thoughtful.

Her suspicions were confirmed only a few moments later, when Mrs Weston approached her and Aunt Bates. "Miss Bates, it is a terribly cold night tonight. Our carriage is at your service to take you home."

"Bless me!" Aunt Bates gushed. "Thank you. I don't think there is anyone in all of England who has such thoughtful neighbors as I do. No one is so fortunate as I am for being surrounded by such lovely, thoughtful neighbors! Many, many thanks for being such considerate neighbors. But, there is no reason to trouble yourself on our account. Mr Knightley has already thought of us, and sent his carriage to fetch us, and he will send us home by his carriage before it takes him home. Is he not the most perfect gentleman to think of Jane, and send his carriage so that she does not catch a chill while walking home? I really, really am completely swept away by how very, very kind he is. All our neighbors are so very kind to us."

Internally, Jane was squirming. Mrs Weston's face was a little too interested. She knew that Mr Knightley's act of gallantry would be the bit of gossip that would replace the gossip about the pianoforte. That was not necessarily a bad thing. But she did not like the way that Mr Knightley's eyes were once again looking in her direction while her aunt and Mrs Weston were discussing the carriage.

Mrs Weston left, to be replaced by Mrs Cole, who began a discussion about cards that seemed to engross the both of them wholeheartedly.

Suddenly, Mr Churchill was right in front of her. "The evening has been a-buzz tonight about the arrival of a mysterious pianoforte at your grandmother's house," he told her with an intimate smile. He had placed himself right in front of her, so that his body was a shield from all the prying eyes in the room. "I hope you are enjoying it."

"It is the most beautiful instrument I have ever seen in my life," Jane answered honestly.

"Perhaps the instrument is not particularly out of the ordinary.

The love that inspired such a gift, however, is a terribly beautiful thing," he said, lowering his voice a little. There seemed to be little danger of him being overheard, there were so many conversations in progress.

"It is, indeed. Every time I put my fingers on the keys, I think about the giver. It is astonishing and humbling to think someone went to such extravagant measures merely for my happiness."

"It is not the least bit astonishing to me. You create so much happiness in others with your music, as well as for yourself. It is only fitting that you should have the means to play under your own roof. You spend so much time pleasing others, you should have the ability to please yourself sometimes."

Jane felt her face grow very warm. "I almost always have listeners," she warned him, her eyes sliding to the back of her aunt's head.

"How unfortunate," he answered with an unrepentant smile. "I am sure there are times you would prefer to practice in private."

Jane was spared the necessity of an answer by a bustle in the room, as the tea things were cleared away and the Coles' pianoforte was opened. "I see you are about to get the chance to display your superior skills," Mr Churchill said. He gave her a mischievous smile, and then he was on his feet, following Mr Cole, entreating Miss Woodhouse to play for them. The guests stood around the pianoforte while Miss Woodhouse seated herself.

To be fair, Emma Woodhouse played and sang a little bit better than Sophia Campbell Dixon. But while Sophia despised playing for an audience of more than two or three, Miss Woodhouse clearly adored attention, and it would behoove her to practice a little more. At least enough to be worthy of the praise heaped upon her when she finished. At least she had enough awareness of her lack of skill to attempt only simple pieces within her power to do with some success. Her fingers only faltered over two or three notes, and her voice only went flat two or three times. She could see it was a bit much for Mr Churchill, who had an excellent ear. She suspected he had perfect pitch. If not, he had an excellent sense of relative pitch.

He had a solution to the problem of listening to Miss Woodhouse sing: when she began the opening bars of a second song, he sang with her.

Jane stood with her hands folded, her eyes politely focused on the performers and tried not to shake with suppressed laughter. Miss Woodhouse was looking delighted. Mr Churchill kept his expression pleasant and bland. But as he sang and looked at Jane, standing on the far side of the instrument, she could see the wicked twinkle in his eye. He had used the same trick at some of the musical evenings they had been to together in Weymouth. He had confessed to her later that it was a dodge he had learned years earlier. He would rather sing with a poor singer than have to sit and listen to a bad singer.

When he seemed to look at her a bit too long, she let her eyes look at the people around her, and then dropped her gaze to the polished top of the pianoforte in front of her. He understood the message, and his eyes traveled over the rest of the assembled guests.

The song finished, there was enthusiastic applause, and even more enthusiastic requests for another song. Well, of course. Miss Woodhouse was a great favorite of all the attendees, most of whom had no musical training of their own. Jane smiled through another song, while Mr Churchill looked at her as much as he dared.

At last, Miss Woodhouse rose from the instrument. "It is about time I relinquished my place to a larger talent than my own," she said. "Miss Fairfax, will you oblige us?"

Without a word, Jane exchanged places with Miss Woodhouse. Mr Churchill stood sorting through the collection of music. "Shall we reprise the duet from Rossini's *L'Italiana in Algeri* that we did at Weymouth?" he asked her, holding out the music.

It took all her willpower to keep her expression neutral. It was the first thing they had sung together after becoming engaged. It was also an extremely technical piece that would show the world of difference between Miss Woodhouse's skills and her own. "That would be delightful."

There was some satisfaction in seeing the faces of their audience when they presented their perfectly blended voices. Since no one in Highbury spoke Italian, no one would understand the significance of the lyrics, as he praised her face and her figure, but at least they dimly understood the skill required to perform it.

Miss Woodhouse left the circle to sit down when everyone applauded, and Jane broke into the introduction for another song that would show off Mr Churchill's singing abilities, as well as her own skills as an accompanist.

From her place at the pianoforte, Jane could see Miss Woodhouse pouting in her seat.

About halfway through the song, Mr Knightley left to sit next to her. It was a relief. Mr Knightley had been staring at her so intently, it was making her uncomfortable.

When the song finished and everyone applauded, Jane saw that Miss Woodhouse and Mr Knightley were busily talking. She could only imagine the conversation between them: Mr Knightley ironically calling Miss Woodhouse out on her poor manners, all the while talking instead of listening respectfully, as everyone did while Miss Woodhouse was playing. Then Miss Woodhouse would give a spirited rebuttal, which was more about Mr Knightley's habit of putting things rather rudely than it was about the actual subject. Jane knew they were longtime family friends, but the ways in which he lectured her, like a big brother, bordered on inappropriate. She rather grudgingly admired the way Miss Woodhouse tended to return fire, rather than accept the criticism, no matter how valid it might, in fact, be.

Mr Churchill selected the next song; a piece for Jane. It was particularly challenging, but Jane delighted in his selection. He had chosen it specifically to showcase her range. It also happened to be another piece they had sung together in Weymouth.

By the end of it, Jane was in need of some water. Before she could ask for some, Mr Knightley declared, "That will do. You have sung quite enough for one evening. Now, be quiet."

Be quiet? He really just told her to be quiet? Jane's incensed feelings were soothed by the chorus of protesting voices calling for at least one more. She wished there was a way for her to thank Mr Churchill for the quick way he presented another song from the stack of music. "I think you could manage this without effort. The first part is so very trifling. The strength of the song falls on the second."

The voices expressing their agreement were not loud enough to drown out Mr Knightley's voice. "Miss Bates, are you mad, to let your niece sing herself hoarse in this manner? Go and interfere. They have no mercy on her."

Jane later wished she had been swifter to start playing. Her hands balled into fists as they hovered above the keys. It was difficult to say which was more rude; telling her to be quiet, or verbally attacking Aunt Bates and asking her if she was mad, allowing Jane to continue singing. But before she could unclench her hands and allow music to emerge from her throat, water or no water, her aunt had pushed her way in and insisted upon an end to the singing.

Dancing was called for, and Mrs Weston took her turn at the instrument. While she was not an accomplished player, she was quite excellent at playing country dances. Even if she stumbled over the melody, she never lost time, and the dance flowed perfectly from one iteration to the next. In the scramble to clear a space to dance, Mr Churchill took advantage of the confusion to touch her on the arm and look earnestly into her face. He felt the rudeness as strongly as she did. Perhaps more so, because he was in no position to protect Jane from it.

It was so swift. A touch, a look that said he would have called Mr Knightley onto the dueling field for his rudeness if their engagement was not a secret, and then he was gone, smiling blandly, asking Miss Woodhouse for the first dance. Mr Cole claimed her, and not a moment too soon. Mr Knightley was behind Mr Cole, already extending a hand as if to claim hers. Jane was only too happy to drop her fingers into Mr Cole's hand, instead. She walked past Mr Knightley, refusing to look at him. He turned to talk to Mrs Cole. Jane thought he would ask her to dance, and was relieved when he simply prevented her from getting a partner. She would not have to interact with him in the course of the dance.

The Duke of Kent's Waltz was followed by Countess of Hardwicke's Favorite. Before partners could be exchanged for a fresh dance, Miss Bates announced that it was late, and they should be leaving. Twice in one evening, her aunt was the means for breaking up everyone's fun. Mr Churchill was among the loudest protests for just one more dance, and she knew why. They were finally going to get to dance together.

Unfortunately, her aunt was firm. "Mr Knightley is right, I am a poor caregiver indeed, if poor Jane can neither walk nor talk tomorrow because I kept her out so late. Besides, Mother is at home all alone. No, indeed, Jane and I must be going. Especially since Mr Knightley has to wait for us to be delivered home before he is able to have use of his own carriage to get home himself. I am afraid we never should have stayed this long. Only it has been such a lovely, lovely evening. Thank you so much for inviting us, Mrs Cole. Mr Cole. Jane and I are the most fortunate people, having such thoughtful neighbors."

As Aunt Bates continued her speech about the generosity of the neighbors, Jane and Mr Churchill's eyes met across the room. They were not going to get their dance tonight.

CHAPTER TEN

Jane did not sleep well that night. After Mr Knightley's rude behavior at the Coles', the last thing she wanted to do was get in his carriage for the ride home. If she had been alone, she would have refused the carriage ride and walked. But there was her aunt to consider. It was late, and the walk was a considerable one, and her aunt was clearly tired.

The feeling of being under obligation to him for the favor galled her. The fact that the favors were starting to accumulate – the apples, the carriage – galled her more.

The entire morning seemed out of sorts. First the rivet came out of her grandmother's spectacles, and she found out that her grandmother did not own a second pair. She offered to take them over to Mr Saunders to get them repaired, but her aunt insisted that she needed to go, since she had other errands to run. But the other errands kept getting postponed. Patty came in to tell them that the kitchen chimney needed sweeping. It was a horrible expense, but the money must be found, or they might burn down the village. Then Mrs Wallis' boy arrived with a fresh pan of baked apples.

Jane had been at the point of convincing her aunt to allow her to run the errand with the spectacles, but when the baked apples arrived, still warm, her aunt nearly pushed her down into a chair to eat. Jane was sure, by the time she left Highbury, she would never want to eat another apple again.

When the bell rang to announce visitors, she was afraid it was going to be Mr Knightley again. She clenched her teeth. She would remain civil. She did not know how she was going to remain so. But she had to. After all, she would be leaving someday; but her aunt and grandmother would continue to live here long after she left for Yorkshire.

"Bless me! Who could that be!" Aunt Bates headed for the door, but Patty let them in and they were already halfway up the stairs. "Mrs Weston, Mr Churchill! Oh my goodness, it is so lovely to see you! This morning has been such a terrible flutter."

Jane stood up, apple forgotten, Aunt Bates's voice fading to a background buzz. Mr Churchill was here! Her fingertips rested lightly on the top of the table – in case she fainted at the sight of him, and she needed to catch herself.

He walked in, all smiles and cheer, and his eyes made the world better.

"Good morning! We have come to hear the new pianoforte," Mrs Weston said, in a voice that suggested they were expected.

"Oh! Of course, well, Mother is asleep in her chair by the fire. But since she has so much trouble hearing, it should not wake her. Poor Mother! The rivet came out of her spectacles, and she has no other pair. I have been meaning to run to John Saunders all morning to get them fixed. But you know how it is, I have been hindered all morning. Poor dear. She has no other pair, and she can hardly see without them."

"Oh!" Mr Churchill exclaimed. "I can fasten the rivet. I like a job of that sort excessively. Allow me to try my hand at repairing them, before you send them out."

"That is so very good of you!" Miss Bates gushed. "Now, where did I put them down? It is so good to have clever friends to help in your hour of need. I wish we had ways to repay everyone for their kindnesses to us. Can I at least offer you a baked apple? They have just come from Mrs Wallis. Perhaps you would be so very obliging as to take some?" She scurried to the pantry door, brought out the pan of apples, and held them in front of Mr Churchill.

Jane was a bit mortified, but by now she had weeks of practice keeping a straight face through Aunt Bates's uncouth behaviors. Mr Churchill's mouth twitched, but he surveyed them with a serious face. "There is nothing in the way of fruit half so good. I must say, these are the finest looking home-baked apples I ever saw in my life."

Aunt Bates was completely oblivious to the satirical tones in his voice. "Indeed they are very delightful apples, and Mrs Wallis does them full justice, even if she does only bake them twice."

"I am sure they are delightful, but perhaps after I keep my promise. You were fetching me Mrs Bates's spectacles, that I might repair them?" he reminded her with a smile.

"Oh!" Aunt Bates would have dropped the pan of apples, but he caught them before they had done more than tilt a little. He took the pan from her, and put it on the table. "Bless me, I was. It has been such a morning. It is so good to have company! Have you business in town, are you taking Mr Churchill to Ford's?" She found the broken glasses on the mantel above the fireplace and handed them to Mr Churchill, who gave Jane a wink when he turned his back to the room and seated himself at the table, across from the apples.

"We came to hear the new pianoforte," Mrs Weston reminded her. "But we were just at Ford's. Miss Woodhouse and her friend Miss Smith are shopping there, right this moment."

"Oh!" Aunt Bates exclaimed. "I must run across, I am sure Miss Woodhouse will allow me to run across and entreat her to come in." It was all Jane could do to keep from covering her face. If she tried to suggest to her aunt that she try to be less sycophantic, it would only cause confusion. "My mother will be so happy to see her. We will be such a nice party, she cannot refuse."

"Aye, pray do!" Frank encouraged her. "Miss Woodhouse's opinion of the instrument will be worth having."

"But – what if she won't come? I shall be more sure of succeeding if one of you will come with me."

"Well, if you want me to go, you shall have to wait half a minute until I have finished my job," Mr Churchill laughed, holding up the bow of the spectacles he was working on reattaching. "This rivet is going to be a bit tricky."

"I will go with you, Miss Bates," Mrs Weston offered. "Come, we had better hurry, or we shall miss them entirely!" With that encouragement, the two ladies scurried down the stairs.

They were alone.

There was a moment of stunned silence, as the two of them stared at each other. Then, somehow, he stood up, and she crossed the room, and they were in each other's arms. "My darling," Mr Churchill's voice murmured in her hair. "I lied to Mrs Weston that she had promised to come see the pianoforte this morning, just to be able to see you. But I never dreamed I would manage to see you alone."

Both of them paused at the word, and looked at the chair by the fire. As if in response to their unasked question, Grandmama started snoring. They both smiled at each other.

With their arms still wrapped around each other, he touched his forehead to hers. "How are you faring, my love?"

"Better, now that you are here." He tightened his arms around her. "But you can see for yourself what I have described."

"I do, indeed," he said. "You have the patience of an angel. Do you have days when your voice is hoarse because you have not spoken at all?"

"Thanks to your gift, I now have a chance to sing, as well as play, while my aunt either listens with Grandmama, or leaves, so that she can talk to someone else."

"As soon as I get back to Enscombe, I will work harder to get my aunt to agree to my getting married," he promised. "Thus far, I have been getting her used to the idea in general terms. Now I will tell her I want to bring her an angel who will sing and play for her all day long, if she likes, who will mend her caps and do her fancywork for her, and all the other little things you do for your aunt and grandmother that have won such approbation here. You really are the village's favorite topic of conversation. I give people only the slightest encouragement, and they are delighted to talk about you. So, there is something useful in their fondness for gossip. At least I can talk about you, when I cannot be looking at you."

"Perhaps I was the favorite topic of gossip, but you have supplanted me, I believe, with your arrival," Jane teased him. "Of course, the pianoforte is, in a way, talking about both of us. They just don't know it."

"It is delicious sharing a secret with you," he told her.

"You say that, but secrets have a way of getting out. People are suspicious, and they have nothing to do but watch each other and talk about each other. We must be very, very careful," she warned him.

"Well, then, Miss Woodhouse will serve as a useful blind. I can see pretty clearly all the matchmakers want me to court Miss Woodhouse, and I can see that Miss Woodhouse is not interested. I can be a charming friend, but while I hear from my new mother that Miss Woodhouse likes making matches for other people, she has no such plans for herself. I was half wondering if we should take her into our confidence?"

"Miss Woodhouse?" Jane was scandalized at the idea. "Goodness, no. She is a horrible gossip. She is also very immature. If you are wrong in your estimation, she will report it to the entire village. You would be forced to marry her to silence the gossip, and I would be unable to get a governess position because I would no longer be considered respectable."

"You know her better than I do, so –" there were voices on the stairs, and the lovers hastily broke apart. Mr Churchill sat himself back at the table with the spectacles, Jane moved quickly to stand by the pianoforte.

"This is a pleasure," he greeted them in a low voice. Jane could hear the irritation in it. She had her back to him, so she was unable to give him any sort of warning to compose himself. "Coming at least ten minutes earlier than I had calculated." Jane smiled inwardly at the thought of ten more minutes alone with him, but she closed her eyes and willed him to be more cautious. "You find me trying to be useful; tell me if you think I shall succeed."

"What!" said Mrs Weston, "have you not finished it yet? You would not earn a very good living as a working silversmith at this rate."

"I have not been working uninterruptedly," he answered. "I have been assisting Miss Fairfax in trying to make her instrument stand steadily. It was not quite firm; an unevenness in the floor, I believe. You see we have been wedging one leg with paper."

Mr Churchill's quick mind was certainly more than a match for any wit in the village. Not only had his sharp eyes noted the bit of paper Jane had put under one leg, he had given her a reason to be standing where she was. She began critically surveying the pianoforte from side to side, and gave it the gentlest of shakes, as if testing to see that it was more stable. She was glad she had her back to everyone. While Mr Churchill seemed to delight in telling any number of fibs, she wasn't nearly as comfortable with so much deception.

"This was very kind of you to be persuaded to come," he continued. Jane could not decide if she should smile or cringe at his parody of her aunt's overly-obsequious words. "I was almost afraid you would be hurrying home."

While Mr Churchill had regained his composure, calmly offering Miss Woodhouse a baked apple and talking about the spectacles, Jane discovered she had not regained hers. Her heart was pounding and her hands were shaking. That was simply too close. How long did it take for people to climb those stairs? If they had been discovered, what possible explanation could they offer? They would have to admit to their engagement. Perhaps they could have claimed that he had that very moment proposed? It did not matter. They were not caught.

She lingered over the selection of music to give her heart and hands time to calm down. But she could only put it off so long; she was going to have to play for her guests. She made her choice, and sat at the pianoforte. The first notes grated on her own ears; she sounded weak and unsure of herself. What was she, an eight-year-old playing for adults for the first time? A sixteen-year-old playing in front of a boy she was afraid to talk to? Her self-disgust gave her the means to pull herself together, and she began to do both Mozart and the instrument justice. To apologize to her listeners for the feeble beginning, she followed that with some Beethoven.

Mr Churchill positioned himself behind the others as they crowded around her, so that as they complimented her playing, and the instrument, he could watch her with shining eyes. No one but herself saw him kiss his hand to her as she finished, and they applauded.

"What tone! You look as though you barely have to touch the keys to produce the most magnificent sound!" Mrs Weston exclaimed.

"Indeed," Miss Woodhouse joined in. "Your new pianoforte is altogether of the highest promise."

"Whoever Colonel Campbell might employ," Mr Churchill was studiously addressing Miss Woodhouse, but his voice was a little too loud, so that Jane could hear him over Mrs Weston's enthusiastic praise of the instrument, "the person has not chosen ill. I heard a good deal of Colonel Campbell's taste at Weymouth; and the softness of the upper notes I am sure is exactly what he and all that party would particularly prize. I dare say, Miss Fairfax, that he either gave his friend very minute directions, or wrote to

Broadwood himself. Do not you think so?"

"I had no idea a square instrument could provide such richness of tone," Mrs Weston had been saying.

"I myself am equally surprised and gratified," Jane answered her.

Mr Churchill was not done with teasing her. "How much your friends in Ireland must be enjoying your pleasure on this occasion, Miss Fairfax. I dare say they often think of you, and wonder which will be the day, the precise day of the instrument's coming to hand. Do you imagine Colonel Campbell knows the business to be going forward just at this time? Do you imagine it to be the consequence of an immediate commission from him, or that he may have sent only a general direction, an order indefinite as to time, to depend upon contingencies and conveniences?"

She wished he would not belabor his point quite so much. The less said about the instrument, the better! Drawing attention to it and the giver was courting disaster. "Till I have a letter from Colonel Campbell," she reminded him with a calmness she did not feel, "I can imagine nothing with any confidence. It must be all conjecture."

He nodded his agreement, and with equal calm, he reseated himself at the table and took up the spectacles again. "Conjecture. Aye, sometimes one conjectures right, and sometimes one conjectures wrong. I wish I could conjecture how soon I shall make this rivet quite firm." That statement told Jane that he had finished with the spectacles a long time ago, but he was using them as an excuse to extend his visit as long as he possibly could. "What nonsense one talks, Miss Woodhouse, when hard at work, if one talks at all. Your real workmen, I suppose, hold their tongues; but we gentlemen laborers if we get hold of a word – Miss Fairfax said something about conjecturing. There, it is done." He stood up, and handed the delicate silver wire frames back to Grandmama, who was now awake, no doubt on account of Jane's small concert. "I have the pleasure, madam, of restoring your spectacles, healed for the present."

"What a clever fellow you are!" Grandmama patted his hand, while Aunt Bates broke into raptures. "Oh! How wonderful it is to have neighbors who are as clever as they are generous. They look every bit as good as new. Perhaps even better, for I am sure that now there is no danger of the rivet coming back out. You truly could have a career as a silversmith, Mrs Weston's observations notwithstanding. For who cares if the job is slow, if it is well done?"

"You are very welcome, Mrs Bates," he said, clasping her hand, still on his, between both of his own. When Aunt Bates seemed inclined to continue her speech, he moved over to stand next to Jane. "I would be most grateful if you would play something more. If you are very kind, it will be one of the waltzes we danced last night. Let me live them over again. You did not enjoy them as I did; you appeared tired the whole time. I believe you were glad we danced no longer. But I would have given worlds – all the worlds one has to give – for another half hour."

Jane did not need the music to play Duke of Kent's Waltz. It was a simple enough tune. She embellished it a little differently with each iteration.

"What felicity it is to hear a tune again which has made one happy! If I mistake not, that was danced at Weymouth."

Jane looked up at him. His eyes were dancing so merrily as he teased her, it was all she could do to keep from laughing. She could not think of any words she could say in response, so she plunged into 'Robin Adair,' the song they had sung together so many times.

He smiled at her, then wisely moved away. He scooped up the music she had spread on a chair, and turned to Miss Woodhouse. "Here is something quite new to me. Do you know it? Cramer. And here are a new set of Irish melodies. That, from such a quarter, one might expect. This was all sent with the instrument. Very thoughtful of Colonel Campbell, was not it? He knew Miss Fairfax could have no music here. I honor that part of the attention particularly; it shows it to have been so thoroughly from the heart. Nothing hastily done; nothing incomplete. True affection only could have prompted it."

Jane could not help but smile. She knew she would have to speak – or write – to him in private, and chide him to have a care. He was being much too imprudent. But he was taking such gleeful delight in having the credit for his generosity given to another man! Most men would chafe at such misapprehension. They would want to take the credit for their actions. But then, that would be Mr

Churchill's own fault for giving her a gift that he could not admit to giving!

He had taken the stack of music over to Miss Woodhouse. She whispered something to him. He answered in a not-whisper loud enough for Jane to hear. "I hope she does. I would have her understand me. I am not in the least ashamed of my meaning."

She missed the next few exchanges, but he raised his voice enough for her to hear him say "She is playing 'Robin Adair' at this moment – *his* favorite."

This lopsided flirtation could have gone on all afternoon – Mr Churchill speaking in riddles only she could understand, she answering him in music. But then Aunt Bates saw Mr Knightley from the window, and insisted upon opening the window in Grandmama's room, and shouting an invitation for Mr Knightley to come in. Jane still had no interest in speaking to him, and wished with all her might she had a way to stop her aunt. But it was too late. Then her fingers ran out of notes, and she sat, silent, at the pianoforte, listening to the conversation with everyone else.

"How is your niece, Miss Bates? I want to inquire after you all, but particularly your niece. How is Miss Fairfax? I hope she caught no cold last night. How is she today? Tell me how Miss Fairfax is."

Jane could feel everyone in the room staring at the back of her head. If only none of them had been in the room to hear that exchange! What would Mr Churchill think now? Not that he would be wrong in his assumptions. Mr Knightley was saying her name with much too much frequency. He was talking like a lover. It was mortifying.

As if that was not bad enough, Mr Knightley was now turning Aunt Bates's gushing about the evening's party into more excuses to compliment her. He managed to make a nasty joke of it all: he complimented the dancing of Mr Churchill and Miss Woodhouse, then complimented her dancing, then complimented Mrs Weston's playing, and then said that the others needed to make compliments about him and Aunt Bates, since the room could certainly hear every word.

Jane had to admit it took a special kind of talent to give compliments and insults at the exact same time.

When it seemed the conversation could not possibly get any

worse, Aunt Bates then brought up the apples. Jane could not blame Mr Knightley too much for his rude response, "What is the matter now?"

She thought about banging her forehead against the keys when Aunt Bates brought up the fact that William Larkins had told them everything he was not supposed to about Mr Knightley's generosity in sending all the rest of his store. She pictured putting her things in a valise and running away to Scotland with Mr Churchill that very night, rather than spend another day in this town with her gossiping aunt, the gossiping servant, and the very rude Mr Knightley. She was actually grateful to him for his rudeness on this occasion; he simply rode away while her aunt was still talking, before matters could get any worse.

The idea of everyone in the room noticing that Mr Knightley was being inordinately attentive was too awful. She did not mean to be quite so sharp, but she could not completely control her tongue when her aunt came back in the room, obviously planning on repeating the entire conversation. "Yes!" She simply could not bear hearing it all again. "We heard his kind offers. We heard everything."

The hint was not enough, and Aunt Bates was launching into a repetition, anyway. Fortunately, their guests had manners enough to rise and take their leave. "Goodness me, it is so late!" Mrs Weston exclaimed. "I know I had suggested coming to visit you at Hartfield, Miss Woodhouse, but I fear the best we can do is see you to the Hartfield gates before we set off for Randalls, that is, if we hurry."

As Miss Woodhouse and her pretty friend hurried down the stairs, and Mrs Weston made to follow them, Mr Churchill lingered behind for a moment. "Thank you for showing us your new pianoforte, Miss Fairfax. I can see how well pleased you are with the instrument. It suits you exceedingly well."

"Thank you, Mr Churchill. It suits me very well." Jane answered. One last look passed between them, then he was gone.

CHAPTER ELEVEN

"I am sorry to trouble you, but are Miss Bates and Miss Fairfax at home? I have been sent to fetch them to The Crown, if they are willing to be disturbed." Mr Churchill's voice floated up the stairwell to the surprise of both of the ladies in question. Jane had left her window seat to put away several garments she had just finished mending, and had been about to embark upon the next item on the pile. Instead, she took a hasty moment to check her reflection in the glass to make sure she was not looking a complete fright. She hastily tucked a stray hair back into place, and then he was in the room.

She did not get a chance to say a word of greeting, of course. Her aunt was aflutter with excitement at the visit. "Mr Churchill! How very kind of you to call! Mother was just asking after you while we were having tea. She noticed that we did not see you at all yesterday. Not that you have any reason to bother with us, but you have been so gracious coming to see us so many times since you've come to Randalls!"

"I am quite sorry I was unable to call upon you yesterday. Believe me, I would have called had I been free to do so, I assure you," he jumped in before Aunt Bates could continue. "I come on a mission, Miss Bates. Would you and Miss Fairfax be persuaded to venture some opinions? Right this minute, my father and Mrs Weston and Miss Woodhouse are looking over the rooms at The Crown to see if they would be sufficient for throwing a small ball. There is a great deal of anxiety over the size of the rooms, and the length of the passage between the ballroom and the supper-room, and if the card-room is sufficient, and whether or not there is a draught on the stairs. I have been summoned to bring you and Miss

Fairfax to look over the situation to see if it would suit."

"Bless me!" Aunt Bates was amazed by the invitation. "To think that Mrs Weston and Miss Woodhouse should want my opinion on such matters. I am sure whatever they decide to do would be delightful, I cannot imagine that I can contribute anything to their decisions."

"Nevertheless," he insisted, "Your opinion is being solicited, and I cannot imagine you mean to do a disservice to my father and Mrs Weston and Miss Woodhouse by not hurrying over this minute, when they have asked me to fetch you."

Jane had to smile. She could see how he must use these same powers of persuasion to manage his own aunt. He certainly had the charm and ability to manage hers with great ease.

"Oh! How awful it would be to keep Miss Woodhouse and Mrs Weston waiting. Fetch our bonnets, Jane! Jane has repaired our bonnets. She is so clever with her needle! My word, she reattached my ribbons, one of them had almost completely come off. But now, it is as sturdy as when it was brand new."

Mr Churchill smiled. "I am sure Miss Fairfax is a wonder with bonnet ribbons." His eyes took note of the knots still in the ends of the ribbons on Jane's bonnet, and he looked into her face with special meaning.

"Oh, indeed she is -"

It was Jane's turn to help move her aunt along. "You can tell Mr Churchill about it on the way to see Miss Woodhouse and Mr and Mrs Weston," she suggested. The look of understanding he gave her as he held the door for her aunt warmed her all over.

They hurried down the stairs and into the street, and then, in wordless agreement, Mr Churchill and Jane hung back a little and let Aunt Bates hurry ahead of them. "Since I still have not been able to manage to have a single dance with you since I have been in Highbury, I have had to talk my way into throwing an entire ball. Fortunately, my companions are willing to be persuaded. Now perhaps you can help me persuade them that the accommodations will work, and the hall is not too long, and the stairs are not too draughty. This lot can give my aunt some hefty competition!"

"I have full confidence in your ability to persuade anyone to just about any thing," Jane answered loyally.

"Well, I hope I can live up to your expectations. I can get any two people to agree on something, but the third always seems to voice an objection. Then I get a different two to agree on something else, but a different third party voices a different objection. Your aunt's agreeable disposition will hopefully be of great use in this situation. She is sure to approve of everything, which will help allay whatever the objection of the moment might be."

They fell silent as they climbed the stairs.

The Crown proved to be a haven of privacy for two lovers wanting nothing more than a handful of seconds in which to lock eyes, or touch hands, or whisper a couple of words. There was the hallway to pace to gauge its distance, the large room for dancing to consider how many couples could fit easily, the smaller adjacent room to plan how to set up the card tables, the hallway and stairs that needed to be evaluated for draughts, and the room on the far side of the inn that needed to be contemplated for the supper.

"Do you think it too long a distance from the ballroom to the supper-room?" Mrs Weston asked her anxiously.

"The people you are proposing to invite are all healthy and fit enough to spend an entire evening dancing. They are therefore fit enough to manage the…" Jane finished walking and counting, "…twelve steps it takes to cross this hallway to go to supper," she pointed out pragmatically.

"When you put it that way, it does make my concerns sound trifling," Mrs Weston said.

"No concerns are trifling, when planning for a ball," Miss Woodhouse had walked into the hallway just in time to hear Mrs Weston's last statement. "Speaking of concerns, Miss Fairfax, Mr Churchill pointed out that you are the person most properly qualified to determine where in the ballroom we should have the music. Should the pianoforte stay where it is, or would it be better in the other corner?"

Mr Churchill was standing in the doorway, surveying the room. He managed to brush his fingers against hers as she walked in. "Miss Woodhouse thinks the pianoforte is fine where it is, but I thought perhaps it would be more visually pleasing to have the music on the other side, over there."

Jane admired his ability to make up excuses to bring the two of them together. She nodded soberly. "I see what you mean. But perhaps more importantly, is there an acoustical difference?"

"I can move the pianoforte, so that we can test it in both places," he offered.

"I don't think we need to go to such lengths. Singing will do." She walked across the room and stood next to the pianoforte, and sang the first few notes of 'Robin Adair.'

He laughed, and hurried to her side to sing with her. After a few bars, they crossed to the other proposed location, and continued the next few bars, then they looked inquiringly at their applauding audience. All the rest of the party had assembled in the room as they sang.

"I do believe the pianoforte should remain where it is," Miss Woodhouse declared, even as Mr Weston was saying, "You should move it to the other side, here, let me help you, son."

Aunt Bates, of course, was no help in deciding the debate. "Bless me, both sides sounded so very well! I don't know how you could ever possibly decide between the two. Of course, the pianoforte can only be in one place, so you are going to have to make a choice. Perhaps the light would be better on the other side? But that would not make much sense, there seem to be more sconces where it is right now. It takes ever so many candles to light a room as large as this. Dear me, is it as large as our entire apartment? I am sure it must be. It is so difficult to say, since of course our apartment is divided into so many rooms – this must be larger – Mrs Cole thinks that our apartment is ever so cozy and inviting, and a ball should be inviting, but dancing does take so much room. We could never do any dancing in our little apartment. We are so fortunate there was enough space to fit Jane's new pianoforte, which it was so nice of Colonel Campbell to send Jane –"

"I am going to vote to leave the pianoforte where it is," to Jane's relief, Mrs Weston elected to cast her vote, stopping her aunt from another tribute of gratitude towards people's generosity. "Miss Bates is quite right, the light will be better here for reading music."

"Since you are the one electing to supply the music, I would say yours is the opinion that matters most," Mr Churchill pointed out gallantly. "But we summoned Miss Fairfax here to get her opinion, and she has not rendered one yet."

Jane loved him more in that moment than in any moment since she had first seen him in the music shop. She looked at the pianoforte, unable to trust herself to look at him. If she did, all their companions would surely guess their secret. "I concur with Mrs Weston and Miss Woodhouse. Leave it where it is. It is quite happy there, especially knowing we will all be here to enjoy it together."

"So, it is settled then!" Mr Churchill exclaimed. Jane could hear the pleasure in his voice. He understood what she was trying to tell him. She was not nearly as good at making pretty speeches with hidden meanings as he was. She would never get better if she did not practice. "The music shall be in this corner. What questions remain to be settled? Do we need to summon Mrs Stokes to ask about supper arrangements?"

"I will go fetch her," Mr Weston offered.

"She did say when she brought us up here that the full services of The Crown's kitchen are at our disposal," Miss Woodhouse said.

"Capital! We will have to tell her how many people we will be having. You do think everyone will come? Are we giving too little notice to the Coles, or the Coxes?" Mr Churchill asked.

"The biggest question, I should think, is yourself," Mrs Weston pointed out. "Are you sure your aunt will be willing to extend your absence past your fortnight?"

"I wrote her in the most abject terms of my need to stay here a few days longer," he answered. "She could not possibly deny my entreaty. I was truly at my most persuasive!"

"Well, then, we should be well settled!" Mrs Weston exclaimed.

"Are you sure – are you quite sure?" Miss Woodhouse asked anxiously. "If your aunt cannot do without you any more than my father can do without me, she may not be too willing to allow you an extension of your visit. I can easily imagine her insisting upon your return, and then all our planning will be for nothing. We will lose the entire evening. No ball, no dancing, the entire evening would be lost. I am very afraid we are building sandcastles, and they are going to get washed completely away when you get your answer from Enscombe."

"Why, no, I am perfectly confident that she will allow me just a few more days," he laughed.

"Well, then, for now let us proceed with the assumption Mr Frank Churchill knows his aunt's mind better than we do," Mrs Weston declared. "We still need to decide upon how many card tables we will need." Once again, the party broke up into small groups and wandering individuals, as they scoped out the space and finished planning the card-room, the food for supper, a place to put their wraps as they came in.

He found Jane alone in the hallway. "I thought I ought to engage Miss Woodhouse for the first two dances, if you approve?"

Jane did not like the idea, but she nodded. "That sounds prudent."

"Then may I engage you for the next two dances, and then the last two? If I cannot begin the ball with you, at least we can finish it together."

"A perfect ending to the evening might agree with me even more than a perfect beginning," Jane agreed.

"I will be hard pressed to dance with anyone else all night," he told her. He might have said more, but both Westons and Mrs Stokes the proprietress were walking out of the supper-room.

CHAPTER TWELVE

Mr Frank Churchill got his response from Enscombe the next day, and hurried to see her. He found her just setting out to bring Mrs Wallis more apples to be baked in her ovens, and took the basket from her. "Do allow me, Miss Fairfax! That basket looks terribly heavy."

"It is nothing but a dozen apples," she laughed at him, but she let him take it. It gave them an excuse to be walking together. No one would question his perfect manners. Of course he would be carrying her basket for her!

"I have received a reply from Enscombe this morning," he told her.

"It must be good news, or you would not be looking so pleased today?" Jane asked.

"I am pleased to see you, of course," Frank answered. "But I do have my aunt's permission to remain here in Surrey."

"You have her permission – but is she very cross with you?" she gathered from his tone that all was not perfectly well.

"She is not pleased with me, certainly. But she has not forbidden it. I will take my small victories as I find them. I want to be here, I am allowed to be here. I will soothe my aunt's feelings when I get back to Yorkshire," he answered confidently.

"Will her displeasure at you staying here now make matters more difficult for you in the future?" Jane was more worried than he was. "After all, there are other subjects upon which you are attempting to persuade her. If she is unhappy with you, will she be less likely to agree to your other requests?"

"For the joy of dancing with you, I will risk her displeasure," he laughed. "When I am gone slightly longer than planned, and it does not kill her, I can demonstrate that she does not need me quite so desperately as she thinks she does. When I go back, and she is not glad to see me, I will offer to go away again. Which will make her angry and make her laugh at the same time, and then I will be forgiven. Once I am forgiven, then she will be in a better frame of mind to be persuaded on other topics. Trust me, my dearest Miss Fairfax. My aunt can be managed."

"I do trust you," she said as she stopped in front of Mrs Willis' bake shop. "You know your aunt. I of all people should be the last person to doubt your powers of persuasion."

He handed the basket back to her with a bow. "I am off to Hartfield to share the news that our ball can continue as planned. Mrs Weston believes that Miss Woodhouse is most anxious about the uncertainty, and asked me to go reassure her that all is well."

Jane gave him a knowing look. "Mrs Weston is clearly anxious to see that you spend as much time with Miss Woodhouse as possible."

"She and my father are being shameless matchmakers, there is no doubt about it," he agreed. "But have no fear. My heart is already taken." He left her with an intimate smile that had her humming as she walked into the shop.

When she re-emerged, Miss Woodhouse was talking in the street with Mr Knightley and the ever-present pretty little Miss Smith. Mr Churchill must have missed her. Or else he had found her on the way, and he was in one of the nearby shops doing an errand for her as she stood talking. Jane walked slowly, examining the new bonnets in the window, in case he should re-emerge.

She could not avoid overhearing Mr Knightley's typically unpleasant words to Miss Woodhouse. "If the Westons think it worth while to be at all this trouble for a few hours of noisy entertainment, I have nothing to say against it, but that they shall not choose pleasures for me."

"Does that mean you are not coming?" Miss Woodhouse asked.

"Oh, yes, I must be there. I could not refuse; and I will keep as much awake as I can. But I would rather be at home, looking over William Larkins's week's account. Much rather, I confess."

"What a very dull person you are! You won't dance, and you would rather be looking at accounting books than at dancing?"

Miss Woodhouse asked indignantly. Jane had to agree with Miss Woodhouse's displeasure.

"Pleasure in seeing dancing?" Mr Knightley huffed with derision. "Not I, indeed. I never look at it. I do not know who does."

"Why, everyone enjoys watching fine dancing!" Miss Woodhouse protested.

"Fine dancing, I believe, like virtue, must be its own reward. Those who are standing by are usually thinking of something very different."

"Well, the rest of us in attendance will be having a lovely time, while you are determinedly making yourself miserable," Miss Woodhouse answered. "I only hope that nothing terrible happens between now and then."

By now, Jane was nearly upon them. Mr Knightley caught her eye, and bowed. "Miss Fairfax."

Miss Woodhouse curtsied quickly while continuing her conversation with Mr Knightley. "You would be pleased if Mr Churchill is unable to extend his stay! I am so anxious that he is successful in persuading his aunt, and everything can go as planned. It would be heartbreaking to have to cancel our ball."

Aha, so Mr Churchill had somehow missed her, and would not be in one of the shops in Highbury. There was no reason to be scanning the doorways, so she focused her attention on the conversation. Mr Knightley's attitude set her teeth on edge, as it always did. She felt sorry for Miss Woodhouse. Even though she did not like her, she certainly did not deserve his boorish comments. He'd rather be reading the financial accounts than attending a ball, indeed! Even if he thought such things, no gentleman would say them out loud to a lady. Even a lady he had known for a very long time.

She smiled warmly, and took Miss Woodhouse by the arm. "Oh! Miss Woodhouse, I hope nothing may happen to prevent the ball. What a disappointment it would be! I do look forward to it, I own, with very great pleasure."

She was glad to see Mr Knightley looking a little uncomfortable as she spoke, and Miss Woodhouse looking less crestfallen. "It is quite selfless of Mr and Mrs Weston to take the trouble, not to mention the expense, to bring so much pleasure to so many people. I assume you are on your way to confer with Mrs Weston about the arrangements? Do thank her for me. And thank you, too, for your share of it. I am sure it will be a perfect evening with the perfect company."

Mr Knightley was simply staring at her now, while Miss Woodhouse's face was much brightened by the praise. Jane excused herself, saying she needed to get back to her grandmother, and smiled grimly as she walked away. Mr Knightley found it a burden to stay awake, did he? He'd rather be home with the account books than at a ball, giving pleasure to others? What a completely odious man.

"Miss Fairfax?" She was about to open the door and go inside when Mr Knightley's voice called to her. She thought for a moment about pretending she did not hear him, but what good would that do? Then he would ring the bell and come in for a proper visit, and it would take her longer to get rid of him. She turned around.

"Yes, Mr Knightley?"

He must have run down the street to catch her; he seemed a trifle short of breath. "I fear I might not have acquitted myself well in our conversation with Miss Woodhouse, and I wanted to make amends."

Jane's eyebrows went up. "It seems to me it is Miss Woodhouse to whom you should be making amends."

"Emma? Miss Fairfax, you know that Miss Woodhouse and I have a very long tradition of verbal combat. I was sixteen years old when she was born, and I have a policy of always telling her the truth."

"It is possible to both tell the truth and be a gentleman," Jane told him bluntly. "The gentlemen of my acquaintance make a pointed effort to avoid saying hurtful things. They certainly would not tell a dear friend of many long years' acquaintance that they scorn her efforts to bring pleasure to all their joint friends."

"No, you see, you do not understand. Emma – Miss Woodhouse – suffers from a lack of strong guidance," Mr Knightley explained. "I feel some responsibility to show her when she is being foolish."

"I certainly do not understand," Jane answered as coldly as she could. She thought lovingly of Mr Churchill, who was working so hard to hold this ball. "There is nothing foolish about throwing a ball and giving people, how did you say it? 'Noisy entertainment?' That noise is called laughter. It is something one does with one's close friends. Especially old friends that one has known for sixteen years. If Miss Woodhouse is helping her former governess to create an evening of friendship and laughter and dancing, I would say she is being generous. And you, complaining about having to stay awake when you would rather be at home all alone settling your financial accounts, are the foolish one. Now, if you will excuse me, my grandmother must be terribly hungry waiting for me to get home. Good afternoon, Mr Knightley."

She was angry as she shut the door and climbed the stairs, and then the ridiculous nature of the moment caught hold of her. "I never thought I would see the day," she said aloud to no one on the stairs with a laugh, "when I would be heaping praise on Miss Emma Woodhouse!"

CHAPTER THIRTEEN

Jane had not begun to help with getting her grandmother out of bed when the bell rang. It was so very early; Aunt Bates had gone to Mrs Willis' to get their bread, Patty was in the kitchen starting the fire for tea. She ran down the stairs to answer the door herself.

She was astonished when Mr Frank Churchill walked in, looking quite undone.

The moment she closed the door, he wrapped her in his arms. "My dearest, darling Miss Fairfax," he sounded ready to cry. "I have horrible news."

"Come upstairs," she whispered in his ear. "Grandmama is not awake yet, and Patty is busy in the kitchen, and Aunt Bates just left."

"I saw her leaving," he confessed. "I waited until I was sure she would not see me, hoping I would get a few moments alone with you!"

She took his hand, and they both ran up the stairs. He took her by the shoulders and kissed her as soon as they were in the small drawing room. Then he put his forehead to hers. "I have to leave," he told her. She saw the tears in his eyes, and laid her hand against his cheek.

"What happened?" she asked.

"My uncle has written me, urging my instant return. He claims Aunt Churchill is very ill. He says she was unwell when she wrote her answer to me, and only gave her permission because of her usual unwillingness to give pain." He gave an unsteady laugh. "He wrote that because of her constant habit of never thinking of herself, she failed to mention how very sick she was. But now she is too ill to trifle, and he directs me to set off for Enscombe without delay."

"I am so sorry, my love. You must be very alarmed for your aunt, of course you must leave at once."

There was real bitterness in his sigh. "I wish I truly felt any alarm. But I know my aunt's illnesses. They never occur but for her own convenience. She could not simply tell me no, she would not allow me to have a couple more days of blissful happiness. She could not allow me to dance with the woman I am going to marry. Instead, she toys with my life, saying yes, and then getting so ill that it is the equal of her saying no, without her having to say it."

Jane did not know what to say. She put her cheek where her hand had been. His arms tightened around her, and she could feel his hot tears slide from his face to hers.

"I am so, so sorry, my dearest, darling Miss Fairfax. I wish I were free to simply ask for your hand, and we could be having the banns read and getting married. I wish I were my own man, and did not feel obligated to obey my aunt's wishes. If I were still Frank Weston, instead of Frank Churchill, and I had grown up here in Highbury, we would be getting married as soon as this local vicar returns from his trip."

"If you had grown up in Highbury," Jane put her fingers on his lips to stop his words, "you would not be the same person. You would not have grown into the man that I am in love with."

It did not seem possible for him to be holding her closer than he already was, but his arms tightened around her. His lips found hers again.

"My dearest Miss Fairfax," he murmured. "I hate abandoning you here like this. Is there someone here in Highbury that I can ask to look after you? Someone you would trust with our secret? I wish I could ask my father and Mrs Weston. They clearly have designs on me and Miss Woodhouse – what about Miss Woodhouse? I know you said not to trust her with our secret, but I hear such stories of her love of matchmaking. She is clearly a hopeless romantic, and would be a powerful protector."

Despite her recent pity for her, Jane found the idea of Miss Woodhouse taking her under her wing like Miss Smith repugnant. "No, Mr Churchill. I do not trust her to keep our secret. She is so close to Mrs Weston, the very first thing she would do is tell her. We might as well just make our engagement public, at that point."

"Mrs Cole? Or the Miss Coxes? There must be someone worth talking to. What about Mr Knightley? I own I am not fond of him, but he seems like the best-read man in the village. I would wager he's the only one in Surrey who really reads the books in his library. If he knew our secret, he would also stop paying you unwanted attentions."

"Definitely not Mr Knightley," Jane answered firmly. "Do not concern yourself about me. I will manage on my own, as I have for many years past. You put your energies into placating your aunt, and getting her consent. Then you can come and rescue me, and we can start figuring out how to get my pianoforte to Yorkshire."

"I already have a full grand waiting for you in the music room at Enscombe," he laughed. "I am looking forward to making you a rich woman. You are not going to know how to behave. Well, you know how to behave, better than I do. But thinking like a woman with money at her disposal? I expect you will still be mending your dresses and my socks."

"You will have the finest clocked stockings in England," Jane promised him, "when I have the time for less practical uses for my needle."

"I will give your needles many uses, practical and otherwise," he promised. Any further words were stopped by the sound of Aunt Bates's feet on the stairs.

Jane had put a brave face on it for Mr Churchill's sake. She watched from the window after he took his leave of her aunt, and headed up to Hartfield to say his goodbyes. She watched again until he came back with Mr Weston, and at least they were able to lock eyes one last time before he climbed into the coach, and was truly gone. Then she told her aunt she had a headache, and closed the door to her bedroom.

She would have wailed at the top of her lungs, and punched the pillows, but while Grandmama's hearing was less than perfect, there was nothing wrong with her aunt's sharp ears. So she threw herself on the bed, buried her face in the pillow to stifle her sobs, and gave herself up to the misery of being twenty-one years old, and in love, and parted from her lover, in a place she did not want to be, with people she did not want to be with.

Eventually, the tears slowed to a stop. Her head really was aching. She ought to get up. She had left her aunt with the job of getting her grandmother up and dressed and fed. She would go and help, in a moment.

She needed to pull herself together. She had very little to complain about. She had a roof over her head. An aunt and grandmother who loved her. A beautiful pianoforte that would comfort her through all the lonely hours she was about to face. Friends in Ireland that she should be writing long letters to, as well as letters to the most handsome man in all England, who had given her his post-office directions where she could safely send her love letters. She knew she could expect to receive love letters.

This was temporary. As soon as his aunt felt better, she would feel some sense of gratitude for his devotion to her, and it would be the perfect time for him to convince her that it was time for him to marry. Jane just needed patience.

Fortunately, Mr Churchill had sent her a lot of music.

CHAPTER FOURTEEN

My dearest Miss Fairfax,

The same post which brings this letter to you also bears a much longer letter to Mrs Weston. Being unable to spend too much time at my writing desk, I merely send you a brief one expressing my deepest devotion. Mrs Weston's letter describes my journey, and any number of details that might amuse the town of Highbury as well as you, since of course I see how any letter sent into town is read by absolutely everyone. It is no wonder you direct all your letters as you do through your post-office, that you and Mrs Dixon might share your girlish secrets with some sort of privacy!

Mrs Weston's letter also describes my situation. My aunt's health is improving rapidly. Both my aunt and uncle attribute it to my presence. I know they say it to be appreciative, but it makes me feel like a prisoner. Enscombe is perhaps twice the size of Miss Woodhouse's home at Hartfield, so I have the space to pace like a caged lion, but it is merely a large jail, instead of a small one.

Hardly a moment goes by, dear one, without my imagining you here. Walking these halls, sitting at the dinner table, playing the pianoforte, strolling in the gardens with me. The moon gives me a great deal of comfort; I fancy as I look at it that you are looking at it, too, and the idea of us both looking at the same moon makes the distance between us seem smaller. I wish I had the presence of mind when I left to ask you to set a time at which we can both go look at the moon, together in our separation.

My latest attempt to broach the subject of marriage did not go well with my aunt; I must be honest. Please be patient, my angel, and believe that my charm and determination and my love for you is stronger than all the obstinate objections my aunt mounts against me. I will prevail, and come back to fetch you home with me.

Passionately your own,
F.C. Weston Churchill

Jane read the letter three times walking home from the post-office, and two more when she reached her room. It was so completely him. Romantic and optimistic and cheerful. He could not even deliver bad news without wrapping it in smiles.

It was hard to refrain from laughing when Mrs Weston called that afternoon in order to show Mr Churchill's promised letter. He certainly had made an accurate evaluation of the gossips of Highbury! She tried to memorize every word, every look, every compliment, that she might report them back. It amused and horrified her that she was about to engage in the very sort of gossip she abhorred. At least it should be easy writing, since he knew all the people, and she had merely to fill in the latest news without having to describe or explain who anyone was. And sometimes, the chain the news took was more amusing than the actual news. Like when Mr Perry finally gave in to Mrs Perry and agreed to get a carriage. Mrs Perry confided the news to Grandmama, and Grandmama told Aunt Bates, which was a little bit like telling the entire world. Jane was not sure whom her aunt might have told, but she assumed Mr Churchill would be the last to know since the post-office was slower than her aunt's tongue.

Excitement over Mr Churchill's letter to Mrs Weston turned out to be short-lived, replaced by a fresh subject of gossip; the town's vicar had married. Jane had never met him; she had not come to visit for two years, and the new vicar had occupied the Vicarage for only the past year. If the unmarried women of the village were to be believed, he must be passably handsome. As everyone in the village buzzed with gossip in every conversation about Mr Elton and his bride, she really learned very little else of substance. He was a particular friend of Mr Knightley, and he allowed Grandmama and Aunt Bates to sit close to the front of the church so that Grandmama could hear the sermons better. Having been a bachelor without other obligations, he had been frequently at Mr Woodhouse's card table in the evenings.

It was an indifferent picture Jane could assemble of him as she listened to conversation after conversation. She managed to avoid several social obligations by claiming to have a headache. Sometimes it was true, sometimes it was just an excuse to avoid sitting through yet another session of gossip about a person she had never met.

As tiresome as those conversations were, she would rather have lived them over again and again, once Mr Elton brought his bride home to Highbury.

It was a sacred duty in any society, to pay a visit to welcome a bride to her new home. Mr Churchill's dereliction of that duty was what had raised so many eyebrows when Mrs Weston got married. The elderly, like Grandmama and Mr Woodhouse, were excused from such obligations, and their younger relations paid the proper social calls for them.

Jane accompanied Aunt Bates on the visit to the Vicarage, wondering how difficult it was to enter a dwelling that used to be her home. It was not particularly grand, but it was certainly larger and more comfortable than their current apartment. On the other hand, its larger size required more care and cleaning and servants. It was perhaps just as well that their reduced circumstances resulted in reduced needs.

Mrs Elton received them in the drawing room, clearly enjoying all the attention from the parade of visitors. "My goodness, I am such a popular person! I thought when my sister married Mr Suckling, and she moved to Maple Grove, that she had such tribes of people coming to visit her! But I see that I shall have my hands quite full here in Highbury. I suppose in such a small home as this, I shall have to keep my parties small. But I am sure I shall manage to keep everyone properly entertained. I always say it is not the size of the party, but the quality of the people! I don't know anyone here in Highbury of course, at least, I don't know them more than a first meeting, but I am sure I shall manage to divine in short order who the quality people are."

Jane thought about asking what her criteria were for 'quality people,' but she kept silent. Aunt Bates sat beside her, assuring Mrs Elton that she would be terribly satisfied with all the quality people in town. "Such thoughtful people, such generous people! Mrs Cole is such a thoughtful neighbor, and so kind to Jane! Why, just the other day she came to call on Jane, because she had heard poor Jane has been having so many headaches lately. She even brought soup, and a bit of honey that she swears always helps her when she gets headaches."

"Oh, poor Jane, I can guess how miserable you are! I have never had a headache in my entire life. I can only imagine how terrible it must be to get headaches. My sister gets them from time to time. But I have been blessed with such perfect health, I feel my good fortune, I assure you."

Jane looked at Mrs Elton with some surprise, but said nothing. So, she was not significant enough to be Miss Fairfax, was she, in Mrs Elton's eyes? Even as a governess she would be Miss Fairfax. The vicar's wife was not a terribly elevated position. Comparing herself to her sister comfortably settled in Maple Grove was probably such a blow to her pride that she needed to take it out on everyone else.

"I hope you are not missing your sister too terribly much!" Aunt Bates sympathized. "I remember when my sister married Mr Fairfax, it was such a relief to me that she was not forced to move away! Lieutenant Fairfax was in the army, you see, so my sister Jane was able to remain with us. It turned out to be such a blessing, when Lieutenant Fairfax died in action, and then again when my poor sister died of a broken heart not long after. Who would have looked after my dear niece if she had not been here in Highbury?"

Jane smiled at that, and reached out to touch her aunt's hand next to hers on the sofa. For all the trials of Highbury, she had indeed been lucky to have been born under her grandmother's roof, with an aunt to look after her.

"I must say, such a romantic story!" Mrs Elton exclaimed. "I hear that you are musical, Jane. I have been plotting with Miss

Woodhouse to form a musical club! I must insist that you be a guest, and play for our concerts! I am so passionately fond of music. I told Mr E when I accepted his proposal, that I did not mind living without two carriages at my disposal, and I can live with smaller rooms than I am used to, but I must have my music. Without music, life would be a blank to me. He assured me that I am got into a very musical society, and I have nothing to fear on that score."

"Oh! Very musical, indeed!" Aunt Bates assured her." No one plays so well as my Jane, if I may say so. But Miss Woodhouse also plays charmingly, and I am sure she is thrilled to be forming a musical club with you! Our neighbors are always so generous. We are so lucky to live here, where we are surrounded by so many thoughtful people."

"I have a great many thoughts for Highbury, I assure you," Mrs Elton continued. The conversation was a bit amusing; two women who loved to talk, both competing to do the larger share of it. Aunt Bates rambled on about how wonderful and generous everyone was, Mrs Elton talked about herself. Jane started keeping track. In their fifteen minute visit, not a single sentence emerged from Mrs Elton that did not include the words "I," "me," "my," or "mine."

"Dear me," Aunt Bates observed as they walked home, "what an entirely pleasant person! Don't you agree that Mrs Elton is perfectly pleasant? And terribly pretty. I hope she is going to be happy here. Did you hear what she said about starting a musical club with Miss Woodhouse? And they mean to ask you to play for them. How very exciting!"

"Indeed," Jane answered drily.

CHAPTER FIFTEEN

As if the day had not been going badly enough already, Mr Knightley came across her when she bought more paper at Ford's, and insisted on walking back with her to pay his respects to her aunt and grandmother.

"For your letters to your friends in Ireland? How fares Mrs Dixon and her family?" Mr Knightley asked.

"Quite well, thank you," Jane saw no reason to encourage conversation with him, but he seemed determined to talk to her.

"Did you ever receive a letter from Colonel Campbell, to tell you about the pianoforte?" he asked next.

Of course he would bring that up. Everyone else in town had tired of such old gossip, and had moved on. It did her no small disservice to dredge up the topic, now. "I did write to let him know his letter may have been misdirected, but I have not had a response yet."

"It is a generous, but thoughtless gift," Mr Knightley surprised her by saying.

"Thoughtless? To provide me with hours of joy?" Jane asked. Mr Knightley was possibly the only person in the village with less tact than the newly arrived Mrs Elton.

"It was thoughtless to expose you to the kind of speculation that comes with such a generous gift," Mr Knightley frowned. "I am sure some portion of the gossip has reached your ears. I believe I overheard Mr Churchill and Miss Woodhouse making fanciful guesses at other possible donors to your enjoyment. I dislike the thought of your reputation being damaged over a generous impulse."

Every part of Mr Knightley's statement rankled. She did not appreciate his criticism. She also disliked the picture he was painting of Mr Churchill and Miss Woodhouse giggling together while Mr Churchill encouraged her indecorous speculations. "My reputation can survive a generous impulse from a man who wishes he could do as well by me as he did by his daughter. Miss Woodhouse and Mr Churchill can say whatever they like. They are both people of consequence, and can speculate over things that are trifles to them, but mean the world to me."

"That's what I am trying to tell you," Mr Knightley persisted. "Their giggling about this ill-conceived gift can be a trifle to them, but do you a world of harm. You-" he cleared his throat in an odd manner. "You need a protector. Your grandmother and aunt may be well regarded in this community, but they are ill equipped to offer protection to an accomplished young woman of marriageable age. If you had a respectable home, and a husband, your future would not be in jeopardy."

"Dear God," Jane thought to herself, "he's going to propose to me!" She realized she needed to discourage him, and quickly. "Mr Knightley, pray do not worry yourself on my behalf. I am very content with my future. I am not in need of protection. My aunt and grandmother will do. No one would ever say that they are not perfectly respectable." They had reached her front door. She opened it, and hurried up the stairs, calling, "Auntie! Grandmama! Mr Knightley is here to call upon you!"

As her aunt greeted Mr Knightley, Jane laid aside her parcel of paper, but instead of taking off her bonnet, she headed back toward the door. "I have forgotten I also needed ink," she lied calmly. "Since you are here to pay your respects to my family, Mr Knightley, I will leave you to talk with them. Good day."

She knew all three of them were staring after her for her oddly rude behavior, but she did not care. She wanted to be as far away from Mr Knightley as she could get.

She walked back to Ford's, uncertain what to do next. She did not need ink, and it would be foolish to spend money on something she did not need. Of all people, Mrs Elton came to her rescue.

"Jane Fairfax! My dear Jane, I am so lucky to run into you! Here I am, about to take a stroll all by myself, because my cara sposo needs to tend to his business, and here you are, also taking a walk without anyone to accompany you! Do, let us combine our exercises and walk together! What direction should we take?"

"Mi importa poco, basta che ci porti fuori città," Jane answered.

Mrs Elton blinked at her stupidly. "What?"

"Parla italiano?" Jane asked. "Ho pensato che fosse così, dal momento che ha chiamato suo marito 'caro sposo'."

"I…" Mrs Elton gave a high-pitched little laugh. "I suppose that's Italian?"

"It's such a beautiful language, isn't it?" Jane answered. She glossed over Mrs Elton's ignorance and went back to the original topic. "A walk is a fine idea. Do let us find a nice view outside of the village. Some fresh air sounds lovely."

"I know what you mean, country air is so good for the constitution! Shall we take this way?" Mrs Elton was looking at the road that would take them directly to Mr Knightley's estate at Donwell Abbey.

"I would say not. There are spots that are no doubt still muddy," Jane lied hastily. "I would not chance it without at least one more clear day."

"Well, then, we shall take this road," Mrs Elton pointed. "You see, that is why I am in need of a local guide, to prevent me from making poor decisions. Speaking of decisions, I should let you know I am quite decided to make myself of use to you. Everyone I have met in this town speaks of your extraordinary talents, and your charm, and how horrible your situation is. Everyone talks, as I say, but no one seems to have the least intention of doing anything to actually help you. I am more than a little put out at how the entire village of Highbury can shake their heads over your desperate situation, but not lift a finger on your behalf. Oh, I know they bring your family food, and send their carriages round for you, but that is not what I would call help. I say your talent is like a flower, and while yes, it needs nourishment and water, it also needs sunshine. I think sunshine is less tangible than the other elements. Think of music. You can touch food, and carriages. But you cannot touch sunshine, or music. A person can sit down at a harp or pianoforte and play notes, and yet not really and truly play music."

Jane was more than a little amazed. Not at the declared intention to help her, but that Mrs Elton had actually spoken sentences that did not contain I, me, my, or mine! It amazed her that, buried among the inanities emerging from the fairly pretty mouth, she actually had something somewhat insightful to say. Music was like sunshine. She liked the analogy.

She swallowed her annoyance at the information that everyone in town was gossiping about her. Everyone in town pitied her. It was galling. But, indeed, her situation, as far as they knew, was pitiable. She could not help but smile to herself at the thought of the astonished reactions when she could announce her engagement to Mr Churchill.

"See? I knew you would like that idea. That is why you are such a favorite with me, my dear Jane. We think so much alike."

Jane had no idea what Mrs Elton had been saying. "It would seem so," she responded.

"I am very, very sure that my brother and sister will like you exceedingly well when they come to visit. I will have a musical party when they come, and you will have to play for us."

Jane stopped listening as Mrs Elton's voice continued in elaborate detail about future parties that Jane would have to attend. When she was Mrs Churchill, she would not have to go to anything she did not want to. That made her smile again. And she would be able to choose her own friends to go walking with. No more Mr Knightleys, no more Mrs Eltons.

Mrs Elton noticed, and Jane did not disabuse Mrs Elton of the notion that she was smiling agreement with whatever she was chattering about.

CHAPTER SIXTEEN

There was less and less cause to smile as the days dragged on. Mr Churchill did not return, her aunt talked to her nonstop if she stayed at home, Mrs Elton talked to her nonstop if she went out. Mrs Elton seemed to be lurking about Highbury, waiting for her to emerge on various errands for her grandmother, or on her daily trip to the post-office. When she did manage to strike out for a walk alone, Mrs Elton called upon her aunt and grandmother, and Jane came home to an invitation to the Vicarage, which her aunt had already accepted for her. She took to taking a walk before breakfast, so that she could get to the post-office alone without Mrs Elton waylaying her and compelling her to walk in some other direction.

Most well-beloved Mr Churchill,

> *I hope it is not much longer till you can come free me from my imprisonment! I am feeling so much like a damsel in distress of late. Your princess is locked in the tower, guarded by dragons, and my hair is not long enough to make a ladder to the ground.*
>
> *The vicar's new wife, Mrs Elton, has decided I am her particular friend. Or perhaps she sees herself more as my patroness. I wish I were capable of describing just how awful she is.*
>
> *Instead of leaving me quietly to await the arrival of my knight in shining armor come to rescue me, she harps on*

me incessantly. She takes such an interest in my abilities as a musician, but if she is in the room while I am playing, she talks the entire time. She is making plans for me to come along with her and her brother and sister in his barouche-landau while they go exploring this summer, regardless of my lack of encouragement for her plans to include me.

Worse, she keeps threatening to write letters to her acquaintances in order to find me a suitable position as a governess. I am constantly having to thank her for her kind attention, then beg her to mind her own business and leave me alone. In polite terms, of course. I live in constant fear of letting one harsh word out. Once those floodgates have opened, there will be no closing them again. I will say every ungrateful thing I can possibly think of to say, and all thoughts of charity and good will in Highbury towards my aunt and grandmama will be lost.

When she mailed her letter to Mr Churchill, a letter was waiting from Mrs Dixon.

Dearest Sweet Jane,

Ireland is quite beautiful, and Mr Dixon tells me now that winter is over, it is going to be even more so. Mother and Father love it here, too, and have agreed to extend their visit, and will now stay here at least till Midsummer.

I miss you so fearfully much! I am writing to beg you to set aside your plans for a little longer, and come to Ireland. Say you will visit, and I will send a servant to fetch you, bearing all the funds you would require for travel.

Mr Dixon and my parents all join me in entreating you most earnestly to come to visit! You have had three months with your grandmother, no one would say you have been negligent in your obligation to your family. Now come and spend three months with the people who love you best! I do not suggest that your relations do not love you. But I insist that we love you more! The group of us are not quite complete without you, and we talk almost daily of how much we miss you.

The invitation sat upon her mind for the next several days. She could be in Ireland, with Sophia, playing duets, instead of playing in rooms full of people whose only appreciation of music was the vague notion they called 'taste.' They could be discussing the possible ramifications of the new Importation Act upon both country and city dwellers. They could be discussing the Treaty of Ghent and the new peace with the former colonists in the United States, and speculating on how long this independence thing would last.

She hardly spoke the entire day, barely listening to anyone except to compare their discussions of fashions and gossip about the neighbors with imagined conversations going on amongst the Campbells and Dixons. She realized she had no way of knowing what the neighbors in Ireland were like. Perhaps that was why her company was so sorely sought after: perhaps the Irish were just like the residents of Highbury.

Then she wondered; did living in Ireland make a person Irish? She doubted that the people who had been there for countless generations would call the English who had moved there since the time of Henry VIII 'Irish.'

When she arose for her morning walk, she had resolved to accept Sophia's invitation. But there was a letter from Mr Churchill waiting for her at the post-office.

My dearest Miss Fairfax,

This letter brings at least some portion of good news to your beautiful eyes!

We are coming to stay in London. I have convinced Aunt Churchill that, considering the delicate state of her health, she would be better off having access to the excellent doctors in town, rather than submitting to no better care than our local apothecary. There is a surgeon about twenty miles from here, which is really no better; my uncle has joined me in convincing my aunt that she needs to be under a physician's care.

This will put me within a day's ride of you! Even better, my aunt and uncle have agreed that I may spend half my time in London with them, and half my time in Highbury with my father. We are preparing Enscombe for an extended absence, and I hope we shall be departing in another day or two. I shall need to see my aunt comfortably settled in town, but if I manage things well, I shall be at your side within a week!

Stand fast, my darling. Your knight is coming! I shall find a way to scale all the obstacles, break all the enchantments, and rescue my distressed damsel. I love you too completely to do otherwise.

Your devoted
F.C. Weston Churchill

He was coming! All thoughts of Ireland and the Campbells and Dixons were cheerfully abandoned. If Mr Churchill could move mountains to come to her, she could endure a week of mindless gossip in order to be here when he arrived.

CHAPTER SEVENTEEN

The long week of waiting was filled with the usual distractions; music, letter writing, attending upon her grandmother, and the inevitable visits with the Eltons. Mr Elton was not as supercilious as his wife – it was not possible since he rarely seemed to get a word in edgewise – but Jane instinctively did not like him. She would not have been able to say why. Perhaps it was his taste in wives. Highbury was a distinctly less pleasant place with Mrs Elton in it.

An invitation to dinner at Hartfield made for a change from dinner with her aunt and grandmother, or at the Vicarage. She only accepted with great hesitation when she learned the guests included Mr Knightley as well as Mr and Mrs Elton. The morning before the dinner party, however, she happened upon Mr Knightley's younger brother, Mr John Knightley, on her walk to the post-office.

"Hello! Do my eyes deceive me, or am I in the presence of Miss Fairfax?"

"Mr John Knightley! What brings you from town?"

"I am merely down for the day, delivering my sons to their grandfather," he explained. "Blasted luck of mine, it turns out my sister has plans for a dinner party tonight. I was going to try and beg off, but then I found out you are going to be there. So, we will have a chance to talk at more length."

Jane was surprised and flattered by his attention. He never seemed nearly so pleased to see her when their paths crossed in London, as occasionally they did. "I would be most happy to talk with you tonight, sir."

He squinted up at the skies. "For now, I will wish you good morning. It is starting to rain; I suggest you postpone your walk for a little while, until this clears up."

Jane nodded, although she had no intention of missing her daily trip to the post-office. She looked at the boys. "See the fence post over there? Which one of you can get there faster?"

"I can! Watch!" The younger one tore off as fast as his little legs could carry him. His brother looked surprised at the head start, then released his hand from his father's to lay in a pursuit.

"That will help get them home a little faster," Jane smiled at their father.

Mr John Knightley tipped his hat to her. "Very clever. See you tonight."

It was a good day. Mr Churchill had sent a letter letting her know they had arrived in London, her aunt spent the afternoon with Mrs Cole, and Jane managed to finish the embroidery on the bedroom slippers she was making for her grandmother.

Knowing her friend would be there made the prospect of the dinner party more appealing. She hummed to herself while she dressed and pinned up her hair, and smiled during the carriage ride with the Eltons. Mrs Elton talked about something the entire time, but Jane had no idea what.

Arriving at Hartfield, she smiled with genuine warmth at the speed with which Mr John Knightley claimed her attention. She had not seen the senior Mr Knightley since that awful, awkward day he nearly proposed to her. The elder Mr Knightley handed her out of the carriage, she greeted her host and hostess, then the younger Mr Knightley escorted her into the house, thankfully away from Mr Knightley's eyes and Mrs Elton's endlessly wagging tongue.

"Mrs Knightley has asked me to take careful note of the new Mrs Elton, and bring her a full report," he told Jane quietly as the party walked down the hall to the drawing room after wraps were set aside. "What is your estimation? Is she as awful as Miss Woodhouse has written to my wife?"

Jane smiled at his lack of delicacy. Somehow the familial lack of tact irritated her in the elder brother, but only amused her in the younger. Perhaps it was because his familiarity came from treating her like a friend. Or being married. She was certain he would not be making overtures to her the way his brother had done.

"Perhaps," was all the answer she had time for before they entered the drawing room, where the Eltons were already in conversation with Mr and Miss Woodhouse. "We shall have to compare notes later."

"Indeed, we shall!" he agreed pleasantly. "But in the meantime, we shall need another subject. Otherwise we shall be obvious in our espionage. Come, Miss Fairfax, what is a topic that people find irresistible?"

"There is always the weather," Jane offered. "That must surely be a very popular topic."

"Why, so it is," he agreed. Then he raised his voice a little bit. "I hope you did not venture far, Miss Fairfax, this morning, or I am sure you must have been wet. We scarcely got home in time. I hope you turned directly."

"I went only to the post-office," said she, "and reached home before the rain was much. It is my daily errand. I always fetch the letters when I am here. It saves trouble, and is a something to get me out. A walk before breakfast does me good." Jane imagined her companion would understand the need to get out of the house for some quiet once a day.

"Not a walk in the rain, I should imagine."

"No, but it did not absolutely rain when I set out."

"That is to say, you chose to have your walk," he gave her a knowing look, "for you were not six yards from your own door when I had the pleasure of meeting you; and Henry and John had seen more drops than they could count long before. The post-office has a great charm at one period of our lives. When you have lived to my age, you will begin to think letters are never worth going through the rain for."

Jane thought of the joy that went through her every time she saw the dear, familiar handwriting, the paper that inevitably started with those precious words, 'My dearest Miss Fairfax.' She would walk through much worse than rain for those letters. "I must not hope to be ever situated as you are, in the midst of every dearest connection, and therefore I cannot expect that simply growing older should make me indifferent about letters."

They pleasantly debated the value of correspondence, while Jane internally laughed at Mr John Knightley's crotchety nature.

He was like an old man trapped in a younger man's body.

They had come to no conclusions when Mr Woodhouse approached to pay his compliments to her. Jane had to alter her appraisal; there was a certain kind of manners in old men that was entirely lacking in younger men. Mr Woodhouse would always wait upon each lady in a room, in the proper order, and say something that was meant to be gallant. Neither Knightley male was likely to ever say anything that could be construed as gallant.

Being the dedicated invalid that he was, he chastised her for being out in the rain, and expressed his concern for her health. She had trouble keeping her countenance when, immediately after protesting her being out in the rain, he added, "young ladies are delicate plants."

With great difficulty, she kept from laughing as she reassured him that, yes, she had changed her stockings as soon as she had reached home, and thanked him for his kind concern.

Unfortunately, now the topic of Jane walking in the rain had become the all-absorbing concern of everyone in the room, and Mrs Elton was pouncing upon her. Apparently the weather was not such a safe subject, after all.

"My dear Jane, what is this I hear? Going to the post-office in the rain! This must not be, I assure you. You sad girl, how could you do such a thing? It is a sign I was not there to take care of you."

Jane managed to unclench her teeth long enough to assure Mrs Elton that she had not caught cold, but it was to no avail.

"Oh! Do not tell me. You really are a very sad girl, and do not know how to take care of yourself. To the post-office, indeed!"

Next, Mrs Elton dragged Mrs Weston into the conversation, and the two of them both lectured Jane on the evils of going outside, even the short distance to the post-office. When Mrs Elton insisted that her own servant would pick up and deliver Jane's mail for her, Jane began to feel desperate. The last thing she needed was the Elton's servant reporting to Mrs Elton about whom she was sending and receiving letters from!

"I cannot by any means consent to such an arrangement, so needlessly troublesome to your servant. If the errand were not a pleasure to me, it could be done, as it always is when I am not here by my grandmama's."

She had no hope that Mrs Elton would be swayed from her determination to interfere with Jane's privacy, and Mrs Elton did not disappoint her. "But so much as Patty has to do! And it is a kindness to employ our men."

Knowing there were no words that would sway her, Jane tried a strategic retreat, and refused to discuss the matter any more. She turned a shoulder to Mrs Elton, and resumed her conversation with Mr John Knightley. "The post-office is such a wonderful establishment! The regularity and dispatch of it!"

Even someone as thick as Mrs Elton did not miss the hint, and she left them to discuss the wonders of the postal service. The conversation devolved from admiration of the monumental achievement of the institution into commentary on the quality of handwriting. The announcement that it was time to go in to dinner could not come at a more perfect moment; they were just starting to discuss Mr Frank Churchill's handwriting. The elder Mr Knightley was sneering at it and calling it small and weak, while Mrs Weston and Emma were defending it as clear and strong. Jane wanted to shout at the lot of them for being imbeciles.

Instead, she smiled serenely and took Miss Woodhouse's arm, and they walked companionably into dinner. At least Miss Woodhouse had defended Mr Churchill's handwriting from Mr Knightley's attack; and she now knew, thanks to Mr John Knightley, that Miss Woodhouse despised Mrs Elton as much as she did.

CHAPTER EIGHTEEN

Dinner gave Jane a welcome respite from Mrs Elton, but as soon as the ladies returned to the drawing room to leave the men to their port, Mrs Elton renewed her attacks. First she had to defend herself from the post-office offer, and all the protestations regarding her delicate health. Jane firmly and obstinately refused to allow her to do this "favor" for her.

Getting no appreciation from that quarter, Mrs Elton changed topics, and returned to one of her other favorite subjects, finding a governess situation for her. This was even worse than the subject of the letters.

"Here is April come!" Mrs Elton nagged. "I get quite anxious about you. June will soon be here."

"But I have never fixed on June or any other month," Jane protested. "Merely looked forward to the summer in general."

"But have you really heard of nothing?" Mrs Elton persisted.

"I have not even made an inquiry. I do not wish to make any yet."

"Oh! My dear, we cannot begin too early. You are not aware of the difficulty of procuring exactly the desirable thing."

"I not aware!" Jane exclaimed. The woman really did not know how very insulting she was. "Dear Mrs Elton, who can have thought of it as I have done?"

The conversation took the form of a fencing match; Mrs Elton attacked, Jane parried. Another attack, another parry, followed by a riposte. Mrs Elton feinted, then lunged. Jane had to keep up an obstinate defense against Mrs Elton's equally obstinate unwillingness to take no for an answer. The bout only ended when

Mr Woodhouse led the gentlemen back into the drawing room, and Mrs Elton changed the topic to how much the old gentleman had been flirting with her over dinner.

It was a relief to have Mrs Elton talking about herself again. As tiresome as it was to have her every sentence include I, me, mine, or myself, it was more awful when the rest of the sentence was directed at Jane. Better she preen herself on making her husband jealous because a courtly old man was trying to be polite, than insulting Jane with her insistence of how little Jane knew of the world.

Almost immediately upon the heels of the gentlemen from the dinner table, the party was joined by Mr Weston. He had business which prevented him from being at dinner, but he walked up to join them as soon as he was able.

Jane was immensely gratified that Mr John Knightley came straight to her when he entered the drawing room, separating her from Mrs Elton. Now he looked at her with annoyance. "Mr Weston could have stayed comfortably at home, but instead walked all the way up here to prolong our party? I could not have believed it even of him."

Jane was amused at the sullen reaction, and very glad that the cheerful Mr Weston had not heard the comment. After greeting his wife and reassuring her that when he arrived home, the servants had his dinner waiting, just as she had instructed, he excitedly handed her a letter. "I have a letter from my son Frank!" he exclaimed. He confessed to having opened it, even though it was addressed to her, and then he hurried to bring it to her, so that she could read it to the assembled company.

Jane tried not to stare. The gall of opening someone else's mail! A marriage license did not give a husband license to open his wife's private correspondence. At least it was pleasant to hear the letter read aloud, to revisit the notion that Frank was removing to London with his aunt and uncle, and soon he would be with them again.

Unable to react to either the news, or Mr Weston's method of delivering it, she was glad when Mr John Knightley drew her aside to the comfortable seats in the corner. "What do you women discuss while we men are at our port? There must be something to talk of besides letters from Mr Frank Churchill."

"Fashions and gossip, mostly," she answered honestly. Lowering her voice, she added, "Tonight it was about my disinterest in finding a position as a governess this very moment. My well-meaning benefactress wants me placed as soon as possible, despite my intentions to wait until the Campbells have returned from Ireland in midsummer."

Her companion also lowered his voice. "I can only assume Mrs Elton wants you removed from Highbury with all dispatch, in order to remove you as a rival."

Jane stared at him, then laughed. "A rival? For what?"

"Attention." He watched Mrs Elton from across the room appraisingly. "She may be gleefully wallowing in the attention that is due a new bride, but that only lasts until the new bride is with child, and retires. A lady is never so much the center of attention again. Especially one married to nothing more than a vicar. Notice how much it rankles her that her sister married better than she did. You, on the other hand, are ten times as beautiful, and twenty times as talented, and no matter where you go or what you do in life, you will always inspire the admiration of everyone you know. Mrs Elton will never be admired, so the best she can do is eliminate the competition for people's attention."

"You overestimate both my charms and my talents," Jane answered. "Although there is a great deal of sense in your appraisal of her motives."

"I believe you like people a great deal better than I do," he answered. "Since I have little patience for my fellow man, I size them up quickly, figure them out, and then I can dismiss them and spend my evenings quietly at home. You can trust my instincts."

Jane managed not to laugh at his assessment of her as 'liking people a great deal.' It proved how little he truly knew about sketching people's characters. "I suppose I can, since you have made such a study of human nature, which I have not."

While he continued to talk about his disenchantment with human nature, Jane mostly nodded and tried to look completely absorbed in their conversation. Mr Weston was talking about Mr Churchill to Mrs Elton, and she wanted to eavesdrop as much as she could.

Part Three

CHAPTER ONE

Mr Churchill returned at last! It was not the one week he had predicted in his letters to Jane and Mrs Weston, but eventually he managed to settle his aunt and uncle in London and effect his escape.

Jane was walking back from the post-office, disappointed by the lack of a letter from him, when she was arrested in her tracks by the sight of him approaching on his horse!

She had trouble maintaining her composure. There were so many people in the street preventing her from smiling up at him with more than a polite welcome! The same people were preventing him from leaping down from his saddle and embracing her.

"Good morning, Miss Fairfax! I trust you and your family are well?" he touched his hat to her.

"I am quite well, thank you," she answered. "Welcome back to Highbury. I assume you are on your way to see your father?"

"I am, indeed!" he answered gaily. "My aunt and uncle are settled in town, so that my aunt can get better care from the doctors there than are available in Yorkshire. I fancied I was not needed this morning, so I rode over to pay my father a long-promised visit."

"I am sure he will be most thrilled to see you," she answered.

"I don't have much time, but I will endeavor to pay a complete round of social calls before I must return to town," he told her. "Are your aunt and grandmother at home, that I might come and pay my respects?"

"My grandmother is at home. My aunt is also here at present, but later today she means to be at Mrs Cole's," Jane told him, hoping he understood her meaning.

"Ah, I see," he nodded. "Well, I must be off to Randalls. Good day, Miss Fairfax."

It was a very long rest of the morning. Jane felt dishonest, not mentioning Mr Churchill's arrival in town to her aunt. But she and Mr Churchill would never get to say two words to each other if Aunt Bates remained at home. She lived in dread of a note arriving from Mr or Mrs Weston, alerting everyone in Highbury of his visit. She tried to account for all the people who were on the street when she saw him, and wondered who might have been looking out a window at just the right - or wrong - moment, who might also bring a report of his presence. Any hint of the news, and Aunt Bates would not leave the house.

Even when Aunt Bates left, Jane could not relax, for fear of her crossing paths with him. She played the pianoforte for a few minutes until her grandmother announced she was going to lie down, instead of falling asleep in her chair. After helping her to bed, she sat in the window and darned a hole in her aunt's sock. She called for tea.

At long last, she heard Patty open the door, and Mr Churchill's cheerful voice sounded in the stairwell.

"Are the ladies of the house at home? Excellent! Don't mind me, I know the way. Thank you, Patty!" She could tell he was taking the stairs two at a time, and then he was coming through the door.

"Good day, Miss Fairfax! Are your aunt and grandmother about? I came in to Highbury this morning to see my father. I am trying to make the rounds of all my acquaintances, to let them know I have not forgotten them."

Jane closed the door between them and Patty's ears, and threw herself into his arms. "Mr Churchill!" She closed her eyes for a moment of bliss, feeling his arms wrap around her.

"Miss Fairfax." He held her tightly for a moment, then pulled away to look laughingly and lovingly into her face. "I take it from my reception my entrance has been well timed."

"Aunt Bates is at Mrs Cole's, and Grandmama decided she would be more comfortable taking a nap in her bed, rather than in her chair. So, for the moment, I am the only one at home to receive you."

"I shall have to take advantage of such a rare and fortuitous opportunity," he answered, then, taking her face between his hands, he kissed her.

His mouth was sweet, and warm, and comforting. The long days spent waiting for his letters, for the sight of his face, melted away, and the only thing that existed was the feel of his lips caressing hers.

He broke the sweet contact, and pulled her to sit beside him on the sofa. "That made it worth the wait. I am sure I was as impatient as a bear at my father's house. Then I came to see you, but your aunt was just stepping out your front door, and stopped to talk to someone before she had taken two steps! Since her back was to me, and she had not seen me, I turned aside and rode up to call on Miss Woodhouse. Now, at last, I get to see the person I rode all the way from town for! Let me look at you. You are a vision, you know that?"

They sat there, smiling into each other's eyes, happy to be in each other's company. "So you've made it as far as London," Jane did not want to break the spell, but she did want to know what progress he had made towards getting his aunt's permission for them to make their engagement public. "How fares your aunt?"

She was immediately sorry for her question. A shadow fell across his face. "Not well. My father agrees with my uncle that my aunt is prone to exaggeration, but I earnestly do believe that when she complains about her nerves, this is not her imagination. I know she has a fondness for attention. Now that she can be seen by the best doctors in London, they will be able to tell if there is truly something wrong with her."

"Have you been able to talk to her at all about us – about your intentions? Or has she been too ill?" Of all the awful timing. Jane knew the answer, but she needed to hear him say it out loud.

"I am sorry, my dearest, darling, most patient and long-suffering Miss Fairfax. My aunt is too occupied with her own suffering to talk about anything else." He was holding both her hands in both of his, and he kissed them, then squeezed them gently. "She is a scared old woman, out of breath at the smallest exertion, and then she is anxious about why she is out of breath…it goes in a circle of discomfort and anxiety. I wish the doctors could explain what's really going on when all my aunt can say is that she is suffering on account of her nerves."

"I wish there was something I could do to help." Jane frowned.

"You do help. You send me letters that remind me there are people out there in the world who are healthy. Your aunt may drive you to distraction, but at least she never complains about her nerves."

"Well, if at least I can entertain you with descriptions from Highbury, that will keep the both of us occupied. Me in looking for things to describe to you, you in reading my descriptions and being entertained by them." She leaned her cheek into his hand when he reached out to touch her face.

"There was never before such an angel as you walking upon the Earth." He was looking at her with such love, it made Jane feel very humble.

"I make a terrible angel," she demurred. "Angels cannot possibly think such terrible things as I do."

"Of course they do," he disagreed. "Angels are not like Adam and Eve. They have not eaten from the fruit of the tree that lets them know the difference between right and wrong. They are innocent – therefore they think bad things, and even do bad things, but they don't know they are being terrible."

"I suppose they would be less effective soldiers of God if they were questioning the morality of their orders," Jane speculated.

They were still contemplating the implications of the word innocence in Biblical stories when Aunt Bates came home. At least they had time for one last quick kiss and embrace before she finished climbing the stairs.

CHAPTER TWO

My dearest Miss Fairfax,

I wish I had better news to report to you today. My brief visit to Highbury has incurred my aunt's extreme displeasure. Even though my uncle was at her side the entire time, my absence was felt – and deplored.

I will confess to feeling some guilt at having abandoned my post, even though the object of doing so was to see your sweet face and assure you in most ardent terms of my devotion. My uncle is not exactly the most comforting of bedside companions. He is of the same mind as my father in insisting that there is too much imagination among her complaints.

To be fair, daily observation makes it difficult to see the minute changes taking place. But I am perfectly certain that, while her fancies certainly play a part, she is in a much weaker state of health than she was a mere six months ago.

To that end, I have engaged appointments with multiple doctors all known to be quite excellent at nervous disorders. I am enough of a cynic to realize that the practice of medicine is at least as much of an art as a science, and no two artists ever have quite the same vision.

It should be so much easier to come back to see you once we have some sort of answer as to what can be done for my aunt's comfort. I should have these answers in a couple of days, and then I will be on the back of my horse, galloping to your arms!

In the meantime, my darling, write to me everything you are thinking, everything you see, everything you do. As "terrible" as you say you are, you are incapable of shocking me. In fact, I dare you to try!

Ever your own
F.C. Weston Churchill

The days dragged by slowly. Jane played the pianoforte, read to her grandmother, accompanied her aunt on visits to Mrs Goddard, or Mrs Cole, or Mr Woodhouse. She wrote long letters to Mr Churchill, sending detailed descriptions of the spirited conversations she listened to, as they used a lot of words and a lot of time to talk about very little. She also wrote long letters to Sophia, trying to make Mrs Elton's insistent "patronage" seem humorous, instead of onerous. If she gave any hint of restlessness to that quarter, the Dixons and Campbells would renew their invitations for her to come to Ireland. While she longed to see them, she was only a matter of days away from seeing Mr Churchill!

My favorite Mrs Dixon,

I am so glad to hear how well settled you are at Baly-craig! Thank Mr Dixon for me for all the sketches he put in your last letter. The both of you spoil me excessively with the amount of paper you send with every post. I consider that the biggest proof that you really have married a very wealthy man. The sketches of your new home are impressive, but the paper you send me to show it off? Now that is a real luxury!

I am sorry my headaches are still plaguing me enough to prevent me from accepting your offer to come and see you. I do wonder if I would not be feeling better, faster, if it were not for my aunt's unfortunate propensity for talk. A couple of weeks of quiet, and I might be quite back to myself. But, there it is. I am an orphan child with two well-

meaning and caring relatives; my lot in life could be so much worse than it is. I never wake up in the morning without feeling how lucky I am to have had relatives to take me in when I was orphaned, and then to be raised by your parents, and to count you as a sister of the heart, if not of the blood.

I do wish I had any talents along the lines of your excellent husband. I would love to send you sketches of all the people and places I write to you about. Failing that ability, I shall simply have to continue painting pictures for you with words...

The bell rang, and Jane groaned when she heard Patty greet Mrs Elton at the door. For a moment, she thought about pleading a headache to avoid seeing her, but then she realized she had used that excuse the last couple of visits. She really needed to start going on longer walks – or find someplace else she could go, in order to not be at home when Mrs Elton called. She already accompanied her aunt on social calls, and went on long walks, and finally convinced her aunt to stop accepting Mrs Elton's invitations without conferring with her first. She supposed she could try and cultivate a friendship with Miss Woodhouse, but that did not sound any more appealing than having to spend time with Mrs Elton. Besides, Miss Woodhouse, as her social superior, would need to be the one to cultivate a friendship with her.

The thought that Mrs Frank Churchill would be the social superior to both Mrs Elton and Miss Woodhouse gave her the fortitude to put on a smile while she put down her quill, capped her inkwell, and went to receive Mrs Elton.

"Jane! You dear thing! I do hope you are feeling better. I left Mr E hard at work on his sermon for Sunday, and I thought this beautiful weather was too perfect to ignore. So I thought, 'Miss Fairfax won't have anything to do, surely she can come out with me for a good long walk.' Here I am in Surrey, the Garden of England, in the spring! It would be unthinkable of us not to be outside enjoying it."

Before Jane could answer, Aunt Bates came in the room, escorting Grandmama. "Good morning, Mrs Elton! How thoughtful you are to think of us. Bless me, I wish I could go along, how very thoughtful you are to invite us. Such wonderful neighbors we have, always thinking of us! But I cannot leave Mother here alone, although I suppose she would be well enough for us to walk with her over to Mrs Goddard's, if only we knew if Mrs Goddard would like company! I suppose she is busy with her school, it is a Tuesday after all, and I am sure she is with her students right now…"

"Indeed, I am sure Mrs Goddard would appreciate social calls, but we have to acknowledge that, after all, she is a working woman." Mrs Elton paused delicately over the horrible words. "I think it would no doubt be a terrible faux pas to intrude upon her in the middle of the day. I suppose, if we think about it, my cara sposo could be called a working man, but I say there is simply a world of difference between a man who is responsible for a parish, and a woman who is responsible for a school full of girls. Especially poor girls - "

"Oh, dear, I had not thought about the fact that Mrs Goddard really could not have time for Mother in the middle of the day on a Tuesday," Aunt Bates answered sheepishly. "I guess that really would be just like asking Mr Elton if he would have time for a social call on a Sunday - "

"Of course, I can see it really is not anything alike," Mrs Elton interrupted with a slightly shrill laugh. "From everything I have seen since I arrived here, Mr E always has time for his parishioners - "

"I see what you mean," Aunt Bates did not wait for Mrs Elton to finish. "Mrs Goddard always has time for her students, but her students make a much smaller congregation than Mr Elton's. Mr Elton is responsible for all of Mrs Goddard's students, and Mrs Goddard, and then everyone else in Highbury. Of course, I have never seen him talk to Mrs Goddard or her students. But he's been to Hartfield and Donwell Abbey frequently - "

"I am quite sure the spiritual needs of a bunch of silly schoolgirls are not quite the same as seeing that Mr Knightley and Mr Woodhouse's needs are met - "

"And then there is Miss Woodhouse," Jane was a trifle surprised that Aunt Bates would be quite so tactless. But only a trifle. "About half of Highbury were quite convinced that Mr Elton and Miss Woodhouse - "

"Mr E. warned me that I might hear all sorts of baseless gossip _"

Jane was shaking with mirth by the time Mrs Elton ended the contest over who could talk the most. She walked over to retrieve Jane's bonnet and sunshade, handed them to Jane, and walked down the stairs with a curt 'good morning' to Aunt Bates and Grandmama.

CHAPTER THREE

My dearest Miss Fairfax,

I am not sure if I am writing to you with good news, or bad. I suppose it is a great deal of both.

London has been a complete failure for my aunt's nerves. The doctors have not been able to come to any sort of consensus about what is wrong or what can be done for her. The noise in town, however, has most definitely had a deleterious effect upon her. She is clearly suffering more now than when we arrived here ten days ago. (Ten days? Has it been ten days since we arrived, and a week since I saw you in your grandmother's drawing room? It feels so much longer.)

Since Enscombe was too cold for her, and London is too noisy, she has agreed to a plan which I flatter myself will meet with your approval. I have engaged a fully-furnished house in Richmond, a mere nine miles from your door!

There is an eminent physician who comes highly recommended who has agreed to take charge of her care. Both my uncle and aunt have visited the place previously and liked it; this new plan should put everyone in good humor. Including myself! With my aunt pleased, she will be much more willing to part with me for extended periods of time.

We should be departing within the hour, otherwise I would spend more time in praising your eyes, your skin, your hair, and all your other beauties which I anticipate viewing with my own eyes, very soon!

Yours completely,
F.C. Weston Churchill

Jane had read the letter three times by the time she walked home from the post-office. Nine miles away! He would only be about an hour away from her.

It took all her self control to get through the next few days. If she started laughing and singing and dancing jigs in the middle of the street, people would accuse her of being moonstruck, or some such. Well, perhaps it was a little bit true. A lot truer than the number of times she had begged off of social engagements, claiming headaches or colds.

Now, she happily accompanied her aunt on her social calls, where everyone in the village had one topic of conversation: the Churchills' move to Richmond. Of course he had written to Mrs Weston as well as to her, and Mrs Weston dutifully made sure everyone in town had a chance to read his letter.

Even though she had little regard for the intellectual prowess of almost everyone in the county, Jane still found enjoyment in listening to people praising her beloved. "Such an excellent young man." "He writes such good letters." "He writes with such a lovely, clear hand." It was silly, paltry praise for all the things Jane loved about him; still, it was the most pleasant topic of which Highbury residents were capable.

His approval in certain circles was even higher, when he sent Mrs Weston another letter instructing her to resume their preparations for the ball they had started planning before he was called back to Enscombe. That inspired a tizzy of excitement that infected the streets every time Jane stepped outside. Whether she was walking to the post-office, or the butcher's, or to Ford's, or simply out for a walk, someone stopped her to talk excitedly about what they were wearing, or how they were doing their hair, or how wonderful it was to be going to a ball in May, instead of March.

"Of course, we would throw balls in Maple Grove whenever it suited us, regardless of the month," Mrs Elton narrated as she joined Jane on a walk to collect wildflowers. "I think the dances at Maple Grove were quite wonderful. I wonder that Miss Woodhouse never throws balls at Hartfield. If I had the management of such an estate as Hartfield, I should think I would throw several balls a year. I know their drawing room is much larger than the room at The Crown. I heard a rumor that the Westons and Mr Churchill and Miss Woodhouse originally planned for this ball to be at Randalls, but when Randalls was declared too small, it got moved to The Crown. I wonder that Miss Woodhouse did not offer to take up the project. I would think, if I were the one living at Hartfield, I would have realized my social obligation and offered to host the ball."

"But Mr Woodhouse would never approve of such a project," Jane pointed out. "His health being even more delicate than my grandmother's, I cannot imagine Miss Woodhouse being so inconsiderate of his needs as to plan such a large, noisy gathering as a ball."

There was a brief, shocked silence. "Well, I imagine that would be the case," Mrs Elton did not take long to recover. "I am so glad I have such perfect health. I can only imagine how difficult it must be to have poor health. I know you suffer from it quite a bit, and I must tell you, Jane, how much I worry about you. You are quite a favorite with me, you know, and I cannot stress enough how I think you should be very careful of your health. I would hate to think of you ending up with such poor health as Mr Woodhouse. I think that is something you need to consider when choosing a situation for yourself. I know you have been resistant to starting to find a suitable place, but, my dear Jane, you need to be very particular. I know that you cannot take just any position. It needs to be with a proper family living in a place that will not be detrimental to your health. I insist upon making some inquiries on your behalf now, so that you have the luxury of discarding any position that is not perfectly suitable."

"Please do not trouble yourself on my account," Jane insisted. "It would not do for me to have a family waiting for my arrival, when I have no intention of starting as a governess in the immediate future." *Nor in the distant future*, Jane added in her own mind. *Mr Churchill is my knight in shining armor who will rescue me from such an awful fate.*

Of course Mrs Elton would not hear of any delays. "I am determined to be of use to you, my dear Jane, and I know you are simply too ignorant of the ways of the world. Trust me, I will find you the most perfect situation. I have so many connections. I will find a family that will not be taxing on your health, who will find it an asset that you have such great musical skills. I think perhaps a family that does not have too many children. I have seen governesses who have been run ragged, caring for large families of eight or ten children. I should think that would be much too difficult for your delicate health. I know your health will be something of a detriment for some employers, but I shall phrase the inquiries properly, so that it should not come up."

"You are welcome to make all the inquiries you like, Mrs Elton," Jane answered firmly, "but please keep in mind that I shall not accept any positions until I am ready to. It would be an embarrassment to yourself, and me, and the family looking for a governess, if they make me an offer I do not intend to accept."

"Nonsense," Mrs Elton was not fond of listening to anyone not perfectly in agreement with her. "When the perfect family finds the perfect governess, it is like a happy marriage. I know you will be quite happy when I find you the right position."

Jane saw no point in wasting her breath any longer, and knelt down to pick a collection of cowslips that were growing in great profusion around them.

CHAPTER FOUR

Most well-beloved Mr Churchill,

I am counting down the hours, minutes, and seconds until I shall be able to dance with you at the ball! Has it really been six months since we were dancing together at Weymouth? It seems like a lifetime ago.

Knowing you will have so much to do as a host, with your father and Mrs Weston and Miss Woodhouse in tow, I will not expect to see you until I arrive at The Crown. Mrs Elton has insisted upon collecting me and Aunt Bates in her carriage, so we should be timely. Mrs Elton is not the sort to be late to any event – she would hate to miss out on a few moments of talking about herself.

I am anticipating your impressions of Mr and Mrs Elton. Mr Elton speaks little outside of his sermons on Sundays. I gather from what I have heard from others that he used to have more to say for himself, but Mrs Elton does not brook much conversation. She requires an audience, not a lord and master, and since she brought more money into the marriage than he did, he has no choice but to oblige her.

I look forward to our first two dances together! I know it shall not be the first two, but I know ours will be the best dances of the evening.

Ever your
J. Fairfax

Jane re-did her hair three times before she was completely satisfied with the outcome. She might not have money or family, but at least she could make the most of what assets she did possess. Little ringlets around her face framed her dark eyes, and a few curls dangling from the knot at the back of her head would bounce amusingly while she was dancing. The loops of braids were hopefully tight enough that the spring flowers tucked into her hair would not fall out.

She hurried into her shoes when she heard a carriage stop at the front door, but it turned out to be the Westons, who paused to collect them. Jane was crestfallen when Aunt Bates turned them away. She would much rather have ridden with the amiable Westons than the overbearing Eltons.

The appointed hour arrived, but no carriage. "Of course, Mrs Elton must be longer at her toilet than she imagined," Aunt Bates worried aloud for the both of them. "It is so thoughtful of her to insist on bringing us with them. Mr Elton's carriage might not be as grand as Mr Weston's, but it is every bit as comfortable! Such wonderful, thoughtful neighbors we have! It was so good of Miss Woodhouse to send for Mother, so that she could spend the evening with Mr Woodhouse while we are away at the ball! I am so glad for the new shawl from Mrs Dixon that you brought home from Weymouth. The evenings are not warm, and it would not do for Mother to catch a chill. Although I cannot imagine Mr Wood-house would be so unsolicitous of Mother's health as to allow her to catch a chill while she was visiting. I have never met a person more careful of everyone's health than Mr Woodhouse. Just the other day, while Mother was visiting to play loo, Mr Woodhouse insisted upon turning the table a little so that he and Mother were both warm enough by the fire. And then later he had the screens moved so that neither of them would get too warm. Being too warm can be as bad for one's health as being chilled, I should think. Bless me, I hope Mother is not too warm with her shawl. Perhaps I should have sent her with the smaller one."

"By the time she comes home, she will be glad for the warmth," Jane tried to soothe her.

"I am glad we thought to set a time, so that I can run home to get her to bed, even though the ball will still be in progress," she continued to fuss. "It won't take me long, but I can run home for her, and then come back well before supper."

"Remember what I told you, Auntie, be sure to slip out quietly. As soon as people begin leaving a party, inevitably the whole thing will come to a stop. You would feel terrible if people felt obliged to leave because you have, and the Westons and Miss Woodhouse and Mr Churchill would be so hurt that they planned such a grand evening, but then people did not even stay till the supper they have waiting."

"I will leave without saying a word, I promise you!"

Jane wished she could believe her. Restless, she could no longer sit in her chair, watching the clock and listening while her aunt's voice hammered continually at her ears. She went to the window. The carriage coming up the street was not the Eltons' less grand carriage. Restless, she began pacing from one end of the drawing room to the other. She paused at the mirror to check her reflection. Not a hair out of place. She checked her reticule to make sure she had her dancing slippers and her fan. Out of things to do, she looked at the clock one more time, and began pacing the room again.

"Do you think we have been forgotten?" She broke in on her aunt's soliloquy. "Perhaps we ought to start walking."

"Oh, that would be terrible to miss the ball!" Aunt Bates exclaimed. "I don't suppose Mrs Elton would be so late as this. It is truly such an honor she does us, sending you a note to say she would collect us. But perhaps in the excitement of the moment, she might have forgotten us. We are not so significant, I am sure we could easily be forgotten. If only Mother had not gone to Hartfield quite so early, perhaps Miss Woodhouse would have made the offer for James to take us to the ball before he took Mother back to Hartfield. But we were not dressed yet when Mother left for Hartfield, we would have been much, much too early."

"Are your shoes sturdy enough to make the walk?" Jane redirected the conversation back to the matter at hand. "I think there was talk of rain; we ought to collect our umbrellas. We can fetch them, and start walking. If we hurry, we might not miss any of the dancing."

At that moment, she heard carriage wheels approaching. She

hurried to the window, and sighed with relief. The Eltons' carriage stopped at the door.

The Eltons were not inside as the coachman handed them in. Jane was annoyed that they had, indeed, been forgotten. It did not say much of one's manners when a person offered a service, and then neglected to follow through. They could have gone with the Westons, and then Jane would already be watching Mr Churchill from across the room, listening to his cheerful voice, feeling the occasional brush of his hand against hers when he would pass her in the hall. Well, as Aunt Bates had said, they were not significant. And, this way, she did not have to listen to Mrs Elton on the ride to The Crown. It was an awful feeling, to owe gratitude to a patroness to whom she did not feel grateful.

At least it was a short ride to The Crown, and by the time the carriage door was open, there was Mr Churchill, standing by with an umbrella, waiting with shining eyes and his warm smile to hand her out.

"It was starting to sprinkle; it would be horrible to have your gowns ruined before the ball even started!" He squeezed her hand before he tucked it under his elbow, then led her inside, making way for his father to collect Aunt Bates.

"Thank you so much for being so considerate of us!" Jane was able to smile up at him unreservedly, there being no one to witness her show of unabashed affection. The footman and Mr Weston were both occupied with her aunt.

"I was glad to do so. And I am so relieved that Mrs Elton's oversight was so easily rectified." He lowered his voice as he took her shawl from her. "I see she is at least everything you described, if not more so."

"She does make a fearsome first impression, does she not?" Jane answered, and then all private observations would have to wait until a later time as they entered the ballroom.

Mrs Elton was standing ahead of Mrs Weston, for all the world receiving the guests as if it were her place, not Mrs Weston's, to greet arriving guests. If Jane wondered what excuse Mrs Elton was going to offer for forgetting them, she would never know the answer, for Aunt Bates entered the room already talking, and loudly enough to make other conversation a trifle difficult.

"Well! This is brilliant indeed! This is admirable! Excellently contrived, upon my word. Nothing wanting. Could not have imagined it. So well-lighted up. Jane, Jane, look! Did you ever see anything?"

Mortified at being shouted for in the midst of genteel company, Jane wished for one small moment that she was not related to Aunt Bates. She wondered if there was a way she could contrive to draw her aunt aside to try and convince her to lower her voice, and perhaps not chatter away quite so much. But then she watched her aunt greet Mrs Elton, and she calculated that, faced with a rematch, Mrs Elton would insist on proving her dominance in the talking contest.

She should have realized Mrs Elton's vanity would be far more engaged by usurping Mrs Weston's place in receiving guests. A few comments, the usual courtesies in asking after Grandmama, and Mrs Elton surrendered. Aunt Bates talked merrily on, addressing Mrs Weston, then Jane herself, then Mr Churchill, then Miss Woodhouse, then Dr Hughes and his wife, then Mr Richard.

At long last someone thought to serve her coffee, and finally the painful soliloquy came to an end. Jane's relief was short-lived; as her aunt was in the process of asking for tea instead of coffee, Mrs Elton had clearly concluded all the guests had arrived, and abandoned her station in order to corner Jane.

"My dear Jane, I must tell you how lovely you look tonight! I swear you must have spent absolutely hours on your hair, it is quite perfect. I do say it takes a great deal of skill to make such perfect ringlets. My maid does not have your patience, or your skill. You see how she settled for only a few curls for my hair tonight. I suppose as a married woman I do not have as much time to sit at my dressing table as you do. That is the price we pay as married women, I suppose. I have too many other important duties for me to be able to spend much time upon my appearance. But truly, you really do look very lovely, believe me! And I have seen many a lovely woman at the balls they throw at Maple Grove."

"Thank you," Jane answered simply when Mrs Elton stopped for breath. "I am honored to be compared to your friends at Maple Grove."

Mrs Elton found her response to be encouragement to continue. "I do not believe I have seen this gown before? Red is not a color that suits everyone, believe me when I say many a complexion should not wear red. But I say you do it justice. I assure you, even at Maple Grove only a few ladies would try to wear red. I swear, some of the other jewel colors, blue and green, are much more forgiving, I think, to a larger range of complexions. I do think women with blue eyes, like me, should wear blue as often as possible. But I think, with your coloring, red was an excellent choice on your part."

"Thank you," Jane answered again. She was unsure what else to say, and did not bother trying to think of anything. Mr Churchill and Miss Woodhouse were standing nearby, and Jane wanted to eavesdrop on anything they were saying.

There was a brief awkward silence, but Mrs Elton failed to use it to excuse herself and go find someone else to annoy. "How do you like my gown?"

Ah, of course, Mrs Elton was one of those people who only gave compliments in order to solicit compliments from other people. She did not give compliments in order to give people pleasure, or to make them feel more comfortable.

"The lace is quite lovely," Jane answered.

Her compliment was clearly much too brief for Mrs Elton's vanity, so she went on to request compliments about her trimming, her hair, her slippers, her complexion, and every other minute detail she could think of. Finally she got tired of asking for compliments and went back to chattering, and Jane had to admit defeat. Her strategy for discouraging Mrs Elton into finding someone else to give her wordier compliments had failed.

"The Westons are giving this ball chiefly to do me honor. I would not wish to be inferior to others. I see very few pearls in the room except for mine."

Jane could not help but stare at Mrs Elton incredulously. Did she seriously think that this ball, which was planned by the Westons, Mr Churchill, and Miss Woodhouse before they knew there was a Mrs Elton, was for her?

Self-centered as Mrs Elton was, she must have realized that she had overreached herself, and changed the topic. "So Frank Churchill is a capital dancer, I understand. We shall see if our styles suit. A fine young man certainly is Frank Churchill. I like him very well."

If Mrs Elton thought that complimenting Mr Churchill would

compel him to turn around and start talking to her, she was very mistaken. He looked at Miss Woodhouse, and exclaimed, "I am so glad that we declared Randalls too small for holding our ball! This is ever so much nicer! I will even say that I am glad for the delay. If we had had our original plan back in February when we first started planning this, it would have been so much more difficult for people to travel here to join us. Just think, Dr and Mrs Hughes would not have been able to be here, for sure. And I believe Mr Elton was in Bath at the time? I had not yet met him at all when we started planning our party. Your father also had more objections to our plans when the weather was colder, did he not?"

"He did indeed," Miss Woodhouse answered. "It is hard for me to say if he is more resigned to our determination to hold a ball because he has had time to ponder the idea and conclude he might as well give in, or rather because the weather is indeed less objectionable."

Jane wanted badly to giggle at Mr Churchill's unsubtle reply to Mrs Elton's assumptions. She looked down at her fan, and sternly clenched her teeth together. She was going to fail. She had to pass her hand over her face to keep from breaking out into most unladylike laughter.

Mrs Elton's face was not in danger of breaking into merriment. "I do wonder where my cara sposo has gotten to? I had gone in to check my gown and my hair; he must be wondering if I was ever going to emerge. I had thought he would meet me here, since this is where the dance shall be. Perhaps he had thought that Mr Woodhouse would be here this evening, and he went to go find him at the card tables? I have no doubt Knightley has waylaid him, and all they would need is a fourth for a game of whist. Oh, except of course, Mr Woodhouse did not come this evening, did he? I remember your aunt did say your grandmother was spending the evening with him. They do seem to be such friends. Do you ever wonder, Mr Woodhouse lost his wife, and then your grandmother lost her husband, why the two of them did not get married? I suppose it is a little disgusting, to think of old people getting married, but they would have each other for company."

"Neither of them is wanting for company," Jane said, a little more sharply than she meant to. The idea of Miss Woodhouse being her step-aunt did not please her. "My aunt is almost as solicitous of my grandmother's needs as Miss Woodhouse is of her father's."

She was glad when Mr Elton came into the room, and provided his wife with a distraction. As he approached, Mrs Elton greeted him. "You have found us out at last, have you, in our seclusion?" Jane wondered how much sarcasm was buried in that sentence, and realized that Mr Elton had been deliberately avoiding the ballroom to have some time away from his bride. He was going to pay a heavy price in exchange for her dowry, she thought, as Mrs Elton continued, "I was this moment telling Jane, I thought you would begin to be impatient for tidings of us."

While Mr Elton answered his wife, Jane was watching with appreciation as Mr Churchill bristled over Mrs Elton's familiarity. "Jane!" Frank was saying to Miss Woodhouse. "That is easy. But Miss Fairfax does not disapprove it, I suppose."

Jane watched Mrs Elton to see if she had heard his reproof. Sadly, she had not. She was busily looking at Mr Elton while some silent communication was passing between husband and wife. She was hoping the two of them would excuse themselves so that they might continue their quarrel in private, but neither seemed inclined to move. Instead, they were joined by Mr Knightley.

CHAPTER FIVE

"Miss Fairfax. I trust you are well this evening." It was not so much a question as a statement.

"I am," Jane answered with equal gravity and brevity. "I trust you are equally well."

"I will be, if you are available for the first two dances," he responded directly.

Jane wondered if this was his attempt at gallantry. It might have been a possibly charming thing to say, if she had liked the man.

She was surprised when Mr Elton came to her rescue. "I am sorry, but Miss Fairfax is not available for the first two dances. I have claimed her for them."

Jane saw the look that Mrs Elton gave her husband, and realized he was not acting out of any sort of altruism, but rather it was a response to his wife's glare. "Why, yes, Mr Elton, I had not forgotten. I am sorry, Mr Knightley, but as you see, I am not available." In a moment of perfect timing, the call was made for the dancers to line up, and Jane was able to walk away with Mr Elton before Mr Knightley might possibly have asked her to dance later in the evening. For all her dislike of Mr Knightley, she did not think him a stupid man, and she thought it seemed highly likely that he understood her meaning. She was not available. Not to dance with, not for marriage.

Jane was amused to see that Mrs Elton had now usurped Miss Woodhouse and Mrs Weston's places at the head of the line. Jane supposed that she did have the honor as the newest bride in the room, but good form would have inspired any woman of breeding to give way to the hostesses to begin the ball. Instead, Mr Weston, as host, led her to the top of the line, while Mr Churchill followed with Miss Woodhouse.

"For a village that dances very seldom, we have certainly filled The Crown tonight," Jane commented, before the silence between them proved to get too awkward.

"Yes, indeed," Mr Elton answered, then fell silent again.

Jane took this as permission to say little, herself.

She could not help noticing that, since she declined to dance with him, Mr Knightley had elected not to dance at all. While several of the ladies were lacking partners, there he was, standing among the onlookers. While the rest of that group were stooped, squat, elderly men with gouty legs, lumbago and other excuses not to dance, there he was, tall, young and fit, unsmiling, watching the dancers and ignoring the ladies across the room whom he should have been inviting to join the end of the line.

As the dance progressed, she could not help but be amused that whenever Miss Woodhouse was able to catch his eye, she glared at him with a forced smile, compelling him to smile back at her. It never lasted once her back was turned to him while she was engaged in the dance, and his face returned to its natural ill-humored expression. Jane had to look studiously away when his eyes turned in her direction.

If Mr Knightley had harbored any last hopes of paying some sort of addresses to her, Jane was fairly convinced that this last snub on her part was finally enough to end any interest on his part. If he was interested in marrying, he would have to look elsewhere. Perhaps there was some other woman in the world who would put up with his lack of manners. But it would not be her.

At that moment, the dance shifted, and Mr Churchill and Miss Woodhouse were now dancing with her and Mr Elton. She dismissed Mr Knightley to focus on the pleasures of the moment, and laughed with pure joy.

That joy increased two dances later, when at last she was claimed by Mr Frank Churchill. "Miss Fairfax? I believe we are engaged..." he paused significantly, with a smile, before continuing, "for the next two dances?"

There was no use chastising him for being incautious. She was as happy as he was to be dancing together again at last. "I believe we are engaged, yes." For more than the next two dances, she thought happily as he took her hand and led her to the line.

Those two dances floated by in a cloud of happiness. Their hands met, and parted, and met again. Their eyes did the same. Jane was glad he was such a congenial spirit; with any other man in the room, people might have commented upon his manner of taking her hand every time they cast, even though it was not completely necessary. But he was always attentive and a trifle flamboyant; Mrs Elton would call it his "style."

It was a fresh thrill every time they came together, every time he took her hand and gave it an imperceptible little squeeze, every time he came a trifle too near before they parted again. The way he looked into her eyes with a smile that was just a little warmer, a little brighter, than he gave to everyone else, made her feel light and happy all over.

She was glad he had managed to whisper in her ear that he would claim her again for the last dances of the evening. Otherwise, the entire rest of the night would have been less wonderful.

Relaxed and happy, she danced with Mr Weston, then Mr Arthur. She was dancing with Mr George Otway when she saw her aunt slip out the door at the appointed time to help Grandmama to bed. It was a pleasant surprise, and a relief to see her keep her promise to leave without a word to disturb anyone.

She noticed with amusement that Mr Knightley had, at some point, come back to the ballroom and was dancing with Miss Woodhouse's particular friend, Miss Smith. Jane did not know Miss Smith terribly well, but she did think the girl would make a much better wife to Mr Knightley than herself. She seemed very sweet and amiable and appreciative; if Mr Knightley did not destroy the poor girl with his bad temper, she would weather his manners without reproach.

Jane felt sorry for the girl; if Mr Knightley made her the proposal he looked ready to have asked Jane, Miss Smith would be forced to accept him. At least since Miss Smith was an intimate of Miss Woodhouse, and Mr Knightley was a longtime friend of Mr Woodhouse, the Woodhouses would surely offer Miss Smith some amount of protection. If Miss Woodhouse could remind Mr

Knightley in public at a ball to mind his manners and stop scowling, hopefully she would remind him in private to be kind to a wife.

Aunt Bates returned just in time for the announcement to go to supper. Jane and Mr Churchill were both quietly lingering back, letting other guests go in, hoping they might have a quiet moment alone in the ballroom. Aunt Bates made that impossible, as she called to her from across the room, waving Jane's tippet. "Jane, Jane, my dear Jane, where are you? Here is your tippet. Mrs Weston begs you to put on your tippet. She says she is afraid there will be draughts in the passage."

"Don't worry about me, Auntie. I don't need it. I am sure I will be quite fine," Jane answered, wishing her aunt would be a little less attentive. Or at least a little less loud and less likely to draw unnecessary attention.

"My dear Jane, indeed you must," her aunt answered.

Mr Churchill crossed the distance in a moment, and relieved her of the contended garment. "Allow me, Miss Fairfax." He stepped in front of Jane, and carefully draped the long, warm scarf around her neck, without mussing a single curl. He was so close to her, she could smell his scent. He smelled of soap and sweat and something…earthy. She did not know what it was. But it struck her as quintessentially male.

Through it all, her aunt had continued talking. "Mr Churchill, oh! You are too obliging! How well you put it on! So gratified!"

While most of the other guests filed out of the room and down the hall to supper, Aunt Bates reassured Jane that she had left without saying a word, and was giving a detailed account of her grandmother's evening. Mr Churchill tried to distract her with the offer of escorting her in to supper, but she was hardly deterred. When he offered one arm to Jane, and the other to Aunt Bates, and proposed to take them both in to supper, she was only impressed into talking a little bit louder. "Sir, you are most kind. Upon my word, Jane on one arm, and me on the other!"

Jane was uncomfortably aware that the attention of everyone still in the ballroom was on them. Even when Aunt Bates proclaimed Mrs Elton the queen of the evening, it did not shift attention away from them. Jane squirmed internally while her aunt returned to the subject of Grandmama's visit to Mr Woodhouse, and loudly proclaimed that she was disappointed by a dish of asparagus that Mr Woodhouse sent back to the kitchen. "But we agreed we would not speak of it to any body, for fear of its getting round to dear Miss Woodhouse, who would be so very much concerned!"

Jane closed her eyes for a moment. She wondered why on earth she had not agreed to go to Ireland. Surely they could have found a way for Mr Churchill to have come to her in Ireland, instead of Highbury. Only ten steps away, Miss Woodhouse met her eyes. At least the glance they exchanged was one of recognition, and sympathy, rather than censure over the tactless announcement to the entire room. They both of them had very ridiculous elderly relatives to care for. The only difference between them was that Mr Woodhouse was very rich, and the Bates women were very poor.

Still mortified, Jane smiled an apology to Miss Woodhouse, who had the grace to look amused. She gave a small shrug, then turned away with her friend Miss Smith, while Aunt Bates and Mr Churchill found them a place to sit. Not in a draught, of course, on account of Jane's delicate constitution.

The fuss, she reflected as she sat, smiling at Mr Churchill as he held her chair for her, was only her due punishment. She should have lied less often about colds and headaches, to get out of various social engagements with people who had nothing else to talk about except the health of their neighbors.

Supper improved once the soup was served. Her aunt took up her spoon and finally ceased talking, and Mr Churchill spent the entire meal with his foot pressed against hers.

CHAPTER SIX

The morning after the ball, Mr Churchill called to say his farewells before undertaking the journey back to Richmond, under the guise of returning a pair of scissors he had borrowed from Aunt Bates, which he had "forgotten" to return.

"It was very fortunate I keep that small pair in my reticule," Aunt Bates received him with her usual verbosity. There was no hour of the day when she might be counted on to be less ready to talk. "Mrs Cole is the one who taught me to always keep scissors in my reticule. In fact, I think she may be the one who gave me this very pair! There was a thread loose on my spencer, I had just repaired it – no, perhaps it was my gloves. I remember I had several things that I had repaired all at once. Jane was not here at the time to help keep everything so well mended. She always does so much mending whenever she visits. And she remembers to clip her threads. But I forgot to clip my thread, and it was dangling, and Mrs Cole pointed it out while we were shopping in Ford's, but when I had no scissors, she used hers to clip the threads, and then gave me the scissors. Can you imagine? Right there in Ford's. She gave hers to me, and bought a new pair for herself, right then. She said she had been wanting to get the pretty new ones with the curled handles, and now she had an excuse to do so."

Jane and Mr Churchill just smiled at each other while Aunt Bates talked. The ball had been so perfect, there was no need for words.

"Well, your scissors did the trick in my hour of need last night, thank you," he jumped in when Aunt Bates almost paused for a breath. "I am afraid I cannot linger, I am expected back in Richmond this morning. I would not like to risk my aunt's displeasure, when she has been so gracious in letting me away for our wonderful ball last night."

"It truly was wonderful! I cannot wait until Mother is awake. Jane and I have so very much to tell her! The supper alone is going to be so hard to describe, it is going to take both Jane and me to remember it properly. Mother will enjoy hearing about it so very much."

"Speaking of Grandmama," Jane wanted a moment alone with him, before he drove off. "Do I hear her stirring? Why don't you check on her, see if she is fit to say goodbye to Mr Churchill before he starts his journey?"

"Bless me! Your ears are so much better than mine, Jane. Thank goodness for it, Mother is always saying how nice it is to have you with us. If you will excuse me, Mr Churchill."

"Of course, Miss Bates," he bowed with a laugh.

The moment Aunt Bates left the room, they collided together.

"Last night was perfect," he whispered, his lips buried into her hair just above her ear. "You were the most beautiful woman in the ballroom."

"I fear that is not saying much, in Highbury," Jane whispered back, teasingly.

"You would be the most beautiful woman in any ballroom. I have seen you in other ballrooms, I know," he answered.

"I love you so much," she snuggled her cheek against him, squeezing her arms around his waist.

"The word 'love' does not even begin to cover how I feel," he answered. They both heard Aunt Bates's footsteps, and they separated with as much force as they had come together.

"Well, Jane! Perhaps your ears are a little too good this morning. Grandmama is still sleeping. Perhaps you heard something from the street?"

"Perhaps," Jane agreed. "I am sorry, Auntie. At least you did not wake Grandmama when you checked on her? In that case, no harm done. Except for the fact that we have delayed Mr Churchill, when he needs to be leaving."

"Thank you once again for such a lovely evening last night, Mr Churchill!" Miss Bates shook his hand in parting. "It was completely wonderful! It was magical, like something from King Arthur's court!"

He smiled down at Aunt Bates, but his eyes drifted up to Jane as he answered, "It *was* a magical evening. Nothing could have been more perfect."

After he left, and Aunt Bates had gone to get Grandmama when she really was stirring, Jane stood precisely in the spot where Mr Churchill had been standing. She could swear the floor was warmer where his feet had been. She closed her eyes and stood there a long while, her eyes closed, smiling.

CHAPTER SEVEN

Dearest Sweet Jane,

Ireland is proving to be so delightful, my parents are now planning on staying all through August, instead of coming home at Midsummer.
Are you sure you cannot come for a visit? If you were to come now, you would be able to see Ireland in its greenest glory, then come back home to England with my mother and father. We still miss you terribly, all of us, even Mr Dixon who does not claim to know you as long or as well as the rest of us. He loves you because I love you, dearest sister of my heart, and entreats you to pack your things and bring us your delightful company.

Sophia's letters were less tempting with Mr Churchill's frequent visits. Once or twice a week, he contrived to be in Highbury; he was visiting his father, or accompanying his father, or accompanying Mrs Weston, or accompanying both Westons to dine with some other family in the county.

Even now, the post-office served to facilitate private communications back and forth between the lovers. They could plot morning walks so that their paths were likely to cross; dinner invitations were accepted or rejected based upon the other guests in attendance.

It was not terribly difficult to contrive frequent meetings. There was really only one social circle of note in the village, and the core of it was the Woodhouses, the Coles, the Otways, and Mr Knightley, supplemented heavily with the friendships of the Eltons, the Perrys, the Coxes, and the Bateses.

The secret moments for a special glance across the dinner table, the squeezing of a hand during a dance that might break out of an evening's dinner party, a stolen embrace behind a door, were frequent, but at the same time, seemed more and more fraught with peril as time dragged on, and Mr Churchill reported no success in talking to his aunt and making their engagement public.

"I am sorry, my sweet and patient angel," he confessed to her when they had a brief moment alone in the drawing room. "My aunt is not well, and it is nearly impossible to talk with her about anything but her health. If I try to talk about myself at all, she threatens to disinherit me because I am showing I do not love her."

"Perhaps you would be better off disinherited. Then we could stop hiding and get married," Jane pointed out.

"And how would I provide for you, my angel? Please, be patient and have faith in me. I know I can convince her to listen. I am sorry about this dismal timing. If she were not so sick, we would be married by now. I am sure of it. I am watching her like a fencer. I will lunge at the first opening she gives me. Trust me, my love."

"You know I do," Jane sighed. "I am just – tired of being here. I have never visited here for more than a fortnight. Now it has been months. I miss the Campbells. I miss Sophia. I miss good conversation. I never spent so much time with people who use so many words to say so little."

He took her face in both hands and kissed her before Aunt Bates's footsteps finished climbing the stairs.

The longer they had to keep up the pretense that there was no attachment between them, the harder it got. Whenever Mr Knightley was present at the same dinner, Jane got the uncomfortable feeling he was watching them. Since the ball at The Crown, he never spoke to her more than to exchange common courtesies, but he still gave her the impression he was paying her more attention than she would like. She made a bigger effort, when Mr Knightley was in the room, to avoid looking in Mr Churchill's direction. She warned Mr Churchill to be more careful, but he laughed at her fears and told her there was nothing to worry about.

When Mr Churchill mistakenly attributed news about Mr Perry getting a carriage to Mrs Weston's letters, instead of hers, the blunder seemed potentially disastrous. So many people had come upon each other while out walking, a large party consisting of Miss Woodhouse, Miss Smith, Mr Knightley, Mr and Mrs Weston, Mr Churchill, Aunt Bates and herself had all agreed to follow Miss Woodhouse home to Hartfield to call on Mr Woodhouse. So there was a very large party to listen when he insisted Mrs Weston had been the one to write him the news of Mr Perry setting up a carriage, after they saw the good man on horseback instead of in a carriage.

There was no way for Jane to signal to him to stop talking. He gave all the particulars Jane had written to him, which Mrs Weston denied knowing. He tried to laugh it off as a dream, which of course was when Aunt Bates had to spill out all the news as it had been confided from Mrs Perry to Grandmama, and Grandmama to Aunt Bates and herself.

If only they could have reached Hartfield a tiny bit faster! The entire story was out, right down to Aunt Bates denying that of course Jane was not the one to have shared Mrs Perry's secret. Jane could feel Mr Knightley's eyes watching her suspiciously. She felt Mr Churchill beside her as she passed through the door, and she knew he would be trying to catch her eye to apologize. But with Mr Knightley watching them intently, that would only make matters worse. She fussed with her shawl, and greeted Mr Woodhouse, and sat at the new round table without making any eye contact whatsoever.

Mr Churchill would not be denied his apology. With no means for them to talk while seated at Miss Woodhouse's large table, he requested the box of letters that Miss Woodhouse had been using with her nephews, and he made puzzles by putting a pile of letters in front of Miss Woodhouse, and she had to figure out the word. He made one for Miss Smith, and then put a pile of letters in front of Jane.

She smiled a little when she saw that the seven letters he had put in front of her spelled 'blunder.' After working it out, she pushed the letters back to the center of the table. It was a mistake not to have scrambled them in with the rest of the loose letters; Miss Smith pulled the pile back out, and when she and Mr

Knightley worked out the word she announced it loudly to the whole table. Jane could feel her face getting warm when Mr Knightley gave both her and Mr Churchill some clearly speculative looks. It would have been better if Mr Churchill would have simply left it alone, and waited until it was safer to apologize in private.

She sat at the table, miserably watching the others laughing and playing with the little alphabet letters, furious with Mr Churchill for piling one indiscretion on top of another. Mr Churchill seemed impervious to the danger of discovery they were in. He had explained away his gaffe by saying it was a dream, he had apologized to her, and she could see in his mind, he was done with the crisis. He was cheerfully creating new puzzles, and making Miss Woodhouse laugh with them.

Mostly the popular village misconception that Mr Churchill was courting Miss Woodhouse did not bother her. She could even pity Miss Woodhouse a little; he was using her in a somewhat disgraceful manner in order to hide his real reason for coming to Highbury as much as possible. If Miss Woodhouse was expecting an offer from him, she was going to be sorely disappointed.

At the moment, however, she was not amused by his deception. She was tired of it. She was tired of the hiding. Every time they were nearly found out, like this, it was going to take an armful of lies to put suspicions to rest. If, indeed, they were put to rest. Suspicions were cumulative. The longer they played at this game, the more likely they were going to be found out by someone. Or several someones. And once a few someones found out, the way everyone in the village gossiped, absolutely everyone would know their secret.

Miss Woodhouse was giggling and protesting at the word Mr Churchill had now given her. "For shame!"

"I will give it to her, shall I?" he asked, after throwing a mischievous glance at Jane.

"No, no you must not, you shall not, indeed," Miss Woodhouse protested.

The five letters Frank put down in front of her spelled 'Dixon.' He meant to reassure her that, if he could keep Miss Woodhouse convinced that Jane had been somehow involved with Mr Dixon, she would not be suspecting any romantic connection between

Jane and himself.

Perhaps he was right. But Miss Woodhouse was not the only person they had to fool, and some, like Mr Knightley, were more discerning.

The fact that everyone at the table was watching her only heightened her displeasure. She had not appreciated the scandalous assumption of Miss Woodhouse's when Mr Churchill had first reported it to her, and it was no funnier with the passage of time. No matter how much it amused Mr Churchill, it did not amuse her. She pushed the letters away. "I did not know that proper names were allowed." She turned and looked at her aunt.

By some small miracle, her aunt perceived her desire to leave. "Ay, very true, my dear. I was just going to say the same thing. It is time for us to be going indeed."

As Jane had observed to her aunt about leaving during the ball, one departure often leads to the breakup of the entire party. Everyone stood, made their thanks to Miss Woodhouse for the invitation, wished Mr Woodhouse a good evening, and made their goodbyes among members of the party. Mr Woodhouse made a great deal of protest over the departure of Mrs Weston, whom he still insisted upon calling Miss Taylor, and insisting that she should not have to leave at all.

Under the cover of the confusion of motion, Mr Churchill tried to deliver another handful of letters, but she pushed them away, irritated at his inability to be discreet, making sure they were better stirred back in with the other letters.

The light was fading with dusk as Aunt Bates said her wordy goodbyes, and the descending darkness made it difficult for Jane to find her shawl. She could have sworn she had draped it near the door, but it was not to be seen. She knew it was a special dodge of Mr Churchill's when he began to help her search for it. Of course, eventually, he was the one that 'found' it, claiming it had fallen on the floor behind the sofa.

"Forgive me, my love, I am so sorry," he whispered as he handed it back to her.

She gave him an angry, miserable look, but said nothing.

CHAPTER EIGHT

May turned into June with little to offer Jane any cheer. She and Mr Churchill made their peace before he drove back to Richmond, but the news in his letters regarding his aunt were merely alternating reports regarding her health. She would have a good day, and then a bad day. Never a day when she seemed truly on the mend, which would embolden him to speak to her about his intent to marry Jane.

She wished the Campbells had not delayed their departure again; she could have run off to London and awaited Mr Churchill with them, if that option was open to her. Of course, that would have made it more difficult for him to come and see her.

On the other hand, when an entire week went by when Mr Churchill was unable to leave Richmond, Jane thought it did not matter if they were only nine miles apart. Nine miles might as well be ninety. She was still left, alone, in Highbury, abandoned to the company of her silly aunt, the gossipmongers of Highbury, evenings trying to make polite conversation with the vacuous Miss Woodhouse while Grandmama played cards, and the daily attentions of Mrs Elton.

For a while, she used music to discourage Mrs Elton's visits. "Her practice at the pianoforte is very important if she is going to keep up her skills," Aunt Bates would explain in a loud whisper to Mrs Elton when she came calling. Jane played every morning, but she would happily play all afternoon, as well, if it kept her from having to go for a walk with Mrs Elton. But then Mrs Elton worked around that excuse by inviting Jane to dine with her and Mr Elton. Jane would be hard pressed to say she would not be eating because she was practicing Mozart.

She also felt obliged to accept all dinner invitations. It made her less of a financial burden on her aunt and grandmother. In a way, it was hardly different; the neighbors donated so much food to them over the course of a year. Either the neighbors sent food to them, or Jane went to eat with them. In either case, the neighbors were feeding them.

Every morning, when a letter from Mr Churchill did not bring news that there was any change in his situation, Jane felt a little more hopeless. How long was this going to go on? When she accompanied Aunt Bates to call on the Westons after Mrs Weston announced there would be a new Weston in the family soon, Mr Weston insisted adamantly that there was nothing truly wrong with Mrs Churchill.

"The woman has suffered for years from an ill temper, but no doctor in the world knows how to cure that!" Mr Weston huffed, when Mr Churchill's latest letter had been read to the assembled company. "A fine thing, her constant claims that she does not wish to give pain to anyone else with her complaints! That is her modus operandi, if you ask me. She uses claims of ill health to control everyone around her. If I remember correctly, she tried to use her delicate health as a reason Frank's mother should not have married me." He bowed to his wife. "Not to bring up the past, my dear."

"It is not a secret that you have been married before, Mr Weston." Jane's heart melted a little at the way Mrs Weston, who was positively glowing with health and happiness at her current condition, looked at her husband. It was the exact same way Jane looked at Mr Churchill. "I am very glad of it. If you had not been married before, you would not have provided me with a son who is excellent company when he is here, and a most diverting correspondent when he is absent."

"He is a most excellent young man, I am glad you agree!" Mr Weston beamed. "I suppose I cannot fault him for being compassionate towards the woman who has been so generous to him. It speaks well of his character, not ill. Still, I deplore his absence. I suppose we shall have to endure it as best we can. At least we know how truly and honestly he longs to see us as much as we long to see him."

Knowing Mr Churchill's real attraction to Highbury was her, the words were a balm to Jane's spirit. It was good to hear the words out loud that he truly longed to be there with her. She wished she knew how to become better friends with Mr and Mrs Weston.

"Of course, Miss Woodhouse must surely be a strong enticement for him to return as soon as he can!" Mrs Weston said with a complacent smile. "We mustn't forget that."

Jane stopped wondering how she might become better friends with Mr and Mrs Weston.

At least while she was enduring Mrs Elton's company, there was never any talk of Mr Churchill and Miss Woodhouse. Mrs Elton only had one topic of conversation, and that was Mrs Elton.

"Oh, Jane, it is positively tragic, the letter I just received from my sister," she sighed as Patty let her in the room the day after the visit to the Westons. She sank down into a chair and assumed a despondent pose. "I warn you – prepare yourself for the most horrid news. Mr Suckling tells my sister to tell me that they cannot possibly come visit until autumn. Just think of it, Jane! I cannot bear to think of it. All our plans, all the anticipated adventures we have been planning! Dashed! I cannot fathom how my sister has been unable to prevail upon Mr Suckling to keep his promise. All the exploring in the barouche-landau that we have looked forward to with so much pleasure!"

Jane was amused how Mrs Elton had changed from "I" to "we" in describing the depths of her disappointment. Hopefully by autumn Jane would have some form of resolution on the personal purgatory she was living in, and she would never have to be trapped in a carriage for weeks on end with Mrs Elton and her sister and brother. She had never been sure whom Mrs Elton was omitting from her plans: if the carriage comfortably held four, how was she planning on accommodating Mr and Mrs Suckling, Mr and Mrs Elton, and herself?

"I am sure you will bear it with great fortitude, Mrs Elton," she said gravely.

"Oh, Jane, that is so true. I am not the sort to be put off by disappointments, believe me. I shall rally. I am devastated by the postponement of so many introductions and recommendations I have been so eagerly looking forward to making. Such a merry party as we were going to be! Well, we still shall be, but not until autumn."

"Autumn will be here soon enough," Jane answered. She imagined being Mrs Frank Churchill by autumn, and she would never have to sit in a carriage with Mrs Elton. She would have her own barouche-landau. Or, at least she believed his aunt and uncle had one. Perhaps once his aunt had regained some strength, they could do some traveling. It might lift his aunt's spirits to see some of the most beautiful places in England, the ones she had read about with the Campbells. She had accompanied them to a few of them; there were plenty of places where people went to improve their health and spirits.

"Well, it is not autumn yet, summer has barely begun. I am determined we should enjoy it to its fullest. Come, Jane, I think a walk is very much in order." She held up her hand before Jane could make any of her usual excuses. "I know you have your music to attend to, but it can wait until we come back from getting our fresh air and exercise. The wildflowers will not be here forever. They are here now, and we should enjoy them now."

Jane looked at her, and for once she gave her a genuine smile. She was sure Mrs Elton would have no idea what the words 'Carpe diem' meant, but it was good enough advice from multiple poets. It should be followed, even when that advice came from the likes of Mrs Elton. "You are right. Let us live in the present, and enjoy what beauties of the present are available to us. Tomorrow will take care of itself."

CHAPTER NINE

Most well-beloved Mr Churchill,

I told you all about Mrs Elton's sorrows because her sister and her husband have found a way to avoid her for a few more months... well, she has put all her energies into "rallying" from this disappointment. The result is an invitation to pick strawberries at Donwell Abbey.

I can only imagine the verbal gymnastics Mrs Elton must have used to procure such an invitation, since it includes me! Mr Knightley has not spoken to me since your ball at The Crown. I am taking this as a sign that he has finally taken the hint. At least, I hope he will leave me alone now.

I know that Mr Weston has written you to beg your attendance at this outing, and I am writing to add my voice to his! I know you do not like Mr Knightley or Mrs Elton any more than I do, but I would greatly appreciate your protection from both parties! You can use your considerable charms to keep all the dragons at bay.

This invitation from such a quarter is a considerable surprise; Mr Knightley clearly has the disposition of a hermit. He is not inclined to like many people. I suppose I should be flattered that he likes me, but I am not. Why he put forth an invitation to Mrs Elton, whom he clearly does not like, is beyond me.

Please, please accept your father's entreaty to come and join us!

Your desperate
J. Fairfax

The Hermit of Donwell Abbey was at least very civil to her, Aunt Bates and the Eltons as he handed them out of the carriage when they arrived on strawberry picking day. "My carriage block being as historical as everything else about Donwell Abbey, it has worn down considerably," he cautioned them in his serious way. "It is a very steep step."

It was amusing to see what a large party was assembling for the raid upon his strawberry beds. Besides herself and her aunt and Mr and Mrs Elton, Mr and Miss Woodhouse were there, plus Miss Smith, and then Mr and Mrs Weston walked up the lane.

"Goodness gracious, Miss Taylor!" It was very amusing to hear Mr Woodhouse continuing to insist upon calling Mrs Weston 'Miss Taylor,' when she was now a married woman with a child on the way. "You did not walk all the way here, did you? You will be too worn out to enjoy picking strawberries. Not to mention, you will have had much too much sun."

Mrs Weston smiled at him from under the shade of her parasol. "Perhaps I am a bit too tired to feel like bending over to pick strawberries. Will you keep me company in the Abbey, while our host sees to his guests in the garden? I would not be sorry for some quiet time to talk."

Jane saw the look that passed between Mrs Weston and Mr Knightley, confirming that this ruse was planned ahead of time. He may not like many people, but he did have a great fondness for Mr Woodhouse, for some reason. "I have had a fire set for you in the library," Mr Knightley reassured Mr Woodhouse in the most gentle tones Jane had ever heard him speak. "Come, we can get you settled. You should find it very comfortable in there by now."

"Yes, indeed, papa," Miss Woodhouse added her assurances to Mr Knightley's, "you see, Mr Knightley thought of everything to make you comfortable. Shall I see you settled by that fire?"

"Bless me, Mr Knightley did think of everything! He is such a thoughtful neighbor. Always so very thoughtful," Aunt Bates wandered over to join the conversation. "The weather is so perfectly dry, there should not be the least bit of danger for anyone to catch a chill. Not on such a perfectly fine morning as this..." Aunt Bates wandered into the house with Mr and Miss Woodhouse and Mrs Weston, and the door closed on her voice.

Knowing his wife would be well cared for inside, Mr Weston cheerfully greeted Jane, the Eltons, and Miss Smith. "Perfect day for an outing, would you not agree? And perfect weather for traveling, it has been so dry. Which I am glad of – my son is going to join us, and it is quite wonderful for him to have good weather for the ride."

Jane was relieved to hear he was coming. "I take it Mrs Churchill is feeling better, then, if he is able to ride out from Richmond today?" she asked.

"Yes, yes indeed," Mr Weston answered. His son was his favorite topic of conversation. "I wrote to beg him to join us, and he answered that his aunt seemed to be greatly improved, and he anticipated that he would ride over first thing this morning. He should be here any time now!"

"How very excellent," Mrs Elton answered. "Quite splendid of him to join my strawberry party. I feel the compliment quite exceedingly, I assure you." She looked back at the Abbey. "I wonder what is taking them so long? Mr Woodhouse only needs to be sat down in a chair, I think that should not take so much time. I suppose I need to go in and flush everyone out, or they might spend the entire morning in talking, and we would miss the most perfect time to be outside picking strawberries. I don't see how anyone could want to be indoors on a glorious morning like this!"

Jane hardly listened as Mrs Elton continued to narrate about the perfect weather, and her perfect large bonnet and her perfect basket with its perfect pink ribbon. She was trying not to feel hurt that Mr Churchill had not communicated with her, as well as with Mr Weston. Usually, she was the one who knew everything that was going on, and his letters to the Westons might fill in a detail here and there.

Jane tried to put aside her displeasure. For all she knew, he had written her a letter and it had been misdirected. Or it had been placed in the wrong box at the post-office. So many things could go wrong when sending a letter.

She sighed. Their correspondence had seemed exciting and romantic after they had parted from each other at Weymouth. But the secret had lost its charm. She was tired of concealing the truth from everyone. It was not quite lying, but it was not NOT lying, either. She had to remain silent whenever the Westons were speculating about a romantic attachment between Mr Churchill and Miss Woodhouse. She had to make excuses about why she went to the post-office every day. She had to hope they weren't caught in an intimate moment when they were alone in the drawing room. She had to NOT tell the Dixons and the Campbells why she did not accept the invitation to come to Ireland. And she had to constantly explain to Mrs Elton why she was still visiting her grandmother, instead of embarking upon a situation as a governess.

Sure enough, after a half hour of picking, and listening to an endless monologue by Mrs Elton on the topic of strawberries that did not even pause long enough for Aunt Bates to chime in, Mrs Elton was quite done with the process. The party moved to seats in the shade, and Mrs Elton placed herself beside Jane.

"Jane, dear, I have been so excited about our strawberry outing this morning, and absorbed in our plans for Box Hill tomorrow, that I have shamefully neglected in telling you about my letter! I have the most wonderful news! I got a letter this morning from my sister. You know I had her write to her husband's cousin, Mrs Bragg, about a position for you."

"I did ask you not to make any inquiries on my behalf right now," Jane reminded her.

"But, my dear Jane! Now is the time to start looking for these positions! I know you are very ignorant of the world, but that is why I am here to take care of you. She wrote to Mrs Bragg, and Mrs Bragg is not in need of a governess right now. But Mrs Bragg has a cousin who IS looking for someone. My dear, I cannot tell you how perfect this is! My sister, Mrs Suckling, is acquainted with Mrs Bragg's cousin. She has been to dine at Maple Grove on several occasions! Now, in terms of a perfectly felicitous arrangement I believe it is not quite as perfect as having a situation with Mrs Bragg. I believe her cousin's estate is a little less splendid. Although perhaps it is similar to the difference right here between Hartfield and Donwell Abbey. The one might perhaps be a little more splendid, while the other is larger. But Mrs Bragg's cousin is a delightful, charming woman, at least, according to my sister."

"What is her name?" Jane asked. It was somehow irksome to have the woman continually referred to as 'Mrs Bragg's cousin.'

"Oh, I don't honestly remember. I cannot remember the name of the estate, either. It is all in the letter. I meant to bring it with me, so that you can read it all yourself. But I was so enthralled with the pleasures of this morning's adventures, I completely forgot it. You can believe me, this is a highly advantageous situation! I assure you, you will be working for people who travel in the first circles! You will surely not even need to bring your pianoforte, I am sure they will be able to offer you a place to play where you will not disturb anyone. I swear to you, there will not be another situation so perfectly ideal for you this year! I shall write my sister in the morning to tell her that of course you will accept the position, and ask when you can start!"

"I cannot authorize you to do any such thing!" Jane responded firmly. "I will begin my search when I am ready. I shall not begin until after the Campbells return from Ireland, and they will not be back from Ireland until the end of the summer."

This was, perhaps, the hardest of all the things Jane had to face in keeping her secret. She wished she could simply tell Mrs Elton to stop looking for a situation for her, because she was not going to be a governess. She would be marrying Mr Frank Churchill, and be helping him take care of Mr and Mrs Churchill, until the time they had their own children to take care of – and find a governess for.

Unable to simply stop Mrs Elton's intentions of helping by telling her the truth, she had to settle for the same excuses and vagaries she had been using over and over again, assuring her she would not at present commit to any engagements with any families. Mrs Elton refused to respect her wishes, and pressed her for the authorization to write to her sister on the morrow to accept.

Jane was uncomfortably aware that everyone in the party had now stopped talking, in order to listen to them arguing. It was time for a strategic retreat. "We have been sitting here so long, now, our legs are going to get stiff," she stood up. "Shall we walk?" If Mr Knightley had been a gentleman with any manners, he would have long since interrupted Mrs Elton's clearly unwelcome advances with a distraction. She appealed to his duties as a host. "Would Mr Knightley do us the honor of showing us the gardens? All the gardens? We can see how extensive and perfectly cared for his strawberry garden is. I should like to see the whole extent of the other gardens."

"Of course," Mr Knightley said, standing up. "Everyone is quite welcome to tour the rest of my grounds. I am sure the ladies would like to see the flowerbeds. The rose bushes are doing quite well this year! There is also a perfectly shady walk up the avenue over there, you can walk in the shade of the lime trees to an extremely pretty view."

"Come, Auntie," Jane hurriedly helped Aunt Bates from her seat. "Shall we go and see Mr Knightley's rose bushes?"

"Bless me! That does sound quite fine. I do miss the days when Grandmama used to grow such lovely roses." Her aunt took Jane's invitation to walk as an invitation to talk, as well. For once, Jane did not mind it. Her aunt's voice would drown out any more attempts on Mrs Elton's part to talk about sending Jane off to be a governess. And if she happened to talk about things that her grandmother used to do to keep the Vicarage feeling welcoming and homey, which Mrs Elton was clearly not doing, well, Jane refused to be embarrassed about such topics.

The entire group ended up taking the walk in small groups; Miss Woodhouse was walking with Mr Weston and Mrs Elton, Mr Knightley walked with Miss Smith (a detail Jane noted with some amusement) and Mr Elton. Then the Eltons broke off from their other groups to walk along behind everyone else. In their splintered groups, they wandered past the rose bushes and the other flower beds, then down the wide shady lane of lime trees to admire Mr Knightley's accurately described "pretty view."

Next the group adjourned to the house, where Mr Knightley had a cold luncheon waiting for them. Food failed to be a distraction for Jane's state of unrest; the main topic of conversation was Mr Churchill's continued absence. He had told his father he would be there in the morning, and now it was well past noon. Mrs Weston fussed, and popped up multiple times to watch the road from the front door, and worried some more. "I am sure something has happened," she insisted. "I know he is a good horseman, but that black mare of his is simply too wild. What if he has been thrown from his horse? Even good horsemen have accidents."

"You have not taken into account the state of Mrs Churchill's health," Miss Woodhouse reminded her. "Perhaps she has taken a turn for the worst, and he won't be coming, after all."

"He was so uncommonly certain," Mr Weston insisted. "He wrote to me that his aunt was so much better, that he had not a doubt of getting over here."

"That mare has thrown him," Mrs Weston fretted. "Perhaps we should send someone to find him. What if he is injured, and lying on the road?"

"Stop making yourself uneasy, my dear!" Mr Weston laughed. "There might be any number of reasons why he has been delayed."

"Perhaps the weather in Richmond is not so pleasant as here, and Mrs Churchill has taken a chill," Mr Woodhouse contributed to the conversation. "Or Mr Frank Churchill himself."

Jane listened to everyone's speculations with her stomach in knots, unable to eat anything on her plate. She was worried, too, but she was not in a position to worry out loud, as everyone else was doing. She had more right to worry about Mr Churchill than anyone at the table, excepting his father, but she had no right to say anything. And, still, unlike his father, she had no letter from him telling her that he was coming at all.

Of course, perhaps his misdirected letter would be the one to tell her that, while he had told his father to expect him, he would not be coming, after all. There were always plenty of obstacles. The majority of the people at the table pointing out the uncertainty of Mrs Churchill's health were not wrong.

The meal dispensed with, the party agreed that such perfect weather should be enjoyed out of doors. Miss Woodhouse elected to stay indoors with her father, in order for Mr Weston to persuade Mrs Weston to take a turn about the gardens. Aunt Bates wanted to see the fish ponds; Mr Knightley suggested any who wished for a longer walk could continue along the same path as far as the clover field, which they were going to begin cutting on the morrow.

As they returned outside, and again broke into small groups, Mrs Elton sought Jane out to renew her attack. "Jane, dear, I simply must insist you give me leave to send a letter to my sister tomorrow morning! This position is simply too perfect, you must believe me! An ideal family, an ideal situation! Very generous terms. Wait until you see the letter! I assure you, they are offering very generous terms. If you squander this opportunity, I cannot promise I will be able to find anything else nearly as nice."

"I appreciate your concern, Mrs Elton, but truly, I am not going to begin any situations at present," Jane answered. "It was premature of you to write any letters on my behalf. I asked you not to write any letters on my behalf. Now that you have done so without my consent, you must now make your apologies to your sister's cousin. I am not, at this moment, interested in beginning any new position."

"My dear Jane, I do not think you understand what a mistake you are making. I know you are very ignorant of how these things work," Mrs Elton began, but Jane cut her off.

"You are wasting a beautiful day in standing and arguing instead of admiring Mr Knightley's gardens," she pointed out. "You must excuse me, Mrs Elton." Jane turned and walked rapidly away. If she did not, she was going to say things she might regret later on. She might not regret them in the short term, but she might regret them someday. She did not know where she was going, but she needed to get away from Mrs Elton. Another word from that quarter was intolerable.

She broke into a run. She wanted to flee from here. Away from them all – away from Highbury. Away from her aunt's and Mrs Elton's nonstop chatter. Away from the gossip-laden conversations without a single topic of substance. Walking away from their tiresome conversations was not enough. She had had all she could take. She needed to escape. Now.

She tried walking in other parts of the Abbey's grounds, but there were always other people, who would no doubt expect her to walk with them if they saw her. She turned her feet to the house itself. It was a large building, surely there was a corner inside where she could hide, and think.

She walked through the entrance, and when her eyes adjusted after the brightness outside, she was facing a surprised-looking Miss Woodhouse. Even in the rambling Abbey, she could not be alone. Looking at the other young woman, she made a decision to leave the party altogether. "Will you be so kind, when I am missed, as to say that I am gone home?"

"Going? Now?" Miss Woodhouse asked. She looked confused.

"I am going this moment." Jane realized if she was going to make an escape, she needed to hurry, before Mrs Elton tracked her down and continued her attack. "My aunt is not aware how late it is, nor how long we have been absent. But I am sure we shall be wanted, and I am determined to go directly."

"And you did not take leave of your aunt?" Miss Woodhouse asked.

"I have said nothing about it to anybody," Jane explained as patiently as possible. "It would only be giving trouble and distress. Some are gone to the ponds, and some to the lime walk. Till they all come in, I shall not be missed; and when they do, will you have the goodness to say that I am gone?"

"Certainly, if you wish it," Miss Woodhouse answered. "But you are not going to walk to Highbury alone?"

"Yes." Miss Woodhouse was looking oddly distressed at the idea, so Jane hastily tried to reassure her. "What should hurt me? I walk fast. I shall be at home in twenty minutes."

"But it is too far, indeed it is, to be walking quite alone," she protested. "Let my father's servant go with you. Let me order the carriage. It can be round in five minutes."

"Thank you, thank you." An odd mixture of feelings flooded Jane's heart at Miss Woodhouse's insistence. "But on no account. I would rather walk." She felt unexpected gratitude to her for treating her like an equal. Not like a servant, or someone about to become a servant. Miss Woodhouse treated her like a lady, who would have a servant walking with her. Well, for now, she still needed to keep up the tired pretense. "For me to be afraid of walking alone!" she exclaimed. "I, who may so soon have to guard others!"

"That can be no reason for your being exposed to danger now," Miss Woodhouse answered with a concerned frown. "I must order the carriage. The heat even would be a danger. You are fatigued already."

"I am," Jane admitted. "I am fatigued, but it is not the sort of fatigue..." How did she explain that she needed to be alone, to think, to have a moment without everyone pressing in upon her? "Quick walking will refresh me." The genuine worry on her companion's face touched Jane, and she reached out to touch her arm. "Miss Woodhouse, we all know at times what it is to be wearied in spirits. Mine, I confess, are exhausted. The greatest kindness you can show me, will be to let me have my own way, and only say that I am gone when it is necessary."

She could see the compassion and comprehension in the other eyes at her appeal. Miss Woodhouse nodded, walked to the door with her, and made her wait until Miss Woodhouse had checked outside to make sure no one would see her leaving. "There, you are safe. No one should be able to see you if you walk straight up the drive, then you should be able to continue quite alone."

Jane gave her a grateful look. "Oh, Miss Woodhouse, the comfort of being sometimes alone!"

CHAPTER TEN

Jane had barely escaped to the Donwell road when she heard hoofbeats. The black mare that had been the discussion of so much of the luncheon conversation rounded the bend, and Mr Churchill was galloping up the road.

"Miss Fairfax!" He saw her, pulled his horse to a stop, leaped down from the saddle, and reached out to wrap her in his arms.

Madly sniffling back tears, she shook her head and stepped away from him. "Not out here in the middle of a field! People could see us for miles. Go on to Donwell, leave me to walk home."

"Not until you tell me what you are doing here," he insisted. "Here, I will walk with you."

"That's even worse," Jane answered. "You have been insulting me in public with Miss Woodhouse to keep people from suspecting our engagement, but now you are going to risk being seen walking with me?"

He ignored her point. "Why have you left the strawberry party?"

"I could not stay there another minute," Jane sniffed hard, but it was no use. The first tears began to slide down her cheeks. "I cannot do this any longer – I cannot stay here with these people. When are you going to be able to get an answer from your aunt? How much longer am I going to be fending off Mrs Elton's persistent attacks? She has found me a position within her family, and I am running out of ways to say no."

"I thought you told her not to go looking for anything on your behalf," he sounded perplexed.

"I did! I told her in no uncertain terms not to make any inquiries. But she is not the sort to listen to other people. When she takes an idea in her head, she is extremely tenacious."

"Well, ask her to leave you alone."

"I have! If I stay home and play the pianoforte, she comes and sits in the drawing room and talks loudly over my playing. If I claim to be sick, she comes and brings me her favorite remedies and sits by my bedside lecturing me about my health. If I try to make sure I am out walking so that I am not at home for her visits, I get waylaid by every person in town. By being waylaid, Mrs Elton is then able to accost me, and then of course the two of us can walk together."

"Well, tell your aunt to send her away after she delivers her remedies," he offered, looking a little at a loss to offer any useful ideas.

"You think I have not tried that? This is Aunt Bates we are talking about. She does not know how to tell a lie. Telling her to lie only puts it at the top of her mind to be sure to tell that person the very thing she should not be telling. I am completely out of resources to put people off any more. I have feigned so many colds and headaches since I first arrived here, in order to avoid people. Then I have to endure the endless lectures – from every human being in Highbury - on how I am endangering my health, every time I walk to the post-office to send you a letter!"

Her nose was starting to run. Jane found her handkerchief, wiped her eyes, blew her nose, and stared back at him. "How much longer am I going to have to do this? Another week? Another month? When are you going to rescue me from this purgatory? Do you expect me to live like this for years? When? Can you please tell me anything about how much longer I have to be here?"

He made a helpless gesture with both hands. "I don't know, my love. There is no predicting how long it is going to take my aunt to get well. I told you how sick she is."

"Mr Weston continues to say she is not very sick, she just likes to have her episodes to keep the people around her under her control." Jane knew that was not completely fair; Mr Weston did not see Mrs Churchill every day, and Mr Frank Churchill did. But she did not feel like being fair. It was not fair to her to have to live here, week after week, month after month. She could have been spending this entire time in Ireland, surrounded by people she loved, who loved her, who had more to talk about than strawberries, who treated her like an equal, instead of addressing her by her first name and telling her how ignorant she was of the world.

"Mr Weston knows little about the matter. He does not see her get stronger one day, and weaker the next. In the time it takes to write a letter to say I am able to come for strawberry picking, she can go from sleeping comfortably in a chair to struggling for breath. She gets extremely agitated when I am not there. She stays much calmer when I am sitting with her."

"I could be there with you, helping you and your uncle take care of her," Jane pointed out. "Instead of here, doing nothing except holding off everyone with small deceptions that get bigger and bigger every single day."

"I know, but I cannot get married without my aunt's permission, and she is so sick, she is out of humor and not likely to give her permission," he answered. "You are just going to have to be patient."

"I have been patient!" Jane snapped. "But sooner or later, I am going to run out of excuses and lies. I *am* running out of excuses and lies. I need to leave Highbury before too many more questions are asked. With Mrs Elton making a huge fuss over this position she has found for me, everyone is going to start asking why I am not taking it. It is a perfectly reasonable question: why am I not eager to accept an offer with a very prestigious family who has a great appreciation of music, with few children, comfortable accommodations, and a generous income? How am I supposed to explain my refusal? I can say that I am waiting until I can see the Campbells again, but when is someone going to point out that this makes no sense? I can go to visit the Dixons and Campbells in Ireland before taking this position. Or, what happens when the Campbells delay their return yet again? What if Mrs Dixon is *enceinte* soon, and her mother and father elect to stay until the baby arrives? What excuse do I offer every pushy, gossiping neighbor in Highbury then? I am out of time, Mr Churchill. There is almost nothing left that I can say. You need to get your aunt's permission so that we can announce our engagement, or we need to get married without your aunt's permission, or I need to go to Ireland to wait until you are free, or I need to accept that you are not actually going to be marrying me any time in the next year, and I should be accepting this position as a governess. Which of these options should I follow? Can you tell me that?"

It was more words than Jane had spoken altogether within the same hour since she had set foot in Highbury. She stared at him, angry at the tears that insisted upon leaking out while she talked.

He was staring angrily back at her. "You follow whichever option you like! I told you that you should have made better friends with Miss Woodhouse. Beats me why you chose to be friends with that awful harpy, Mrs Elton. Miss Woodhouse would not have pushed you into a corner like this."

"I am the granddaughter of the old vicar, not a young woman of any means, who can make friends with whomever I choose," Jane reminded him. "You are the chosen heir of privileged people. You can make friends with whomever you like, do whatever you like, go wherever you like. I don't have those options. If Miss Woodhouse does not invite me, and Mrs Elton does, I do not get many choices."

"Fine thing to say I have any options!" he responded angrily. "If I had any choices, you think I would be galloping from Richmond hours and hours after I said I would come? You begged me to come: here I am, as quickly as I could get here. My aunt had a terrible spell this morning. What am I supposed to do, rip my hand out of hers in the middle of a seizure, to leave the sickroom for a pleasure excursion?"

"If we were engaged, I could be there, holding her other hand!" Jane pointed out.

"We are engaged!" he pointed out. "But things are not as simple as all that."

"Are we? Are we truly engaged?" she asked. "If we were truly engaged, no one would be treating me the way they are. I would not be putting up with the indignity of Mrs Elton calling me 'Jane,' and fending off Mr Knightley, and listening to everyone raising their eyebrows and pairing your name with Miss Woodhouse's at every single opportunity, and you would not be encouraging Miss Woodhouse to think there was something inappropriate between me and Mr Dixon!"

"Is this what it all really comes down to, jealousy?" He threw up his hands. "You are jealous because Miss Woodhouse is the shield guarding your reputation? Are you also jealous of my aunt because she needs me? I know my father does not understand. But I thought you would! She is a sick old woman, and I am her greatest comfort. She has been very good to me from the moment she took me under her roof. It is not that different from your relationship to the Campbells. You, of all people, should understand! If it was Colonel Campbell who was very sick, I cannot imagine you would be running off to pick strawberries when he needed you to be there, holding his hand and reassuring him that he is going to recover!"

"At least I hope I would make the time to tell the person I was engaged to whether I was coming or not," she answered. "Did you send me a letter that got misdirected? Or did you neglect to send me one, and assume I would simply hear the answer through your father, once we got here?"

"I assumed you would realize that with a sick aunt, I had little time to write letters, and I was considering myself fortunate to have the time to write one letter, and I was considering myself very fortunate to be able to come at all – because my intended desperately wanted me to. But, if you are so little pleased to see me," he turned to remount his horse, "I shall continue to Donwell Abbey and spend time among people who will be better pleased by my arrival."

"Fine," Jane said. She did not bother to watch him ride away. She turned toward Highbury, and forced her legs forward, one step after another, in that direction.

CHAPTER ELEVEN

It was a long, horrible, sleepless night. Jane relived the argument over and over in her head, then recalled every promise in every letter Mr Churchill had sent her, then rehearsed every possible option she currently had available to her.

Painted over all these thoughts was the horrible dread of sunrise, which would soon be followed by the arrival of the Eltons' carriage to take her and Aunt Bates on an outing to Box Hill.

Even that had a variety of options to mull over and dread. Perhaps Mrs Elton would take umbrage at Jane's desertion from Donwell Abbey, and would not send the carriage to collect them. The idea suited Jane, but she did not hold out much hope for that outcome. The Eltons had brought Aunt Bates home, and she had brought Jane solicitous messages full of the usual scoldings about her health, and promises to pick them up early, so that the seven mile journey should not deprive them of a full day's enjoyment.

Jane could only imagine that Mrs Elton would use the entire drive with Jane trapped in a small space with her to press her to accept the governess position. While yesterday, Jane's only thought was to keep Mrs Elton at bay, now the matter was much more complicated.

Was Jane still engaged? Did she want to be?

When Mr Churchill remounted his horse and rode away, they had not broken off their engagement. Was this merely a bad fight, or was their private agreement terminated?

If this was merely a fight, they would consider the points that had come up during the argument, and come to some plan of action. This inaction was not tolerable. Perhaps Jane should go to Ireland, and Mr Churchill could send for her when his aunt recovered and he could receive her blessing.

If their fight signaled the end of their engagement, Jane faced different choices. She could still go to visit the Dixons, but then what? The position Mrs Elton had found was not without merit. She hated the idea of being beholden to Mrs Elton. But it would be foolish to throw away a truly generous offer simply because she disliked the messenger. It would be rather horrible if she ever had to see Mrs Elton while being governess to Mrs Suckling's cousin's children. But the connection seemed remote enough, Jane would probably be safe. Maple Grove was not exactly sending invitations for the Eltons to visit there. Even if Jane ended up at Maple Grove accompanying the children under her charge, there was probably only the remotest chance that Mrs Elton would be there, as well.

So, she summarized as she rose to dress, the first thing she needed to do was figure out whether or not she and Mr Churchill were still engaged. Once that was more clear, then she would know which options were open to her.

The carriage arrived to collect them, exactly as promised, and Jane was spared the humiliation of having to ask Mrs Elton to show her the fateful letter by Aunt Bates's excessive cheer, which did not allow Mrs Elton to get a word in.

Aunt Bates was talking from the moment they stepped out their door. "Bless me! What uncommon luck! Two perfect mornings in a row! One would think, after yesterday's perfect morning, something should surely go wrong this morning to prevent us from enjoying such a perfect excursion! We are so very fortunate to have such considerate neighbors to include us in their outings! So very, very thoughtful. We have such very thoughtful neighbors. Mrs Goddard is so thoughtful to take care of Mother for us today. She had a pot of tea waiting when we arrived this morning, and an extra cushion on her most comfortable chair. Such a neighbor! I believe one of the young ladies from her school embroidered the cushion, and such fine needlework it was, too!"

She chattered happily away about thoughtful neighbors, and embroidery, and strawberry jam, and the flowers they saw along the drive, and the comfort of the Eltons' carriage, and the sight of Box Hill towering over the Surrey landscape. The other three occupants of the comfortable carriage did not make much effort to stop the river of words. Mrs Elton made a couple of attempts, but even her determination was no match for Aunt Bates's energetic observations.

Everyone in the carriage, however, had to exclaim with delight once they started the ascent on the winding road that would take them up Box Hill, and the exclamations became more fervent once they alighted and got their first look at the views from the top. The view was spectacular. The Surrey hills undulated below them in gentle green waves, and, being on the tallest hill, one could see for miles and miles.

"I see why everyone makes such a fuss about coming to Box Hill," Jane heard Mr Churchill's voice before she saw him. He was standing with Miss Woodhouse and Miss Smith, not terribly far away, but not close enough for her to assume that he was deliberately speaking for her benefit, while seemingly talking to someone else. It had been a trick he had employed frequently over the past several months.

"Indeed!" Miss Woodhouse replied. "I feel like we can see to the ends of the earth!"

"I suppose I do feel a little as though I am looking at the end of the world," he agreed. Jane had to believe that comment was indeed meant for her.

He did not, however, say more than the briefest greeting to her and Aunt Bates as he strolled past with Miss Woodhouse and Miss Smith. Mr Knightley, however, could not be persuaded from going away after he had greeted them. "We were all so distressed by your sudden departure yesterday afternoon," he told her with a concerned frown. As opposed to his disapproving frown, or his thoughtful frown, or his other frowns. All she could think of while he talked was that he frowned a lot. "I do wish you would have let me know you wished to leave. I would have sent a servant with you. Really, Miss Fairfax, it is not safe for you to be walking about alone. After the event with Miss Smith and Miss Bickerton-"

Jane had been thrilled by Mr Churchill's heroism in rescuing the two frightened girls, but now she wondered how much danger they had really been in. The gypsies were not armed, they were desperately poor, they were apparently mostly children. What were they going to do to two young ladies who were out for a walk? They ran away frightened – of what? Of the begging? Of their need for a bath? Of their numbers? Jane had a few questions.

"As you see, Mr Knightley, I made it home quite safely. No harm came to me," she answered him.

As if in penance for perceived neglect, however, Mr Knightley determinedly squired her and Aunt Bates around the top of Box Hill, talking gravely about the beauty before their eyes, when Aunt Bates let him get a word in. Jane gave up trying to discourage him. At least for the day. The group had splintered into small parties. Mr Churchill was walking with Miss Woodhouse and Miss Smith, and Jane could not tell whether or not he was trying to avoid her. The Eltons were walking together, and Jane was trying to avoid them. That left Mr Weston. She tried to entice him to come and walk with them, but his energies were engaged in trying to corral all members of the party into a more cohesive group. His cheerful entreaties were not enough to conquer the disinclinations of the various members to all walk together.

As awful as it was to walk around with Aunt Bates and Mr Knightley, things were infinitely worse when they all sat down together with the cold collation that had been supplied by the combined planning of Mr Weston and Miss Woodhouse.

Whereas in the past Mr Churchill would be trying to catch her eye, and finding a way to sit near her, now he hardly glanced her way while he flirted with Miss Woodhouse. "How much I am obliged to you for telling me to come today! If it had not been for you, I should certainly have lost all the happiness of this party. I had quite determined to go away again."

Well, at least he was still talking to Jane while talking to others.

The two of them sat, giggling and talking, while everyone else sat around, listening to them while they picked at their food. While food usually gave her mouth a different occupation than talking, even Aunt Bates had absorbed the general mood, and sat, eating little, watching the others, looking at the scenery, and saying nothing.

Jane's first hint that Mr Churchill wanted to talk to her, possibly to make up with her, came when he stood up and announced that Miss Woodhouse ordered him to say that she desired to know what everyone was thinking.

Was he still using Miss Woodhouse? Jane felt a little sorry for her, if he was. On the other hand, if this flirtation right in front of her was his signal to her that she was dismissed from his affections and he was going to start pursuing Miss Woodhouse, instead, Jane supposed she still felt sorry for her. Mr Churchill had toyed with her in the past, and was either toying her still, or was toying with Jane now. Perhaps any woman who was willing to accept Mr Frank Churchill was doing so at her own risk.

Everyone else was reacting to his announcement. Aunt Bates was wondering out loud about what she might be thinking, Mrs Elton was muttering – mostly to her husband – about the fact that Mr Churchill had said that Miss Woodhouse was presiding over the party, not her. Mr Weston and Mr Elton merely laughed. Beside her, Mr Knightley answered loudly enough to be heard above everyone else, "Is Miss Woodhouse sure that she would like to hear what we are all thinking of?"

Jane wondered if it was a warning, or more of his usual bad manners. Although, strategically, she realized, it gave Miss Woodhouse a way out of the awkward position Mr Churchill had just put her in.

"Oh! No, no," she laughed, "Upon no account in the world. It is the very last thing I would stand the brunt of just now. Let me hear anything rather than what you are all thinking of. I will not say quite all. There are one or two, perhaps," she continued, glancing at Miss Smith and Mr Weston, "whose thoughts I might not be afraid of knowing."

Jane could see Mr Churchill was determined to break the sullen mood of the party. She wondered if he was also trying to get her to say something, anything. The only words they had exchanged thus far were the initial greetings. "Ladies and gentlemen, I am ordered by Miss Woodhouse to say, that she waives her right of knowing exactly what you may all be thinking of, and only requires something very entertaining from each of you, in a general way. Here are seven of you, besides myself (who, she is pleased to say, am very entertaining already) and she only demands from each of you either one thing very clever, be it prose or verse, original or repeated, or two things moderately clever, or three things very dull indeed, and she engages to laugh heartily at them all."

"Oh! Very well," Aunt Bates spoke up immediately. "Then I need not be uneasy. Three things very dull indeed. That will just do for me, you know. I shall be sure to say three dull things as soon as ever I open my mouth, shan't I?" She looked around. "Do you not all think I shall?"

"Ah! Ma'am, but there may be a difficulty. Pardon me, but you will be limited as to number. Only three at once," said Miss Woodhouse.

CHAPTER TWELVE

Jane was willing to say that Miss Woodhouse's words were meant to be teasing. She certainly would not say that Miss Woodhouse's observation was wrong. But she did think that the jest was not merely in poor taste; it was cruel.

It took her aunt a bit longer to figure out that she had been cut in a rather humiliating way. Jane hoped for a moment that she would not figure it out. But then a blush spread over her face. "Ah! Well, to be sure. Yes, I see what she means." She turned to look at Mr Knightley, who also blushed when Aunt Bates looked at him. "I will try to hold my tongue. I must make myself very disagreeable, or she would not have said such a thing to an old friend."

'Old friend,' indeed! Jane studied her own hands in her lap, unable to look at anyone in the party. She was trying to decide whether or not she despised everyone there. Miss Woodhouse was certainly despicable for being so cruel to a harmless silly old woman. But she was also not wrong. Her aunt was disagreeable in that she could not stop talking after saying only three very dull things. She could talk all day long without stopping, and never say one thing that did not qualify as dull. She despised having a silly creature for an aunt, instead of a woman of intellect and understanding whom people would respect.

She despised Mr Knightley for being a cranky boor who had an estate, but no idea what was required of him as a gentleman. Somehow, a gentleman should have been able to stop such an insult from being said in the first place. Jane knew that was not fair, but she despised Mr Knightley anyway.

She despised Mrs Elton for being…Mrs Elton. She despised Mr Elton for having married the awful woman and bringing her to Highbury. If he had not married her, she would not be in Highbury, making the village such an awful place to be. Staying with her grandmother would have been much less onerous without Mrs Elton. She despised Miss Smith for being pretty, and stupid. A smarter friend might have stopped things from getting to this stage. As for Mr Weston…she could not think of any reason to despise Mr Weston, except he was Mr Churchill's father, and she despised Mr Churchill. Mr Churchill, who had thought he could enliven the party by flirting very loudly with Miss Woodhouse and instigating this game which led to the insult to her aunt.

Mr Weston did not even realize an insult had been given, and cheerfully played his game first, a conundrum that turned into a compliment for Miss Woodhouse. So, Jane did have a reason to despise him, after all.

Miss Woodhouse laughed, as did Mr Churchill and Miss Smith. The rest of the party simply looked on. Mr Knightley frowned at their laughter – of course – and observed critically, "This explains the sort of clever thing that is wanted, and Mr Weston has done very well for himself. But he must have knocked up everybody else. Perfection should not have come quite so soon." Jane felt the smallest bit of appreciation for his bad manners, this time. Giving Miss Woodhouse compliments seemed an inappropriate reward at this particular moment.

Mrs Elton, of course, was in a perfect snit because Miss Woodhouse was getting all the attention, not her, and started protesting profusely. If she was expected to give a compliment to Miss Woodhouse, this was going to be absolutely and completely unsupportable! After making sure to list past experiences when she was the recipient of compliments, not the giver, she continued, "Miss Woodhouse must excuse me. I am not one of those who have witty things at everybody's service. I do not pretend to be a wit. I have a great deal of vivacity in my own way, but I really must be allowed to judge when to speak and when to hold my tongue." Jane gave a mental snort at that. Was Mrs Elton capable of holding her tongue? She rather doubted it.

Jane unfolded and refolded her hands in her lap and squeezed them together when Mrs Elton continued, "Pass us, if you please,

Mr Churchill. Pass Mr E, Knightley, Jane, and myself. We have nothing clever to say. Not one of us." Jane wondered how many insults were contained in those short sentences. Next to her, she heard Mr Knightley take a breath, and she knew he was every bit as irritated and insulted as she was. It was odd to be in agreement with him on anything, whatsoever.

Mr Elton stood up and invited Mrs Elton to resume walking. She joined him, then gestured to her. "Come, Jane, take my other arm."

As if there was any power on earth that would persuade her to do so! Mrs Elton spoke to her almost as if she was calling a dog to heel. With difficulty, Jane managed to say, "I am content where I am, Mrs Elton, thank you."

The rest of the group watched the couple walk away. "Happy couple! How well they suit one another!" Mr Churchill exclaimed. "Very lucky, marrying as they did, upon an acquaintance formed only in a public place! They only knew each other, I think, a few weeks in Bath!" Jane did not need to look up from her hands to know he was looking at her, not the Eltons, as he continued, "for as to any real knowledge of a person's disposition that Bath, or any public place, can give – it is all nothing. There can be no knowledge. It is only by seeing women in their own homes, among their own set, just as they always are, that you can form any just judgment. Short of that, it is all guess and luck; and will generally be ill luck. How many a man has committed himself on a short acquaintance, and rued it all the rest of his life!"

So, that was where they stood. Mr Churchill had just told her that their engagement was over, and he was simply glad they had not been married soon after meeting in Weymouth, the way that the Eltons were married soon after they had met in Bath. She was going to have to respond. She took a breath.

"Such things do occur, undoubtedly," she was cut off by a cough.

When she stopped, Mr Churchill made sure no one else started talking, to interrupt her answer. "You were speaking."

She looked up at him. "I was only going to observe, that though such unfortunate circumstances do sometimes occur both to men and women, I cannot imagine them to be very frequent. A hasty and imprudent attachment may arise – but there is generally time to recover from it afterwards. I would be understood to mean, that it can be only weak, irresolute characters, whose happiness must be always at the mercy of chance, who will suffer an unfortunate acquaintance to be an inconvenience, an oppression forever."

There. She had given her answer. He bowed. "Well, I have so little confidence in my own judgment, that whenever I marry, I hope somebody will choose my wife for me." He turned to Miss Woodhouse. "Will you choose my wife for me? I am sure I should like anybody fixed on by you. You provide for the family, you know." He smiled at his father. "Find somebody for me. I am in no hurry. Adopt her, educate her."

"And make her like myself?" Miss Woodhouse asked.

"By all means, if you can."

"Very well. I undertake the commission. You shall have a charming wife."

"She must be very lively, and have hazel eyes. I care for nothing else. I shall go abroad for a couple of years, and when I return, I shall come to you for my wife. Remember."

Jane was back to looking at her hands – with her dark brown eyes. Well, that was it. Their engagement was well and truly broken. All these months of delay, the deceptions, the fears and the exhilarations, were over. All for nothing. Well, she knew more now than when she woke up this morning. Now she had to pick up the pieces and rebuild her life.

Might as well make a start of it, right away. "Now, ma'am," she stood up and offered a hand to her aunt. "Shall we join Mrs Elton?"

The pathetic, grateful smile her aunt gave her was a little heart-breaking. "If you please, my dear. With all my heart. I am quite ready. I was ready to have gone with her," Jane was sorry she had not tried to rescue her humiliated aunt earlier. But, she had needed to stay to see things through. To the end. "But this will do just as well. We shall soon overtake her."

They walked away with long strides, equally eager to quit the party. Aunt Bates pointed out someone walking in the distance, thinking it was Mrs Elton, but she was mistaken. Jane was not particularly eager to find the Eltons, but felt a little more so only moments later when Mr Knightley joined them. "Shall we continue our explorations where we left off?" he asked, with something vaguely like a smile on his face. "Or are you more concerned with finding Mr and Mrs Elton?"

"Oh, you needn't feel that you must walk with us, if there are others in the party you would rather be with," Aunt Bates answered pitifully. "I know what an irksome creature I am. Poor Miss Woodhouse always shows such forbearance, extending invitations to me and Mother and Jane! Oh, how many times in a month do you suppose she has extended invitations that she wished she had not! She is the soul of generosity." Aunt Bates was clearly listing in her own head how many times Miss Woodhouse had extended some form of kindness or other towards her and her family. She gripped Jane's arm. "And Mr Woodhouse, too! So many evenings he has spent with Grandmama, Jane. He would send the carriage to collect us, and we had our merriment while he spent the evening with her! We have been such a burden to the Woodhouses, and they have been so patient and forbearing."

"Nay, Miss Bates!" Mr Knightley contradicted her firmly. "You underestimate the bonds of friendship. It is no burden for Mr Woodhouse to spend an evening with Mrs Bates. Your mother and Emma's father are very old friends. They both take great delight and comfort in spending their evenings together. They both prefer cards to dancing, and a little basin of gruel to an evening's supper, and a warm fire to the chills and damps of the out-of-doors."

"Oh, but Mr Knightley! I have been forever receiving such attentions from Miss Woodhouse – and her father – that go well beyond the dues of friendship. Why, just this year! The ball at The Crown, the dinner parties, the hind-quarter of pork! So much generosity, so much forbearance! And me, I repay her kindness with so much dullness. She really is a most excellent creature."

Mr Knightley opened his mouth to try again to soothe Aunt Bates's feelings, but was interrupted by the arrival of Mr and Mrs Elton. "Ah, there you all are! For shame, Knightley, keeping Jane from us! But, since you are all gathered together, you save us the trouble of having to deliver more than one invitation. Mr E and I were talking, and we have hit upon a most delightful plan! After we get back to Highbury, you must all spend your evening with us!"

"After we have already spent most of the day with you?" Mr

Knightley asked. "I should think you have other things to which you need to put your energies. I certainly do. Thank you for your kind invitation, Mrs Elton, but I shall beg off."

"Nay, I positively must have you all come!" Mrs Elton was not to be so easily put off. "I shall not let you off, Knightley. Bachelors should never turn down invitations. We shall have such a nice time, but it won't be nearly as nice if you are not with us."

Jane kept her eyes focused on the hills, and silently hoped Mr Knightley would continue to refuse. Aunt Bates did not need any more of his inept attempts to cheer her by telling her she was wrong to feel humiliated by Miss Woodhouse's cruelty. She could not decide whether he was acting from an attempt at kindness, or if it was his way of defending the Woodhouses, since he was so intimate with them. Or, was he not yet done with trying to ingratiate himself with her? Well, there was one way to find out.

"My aunt and I would be happy to accept your kind invitation, Mrs Elton," she answered. "Unmarried ladies should no more turn down invitations than bachelors, don't you think?" There. If Mr Knightley showed up at the Vicarage, then he was not done with her. If he did not show up, he had taken her hints and she had nothing to fear from him. Then her face fell with realization. "Oh, dear."

"What is it, Jane?" Both Mrs Elton and Aunt Bates asked her at once.

"Grandmama has been with Mrs Goddard for the day, but we cannot expect her to visit all this evening, as well. Mrs Goddard has her own interests she will need to tend to." She shook her head with something like honest regret. "Thank you for your invitation, Mrs Elton, but we cannot join you."

"I cannot believe you would assume my invitation did not include Mrs Bates!" Mrs Elton exclaimed. "Of course I insist you should bring her as well. Our evening party could hardly be complete without her!"

"Are you so sure you wish to have us, Mrs Elton?" Aunt Bates asked, a little wistfully. "After such an excursion as this, you must surely be tired of our company. We can stay home as we ought, after we collect Mother from Mrs Goddard's."

"I shall no more allow you to put me off than Knightley!" Mrs Elton exclaimed. "The lot of you are coming to spend the evening.

I am completely determined to have my way in this, and you all know me well enough to know that when I am determined to do a thing, it is useless to resist me. We shall have a most excellent evening together." She looked up, and saw the servants waving from the top of the hill.

"Look, the carriages are on the way. Mine shall be first, so we should hasten ourselves to be sure we are ready to be collected. I do hope you have had your fill of the fine views of Box Hill. I am sure we have had our fill, enough to last quite some time! It is not as fine as the views to be had around Maple Grove, to be sure! I profess myself rather disappointed. I was expecting something much more sublime, after everything people always say about Box Hill! But of course I am not one to complain. Travel is always broadening, I always say, and now I know what it is people are speaking of when they talk of Box Hill."

While she talked, Mrs Elton had taken Jane by the arm, and firmly guided her to where she could see the carriages pulling in. Since Mr Elton had Miss Bates in a similar grip, Mr Knightley's services were not needed as an escort. He excused himself with a curt bow, and strode off with a much longer step than the rest of their party could take with Aunt Bates's short legs. Jane watched him walk away. There was something in his posture that indicated displeasure, and for some reason she found herself wondering which of the many possible options he was displeased about.

Her rational mind forced her to ask; could she get over her dislike of him? Marrying Mr Knightley would have more social and economic advantages than becoming a governess. She gave a small, involuntary shudder. Would the advantages outweigh the horrors of being married to a man who was the exact opposite of Mr Frank Churchill? Perpetually grumpy, instead of perpetually cheerful. Critical, instead of supportive. Never remembering what is expected of a gentleman, instead of always knowing and doing what is expected of a gentleman.

It made the awkward, awful isolation of being a governess seem less terrible. Once the four of them were seated in the carriage and started back to Highbury, Jane looked at Mrs Elton, and took a deep breath. "I don't suppose, Mrs Elton, you brought that letter from your cousin with you?"

CHAPTER THIRTEEN

It was, surprisingly, 'a very good letter.' The family's name was Smallridge. Mrs Suckling wrote in the warmest, most affectionate terms about them. Jane would be in charge of three small girls, and Mrs Suckling assured her they were all amiable, well-behaved creatures. Mrs Smallridge was excited by Jane's musical gifts, and offered a very generous salary with the respectful request that she impart her knowledge to the girls. The grand pianoforte in the drawing room was at her disposal as often as she wished the use of it.

Jane merely nodded after reading the letter, but refused to commit herself on the carriage ride home. "Surely you understand I wish to think about this a little, first, Mrs Elton," she said in response to the lady's persistent requests to write a response at once. "She wants someone to start within a fortnight, and you know I had my heart set on seeing the Campbells before I embark upon any position. I would have to forfeit my dearest wish in order to accept this offer."

Aunt Bates and Mr Elton were both asleep in the carriage by now, and Jane discouraged any further conversation on the drive by showing a disinclination to waking them up.

Home again at last, she asked Aunt Bates to go alone to fetch Grandmama so that she could lie down. For once, it was not a lie when she claimed a headache. Behind the closed door, she buried her face in her pillow, and cried.

The future she had known about all her life had come for her at last. Earlier she had compared being a governess to the slave trade; that was unjust of her. The misery of her life did not compare to the miseries of being a slave. A slave was a human being who had been captured and was then sold, and someone else collected the money. She was the one doing the selling, and she would be the one to command the wages that were given to her. So, in truth, what she was doing was a form of intellectual... prostitution. Harlots sold their bodies for money. She was selling her mind.

Well, what was marriage, if she was really, brutally honest? Was that not also the sale of women's bodies? Perhaps, but the dowry a bride brought with her kept matters a little more equal. If she looked at the Eltons, it was unthinkable to say that Mrs Elton was bought or sold. If anything, Mrs Elton was the one doing the buying. She wondered how many other suitors Miss Hawkins had had. Were other men attracted to the money? Were other men repulsed by the personality? Were other men willing to put up with the one, in pursuit of the other? Jane laughed in the middle of crying to think that, if she were to marry Mr Knightley, she would be in the same position as Mr Elton.

While Mr Churchill had pointed out at the strawberry picking party how well suited the Eltons were for each other, Jane had to wonder. She detected some amount of self-satisfaction in Mr Elton that he had managed to acquire an heiress; she did not detect a great deal of happiness emanating from him. If Mrs Elton was willing to say, in company, so many times, that she did not hold it against him that she had given up so many comforts and luxuries in order to marry Mr Elton, how many times in private did she upbraid him for the loss of comforts and luxuries?

She would happily have spent the entire night alone in her room, giving vent to all the tears she had been accumulating over the last few days. But the luxury of time to think was a privilege of the monied classes. As Mr Frank Churchill's betrothed, she could presume a life of luxuries. That was no longer the case. She was alone, but not friendless. She needed to take stock of her situation, evaluate her resources, and do what needed to be done.

When she dressed for the evening, her mirror told her no lies. She looked very ill. A little water splashed on her face could not hide the red eyes. She dressed her hair simply, not caring enough to bother to heat the curling tongs. Governesses were not seen in public enough to bother with dressing for dinner, or for evenings out with respectable friends. She should use these last opportunities to their advantage, but she could not bring herself to take the trouble.

The carriage was at the door in a timely fashion, and the three generations of Bates women were delivered at the Vicarage. Walking inside, Jane felt as though she was walking up the scaffold to her execution. That was not right. Her fate was not fixed yet. If Mr Knightley was there tonight, perhaps she could mend that fence and marry a man she despised. It was still an option. So it was more like she was a prisoner during the trial. Either she would be sentenced to death, or sentenced to deportation. The judge had not declared what her sentence would be yet.

Jane felt like a sleepwalker. She smiled, she walked, she helped her grandmother to a seat by the fire. She sat. People around her moved their mouths. There were sounds. She forced herself to listen, to force the sounds into words.

"Still no sign of Knightley! I declare to you, I am most displeased with him! Most displeased, indeed! I am not in the habit of being disappointed. And here I thought that everyone in Highbury was so welcoming, so very observant of those niceties that are due to a bride! But then, I suppose, Knightley is so very intimate with the Woodhouses. Mr Woodhouse never did come to call when I first came to Highbury. I had to pay a call to Hartfield for him to give me those attentions that are due to me! So for Miss Woodhouse to usurp my place today, it only stands to reason for the father to impart his lack of manners to the daughter."

Jane speculated that if Mr Knightley meant to come, he would not be late. He had told Mrs Elton that he did not intend to come. Apparently the information that Jane would be there did not change his mind. On the other hand, he was late plenty of other times to other social gatherings on account of his managers, or his tenants, or other things. Well, if they were more of an enticement than she was, she could count herself fortunate that she would not have to make that unpleasant choice.

It appeared that marrying Mr Knightley was not one of Jane's options. Mr Elton was summoned out of the room, there was more talking. Jane did not bother trying to turn the sounds into words while she examined her heart. No, she was not sorry she did not have to try to convince herself to accept Mr Knightley. The process of trying to repair the damage done by her discouragement sounded worse than the idea of marrying him; it was, somehow, even more dishonest.

Mr Elton returned to the room. There were a lot of sounds emanating from him. The two words, "Frank Churchill," shook her out of her stupor, and forced her back to listening.

"That's what John the ostler said. He said that Tom said that the servants at Randalls said that Mr Churchill had sent Mr Frank Churchill a note concerning Mrs Churchill, which arrived soon after he returned from Box Hill, and he immediately sent for his horse. But the horse seems to have caught a cold, so Mr Frank Churchill sent to The Crown to hire the chaise. Mrs Weston's maid said that the letter gave a tolerable account of Mrs Churchill's health, and Mr and Mrs Weston were extremely puzzled that Frank Churchill insisted on leaving immediately, even though the letter said he need not leave until tomorrow morning. There was no need to leave with such haste."

Jane knew the reason for all the hurry. Mr Churchill wanted to get as far away from here – and her – as possible. He was finished with her, and he was finished with Highbury. He had managed to avoid Highbury for so many years, until he needed to use his connections to be able to be close to her. Now that their association was over, he no longer needed to maintain the ties. He could go back to the luxuries his aunt and uncle provided.

Automatically, she held out a hand to accept the cup of tea that was offered to her. He was gone. She shook her head when someone tried to hand her a plate of cake. It was really and truly over. She knew it was over, but his departure felt like the final nail in the coffin. She was climbing the scaffold, looking at the noose before her hanging.

During the shuffle when the tea things were cleared away and the card table was set up, she pulled Mrs Elton aside. "Mrs Elton," she had to take her hand off of Mrs Elton's arm, because her hands were shaking so badly. She clasped them behind her back. "Thank you for giving me the time to reflect. You have convinced me that the situation you have found for me is truly too ideal of an opportunity for me to decline. Would you please write your letter on my behalf, accepting the position with Mrs Smallridge?"

CHAPTER FOURTEEN

It was done.

Mrs Elton's elation was unbearable. Aunt Bates's confusion when Mrs Elton immediately went to congratulate her for Jane's decision, before Jane could sit down to tell her aunt the news herself, was almost equally awful. She had just agreed to sell her brain, the way a harlot sells her body, and the Eltons were congratulating her. The vicar of Highbury and his wife, approving of her selling herself like a whore! They were the ones to arrange for Jane to sell herself. There were words for that, too. Not generally words considered moral by the church.

Jane insisted that her aunt and grandmother played cards with the Eltons, while she sat watching, wallowing in her misery. She tried not to listen to Mrs Elton's endless prattle about first circles and wax candles in the schoolroom, which finally stopped at a stern admonition from Mr Elton that she was neglecting the game.

She tried to focus her thoughts on Colonel Campbell. There was no man in England so upright and respectable as he was: he was the one who educated her to be an educator. He picked out her future as a governess out of love and the desire to give her the best future possible. It was not immoral. Nor improper. He would never have planned for anything disgraceful. While she would be isolated, she would be well provided for. She would have a good roof over her head and an income. She would have a much larger income than her aunt and grandmother did, and fewer expenses. She would be able to send a large portion of it back to Highbury, and make the two elderly ladies' lives more comfortable. It would be good to have them less dependent upon the charity of the neighbors.

As much as Jane despised the majority of them, she had to admit they were generous and kind to her relations. And to her, too. Even Mrs Elton, as unpleasant as her company was, had kind-hearted motives. Well, her motives weren't kind. She wanted attention, and she wanted it at any cost. But the outcomes were kind. The long-abandoned plan to form a musical society would have benefitted the local society. Perhaps it would even have improved the quality of everyone's playing, since the ladies who would have been expected to exhibit would no doubt have felt pressured to practice more beforehand. Her insistence upon sending the Eltons' carriage to bring Jane's family to various parties seemed like an act of control on her part, but it was also an act of generosity. Then of course, there were the energies she had put into looking for a situation for her. She hated being beholden to Mrs Elton, but it was an extremely generous salary. If Jane had merely put in her application in London, she might not have found its equal.

She could not bear to think of her upcoming exile anymore, and her mind drifted to thoughts of Mr Churchill. The hands, the cards, the table in front of her became blurry and hard to see. She quietly got up to take a turn about the room. She absolutely could not cry in front of them. She absolutely could not think about him until she was alone. She missed him too much; the pain was too great.

When she was able to master herself, she sat next to her grandmother, who showed her the cards she was holding. She really was a dear old lady. Jane realized she had wasted an opportunity during her long visit: she should have asked more questions. What was her grandfather like? How did they get engaged? What stories were there of the days when she was living here in the Vicarage? She had avoided asking anything about it, assuming it would be painful to talk about the old days when life was more comfortable. But perhaps that was wrong. Perhaps Grandmama would have enjoyed reminiscing, telling stories of when she was the bride, not Mrs Elton.

At long last, the evening was over, the carriage was called for, and they were able to go home.

There was nothing but a stunned silence in the carriage for a moment, before Aunt Bates found her voice. "I confess I am breathless at this news! You have been saying for months you did not want to find a position until after Colonel and Mrs Campbell returned from Ireland. Are they not going to be exceedingly sorry to find you have engaged yourself before their return?"

Engaged. What a very unfortunate choice of words. Jane had to clench her teeth together a moment before she could answer. "I am very sure they will. But yet, this is such an advantageous situation, I cannot feel myself justified in declining. I am delighted and happy to have been able to secure such a position."

"But we are going to miss you so very much, my dear," her grandmother said, patting her hand.

"I know, Grandmama." Jane tried to smile. "But we should be thankful for having had such a long visit before I started. It is so much more time than we ever thought we would have."

Aunt Bates was perceptive enough to tell Jane to go to bed once they got home; she would see to Grandmama. Jane did not argue. Aunt Bates undid the buttons on the back of her dress for her, and Jane was able to close the door on the world and be alone.

The tears started the moment the latch on the door clicked shut. She put both hands over her mouth to stifle the sound of her sobs, and she ran to throw herself face down on the bed. Mr Churchill. She could say his name inside her head now. She buried her face in the pillow and let out a sound that was somewhere between a moan and a scream.

There was so much to love about him. His endlessly cheerful, optimistic, sunny disposition. His wit. His intelligence, which was different than wit. Miss Woodhouse could be witty (albeit at the expense of others' feelings), but Jane would not call her very intelligent. Mr Churchill was intelligent, well-read, a man who knew both poetry and the news of the day. He would have been able to hold up his part of the conversation at the Campbell dinner table.

He was so handsome. He made her heart flutter every time she looked at him. He made her heart flutter even more when he was looking at her. That look of love, of admiration, of joy in knowing that, someday, they would be man and wife. He had a smile that lit up his eyes. His laugh was infectious: it made everyone who heard it a little bit happier in that moment.

He was so romantic. No novel could capture the thrill of his letters. Or the feeling when they had a moment alone, and his arms or lips eagerly found her. Even the secrecy of their engagement had been romantic, in a way. As terrifying as the secret was; the clandestine passing touch of hands, the messages buried within conversations in public with others, the meaning in their eyes when they looked at each other with a special understanding; it was in itself the stuff of a romance. No conventional engagement, all proper and aboveboard from the beginning, could match the romance of the meaning in the knots on the ends of the ribbons of her bonnet.

Jane moaned again. She would have to untie those knots, and iron out the creases. That is, if they would come out. They might not - they had been there for months, now. Well, she could always just cut them off.

When the first light began showing through the window, and she realized that she had cried all night long, she got up and changed out of her gown from the night before.

Dressing herself in a front closing gown she could pin herself into, so she did not need to wake anyone, she gathered her ink, quill, and paper, and sat herself at the table in the drawing room. Even though their engagement had been secret, she knew what she had to do. The formalities, still, had to be observed.

Dear Mr Churchill,

While we both have our share of difficulties in fulfilling our obligations to our families, those difficulties would seem to prove to be insurmountable.

In light of recent events, I feel that our engagement has been a source of repentance and misery to each of us. With the assumption that my understanding is correct, I am writing to you to dissolve it.

Please write to tell me if I am mistaken in my apprehension of our relative situations.

Your obedient servant,
J. Fairfax

There. The words were on paper.

In a way, it was the easiest of the letters she needed to write. She wished she had confided in Sophia and Colonel and Mrs Campbell from the start. They would have sympathized, cried with her, offered both comfort and counsel. Perhaps she would tell Sophia everything someday, but for now, at least, she should send word that a very good position was now hers, and in a fortnight, she would be starting her new life.

It was hard to sound cheerful and grateful. She thanked Colonel Campbell with all due honesty and gratitude, and painted as good a picture of the position as had been presented to her. But she had to be careful not to ruin her letters with the tears that occasionally dripped from her face. She had to get up to find a new handkerchief between her letter to the Colonel and her letter to Sophia.

"Oh! My dear, you will blind yourself, writing and crying at the same time," Aunt Bates exclaimed when she came into the drawing room and found her there. "Have you already been to the post-office? Is there bad news?"

Jane sat back in her chair, sniffed violently to try to control her running nose, then gave up and used her handkerchief to mop everything wet on her face. "Need I list all the bad news? I am leaving you and Grandmama in a fortnight. Who knows when I will be able to see you again? I am writing the Campbells to let them know I cannot wait until they get back from Ireland. When will I ever see them again, since I won't get to see them now?"

"Oh, bless me, I had not thought of that. I don't suppose we will see you again until the children are very much grown up." Tears began to form in Aunt Bates's eyes. "Mrs Weston was with Miss Woodhouse until very recently. Governesses don't always stay with their pupils until they are twenty one, do they? Oh, dear, oh dear. How old is the youngest of your charges?"

"Three," Jane answered. "And of course, Mrs Smallridge could still have more children. If the position is a good one, and they like me, I could potentially be there for twenty years."

The two women stared at each other. "Bless me, I had not thought of that. Grandmama might never see you again, once you leave us."

"If she were to get sick, and they are kind people, I might be able to get leave to travel back for a short visit," Jane answered.

"But I will be their servant, and I will have no liberty to come and go as I please."

"Oh, dear," Aunt Bates hurried forward to put her arms around Jane. "I was thinking that parting with you now is really not any worse than all the years you've been with the Campbells. But this really is a great deal different, is it not?"

"It is a world of difference," Jane answered. "I am not leaving to be the bosom companion of a gentleman's daughter. Or, if you will, the adopted daughter of a gentleman. I am leaving to become the governess of a gentleman's children. I will be a gentleman's servant."

"I had not thought about that," Aunt Bates repeated. "It has been so lovely with you here, I was thinking how difficult it is going to be to part with you after having you for so long."

They both turned at the sound of noise from Grandmama's room. Out of habit, Jane made to get up. "You stay and finish your letters, I will tend to Grandmama," Aunt Bates told her. Jane would have protested, but she knew she was in no condition to be of much use to anyone, so she acquiesced.

She was just sealing her letters when Patty brought in the tea from one door, and Aunt Bates and Grandmama came in from another. She realized from the concerned way all three of them stared at her, she could not be seen in public in her current state. "Could you please take these to the post-office for me, Patty?" she asked. It was something of a risk entrusting someone else with a letter to Mr Churchill, but Patty was illiterate. As long as she did not show them to anyone along the way, no one would know she was writing to a single gentleman.

"I will take them right away, ma'am," Patty said, as Jane handed her the finished letters. She hurried out of the room.

"Are you quite well, Jane?" Grandmama asked. "You do not look well."

"Do not worry about me, Grandmama. I am well." She paced the room, looking out the window as Patty hurried up the street, looking at the pictures on the walls of the room that had become very familiar over these last months of waiting.

"Are you sure? You do not look well." Grandmama looked at Aunt Bates. "She does not look well. She looks quite ill."

"Oh, dear Jane is quite well, I assure you. She is dreading her departure from us, you know. So soon, it is a bit of a shock. For all of us. She will be leaving us within a fortnight."

"That soon?" It was awful for Jane to hear the grief in her grandmother's voice. "How are we going to bear parting with her with so little notice?"

"Do not let us think about it any more," Aunt Bates answered. "We can think about it later, after Jane is gone. She is still with us for now. This is not the time for us to be sorry that she is leaving us. We should make the most of our last few days together."

Jane stopped pacing in front of the pianoforte. She had loved that pianoforte like she had never loved a musical instrument before. Never mind the stir it had created among the neighbors: it was the most overwhelming gift of love she could ever imagine. One more demonstration that Mr Churchill was the most romantic man that ever lived.

It used to be a symbol of his love for her. What did it stand for now? A broken heart? Shattered dreams? She ran her fingers sadly over the beautiful wooden inlays. "You must go," she told it. "You and I must part. You will have no business here." She realized her aunt and grandmother were watching her. "Let it stay, however, until Colonel Campbell comes back. I shall talk about it to him. He will settle for me, he will help me out of all my difficulties."

She had no idea what she was going to say to Colonel Campbell, but she was going to need his help. She could not afford to move the pianoforte, and yet it had no business staying in her grandmother's drawing room. She would have to confess every-thing to Colonel Campbell, or to Sophia. They might be able to help her sell it, and the money would be dearly welcome in the little household. Her heart sank. It did not feel right. She would have to find a way to talk to Mr Churchill, to have him take the gift back. If he could spread the lie that the gift was from Colonel Campbell, he could find a way to retrieve the instrument and keep the story intact.

Her eyes focused on the sheet music on the top of the stack. It was 'Robin Adair.' Grief, anger, frustration and hopelessness washed over her. With a wail, she reached out, and swept the entire stack of music onto the floor. Then she sank down among the pages, sobbing.

The demonstration would have been quite enough to alarm the

two old ladies staring at her, but then they heard the voices at the bottom of the stairs. The three of them stared at each other.

"It is only Mrs Cole," Aunt Bates assured her, coming to start collecting up the scattered sheet music. "Depend upon it. Nobody else would come so early."

Jane hastily wiped her handkerchief across her face, and began helping. "Well, it must be borne some time or other, and it may as well be now."

Patty opened the door. "Miss Woodhouse is here to see you."

Jane scrambled to her feet, dropping some of the gathered music in her haste, which fluttered all over the drawing room floor.

"Oh, dear, oh dear," Aunt Bates murmured as she chased the errant pages. "We should hurry and pick these up. Patty, do tell Miss Woodhouse I hope she will be pleased to wait a moment."

"We can put these in your room, Jane, for now, while we visit with Miss Woodhouse. I am sure you will like to see her."

Jane shook her head. She would have tolerated Mrs Cole, but not Miss Woodhouse. "I can see nobody."

Aunt Bates followed her as she headed for her room. "If you must go, my dear, you must. I shall say you are laid down upon the bed. I am sure you are ill enough."

"I am ill, I am sure. I am ill of spirit. But no amount of lying down will do me any good," Jane cried. She paced her small bedroom, her hands over her eyes. She had such a headache. "Go and see to your guest, Auntie. There is nothing you can do for me. I just need to be alone."

"But surely lying down will help your headache," Aunt Bates persisted. "You should not have spent the whole of the morning writing. I can see what a headache you have."

"Now that my letters are written, I shall soon be well," Jane answered patiently. "Now, please, go talk to Miss Woodhouse. I can only imagine the reason she has come to call so early this morning is to apologize for teasing you so meanly yesterday."

"Oh! I am sure Miss Woodhouse has no need to apologize to me-" Aunt Bates protested.

"Just, go, Auntie," Jane interrupted. "You don't want to be rude and keep Miss Woodhouse waiting."

The horror of being rude to Miss Woodhouse had the desired effect of hurrying Aunt Bates out of the room.

CHAPTER FIFTEEN

Jane paced the confines of her room for hours, long after she saw from her window that Miss Woodhouse had finished her visit. What an awful creature. She hoped, at least, that she had given Aunt Bates a proper apology for her insolence of the day before.

On the other hand, when Aunt Bates came back into her room to check on her, Jane admitted to herself that Miss Woodhouse was not the least bit wrong.

"Oh! Bless me, Jane, why are you still walking about? I really wish you would have come out to see Miss Woodhouse. She was very concerned for you. Such a kind person she is! She asked about you in such a concerned manner! I told her you had such a terrible headache from writing all morning, and how upset you are to be leaving us so soon. I told her I implored you to lie down upon the bed for a while, but that you were walking about the room. I told her you assured me that now that your letters are written you will soon be well. She asked about your new situation. She remembered that you had wished to delay until Colonel Campbell's return. Such a thoughtful neighbor! Miss Woodhouse is always so thoughtful. She asked where you were going, I told her all about Mrs Smallridge, and how you will only be four miles from Maple Grove. Such a comfort it will be for you to be only four miles from Maple Grove, and Mrs Elton's sister!"

Jane stopped her pacing, and covered her ears for a moment with a cry of pain. Why, on earth, would she find it comforting to be four miles from the sister of an unbearably awful woman whom she despised, but was indebted to? It made matters worse. Better to be four hundred miles removed from anyone she knew. No one could gossip about her awful reduced circumstances if no one knew anything about her.

Aunt Bates mistook her cry of agony to be coming from her headache, not her heartache. "Oh, my dear! Please, you should really lie down. I will ask Patty to bring you some tea. Would you like a cold cloth for your head? Dear me, I hate to send for Mr Perry, but I know he will come. Such sweet and generous neighbors we have! We are completely surrounded by the kindest people. Miss Woodhouse was so completely kind in asking about you. She asked all about you – about how Mrs Elton found your position for you, and how Mrs Elton was so kind to have all of us come to spend the evening with her after our pleasant excursion to Box Hill. I told her everyone seemed a bit fatigued, and I cannot say that anyone seemed very much to have enjoyed the trip. But I thought it was a very pleasant party, and feel extremely obliged that our kind friends included us in it."

Jane desperately wanted to get away from the sound of her aunt's voice. "Do not trouble Mr Perry on my account. You know we cannot afford his visit, and I cannot bear the idea of being indebted to his kindness. I think I will lie down. If you will draw the curtains, I will try to sleep for a while."

Lying down was the only way to stop the endless flow of terrible words. While she buried her face in her pillow, Aunt Bates drew the curtains and tiptoed out of the room.

The darkness and quiet closed in around her. Perhaps it was a mistake to induce her aunt to leave. Instead of the barrage of words illustrating the hopelessness of her future, Jane's imagination took up where her aunt had left off. Unfortunately, her imagination was more fertile than her aunt's tongue.

Her aunt had echoed Mrs Elton's assurances that Mrs Suckling's neighbor was an amiable woman with three charming daughters. What was the truth of the matter? Mrs Elton also thought she could play the pianoforte well, and speak Italian. The daughters would be as rich and pampered as Miss Woodhouse, and probably grow up to be every bit as privileged and arrogant. Jane knew that a child as young as three understands the concept of a pecking order. What was Mrs Smallridge's concept of discipline? When the daughters misbehaved, would she side with Jane, or the daughters? Jane had seen parents who could not grasp the idea that their angelic children could ever do anything wrong.

Jane tried to focus on the good parts of the arrangement. It really was a lot of money! She would be able to send so much back. Grandmama's last years would be comfortable, and Aunt Bates could stop relying so heavily on the charity of the thoughtful and kind neighbors. Of course, then she would have to find something else to talk about. Well, no doubt she would tell the neighbors about how generous and kind Jane was, and exactly how much money she had sent. The idea of giving out the details made Jane squirm internally, but she knew there was no getting away from that fact.

She tossed about. She wanted to get up and go play the pianoforte. But then, she did not want to touch Mr Churchill's gift. Perhaps she never wanted to touch it again. Since its arrival, it had been a symbol of his love. Beautiful to look at, exquisite to listen to, generous to a fault in its tones. Playing it had filled her soul and completed her. Touching the keys had been a thrill. Now, what did it stand for? By all rights, it should be thrown out the window and smashed to pieces.

At some point in time, she must have fallen asleep. She opened her eyes to darkness, but even the darkness seemed to stab her eyeballs. She pressed her hands over them and sobbed from the pain. This was a very different kind of headache than the ones that plagued her after the boating accident in Weymouth. This one burned, instead of throbbing. This one made her want to retch. But she had not eaten anything for a couple of days, and she knew there was nothing in her to actually throw up.

Aunt Bates came in as soon as it was light, and sat beside her, once more pressing her to eat something, to have some tea. Over and over Jane refused. When Aunt Bates's unending chatter would not let her sleep again, Jane got out of bed and walked the length of the room back and forth for what seemed like hours. It might have been minutes, it might have been days. Jane could not tell the difference.

A knock on the door admitted Patty, providing a moment's distraction from her agitation. "Here's a note from Miss Woodhouse, Miss Fairfax."

Jane waved the note away. "Tell Miss Woodhouse that I am not well enough to write."

Aunt Bates stared at her when Patty closed the door. "Oh! My dear. You who write so many letters! When you are too ill to write, you are very ill, indeed! I hate to trespass on his time, but I do believe it is time to summon Mr Perry."

"No!" Jane protested firmly. "There is nothing Mr Perry will be able to do for me. I do not consent to a visit from him. It will waste his time, and do me no good, and we will be once more beholden to your kind neighbors."

This set her loquacious aunt on a long soliloquy about the kindness and generosity of the people of Highbury. When she could not stand the endless flow of words anymore, Jane curled up on her bed, and put her hands over her ears.

Unfortunately, while this sent Aunt Bates away and gave her a brief respite from her voice, it was only to fetch Mr Perry.

"I told you I did not need to bother the good Mr Perry," Jane protested.

"Nonsense, my dear," Mr Perry did have a very soothing voice, very fitting for his profession. "Your aunt is very concerned about you." He put a hand on her forehead. "You do have a little bit of a fever. How many days have you now had this headache?"

"Three," Aunt Bates answered for her. "Or, dear me! It might be four. Bless me, the days and nights start to run together. And she hasn't had a single thing to eat in all this time. I have implored her to take a bit of something, and she refuses everything. Her appetite has dwindled away to nothing." She had been twisting her handkerchief in her hands as she talked, now she flapped it in alarm. "I hope it is not her heart. Her grandfather died of a complaint of the heart, you know. I think the poor dear is simply overwrought. She is completely overcome by the thought of leaving us."

Mr Perry held up a hand to stop the anxious flow of Aunt Bates's words. "Would you be so good as to fetch me both a hot compress, and a cold one, Miss Bates?"

"Oh, certainly, let me ring for Patty."

"No, do see to it yourself, to make sure it is just right. The hot one should not be so hot that it is scalding, and the cold one should be about as cold as one can manage at this time of year, but not so cold as ice straight from the ice house," Mr Perry instructed her.

"I see! Yes, of course, I shall make sure they are quite perfect," Aunt Bates promised, and hurried out the door.

Mr Perry smiled at Jane in the quiet. "That's better. Now, my dear, I would like to hear from you directly, did this headache start when you accepted Mrs Elton's position?"

"Yes," Jane answered reluctantly.

"And you lost your appetite at the same time?"

"Yes."

"Have you been able to sleep?"

"Not much," Jane admitted. "A little."

"But the smallest sound wakes you up, once you are able to fall asleep?"

"Yes."

"I assume your headache has not allowed you to get out of this room much, not even for a little fresh air?"

"No."

He felt her forehead again, put his fingers on her wrist to feel her pulse, asked if he could open the curtains to better look at her eyes. The sun coming in the window made her squint, but she endured his examination as patiently as she could. Since he was here, and determined to try to help her, the least she could do was not be a troublesome patient.

"Well, my dear, if this persists, you might need to see a doctor or barber-surgeon to apply some leeches. For now, try hot and cold compresses, to see if one of them helps. I will also suggest getting some lavender or rosemary to put in your pillowcase. Please try and get out of this room a little, if you can. Some fresh air and sunshine may help your spirits, as well as your head."

Jane shook her head. "I don't think I can stand to go out. Everyone will want to talk to me, which will only make my head worse." She flinched a little as Aunt Bates came back in the room, loudly proclaiming that she tried her best, but the hot compress might be either too hot or not hot enough, and the cold compress was probably not sufficiently cold.

"It will do for now," Mr Perry reassured her.

CHAPTER SIXTEEN

Predictably, once Mr Perry had left, there was a parade of concerned friends showing up at the door. Jane insisted that she could not bear to see anybody. This only made the well-intentioned matrons of the town all the more insistent that they gain entrance to her room, and sit beside her bed holding her hand and loudly exclaiming over her. Of course Aunt Bates did not have a forceful enough personality to keep Mrs Elton away, but Jane would have thought at least Aunt Bates might have held off Mrs Cole and Mrs Perry.

Jane hated knowing the entire village was gossiping about her. She owned that their concern was genuine, and their gifts of food and medicinal remedies were well-meant. Well, mostly. Miss Woodhouse sent a second message offering to pick her up in the carriage and take her anywhere she would like to go for a couple of hours. The note made it clear Mr Perry had asked her to do it, so no doubt the offer was made with the greatest of reluctance.

She told the servant who brought the invitation to give Miss Woodhouse her compliments and thanks, but she felt quite unequal to any exercise. Not to be outdone by the other women who had pushed their way into her privacy, Miss Woodhouse responded by showing up at the front door with her carriage.

It was enough to make Jane wish that, among everything else Colonel Campbell had taught her, he had taught her some curse words.

Aunt Bates went down to the carriage to greet Miss Woodhouse, and came back up to tell Jane that she implored her in the most earnest terms to come take the air with her.

"She is most concerned about your health!" Aunt Bates reported. "Indeed, she may be more alarmed for your sake than anyone else in Highbury. She is always kindness itself. Do consider- "

"I have no intention of going out!" Jane interrupted her. "And I want you to promise me, Auntie, solemnly swear, that you will not, under any circumstances, allow Miss Woodhouse to come in. I have had quite enough visitors for one day. I do not need to see any more. I want to see absolutely nobody."

"Oh! Oh, dear," Aunt Bates said unhappily. "I so hate to disappoint Miss Woodhouse. She is so anxious to see you."

"So is every other gossip in Highbury," Jane answered with some asperity. "They will have to be satisfied with the reports from the four visitors I have endured so far."

Aunt Bates reluctantly left to deliver Jane's regrets, taking so long to return that Jane had no illusions that Miss Woodhouse had been supplied with plenty of gossip to feed the hungry mill of Highbury.

A short while later, one of Miss Woodhouse's servants delivered some arrow-root from the Hartfield stores.

"See how kind Miss Woodhouse is! Here, Jane, read her note. Such a well-written, friendly note! Bless me, what a wealth of kindness we are surrounded by."

Jane angrily waved aside the slip of paper. "Send it back."

Aunt Bates looked at her with some bewilderment. "What?"

"I cannot take it. Send it back to Miss Woodhouse. Send it back, and tell her I am not at all in want of anything."

"But..."

"Send. It. Back," Jane repeated firmly.

"Oh, I shall return it to Miss Woodhouse with a thousand thanks for her thoughtfulness. Perhaps if I hurry, I can catch the servant who brought it." Aunt Bates hurried out of the room.

Alone again, Jane paced her room. How much time had passed since she had sent her letter to Mr Churchill? Enough for him to have sent an answer. She wandered out into the drawing room.

Aunt Bates was gone, but Grandmama was still there, in her favorite chair. Jane knelt in front of her.

"Grandmama, I am sorry I have been ill. I have not been going to the post-office for your letters."

She looked at her with some surprise, but then patted her hand reassuringly. "Of all the things for you to worry about! Patty has been going every day since you sent her with your letters, in case you received any answers. There has been nothing for you, yet. She goes very faithfully every day, hoping a letter will come to bring you some cheer."

Jane smiled, kissed her grandmother, and resolutely returned to her room. There was only one meaning to Mr Churchill's silence. There were no tears this time. She gathered up every letter he had ever sent her, and carefully checked to make sure every letter was included before she sealed the parcel. Then she uncapped her inkwell.

Dear Mr Churchill,

I am extremely surprised to have received not even the smallest reply to my last letter.

Silence on such a point cannot be misconstrued. It must be equally desirable to both of us to have every subordinate arrangement concluded as soon as possible, and thus, I am sending back all your letters by a safe conveyance. If you cannot directly command all of mine so as to send them to me at Highbury within a week, please send them to the enclosed address at Mrs Smallridge's, near Bristol.

Your obedient servant,
J. Fairfax

She dressed quickly, laced her shoes, grabbed her bonnet and the parcel and the letter, and nearly ran out of her room. "Patty, please keep an eye on Grandmama until I return," she called into the kitchen. As soon as Patty replied, she hurried outside, before Aunt Bates could return and ask where she was going.

She nearly ran all the way to the post-office. Once the letter and parcel were dispensed with, she found she was reluctant to go back to the confines of her room. Her feet insisted on going the opposite direction, until she had left the village, not pausing until she had found a sunny meadow.

It felt good to wander through the meadow, warmed by the sun, listening to nothing but the breeze rustling the grasses and the chirping of birds, seeing and smelling flowers and the scent of sun-warmed grasses. There were no voices, no Mrs Eltons or Miss Woodhouses or Aunt Bateses to annoy her with too much talk.

Part of her wanted to lay down in the tall grasses and sleep. There must be something a little wonderful, sometimes, about being a gypsy, living out of doors, with no walls to confine one's life and spirits. Until it rained, or until foolish young women got scared when you begged for some money to get something to eat, and you were driven away under threat of violence. She had never heard the full story from Mr Churchill.

Her heart ached at the thought of him. She missed the days when they were in love, and engaged, and she believed his promises that it would only be a month or two until they could make their engagement known. The days when she trusted him, and believed everything he told her.

She pulled three long pieces of grass, and braided them as she walked. Well, to be fair, he had never lied to her. He had told her his aunt was difficult, and sickly, and that it would take him some time to persuade her that he could get married. The real problem was Mrs Elton, and her incessant harping on the subject of a position. If Mrs Elton had never moved to Highbury, it would have been a little less unpleasant. There still would have been Mr Knightley to contend with, and Miss Woodhouse, and Aunt Bates's endless chatter, but she would not have been constantly under pressure to make a commitment she had no intention of honoring.

So the circumstances had piled up against her. If only they had known from the start how long it would take Mr Churchill to talk his aunt into the match, she would have gone to Ireland to wait for him. Of course, the reason for going to Highbury was so that they could be near each other in the meantime. Separating from him at the start of their engagement had been unthinkable.

She tucked the ends of the braid back into the beginning, making a little ring which she slipped on her finger. Mrs Frank

Churchill. They had both imagined that they would be married by now. If his aunt had not taken so ill, would they have been married by now? Would his aunt ever have given her consent? Or would Jane have been every bit as stranded alone? Would she have spent the last months every bit as miserable?

Guilt pricked her conscience. All the misery of the last months was not because of him. It was not his fault Mrs Elton had moved to Highbury to make her life unbearable. Mr Elton had not even been married when she first arrived in Highbury. She should have found a way to discourage Mrs Elton's attentions. After all, Miss Woodhouse had also received overtures from Mrs Elton, and she managed to avoid any social expectations. Whatever sort of rudeness or impertinence she had employed, Jane should have done the same thing.

Well, what was to be done now? The engagement was over, she had accepted the governess position, soon her life would be very different. She had managed to put it off for so many years, she would simply have to treasure the memories of all those years of conversations, of laughter and music, of people she loved and respected, who loved and respected her.

She would have simply kept walking, never to return to Highbury, but the skies turned very dark and threatening, and she had not brought her umbrella.

CHAPTER SEVENTEEN

Jane slept better the next night, which was not to say that she slept well. The walk in the meadow had done her good while she was there, but back in the confines of her room at her grandmother's, the headache returned with full force, and her hovering aunt's anxious attentions only served to make her irritable and unhappy.

Perhaps two days later, she was up with the sun, unable to lie in bed any longer. She threaded a needle and repaired a rip she had acquired in her front-closing gown in the light from the ray of sunshine that was streaming into her room. She had caught her hem on some gorse leaves on her walk in the meadow. Without her worried relatives to entreat her, she managed to eat the toasted bread and tea that Patty brought her, then reclined on the sofa in the drawing room, Mr Perry's warm compress on the back of her neck and the cold compress on her forehead. She did find that combination oddly soothing.

She sat up in surprise, compresses flying, when the bell rang. Who would be calling at such an hour? Everyone knew her aunt and grandmother would not be up yet. She froze when she heard Patty answer the door, and Mr Churchill's voice answered her.

It all happened in a confusing rush of mere seconds. There were footsteps pounding up the stairs, two at a time, then he was in the room, his eyes looking positively wild, tears streaming down his cheeks. Abandoning all propriety, all pretense, he threw himself on his knees in front of her and took both of her hands in his.

"Miss Fairfax! My dearest, darling Miss Fairfax!" He kissed her hands, then lay his face on her knee and sobbed.

Astonished, Jane stared at the top of his head. Instinct wanted to reach out and stroke the thick hair soothingly, but a different instinct, informed by experience and self-preservation, refused to allow her to make any gestures until she knew what he was going to say next.

"I was afraid you were already gone to the Smallridges," his voice was muffled against her skirts. "I was afraid I had missed you."

"You nearly did. I leave in just a few days." She hesitated, then asked, "I take it you are not here to return the letters I asked for?"

He looked up at her, taking her hands. "I am here to beg your forgiveness, and to apologize for being such a blundering idiot."

Jane studied his tear-stained face for a long while before she answered. "Now, if I forgive you, then what?" Anger flared as she thought of him snickering with Miss Woodhouse while they muttered about improprieties between herself and Mr Dixon. "You go back to insulting my complexion in public, while I look for ways to keep Mrs Elton away from me?" She pulled her hands out of his grasp. "It is too late for that. I am already committed to this position. Quite frankly, I welcome it. I would rather be a governess in Bristol for the rest of my life than spend another week in Highbury. I hate being beholden to Mrs Elton, but even if Mrs Smallridge is as awful as she is, at least I won't see her as many hours of the day. Being alone with three small children cannot be nearly as bad as living here."

Jane had not even thought those words to herself, but when they fell out of her mouth, a sudden calm descended on her spirit. The truth of them made her life seem simpler, better. The company of three girls might be delightful. They were young enough to be guided by her education. She could teach them to value good conversation over gossip. She could teach them to play the pianoforte, how to listen to good music with a discerning ear. She could talk to them in Italian, and they would soon be able to speak it in complete sentences, unlike Mrs Elton.

She was ready to leave, even eager.

"Would you consent to moving to Enscombe?" Frank asked.

"And what then?" Jane asked, a little mystified. "Under what pretense am I to be maintaining in Yorkshire?"

Frank looked a little confused. "As my wife."

"How do you propose to pass me off as your wife in Yorkshire?" Jane wanted to stand up and move away from him, but he was still on the floor leaning against her legs.

"Not in Yorkshire – in Enscombe," he answered. "As soon as I got your parcel with my letters, I found out that I had never sent my answer to your previous letter. It was locked up in my writing desk. I went straight to my uncle and got his blessing, and now I come straight to you to ask you to marry me."

"Is your aunt so sick you don't imagine she is going to object anymore? What will she say once she recovers?" Jane shook her head. "This is a terrible way to get what you want. There would be no domestic tranquility. She would hate me, and possibly you. I would be trading one awful home for another."

"Wait – you don't know!" Frank exclaimed. "I sent word to Mrs Weston. I thought everyone in Highbury would know by now. My aunt passed away the very morning I got your letter."

Stunned, Jane stared at him.

"You see, this changes everything. I am amazed you did not already know. The whole way here, I was sure at least I would not have to explain that much, knowing the town's fondness for gossip."

"I have been very ill," Jane stammered. "All I have heard for a week is people talking about how ill I am, and how worried they are about me."

"My poor darling, I can see it!" he cried. "What a beast I am! But at least excuse part of it as unwitting. I swear, I answered your first letter within an hour of receiving it, even though I was writing it as my poor aunt was lying there, dying.

"I thought I had discharged my obligation to you, and was absorbed in caring for my uncle, and making arrangements for my aunt's burial in Yorkshire. He is in Windsor now, seeing a friend he has been promising to visit for ten years. That was where your letter and parcel caught up with me, and where I discovered that I had not sent the letter still in my writing desk. I was shocked, and horrified at my blunder. I threw myself on his mercy at once.

"He gave me his blessing, and wished that I might find as

much happiness in the marriage state as he had done. I should hope we shall do better than the example of my aunt and uncle; that is, if you will take pity upon me and make me the happiest man in England."

"A proper, public engagement this time?" Jane asked.

Mr Churchill's face fell a little. "Well, my uncle does request that we delay a public declaration of our wedding until after my aunt is buried. It would seem indecent to proclaim to the whole world that, the moment my aunt died, I proposed to you. But I have leave to make a proper proposal, and we have leave to inform our immediate families. Including the Campbells and the Dixons, of course."

Jane was not sure her heart could stand another secret engagement. But she could see the lack of decorum in announcing a death and a marriage at the same time. "It is not an unreasonable request," she sighed.

"Miss Jane Fairfax, would you do me the great honor – would you deign to take pity upon this poor soul – would you forgive me – would you give your consent to become my wife?"

She could hardly see his face in front of her for the tears in her eyes. "Yes. Yes I will."

Somehow, he was beside her, instead of on the floor at her feet. Somehow, she could taste the saltwater on his lips. There was no way of telling whose saltwater it was; perhaps it was a blend of both of theirs.

CHAPTER EIGHTEEN

My favorite Mrs Dixon,

I have such a tale to tell you!

I am engaged to Mr Frank Churchill! Before you celebrate too thoroughly, I have the most horrid of confessions to make. Mr Churchill and I have been engaged since Weymouth. We were prevented from informing our families and friends immediately, because first he needed the consent of his Aunt Churchill, which was not immediately forthcoming...

It took Jane a very long time to write even the first page of her letter to Sophia. She only had so many sheets of paper, and so much ink! Confessing to such an awful concealment, knowing how much pain she would be causing, was the most difficult correspondence she had ever attempted. It took her hours of pacing, and writing, and stopping to send a letter to Mr Churchill, then more pacing and writing to find the right words. The idea of communicating with Colonel Campbell was even worse, and she did not feel equal to the task quite yet.

It helped that Jane ate her first real breakfast since her arrival, and she felt she had more physical strength and mental clarity than she'd had in months. Aunt Bates might have been more excited by the return of Jane's appetite than she was about the news of her engagement.

It felt good to be clean, and dressed, and upright, sitting in the drawing room with Grandmama and Aunt Bates instead of lying in bed. She had her first real night's sleep in a very long time. When the bell rang, she felt ready to face visitors.

She felt a little less ready when Patty came in to announce Mr and Mrs Weston.

Mr Churchill had gone to them immediately upon leaving her, and she could only imagine how that conversation had gone. What must they think of her? The fact that they were calling the very next day was probably a good sign. But then, they could be here to offer their recriminations for her share of the duplicity of the past months.

She stood and faced the door. This interview was inevitable, one way or the other. She had to face it as best she could.

For once, when she would have been glad of Aunt Bates's endless gift for talk, the good lady's tongue failed her. The five of them stood staring at each other for a long, embarrassed moment, until Grandmama invited their visitors to sit.

"Mrs Weston! We are doubly honored. You should not be climbing stairs, this close to delivering a child! Please, I think you will find this chair the most comfortable."

Mr Weston was the one to plunge into the topic on everyone's mind. "Well! It would seem my son has played something of a prank upon all of us! I am not the least bit surprised he succeeded in convincing you to play along, Miss Fairfax. We all know how charming and persuasive he is!"

Jane could feel her face get hot. Knowing she was blushing made her guilt all the worse, and she could no longer meet anyone's eyes. She looked at her hands folded in her lap, and wished she had not been presentable to receive company.

"He is, indeed, so charming!" Aunt Bates finally came to her rescue. "Everyone in Highbury is charmed by him. Jane will be so very happy! I am sure everyone in Highbury will be happy for the both of them. That is, once we are able to tell people. Mr Churchill did say that, for decorum's sake, the entire affair is to be kept a secret."

Jane's hands involuntarily clenched around each other. She could only imagine that, by now, absolutely everyone in the village already knew. Or would know before they went to bed tonight. She had not thought about that. She had been too wrapped up in the happiness of Mr Churchill's official proposal. While she was not enamored of the general littleness in the characters of the inhabitants of Highbury, her reputation among them would very much affect the social standing of her aunt and grandmother. She did not wish to be the means of injuring them!

Mrs Weston's brow furrowed. "I do hope our paying this call does not prove a means to betray your son's promise to keep this secret."

Mr Weston was so much like his son. "Nonsense! What harm can there be in a friendly call to our neighbors? We are calling upon Mrs and Miss Bates, not merely upon our daughter-in-law elect. Is that not right, Mrs Bates?"

Grandmama's calm answer had an effect on everyone in the room. Jane could see how she must have been a perfect vicar's wife. "There is no reason to assume malice on the part of our neighbors. We have never given them reason to wish us ill, they do not have a reason to invent mischief on Jane's behalf. If anything, they might assume you are calling because you have heard how ill Jane has been."

"Indeed! I apologize not to have thought of it," Mrs Weston exclaimed. "I can rectify that oversight at once. Mr Perry has declared I should be taking the air as much as possible. Mr Weston has business in town; come take a drive with me while he conducts his affairs. You need the fresh air more than I do."

Grandmama's assurances notwithstanding, Jane deplored the idea of facing the eyes of the gossiping village. She shook her head. "Oh, no."

"What a capital idea!" Mr Weston sat forward in his seat. "My wife cannot handle the reins in her condition, and I am sure she would like someone besides me to talk to for a little while."

"It would do you a world of good, Jane!" Aunt Bates added her persuasions. "I am sure you have been cooped up here far too long."

"The weather is extremely fine," Mrs Weston exerted more gentle pressure. "You and I should both make use of it. We have both been confined a great deal of late, and soon I will be confined a great deal more."

Put in the position of denying a favor if she did not ride with Mrs Weston, Jane nodded her consent.

A mere five minutes later, the two women were in the curricle. Jane took the most direct route possible out of Highbury, to minimize the number of people who might see them.

Mrs Weston was clearly sensitive to Jane's distress, and did all the talking to avoid an embarrassed silence. It was completely different than Aunt Bates's monologues; she talked of the things they were seeing on the drive, and allowed moments of comfortable quiet between them. When they had cleared the village, she talked of Mr Churchill, and told her everything about his visit to them to inform them of their secret engagement. She was perfectly candid about their surprise, and his sincere chagrin, and hoped that she and Mr Weston had not, in their ignorance, said or done anything that had caused any pain to Jane.

"You have never been anything but pure kindness to me," Jane answered earnestly. "I hope you did not find my initial greeting of you and Mr Weston this morning to be terribly ungracious. You surely realize what an agony that moment was, when I knew you are aware of my deception all these months, and I was unsure of what my reception would be."

"My poor, dear girl! What you have been suffering! So many months of concealment, surrounded by the very people you would wish to be celebrating your good fortune with, you must have been miserable!"

Jane's mind flew to Sophia and the Campbells. It truly had been miserable, writing so many letters to them without a single hint of the truth! The Highbury residents did not matter so much; even, if she was honest, her own aunt and grandmother. But this woman was Mr Churchill's stepmother, and she ought to do everything in her power to curry her favor. After all, she was about to become her daughter. Establishing cordial relations with Mr and Mrs Weston would make their lives easier.

"I will not say that since I entered into the engagement I have not had some happy moments. But I can say that I have never known the blessing of one tranquil hour." She was overstating her case a little and she knew it, and felt a little dishonest. But, then, it was not an untrue statement. Highbury had not been a tranquil place for her.

Mrs Weston was an enthusiastic audience. "You have been living in a state of perpetual suffering."

Well, then. If she wanted a tragic opera heroine, Jane was going to give her one. "Yes, but the pain is no expiation."

"Surely you've been punished well beyond the nature of the misconduct. I am married to one of these Weston men. Their charm can be terribly persuasive. I think you can lay a hearty portion of the blame on your co-conspirator."

Jane sighed and looked tragically over the horses' heads as they stopped at a particularly lovely view. "I never can be blameless. I have been acting contrary to all my sense of right, and the fortunate turn that everything has taken, and the kindness I am now receiving, is what my conscience tells me ought not to be." There, that ought to be sufficient for the village gossips. She knew every word she uttered would be repeated, and repeated, and repeated.

She realized that, somewhere in all the retellings, someone might blame Colonel and Mrs Campbell for her behavior. Somehow, she could not bear the idea of anyone, anywhere, ever saying something that would besmirch their characters. She turned and took Mrs Weston's hand and looked earnestly into her face. "Do not imagine, madam, that I was taught wrong. Do not let any reflection fall on the principles or the care of the friends who brought me up. The error has been all my own. I do assure you that, with all the excuse that present circumstances may appear to give, I shall yet dread making the story known to Colonel Campbell."

There, she said something that was absolutely, completely honest without the smallest touch of exaggeration.

"I am sure the Colonel will exonerate you from any censure! He cannot be blind to your merits, surely he knows better than anyone in Highbury what a steadfast character you possess. It is fortunate he is at least a little acquainted with Frank and his circumstances with his aunt. I cannot imagine he would not understand. If it would help, I will happily send him a letter, assuring him that Frank's playful and persuasive disposition meant no dishonor. He was simply trying his best under difficult circumstances."

"Thank you, Mrs Weston. I would be honored and grateful for

your help. It would be pleasant to be able to accept help for a change." She remembered Miss Woodhouse's recent attempts at help, and her own rebuffs to any kindnesses from that quarter. Since Mrs Weston was her former governess, and the two women were as close as any mother and daughter, she ought to try and mend that fence for Mr Churchill's sake, as well. "I know you speak to Miss Woodhouse very frequently; she tried several times during my illness to extend kindnesses which I felt in no position to accept. But I would be most grateful if you would convey my thanks for every wish and every endeavor to do me good. She has never received any proper acknowledgment from me. And, of course, now she is but one more person from whom I am unsure of my reception, once the news becomes public."

Mrs Weston patted her arm reassuringly. "I will happily convey your good wishes. Emma is a very dear and kind person; I will let you know that she already does know about your engagement to Frank, and congratulated Mr Weston most heartily upon acquiring you for a daughter. She called you one of the most lovely and accomplished young women in England."

Jane took up the reins to hide her surprise. Not at the admission that the gossip had already spread so far, but at such a compliment from such a quarter. "Well, that is a relief, then. I hope she has forgiven Mr Churchill as easily. I confess, Mrs Weston, I never supported his trifling with Miss Woodhouse, in order to help conceal our attachment. He was convinced it was harmless, but I never agreed with him that it was a good idea."

"I spoke with Emma most earnestly on this subject. I can tell you Frank was absolutely correct in his assessment. She views him as a friend, that is all. But it must have pained you excessively to watch his attentions to her, when they were the very attentions due to you as his intended."

As Jane guided the curricle back towards Highbury, she carefully steered the conversation around the past months, knowing that every word she said would be repeated to Miss Woodhouse. She tried to make sure Miss Woodhouse's pride would remain intact, without debasing herself too horribly. Eventually, inevitably, the conversation came around to talking about Mr Churchill and all the things about him that were why both women loved him so very much.

CHAPTER NINETEEN

There was one meeting Jane dreaded more than any other: she was going to have to admit the truth to Mrs Elton in order to truly convince her to terminate the agreement with Mrs Smallridge.

No matter how many times she had rehearsed different speeches as she walked to the Vicarage, when she sat facing Mrs Elton, she had no idea what to say.

Of course, Mrs Elton had no idea Jane had any news to impart. It did not occur to her that this was the first time Jane had ever called upon her without an insistent invitation coming from Mrs Elton. Jane let her voice wash over her for a long time, not hearing the individual words, just waiting for a break in the sound when she could enter into the conversation. If one could ever call being in Mrs Elton's presence a conversation.

"I have some rather remarkable news," she finally said when Mrs Elton was distracted by the maid bringing in a message for Mr Elton.

"News? By all means, I do love to hear all the news. But I have already heard that Mrs Cole has a new maid, and that Miss Wood-house's little friend, Harriet, has gone for a visit to Mrs Knightley to get a tooth taken care of."

Jane saw no reason to stall. She needed to be direct, if she was going to communicate all the information. "I need to ask you to write Mrs Smallridge. I am engaged to Mr Frank Churchill, and I will not be accepting the position as a governess."

It was a little satisfying, seeing the astonishment on her face. "Engaged to Mr Churchill! I would have thought for all the world that he would be making an offer to Miss Woodhouse."

Jane had not realized until that moment how her face had been frozen since she arrived in Highbury. It had been thawing the last couple of days for the first time since she'd said her goodbyes to Sophia…but the look on Mrs Elton's face told her this was going to be at least as unpleasant as every other conversation with her, and she could feel her face hardening back into the Highbury mask. "Well, instead of Miss Woodhouse, he has made an offer to me. And, as the future Mrs Frank Churchill, it would be inappropriate for me to be accepting a position as a governess."

"After all the time and trouble I spent, looking for a good situation for you!" Mrs Elton objected.

"If you will recall, I asked you not to trouble yourself on my account. Nay, I begged you not to write any letters on my behalf."

"So you were putting designs on Mr Frank Churchill the entire time? You could have told me," she admonished her. "Instead of writing letters to my family, I could have been doing what I could to assist you in your plans to ensnare such a wealthy match. It is so much better to have Mr Churchill engaging himself to you, instead of to Miss Woodhouse. Truth be told, the two of them are insufferable together."

Well, Jane could not disagree with her on that point. "So, you will send my apologies to Mrs Smallridge? Along with my thanks for her generous offer, and my best wishes for finding someone worthy of filling the post?"

"This is going to be a most difficult letter for me to write," she was agitated enough to rise from her chair and pace the room. "I will have to apologize to her, and to my sister, and to Mrs Bragge, as well."

"Fortunately, they are all family members, and family is more likely to understand and forgive," Jane answered. She hoped in her heart the Campbells and Dixons, closer to real family than her blood relations, would be understanding and forgiving.

"You don't know my sister. She can get into quite a high dudgeon, let me tell you! I cannot count the number of times I have had to go to such extreme measures to calm her nerves. But, I suppose I will simply have to rise to the occasion."

"I am sure that anything you put your mind to, you will succeed at," Jane answered.

"That is so true. I will write the necessary letters, since I suppose I have to, but I am most displeased with you, Jane," Mrs Elton shook a finger at her as if she was a child, or a misbehaving dog. Jane wondered how many times she would have to see this woman again. At least once more, she supposed. There must be a way to avoid many more encounters.

Jane stood up to leave. "I am sorry for it, but I am not breaking off my promise to Mr Churchill merely to oblige you. Remember, this is not public knowledge, please respect Mr Churchill's wishes to keep this private until after Mrs Churchill has been buried. Utmost secrecy is to be observed, for decency's sake. Good morning, Mrs Elton."

"You can rely upon me, Jane, I know how to manage things," Mrs Elton answered.

Jane thanked her, and made her escape.

She saved her trip to the post-office as her reward to herself for surviving the trip to the Vicarage. When a letter was waiting for her from Colonel Campbell, she was less sure this was the right order. She was more afraid of what the Colonel might say than anything Mrs Elton might say.

My dearest child,

I know Mrs Campbell and I should be chastising you for the delayed gratification of your news, but we remember all too well the distress Mr Frank Churchill was under while caring for his aunt at Weymouth.

It is quite impossible to offer any words of reproach, when, upon reading your letter, the both of us shouted "I knew it!" at almost the same moment, and then we laughed and embraced in jubilation.

If you have not received a letter from Sophia yet, it is because she is assembling a package of Irish gifts to send along with her letter. She is equally excited for you, and is sending us home with all due haste, that we might have you with us for a last few precious months until your wedding.

I am sure this secret has been hard on you all these months, and we look forward to hearing all the details.

We shall be leaving for England soon, and will come collect you immediately after we land. We can all go home to London together.

With Mrs Campbell's love as well as my own,
Col. E.F. Campbell

Jane closed her eyes and sighed with relief. She had not realized just how much she was dreading his response!

She wanted to skip like a child as she walked back to her grandmother's house. Unwilling to go back in quite yet, she turned her feet and headed into Ford's. She needed more paper.

Mrs Ford was unpacking a box of new ribbon, and the counter was covered with cheerful colors. Wide ribbon, narrow ribbon, blues, reds, greens, and pinks were piled everywhere.

Mrs Cole was standing on the other side of the counter, hovering over the new selection. She was so engrossed, she only realized Jane was in the store when she came to stand right next to her, eyeing the five different shades of pink.

"Miss Fairfax!" Mrs Cole greeted her with delight. "I hear congratulations are in order!"

Jane smiled. She had no way of knowing whether she was being congratulated on the governess position, or her engagement to Mr Churchill. She had her suspicions. But she was not going to talk about the one, if Mrs Cole was talking about the other. "Thank you."

She did not have long to wait to find out. "When did he propose?"

"Three days ago."

"Well, I would say he has found a miracle cure. You look very well. I was quite alarmed when I visited you a mere week ago."

"I am feeling very much better, thank you. And thank you for your concern while I was sick. It was very comforting to know I have such devoted friends," Jane answered.

"We'd heard you were at death's door," Miss Anne Cox spoke up from across the room. "My sister and I talked about coming to visit you, as well, but we were afraid the intrusion would be more inconvenient than comforting."

"Thank you for thinking of me," Jane answered.

"We'd heard Mrs Elton arranged for a position for you as a governess, and as soon as you accepted it, you collapsed and had to be carried home," Miss Cox continued.

"What nonsense!" Mrs Cole exclaimed. "Who was spreading such drivel?"

"I don't remember exactly," Miss Cox frowned, trying to remember. "It might have been Mrs Wallis. I know we were picking up bread that morning when we heard."

"Oh, you poor dear," Mrs Ford stopped unpacking the ribbons to give Jane a sympathetic look. "I knew you were sick, but I had not heard why."

"Well, nothing could be further from the truth," Mrs Cole huffed, glaring at Miss Cox. Jane knew the more monied set all considered the Miss Coxes vulgar. Jane pitied them. How could anyone consider the two daughters of the village's lawyer vulgar, when the same locale housed Mrs Elton? "You should not believe everything you hear."

Just then, the door to the shop opened, and Mrs Perry came in. "Miss Fairfax!" she exclaimed as soon as she saw her. "I understand congratulations are in order! You and Mr Churchill! It is a rather brilliant match!"

Jane had great difficulty keeping her countenance.

CHAPTER TWENTY

My dearest Miss Fairfax,

Such excellent news to know that the Campbells bear me no ill will for my abuse of your sweet nature! I was fully confident that their love for you would excuse any indiscretion on your part. My faith has been fully justified!

I have similar good tidings to report from Windsor. My uncle is in exceptionally good spirits for a man who has just lost his wife. The dear friend he is visiting has been a tonic for his nerves. I have been able to discuss arrangements in great detail; we have settled upon three months of deep mourning for my aunt. After that time, we are to be married wherever you and the Campbells see fit, and then my uncle insists that you and I reside with him at Enscombe.

I have even obtained permission to begin work immediately on some renovations to a wing of the house that has been a trifle neglected; we shall have some new rooms to move into once we are married! I have already dispatched some letters to that end, and will pause for business in London once we depart Windsor for Yorkshire, to make a start upon the project imme-diately.

I am in hopes of persuading my uncle to pay a visit to Randalls before we turn northward. He wants to be introduced to you (yes, I am afraid he has no memory of meeting you in Weymouth). While I have not yet persuaded him to a trip to Randalls, I have already been successful in getting him to agree to meeting the Campbells as soon as they return to London! That is, as soon as they are settled enough to be able to meet.

Soon, my beloved. I would that it were only a week, not three months, until we are married. I am more than ready to begin married life with you! But November will be here soon enough.

Yours heart and soul,
F.C. Weston Churchill

Mrs Elton called with her letter of response from Mrs Small-ridge only moments after Jane had finished reading her letter from Mr Churchill.

Aunt Bates had gone out, so Grandmama was her only shield from Mrs Elton. "Well, Jane!" she was already talking as she walked into the room. "I must say, my ability to write a good letter has not deserted me. I will admit I am generally an indifferent correspondent at best, but when I have something to say, my ability to say it well is indisputable. I have not heard back from my sister or Mrs Bragge, but Mrs Smallridge wrote back immediately. I suppose, after all, she is the one most affected by the situation. This just arrived, and I hurried directly over to reassure your mind on this subject, since I am sure you have hardly slept a wink for worry over the situation."

"How very thoughtful of you," Jane answered, sternly keeping any hint of a laugh out of her voice.

"Is that Mrs Elton?" Grandmama asked from her chair. Jane pressed her lips together. Leave it to her grandmother to call Mrs Elton rude to her face, without Mrs Elton even realizing it. Belatedly, Mrs Elton dropped a curtsey.

"How do you do, Mrs Bates?" Mrs Elton went over to sit beside her. "I have a letter for Jane. I am quite sure you would like to hear it, too. I shall be sure to read it loudly and clearly enough for you to hear it, too. I am sure you are every bit as interested in the contents as Jane is." She pulled out the letter and began reading.

Dear Mrs Elton,

Such a turn of events! I am astonished that Miss Fairfax received an offer of marriage while she was packing her valise in order to come to us here in Bristol.

You do write a pretty picture, and I can see how a shy gentleman in love would be in a panic when his heart's desire was about to move out of the county and out of reach. It sounds like a romance worthy of Sir Walter Scott. You must fill your sister in on every little detail next time you write to her!

To start with, who is this country swain who has carried off my governess?

Jane jumped to her feet when Patty came in. "Miss Woodhouse to see you, Miss Fairfax."

"Beg her to walk up," Jane answered. "I will stall her if I can, so you have time to put away your letter, Mrs Elton." She hurried out of the drawing room, happy to have the interruption. She wanted to laugh at the absurdity of it all, and was thankful for the moment's disruption to compose herself.

She never thought she would see the day when she would be so happy to see Miss Woodhouse, but she was genuinely glad to greet her on the stairs. She met her with an extended hand. "This is most kind indeed! Miss Woodhouse, it is impossible for me to express," she was still having difficulty controlling her giggles. "I hope you will believe – excuse me for being so entirely without words."

Miss Woodhouse shook her hand warmly, and her face showed comprehension and sympathy when Mrs Elton's voice floated down to them. Miss Woodhouse clung to her hand a moment longer than normal, and their eyes met in mutual loathing of a common enemy. They both made a small nod to acknowledge that it was time to face the dragon, and they climbed up the stairs and entered the room.

"Miss Woodhouse! You are making calls very early, I see. I

suppose we can blame the weather. When it gets this hot, I say better to dispense with everything as early as possible, so that I can languish wherever it is as cool as possible."

"An excellent plan, Mrs Elton. Good morning, Mrs Bates."

Jane was amused to see how much better Miss Woodhouse's manners were than Mrs Elton's. After she made her initial honors, and returned Mrs Elton's greetings, she went straight to Grandmama to pay her compliments, share greetings from her father, and then listened to her answers.

At the same time, she was annoyed to see that Mrs Elton had not used Jane's time on the stairs to put away the letter, and was now doing it as ostentatiously as possible to attempt to draw Miss Woodhouse's attention. When Miss Woodhouse made a show of ignoring Mrs Elton's actions, she put it in her reticule and looked at Jane. "We can finish this some other time, you know. You and I shall not want opportunities."

What a horrible threat to make. Jane did not react.

Mrs Elton was not done with her vulgar display, and kept on talking. "You have heard all the essentials already. I only wanted to prove to you that Mrs S admits our apology, and is not offended. You see how delightfully she writes. Oh! She is a sweet creature. You would have doted on her, had you gone."

What part of that speech was meant to be discreet, in the company of the town gossip? Jane gave Mrs Elton a significant look, and then looked from her to Miss Woodhouse, who was sitting on Grandmama's other side.

Mrs Elton sort of took the hint. "But not a word more. Let us be discreet. Quite on our good behavior."

So, now Mrs Elton was using the royal we? Jane stopped listening as Mrs Elton continued to prattle on the very topic that she should be avoiding. At least it did not matter. Her visit to Ford's had demonstrated that every other inhabitant of Highbury already knew more than Mrs Elton did. Perhaps her displeasure when she figured that out would limit the number of 'opportunities.'

Miss Woodhouse was studiously admiring Grandmama's knitting. Mrs Elton dropped her voice to a half-whisper to tell Jane in the quiet room, "I mentioned no names, you will observe. Oh! No. Cautious as a minister of state. I managed it extremely well."

Miss Woodhouse looked up at Jane with a smile, and came to her aid. "I don't know how you can tolerate knitting at this time of year, Mrs Bates. As Mrs Elton so rightly observed, the weather is so terribly hot. I have trouble generating any enthusiasm for knitting in the summer. The wool sticks to my fingers, and the whole thing is hard to manage."

The topic of the heat transitioned into sympathy for Mrs Weston, and how unpleasant it must be to be close to her time in such weather. "I have helped with many a baby, being a vicar's wife," Grandmama said. "I do believe we ladies are much more comfortable when our time is any other time than summer. But we don't get to plan these events, after all."

There was the smallest, awkward pause while everyone looked at Mrs Elton. No one in the room could imagine Mrs Elton being an angel of mercy at the bedside of women while they were in labor.

Including Mrs Elton. "Do you not think, Miss Woodhouse," she changed the subject abruptly, "our saucy little friend here is charmingly recovered? Do not you think her cure does Perry the highest credit?" She looked meaningfully at Jane. "Upon my word, Perry has restored her in a wonderful short time! Oh! If you had seen her as I did, when she was at the worst!"

"We were all very concerned," Grandmama turned to talk to Miss Woodhouse. Jane realized her grandmother really did not like Mrs Elton. Once again, she wished she had asked more questions during this long visit about her life as a vicar's wife. She could not hear the rest of what Grandmama was saying, because Mrs Elton was insisting upon using her stage whisper to talk about how much the assistance of "a certain young physician from Windsor" helped with her recovery.

When Jane offered no reply other than another look of reproach for Mrs Elton's lack of discretion, Mrs Elton turned to Miss Woodhouse and began planning a repeat of the trip to Box Hill.

She was sorry Aunt Bates returned before she could hear what entertaining thing Miss Woodhouse might have said to put Mrs Elton off. But, now with both her aunt and Mrs Elton in the room, no one else need say anything of consequence. Of course, Aunt Bates was a little nervous at first, finding Mrs Elton in the room. The displeasure from that quarter over the aborted governess position had distressed Aunt Bates exceedingly, and Jane had to actually prompt Mrs Elton to offer some reassurances.

"Yes, here I am, my good friend." Naturally, she could not actually apologize for either her attitude or her past behavior, so instead she changed the topic. "The truth is, I am waiting for my lord and master. He promised to join me here, and pay his respects to you."

She hid in the subject of her husband's business, only deviating once or twice more into inappropriate asides on the topic of Jane's engagement. The asides irritated Jane enough that she could not resist the urge to cast aspersions upon Maple Grove, when that topic reared its inevitable head. "Your parish there was small," she said, mildly.

Of course she would not want to hear that. "Upon my word, my dear, I do not know, for I never heard the subject talked of."

Jane was not in the mood to let the matter slide. "But it is proved by the smallness of the school, which I have heard you speak of, as under the patronage of your sister and Mrs Bragge. The only school, and not more than five and twenty children."

Mrs Elton could only respond by calling Jane a clever creature. She managed a couple more of her characteristic unwitting insults, before Mr Elton arrived to add to the absurdity of the morning. Mrs Elton did not even allow him to greet anyone in the room before she complained to him about how long she had been presuming upon their hospitality, waiting for his arrival. He answered with complaining about miscommunications between himself and Mr Knightley. Miss Woodhouse and Jane exchanged amused glances. Mrs Elton had only moments before been bragging about 'Mr E' being 'Knightley's right hand.'

As the couple continued a bizarre combination of quarreling and heaping insults upon everyone in the Knightley household, including a broad range of the servants, Miss Woodhouse elected to depart. Jane took advantage of the opportunity to have a moment away from the argument to see her down the stairs and out the door. They parted with a far better feeling of friendship and understanding than ever they had felt in all the years of their acquaintance.

CHAPTER TWENTY ONE

When Mr Weston surprised Jane with a morning visit to inform her that Miss Woodhouse was secretly engaged to Mr Knightley, it was all she could do to wait until he left before she threw herself on her bed, and laughed until she cried.

So – now Miss Woodhouse was also in a secret engagement. Jane had no idea why it was a secret: Mr Knightley had no parents whose permission he required, and Mr Woodhouse's blessing had been received. Mr Knightley's brother and Miss Woodhouse's sister (who were married to each other) were already informed, then Miss Woodhouse had told Mrs Weston, who told Mr Weston, who came to tell Jane in the presence of Aunt Bates. Aunt Bates put on her bonnet the moment the door had closed behind Mr Weston, so no doubt the entire village would hear the news within the hour!

That probably explained a little bit about Miss Woodhouse's sympathetic air when she had called the other day. Perhaps she had even been hoping to confide her own engagement, but was prevented by Mrs Elton's presence. Jane wondered a bit at Miss Woodhouse's sense, accepting a man like Mr Knightley. He was such an unpleasant, ungentlemanly person! Well, while Jane had never credited Miss Woodhouse with much intelligence, she was certainly a persevering sort of soul. She might improve him. She remembered the dance, when Miss Woodhouse had stared daggers at Mr Knightley, clearly telling him to smile. The two of them had known each other for so long, and so well, they knew what they were getting into.

Such gossip was not nearly so exciting as the note from Mrs Weston the next day, informing her that Mr Frank Churchill had come to meet his new half-sister, and he begged her to come spend the day at Randalls.

"I insisted to my uncle that I ought to meet my half sister before we depart farther north," he greeted her at the front door. "Not that I need any more inducement than the sight of you to pay a visit. I could not stand the idea of not seeing you until you get to London. When will the Campbells be here to collect you?"

"They will be here in a week," Jane answered. "I am sure I do not need to express to you how eager I am to see them!"

"Well, I hope you will insist upon bringing them here, before they spirit you away from us," Mr Weston greeted Jane heartily. "We are both eager to meet them."

"Of course I will," Jane promised happily. "They will want to meet you, too."

"We can make plans today for their visit. For the moment, my wife is with the baby. Perhaps you two want to take a bit of a walk while we are waiting for her?"

They needed no further encouragement.

"I hear that we are not the only ones secretly engaged in Highbury," Mr Churchill commented as they wandered down the lane. "My father was most eager to impart the news that Miss Woodhouse is also engaged! Would you have guessed that Mr Knightley would settle on her, once he was finally convinced that you were unavailable?"

"Your father told you? Then you did not get my letter with the same news."

"I was too eager to see you with my own eyes to wait for the post. It will no doubt be waiting for me when I return tomorrow. I can pretend to be surprised when I read it, if you like."

"I hope you will find better things to write about by then!" Jane laughed.

"I am sure I will. I know how much you despise gossip. Although, I suppose gossip is much more interesting when you are not the subject of it, but you do know the parties being discussed."

"There is also a difference between gossip and news," Jane pointed out.

"What's the difference?" he asked.

"News is a presentation of the facts. Mr Knightley proposed to Miss Woodhouse. That is the news. Gossip is the speculation without any facts, perhaps spinning stories about how the proposal might have taken place, without any information from a reliable source. Gossip supplies salacious details, not meant to be shared, thereby without a means of confirming the veracity of those details. Or rendering opinions about the facts. In this case, perhaps, discussing the suitability of the match."

"Well, not to gossip, my love, but I do have to wonder about the suitability of the match," Mr Churchill confessed. "While I needed to utilize Miss Woodhouse as an unwitting guard to our secret, I do profess to a genuine affection for her. I know you have little reason to like her, but I hope you can bring yourself to tolerate her. She is like a daughter to Mrs Weston, and Mrs Weston is, of course, married to my father. So she is close to being a sister to me, and seems likely to continue to be so."

"I believe Miss Woodhouse and I have come to a sympathetic understanding," Jane could say with perfect candor.

"I am glad to hear it," Mr Churchill said. "But Mr Knightley? The only person I have ever met in all my life as churlish as Mr Knightley is that awful man at the music shop in Weymouth. Remember the man who was abusing his poor clerk, the day we met?"

"The day we met? It was the very moment we met," Jane remembered. "You looked at me while you were trying to dissuade him from chastising his clerk so meanly, right in front of us." She laughed. "I have trouble imagining Mr Knightley belittling a clerk in front of an audience like that, but we have both heard the gossip that he has belittled you, copiously, outside of your hearing. Considering everything we have heard him say, there seems to be ample reason to believe it is true. I have heard him be perfectly beastly to Miss Woodhouse. But," Jane shrugged. "There is no accounting for other people's sensibilities. If they want each other, they can certainly be under no illusions as to each other's character."

"Are we under any illusions as to each other's character?" he asked her. His tone was playful, but she detected a note of worry in his voice, and knew he was actually completely serious in his question.

"If we were, I cannot think we are anymore. This experience has surely taught us more about each other than most people know upon entering the married state. It seems to me that a good understanding of each other is far more important than people give credit for, and that a happy marriage should be given more consideration than we as a society do.

"Perhaps no one will know as much about each other as Miss Woodhouse and Mr Knightley. It seems to me the lack of any mystery is unromantic, but they certainly know what they are in for. The other extreme seems far more common. Mr Elton knew that Mrs Elton was wealthy. That was all that really mattered to him. That is the one thing that seems to matter for most people. I can tell you from firsthand observation, I don't believe it is a recipe for happiness. I wish you could have witnessed their behavior when they both called upon us last. They were quarreling right there in our drawing room. Mrs Elton attacked him the moment he walked in the door."

"Well, if I am ever such a dolt as I have been in the past to you, you have every right to be angry with me. I beg you to attack me the moment I walk in the door."

Jane could feel her face growing very warm. "If I attack you the moment you walk in the door, don't assume I am angry with you."

Their kiss was interrupted by the sound of carriage wheels. They separated in haste, well before they saw the Woodhouse carriage in the drive.

"Mrs Weston told me that Mr Woodhouse insists upon calling every day. And of course Miss Woodhouse comes along, dutiful daughter that she is. I suppose we should go back. I have not made my peace with Miss Woodhouse yet. Do you think she is very angry with me?" he asked.

"Perhaps a little," Jane answered as they turned their steps back to the house. "But being so happy in her own engagement, I am sure she will forgive you with very little effort on your part. What did you say she calls you? Child of Good Fortune? You will surely make out better than you deserve."

"I am sure I will. I would say I already have."

They had to stop behind a tree for a long, delicious moment before they went back in the house.

ABOUT THE AUTHOR

Jeanette Watts has written television commercials, stage melodramas, dance textbooks, historical fiction, modern satire, and one LGBTQ romance. Little by little, each genre she likes to write keeps merging into the others.

She respectfully requests that you go to your review venues of choice, and PLEASE leave a review. Your honest review makes all the difference in helping every author in their battle with the almighty algorithm.

Made in the USA
Middletown, DE
14 March 2022

62649605R00156